Love Lessons

Love Lessons

Kennedy Shaw

URBAN BOOKS
http://www.urbanbooks.net

This is a work of fiction. Any references or similarities to actual events, real people, living or dead, or to real locales are intended to give the novel a sense of reality. Any similarity in other names, characters, places, and incidents is entirely coincidental.

URBAN SOUL is published by

Urban Books
1199 Straight Path
West Babylon, NY 11704

ISBN-13: 978-1-59983-044-5
ISBN-10: 1-59983-044-2

First Printing: January 2008

10 9 8 7 6 5 4 3 2 1

Printed in the United States of America

Chapter 1

Sunday afternoon, while most people were enjoying the humid north Texas weather, Jenna Bradshaw was adding up her life. She sat at the oak desk in her home office, hoping the numbers on the spreadsheet program on her computer screen would be in her favor if she added them a second time. She glanced out the window and admired the sunshine.

She loved living in Dallas and everything that came with living near the arts district, from the trendy restaurants, to the myriad cultural activities at the nearby Dallas Museum of Art and the Myerson Art Center, to living within yelling distance of so many other artists. Jenna sighed and returned her attention to the flat-screen monitor. Maybe, just maybe, the numbers would be in her favor.

They weren't. In her checking account she had five thousand dollars, in her savings, ten thousand. That would only keep her afloat for a few more months, and her latest project was far from finished; it was still just a thought in her head. She hadn't sold a painting in two years.

For the last ten years, she had survived solely on the proceeds from her art and had done quite well. She had given herself the luxury not only of owning a home in the art section of Dallas but also of paying cash for a new car. But with the sluggish economy and layoffs occurring more frequently, her painting sales had fallen off greatly. Luxuries like a painting were no longer a priority. She didn't even have a gallery show in sight.

She had only one real choice.

With a sigh, she made the call she had been putting off for the last few weeks. She called her friend at the temp agency to see if they had any job openings to tide her over until her sales picked up again. She smiled as her best friend answered the phone.

"Harcourt's Essential Temps, Dawn Castle. How may I help you?"

"Hey, Dawn. It's me. It's time."

"Jenna, girl, it's about time you called me."

"I know. I just kept hoping things would turn around."

Dawn was known for her perky attitude, which at the moment Jenna absolutely hated. "Well, Jenna, it's not like you'll have to work in an office forever. I have an opening at Duncaster and Finch in downtown Dallas, very posh. They are a stickler for proper attire and punctuality. If you're good, you might get to be permanent," Dawn chuckled, knowing that was last thing Jenna wanted.

"I only want temp status. Will I still be able to work on my new project? Is there much overtime?"

"Actually, at this place, temps don't work overtime. They almost treat them as subcitizens."

Jenna laughed as she turned off her computer. "That's fine with me. That means no one will bother me."

"Well, the last temp I sent there ended up meeting someone and getting engaged."

Jenna grinned. "That won't happen to me, Dawn. I don't have time for romance. I have a masterpiece to create."

"So, you think you'll ever get married?" Angela Taylor-Hill asked her older brother, Zyrien.

Zyrien was so tired of everyone in the Taylor family asking about his personal life. He was the oldest of eight, for goodness' sake. "My career and you guys are my main focus right now. I don't have time for relationships. Besides, there are enough grandkids running around this family without my contributing any." He helped his sister clean up after the surprise party for their parents' thirty-fifth anniversary.

Angela shook her head at her brother. "Don't give me that crap. You need to find you a nice woman who understands you and leave those young girls at your job alone. They see a brother in management with no kids and no drama and they pounce like a cat on a mouse. Wouldn't you like someone you could talk to and share some realistic goals with, instead of what you were going to buy them or their kids next?"

Zyrien hastily nodded. He was tired of dating women he had nothing in common with but the color of their skin. He wanted someone who would challenge him on all levels, though he didn't think that was possible. "I appreciate your concern, Ang, but right now I'm focused on work." He was lying, but his very pregnant sister didn't need to know that. She was six months along with her first child. The last thing he wanted to do was worry his sister.

"Have you ever thought in terms of an older woman?"

"Never. Too dull."

She winked at her brother. "Never say never. You just never know. Besides, an older woman would be settled and wouldn't give you all that drama." She waddled into the kitchen.

Later that evening, he was finally in the solitude of his four-bedroom home, reveling in the peace and quiet. He loved his family dearly, but he also loved being away from them.

As he flipped on the TV in the master bedroom, he reflected on his sister's words. The big three-five was approaching and he was still miserably single.

* * *

"Why don't you smile?"

Monday mornings were always hard for her. She dreaded coming to work after such a productive weekend. But Jenna forced a smile at the young black man as she headed to her desk. He spoke to her most days as they passed in the hall. She chalked it up to being a fellow African-American. She had only been employed at Duncaster and Finch a few weeks and was still feeling her way around her job. Most days she didn't feel like smiling.

Most days she was just happy her new bosses hadn't told her that her temporary clerical services were no longer needed. She plopped down in the leather chair and surveyed her work.

Jenna looked at the growing mound of papers on her desk and sighed. Given that she was new to the department and instructions were vague, she did her best. She began working on the stack, inputting the information into the computer's database.

Jenna just didn't fit in. In her other life, back when she was an accountant, she had never fit into the corporate world. She was the round peg trying to fit into a square hole. That was probably why she loved painting so much. She didn't need an audience to paint. She only needed her imagination and sometimes a model.

Most of her work associates were young and had children and husbands or some other drama. Here she was, childless and over forty. She couldn't even boast of getting out of a bad marriage; she was deliriously single—not even a boyfriend.

At lunchtime, she gathered her latest paperback novel, headed downstairs to the company-owned cafeteria, and picked out a salad. She sat at a vacant table. After she fixed her salad to her liking, she took a forkful to her mouth. Delicious. She took a few bites and began to read the novel.

"Do you mind if I sit with you?" a masculine voice asked.

Jenna looked up and stared at him for a moment. He was the same young man from that morning, telling her that she needed to smile. He probably just felt sorry for her, eating alone, she thought, and put away her novel. "Sure, you can sit down."

He sat down with a plate full of diet no-nos: greasy cheeseburger, French fries, chocolate cake, and soda. She wondered how his mocha skin stayed so smooth when he ate that kind of junk. Must be the perks of being young, she thought, as she nibbled on her salad.

"My name is Zyrien Taylor," he said, extending his hand across the table to her.

"Jenna," she said, taking his hand and careful not to mention her last name.

Zyrien took a bite of his burger and downed a few fries before he spoke again.

"So, how are you liking your new job so far?"

She shrugged her shoulders. "It's OK. What do you do?"

"I'm the national accounts manager," he said.

That figured. He was always impeccably dressed in the trendiest business fashion. Today he wore a blue button-down polo shirt and tailored slacks, looking like a male supermodel. Jenna glanced around the room. "Should you be eating here with me? I mean, I'm a temporary employee."

He leaned back in his chair and smiled. He had perfect, straight white teeth and dimples! But those hazel eyes were his best feature. "You're still a human being, right?"

"Yes, but I know the rules are pretty stringent around here. I can't even park in the employee parking lot. I have to walk at least ten minutes just to get to the building," Jenna said, watching her companion.

He nodded. "Yeah, I think that rule stinks, but some of the more tenured employees complained about not being able to find a place to park in the mornings and you know how that is."

Jenna agreed. She noticed the women at the next table blatantly listening to their conversation. They were probably mad, since nothing juicy was being said, she thought.

"Kids?"

Jenna stared at him in confusion. "Oh, I get it. No, I don't have any. No husband. I'd like to do them in the traditional manner. You know, husband, then children."

He laughed. "Yeah, I feel you on that. I have a big family. I think that's why I don't have any. I have four sisters and three brothers and I'm the oldest."

"Wow," she said. "Now that's a big family."

"Yeah, Sundays are always nerve-racking for me. We have dinner at my parents' house after church and the kids run around like they are hopped up on chocolate or something. I'm always happy to go back to my house, where it's peaceful and quiet. How about you?"

"Well, I'm afraid it's just me and my younger brother and he lives in Austin."

"What about your parents?"

"My parents are deceased. I take it yours are still alive."

"Yes. My mom just turned fifty-two last month. She and my dad went to Vegas for her birthday."

"That sounds exciting."

He took another bite of his burger and it was gone. "It was a surprise. My parents were very young when they got married. They didn't get to have a honeymoon. I was on the way," he explained with a wink. "So us kids got together and sent them to Vegas."

"I bet they were surprised," Jenna said, trying to keep her mind on the conversation and not the fact that she was sitting with a very attractive, very young man. A man that made her feel older by the second.

"I'm thirty-four," he volunteered the information.

Jenna almost choked on her salad. "I didn't ask."

"I saw that worried look on your face. How old are you?"

Jenna pondered the question. She could always claim the Fifth Amendment. "How old do I look?"

He shrugged. "I don't know. Thirty or so."

Jenna smiled. People always told her she didn't look her

age. They always swore it was because she had the good sense to avoid marriage and children.

"Jenna, how old?"

"I'm forty-two."

His expression changed from shocked to more shocked. "You look great."

"Thank you, Zyrien." She glanced at the clock on the wall, rising. "I enjoyed talking to you, but I must get back to work."

He rose also. "Yeah, I should be getting back as well. We can walk together."

Any other day the elevator would be crowded with people rushing back to work. Not that day. They were the only two people on the elevator. Jenna better assessed his chiseled features. He was shorter than her five feet, ten inches, somewhere in the region of five-eight, she guessed. But he was muscular. He filled out the cotton shirt perfectly, his biceps straining at the short sleeves.

He leaned against one of the walls, staring at her. His hazel eyes assessed her attributes carefully before he spoke. "So. Since there's no husband, is there a boyfriend?"

"That would depend on your definition of boyfriend," she said softly.

"Do you date regularly? Does he live with you? Are you sleeping with him?"

"No, no, and no."

He smiled. "Well, I guess that means you don't have one?"

"Yes, you are correct."

The elevator dinged for their floor. He motioned for her to precede him. "It was nice chatting with you." He smiled, then went in the opposite direction.

Jenna always prided herself on the fact that she could tell when someone was picking her up. But today her radar was definitely off. He didn't even make a play for her or anything. Feeling even older by the second, she walked to her desk.

She had just started to input the information in the computer when she received an e-mail. In the three weeks she'd been working there, she had gotten a total of ten e-mails. Usually it meant more work, which she didn't need. She opened it with trepidation. To her surprise, it was from Zyrien. He thanked her for letting him sit with her.

How did he know her last name? They weren't required to wear name badges. Had he been inquiring about her? He was a manager; no one would have questioned him if he asked for the information. She didn't reply to the e-mail.

Zyrien sat at his desk, mulling over reports and wondering why Jenna didn't respond to his e-mail. His plan worked wonderfully. He didn't seem too needy and it almost seemed natural. Too bad he didn't normally eat lunch that early. He usually didn't eat until late afternoon, in an attempt to finish all his paperwork and get a jump on the next day.

But for some reason the fact that she didn't reply to his e-mail began to gnaw at his resolve. He had noticed her the first time he saw her in the elevator. She had flawless light brown skin that reminded him of honey. She usually wore stilettos, which made her even sexier to him. He had always wanted to date a tall woman.

"Are you daydreaming or thinking about the meeting you have in exactly five minutes?" Brenna Fitzgerald, his assistant, asked, smiling at him.

"The meeting, of course," Zyrien lied, rising from his desk. He gathered the report he hadn't finished and headed to the elevator.

He walked into the meeting room and took his seat. He watched as the other managers filtered in. At thirty-four, he was one of the youngest managers in the company and one of the few African-Americans in a managerial position. He had worked hard to get to that position and wanted nothing to detract from that. Even the fact that he hadn't finished his report.

"Zyrien, I know you're working on the numbers for some

upcoming projects," his boss told him, "but there's a new development."

"Yes, Mr. Duncaster, what is it?" *There goes the thought of leaving work early.*

"We're in serious competition with one of the larger accounting firms for a government contract. I need you to put aside your other projects, and focus on landing that contract. You know, how much more manpower will be needed, salary projections versus revenue, and how will that affect our budget, since we're almost at the end of the fiscal year."

Zyrien nodded, knowing exactly what his boss was talking about. He always prided himself on the fact that he kept informed of changes in the accounting industry. He knew of the large contract and if his company could land it, that would be quite a feather in their cap. But it would require more manpower than their company had. Duncaster and Finch might not want to lay out that much money up front without the promise of the contract.

"I'll need the updated numbers by the end of the month, which gives you about three weeks to work on it. The first prelim meeting will be July 3. If you need some help with the data, let me know."

Mr. Duncaster dismissed the meeting and Zyrien left the room, already thinking about all the work he was going to have to do to make this report happen. He rang for the elevator. As he stepped inside, he studied his notes, ignoring the other passengers. Until he took a deep breath. He smelled her perfume. She was in the elevator. He discreetly glanced around the crowd and spotted her.

Jenna stared at Zyrien.

He smiled back at her, for lack of anything else to do.

Chapter 2

Later that afternoon, Jenna sat at her desk, looking in disbelief at the e-mail she had just received. Zyrien had asked her to have a drink. Tonight. He was certainly persistent.

So he *was* putting the moves on her. The bar he suggested was just across the street, and she could postpone her workout one night.

She responded affirmatively and sent the e-mail. She laughed when he instantly replied.

Exactly two hours later, Jenna and Zyrien sat in the bar talking as if they had known each other a hundred years instead of one day. Zyrien ordered a Guinness and Jenna had a glass of her favorite Kendall Jackson Chardonnay.

Zyrien played with his beer bottle, as if he were pondering the fate of the world.

Jenna couldn't stand it any longer. "OK, what is it?"

He smiled. "I was just trying to figure out how to ask you to dinner."

Jenna wasn't expecting that. "Why?"

Zyrien took offense. "What do you mean, 'why?'"

"I just wondered why me and not one of the hundred other women at work, like those girls who sat across from us at lunchtime. They stared at you the whole time we ate."

He shrugged it off like it was an everyday occurrence. "Women are attracted to my looks, but then they usually change their tune when the real me starts sneaking out."

"What are you? A serial killer?"

He grinned. "That's what I like about you. Your mouth doesn't have a filter. You say whatever's on your mind and that's that."

"Not true," Jenna countered. She didn't mention the ketchup stain on his tie.

"Yes, it is. You just asked me if I was a serial killer." He leaned back in the wooden chair, signaling the waitress for another round of drinks. "But since you want to know, I'll tell you. I tend to get one-tracked. You know, I get started on a project at work and I forget dates, phone calls, stuff like that."

Jenna shrugged. "Oh, is that all?"

Zyrien looked intrigued. "So, that doesn't bother you?"

"In case you haven't noticed, I do have my own life. I don't have time to run people down. You call if you want to. If work is your primary focus, you should state that up front."

He nodded, taking in her answer. "OK, work is my primary focus. Can we go out to dinner?"

Shock, more than good sense, made her answer in the positive.

"Great. There's a fantastic Italian restaurant just down the street. We could walk there, if you like."

"You mean tonight?" Jenna assumed she would at least have a few days or a week to get ready for it. *Who has a dinner date during the workweek?*

"Yes, I mean tonight. As soon as we finish our drinks."

She had forgotten about that second round. He had unnerved her with the dinner invitation. She really wasn't expecting it. What was she going to do in an intimate setting?

"OK, Zyrien," said Jenna regaining her confidence. "Only because I was going to have to eat out tonight anyway, since I didn't take anything out of the freezer this morning."

"Of course," he said, smiling.

Jenna knew he didn't believe her little white lie. She was ready to confess when the waitress showed up with their second round of drinks. Rather than force the issue, she took a sip of her wine.

After a brief walk to the restaurant, they were soon chatting again. They were seated at the table looking over the menu in silence. Jenna couldn't stand the quiet. "What are you having?"

He chuckled. "I was thinking about chicken Parmesan."

Jenna couldn't contain her surprise. "Me, too. It's my favorite."

"So what does Jenna do for fun?"

"Fun? What's that? Every day of my life is fun. What do I do for excitement should be the proper question."

He smiled at her, revealing those dimples. "OK, what does Jenna do for excitement?"

"I go to art exhibits."

Zyrien's smile became larger. "Really? I'm into some of it, thanks to my little brother. A few years ago, he had to go to some museum for extra credit at school and I got roped into taking him. Now he's a senior at Dallas University majoring in art."

Jenna almost couldn't contain her giddiness. Rarely did she meet someone outside of the art community who liked art. Maybe he had just earned ten points for admitting he liked it. "Well, I love going to the museum. I don't live too far from it and I always end up going on the weekends."

"The only thing I live near is Bachelor's Park," he said.

Jenna nodded, knowing exactly what he was referring to. Bachelor's Park was so named because of the single men who used the park as a pickup spot. It was also in a very expensive part of Dallas and at least forty-five minutes from the arts district.

"Any interesting exhibits coming up?"

Jenna laughed. She had trapped herself with her big ol' mouth.

She couldn't pretend ignorance, because she'd already confessed. "Actually, I think it's Georgia O'Keeffe this weekend."

He frowned. "I've seen some of her stuff. Anything else?"

"Well, there are always the classics. You know, like, Monet, Picasso, and Cézanne. Oh, and they just did one of Jean-Michel Basquiat's work."

"Finally, something of interest. Maybe we should go sometime."

Jenna hesitated.

He held his hand up. "Sorry, I know, I'm pushing too hard. Check that last thing. I'll give you time to fall madly in love with me first."

The next evening, Jenna met her friend Dawn for dinner. Feeling a little out of sorts, she needed the guidance of her best friend since junior high. She walked into the Hill Street Bar and Grill, and searched the crowd of people for her friend. She spotted Dawn quickly. As usual, Dawn was the center of attention in a small circle of men.

Jenna neared the table, and the men scattered. "Why is it I always find a group of men around you? You're married, remember?"

Dawn flashed her left hand at her friend, showing off her ten-carat diamond wedding ring. "Yes, I know. I always tell them, but you know men, they don't care. They just see a voluptuous sister and they go nuts." She stared at Jenna as she finally took a seat. "Now, Ms. Bradshaw, where were you last night?"

"I had a date." Jenna smiled. She couldn't help it. Dinner with Zyrien had been exciting and made her realize what was missing in her well-ordered life. He was easy to talk to and seemed mature beyond his young years.

"OK, out with it," Dawn demanded. "I've been married too long and all the fun stuff has left my dull life." Dawn signaled for the waiter.

"Your life is far from dull, Dawn. You're married to the most popular player on the Dallas Stars. I'm dying to tell somebody. It was a guy from work. He asked me to meet him for a drink. Then we went out to dinner."

Dawn's eyes searched Jenna's face. "OK, I need details."

Jenna opened her mouth, but the waiter appeared at the table to take their order. After he left, she started her story. "Well, he's only thirty-four, but he's a manager already."

Dawn grunted. "So?"

"And he's about two inches shorter than me and I'm not even a permanent employee. You know how strict they are at that place. I honestly thought you were exaggerating about the subcitizen thing, but it's true."

Again, Dawn grunted. "You know that's not where you want to be, anyway. If they told you tomorrow they didn't need you anymore, you wouldn't be the least bit upset. He's a manager, so the rules don't really apply to him, unless you guys start having sex at work. I say enjoy yourself and give the young man some play. I'll have to buy you some celebratory condoms. Maybe some fruit-flavored ones."

Jenna gasped at her friend's comment. She didn't know why she was still surprised at anything Dawn said, but she was. "Hey, we don't know each other that well. Anyway, I didn't hear from him today. Maybe he was just passing the time yesterday."

"Maybe he wasn't," Dawn countered in her usual "the glass is half-full" mentality.

Jenna watched the waiter return with their food order. He placed her salad in front of her, and a juicy steak in front of Dawn. Dawn believed in taking life by the horns. She didn't care about gaining weight, cholesterol, high blood pressure, or diabetes. Dawn's goal was to live life to its fullest and she did.

"Besides, I know you, Jenna," Dawn continued. "Something must have attracted you to this guy. I can't see you spending any time with someone who wasn't up with you mentally." Dawn cut her rib-eye steak into small pieces before drowning them in steak sauce. "You know, there are some advantages to sleeping with a shorter man."

Jenna grunted in disagreement. "Isn't your husband like six-three and you're only five-eight?"

"The advantage I'm talking about has nothing to do with height."

A few hours later, Jenna walked into her house, feeling much better after her talk with Dawn, even if it had wandered into lusty sex talk. Jenna knew she was nowhere ready to travel down that road with Zyrien. She hoped Zyrien wasn't thinking in the same terms as Dawn.

She sat down on the plaid couch to read her mail, but was distracted by the red light on her phone. She quickly retrieved the message.

It was from Zyrien. How on earth did he get her home number? He wanted her to call him back. After twenty minutes of indecision, she did.

His voice was husky, doing silly things to her blood pressure. How could he sound so sexy this late at night?

"Hey, I'm glad you called. I went by your desk, but you were already gone."

"Yeah, I met a friend for drinks and dinner."

"Oh," he said in a tone that wanted more of an explanation, but didn't dare ask.

"Why don't you just ask me?"

Zyrien laughed, his tone rich with sexual magnetism. "You think you know me?"

"Not yet," Jenna flirted back. "But I hope to one day."

"OK, Jenna. Whom did you have dinner with?"

"Why?"

"You know, woman, you're pushing me. I want to know, that's why. If it's a guy, I need to go kick some ass."

Jenna pretended exasperation. "If you must know, it was my best friend, Dawn."

He was silent for a moment. "You're saying 'Dawn,' like a girl's name, right?"

"Yes, Mr. Webster," Jenna answered ironically, liking the jealous tone in his voice.

"Good. See you tomorrow." He ended the call.

The next morning, Jenna exited the elevator and smiled instantly. The first person she saw was Zyrien. He was dressed in a dark blue suit and was walking with another man. They appeared to be in deep conversation until he made eye contact with her. "Hello, Zyrien."

"Ms. Bradshaw." He walked past her as if she were a stranger.

OK, buster. Two can play your silly game. She walked to her desk, turned on her computer, and began her day. Not long after she took her morning break, she received an e-mail from Zyrien. He wanted to meet her for lunch, but Jenna declined his offer.

This started their first fight. By e-mail.

Ten minutes later, her phone rang. A funny feeling told her Zyrien would be on the other end of the line. "Accounting, this is Jenna," she said in her clear, businesslike tone.

"Well, at least you're answering your phone professionally," he drawled.

He ruffled her feathers that quickly. "Yes, may I help you?" she shot back.

Zyrien laughed. "OK, Maybe I deserve the cold shoulder. I was in the middle of an important discussion," he explained.

"And that's your excuse for bad manners?"

"Ouch, tough room."

That made her smile, but she was determined not to let him know that he could make her laugh in the middle of being mad at him. There would be no end to it. Was she actually thinking there was a beginning?

Zyrien was not to be outdone. "So what's do you say, Ms. Bradshaw, we could have lunch and you can tell me how bad my manners are."

"No, I already have plans," she half-lied. She wanted to sketch out an idea for a painting.

"Break them," he said.

"You're not my father, brother, or lover. I see no reason to change my plans."

Zyrien took a deep breath, a sure sign he was trying to keep his temper in check. "Look, I would just like the opportunity to make up for this morning."

"I'll give you ten minutes of my lunch hour," Jenna said. "I really have something I need to take care of for the remainder of my time."

"So I get a whole ten minutes," Zyrien said in a short tone. "Man, I should jump up and down with joy."

"Don't be a jerk."

Chapter 3

Jenna settled at a table in the cafeteria at lunchtime. After their brief fight, she and Zyrien had compromised and decided to spend thirty minutes together. She waited for Zyrien to make his appearance.

But after ten minutes, he hadn't showed up. Jenna decided to work on her sketch instead of brooding over why he hadn't kept their lunch date. She took a bite of salad, and opened the small sketchbook she kept with her at all times, just in case she had a germ of inspiration. She took a pencil out of her pocket and began working on an idea.

She easily sketched the outline of a male model in a very seductive pose and had almost finished when she glanced at her watch. Zyrien was over thirty minutes late. She took another bite of her salad and completed her sketch. Now would come the hard part. She would have to call her mentor for a model.

"I bet you are fit to be tied, aren't you?" Zyrien asked, joining her at the table. He didn't have a tray of food.

Jenna immediately closed her book and put away her pencil. "No, I was working on something while I waited." She glanced at the clock on the wall, which was unnecessary, since she had her mother's gold watch on her left wrist. "I don't have much more time."

Zyrien let out a tired breath. "I was stuck in a meeting. I

left early, just so you wouldn't think I was trying to stand you up or anything."

"Where you were is none of my business, Mr. Taylor."

He spoke through gritted teeth, "Why are you doing this?"

"I'm not doing anything. We're not married. I don't have to know your whereabouts. Just like you don't have to know mine."

He played with the saltshaker nervously. "So what are you doing after work?"

She glanced at her watch. "I have to run an errand."

"What kind of errand?"

"Did you listen to what I just said?"

A muscle moved in Zyrien's strong, chiseled jaw. He was trying to suppress his anger and failing terribly. He spoke in a low voice. "I heard what you said. I also think I should know. What if something happened to you and no one knew where you were?"

"Again, it's not your business." Jenna rose from her seat and picked up her tray. "My lunch is over. Good day, Mr. Taylor." Jenna left the cafeteria.

She expected him to follow her, but he didn't. At first she was upset that he didn't at least stake a claim to her. But later she realized that they were just too different, age being the biggest factor. What was she thinking? He was used to younger, firmer women. Not someone nearing menopause.

She entered the elevator and her least favorite person also entered. Her boss, Kyle Storm, grinned as he pushed the button for their floor.

"Hello, Ms. Bradshaw, I left some forms on your desk. I need them back before you leave today."

Jenna nodded. She knew it was probably something that he was supposed to do himself. "Sure thing, Mr. Storm. Are there any instructions I should have for these papers?"

He grunted. "I thought temps were supposed to know their job." Translation: he had no freaking idea of what she was supposed to do.

"Thank you, Mr. Storm." *Asshole.*

* * *

After Jenna left without so much as an explanation of her plans for the evening, Zyrien pondered the possibilities. Maybe she had a boyfriend after all? Maybe she had another type of obligation and didn't feel he was worthy enough to share the information with. Suddenly, those women his sister warned him against didn't look so bad.

He was used to being the center of someone's universe. He was used to knowing where the object of his affection was at any given time. With Jenna, however, she worked on her own timetable and anyone else apparently had to deal with it and he didn't like it one bit.

"Well, don't you look deep in thought," Katonya Washington said, sitting down in the seat Jenna had vacated earlier.

Zyrien looked at Katonya's dark brown complexion, head full of microbraids neatly pulled back in a ponytail, and a bright smile, instantly comparing her with Jenna. They were direct opposites, right down to the fact that Katonya had two children and Jenna was childless.

"Yeah, you got me," he finally answered. "What's up with you? Where's your man?"

"Will you let that go?" Katonya arranged her food on the table with precision before she continued the conversation. "I saw your friend leave suddenly. You know those temps will do almost anything to get permanent status. And I don't have to tell you about the company rules against dating temps, do I?" She winked at him.

"You should know. You were a temp once and now look—six months later, you're a supervisor. I didn't think you ate lunch this early. Or at least that's what you told me when we were dating." Zyrien stared at the clock on the wall. He hoped Katonya didn't want to walk down memory lane; he wasn't in the mood.

"This isn't about me. This is about that woman. You know

she barely speaks to anyone here. I think she's a snob. I heard she wasn't working before she came here."

"So?"

Katonya frowned as she picked up her cheeseburger. "Don't you take that attitude with me. I don't think she's your type; usually you go after a much younger woman. I do know she's over forty. I heard her tell someone in the restroom one day. You know, Zee, the kids still ask about you. I know I was wrong for cheating on you, but I think we could work out our problems."

Zyrien shook his head. He hated when she used her nickname for him. It reminded him of those paper towels with the same name. "You know, Katonya, I think it was the best thing for both of us. I couldn't be the man you wanted and I definitely couldn't be a stand-in dad for your kids." *And you were cheating,* he thought.

"OK, maybe I was pushing you too fast. I just wanted my kids to like you. You know you liked playing daddy to them."

Zyrien remembered well. He didn't have a choice with those crumb-snatchers. "By telling them I would buy them whatever they wanted. I don't have to buy anyone's love. You shouldn't have used them like that, anyway."

"OK, Zee, gosh," Katonya gushed. "You started hanging around that woman a few days and look at you. You act like that was so wrong."

Zyrien stood, knowing this conversation would only end in a knock-down, drag-out fight. "I've got a meeting, Katonya, maybe I'll see you around."

She waved her hand in the air, dismissing him. "Yeah, you know my number. Why don't you give me a call sometime?"

He nodded and left the cafeteria. He had her number, all right. The more money he spent on her and her kids, the more affection she spent on him. He didn't want that anymore. He'd bought love for the last time.

Zyrien entered his office, thankful that his chattering assistant was out to lunch and he could have some peace and quiet for at least an hour. He sat in his leather chair and closed his eyes, thinking back to his conversation with Jenna.

"What was on that pad?" he asked the room. He remembered the small pad. She was almost hiding it from him. Zyrien didn't like secrets of any kind and he would make sure that Jenna knew her place in his life.

After brooding most of the afternoon, Zyrien decided to go home early and work on the report. The preliminary numbers were due by Monday, and he had not devoted as much time to the report as he would have liked. Mostly due to one Jenna Bradshaw.

He grabbed his briefcase and left his office. He stopped at his assistant's desk. Luckily, she was not there, so he scribbled a quick note and a list of instructions that would keep her busy for the rest of her shift, and left the office.

As he drove home, his stomach reminded him that he hadn't stopped for lunch. Knowing his refrigerator was bare, he pulled into his favorite Chinese restaurant for some quick takeout.

He punched the access code that turned off the burglar alarm, entered his house, and immediately checked his phone for any messages. What was he? Crazy? Stupid? There's no way Jenna would have known he had left for the day. He needed to remember the task at hand, the report. He walked into his home office and began to work on it.

If he could just make the prelim numbers come out in his favor, it would be a feather in his cap. Not knowing how much of a risk his company was willing to take made his job that much more difficult, but he loved a challenge.

The accounting department had 300 permanent employees and there were at least 150 temporary employees. One hundred fifty people who didn't work overtime; seventy-five of those didn't even work full-time hours. How would they figure into the new contract? And as his thoughts betrayed him, he wondered how would or could Jenna fit into his life?

He gave up all thoughts of trying to work on the report and

decided to take a quick nap to reenergize his brain. Too much clutter inside his head was only making his thought process slower. Any other time this report would have been almost completed and he would be on to the next project.

He turned off his computer and headed upstairs to his bedroom. After he stripped down to his silk boxer shorts, he eased under the covers and quickly fell asleep.

Jenna took a deep breath as she finished the project Mr. Storm had left on her desk. It wasn't as difficult as he made out. It was simply a matter of knowing which column was the debits and which was the credits. But, as usual, Mr. Storm didn't want to spend the few minutes it would have taken to adjust the columns in the Excel spreadsheet.

Now that she had a free moment, she called her mentor, Gunter Prodder. She laughed as she heard him greet her in his thick Austrian accent.

"Jenna, dahling. It's been much long since you have seen me. How are you?"

"Fine, Gunter. And yes, I'm painting." She laughed. "That's actually why I called. I need a model."

"Are you still doing ze nudes?"

"Yes. I had a creative moment at work and have finished my drawing. So I'm ready to get busy painting."

"Vonderful," Gunter said proudly. "I know zis vill be another masterpiece in the making."

"Yes, I need a male model, if you know of anyone needing some quick cash. I'll only need him a couple of nights." Jenna gasped at her own words. "My goodness, if someone overheard my conversation they would think I'm in the market for a stud or something."

"Yes, I zink zey vould. As stuffy as zose monsters are at that place, I can imagine," he said, making his usual mockery of the English language. "I zink I can get someone to be at your home tonight."

Jenna couldn't hold back her laughter any longer. "Stop that. You're doing that on purpose. Your English is much better than that." She covered her mouth, hoping her laughter didn't attract any unwanted attention from any of her co-workers or her supervisor.

Gunter finally started using proper English. "All right, all right, I'll tell him to be zere about seven. Gives you time to work out, even if I happen to zink you don't need to. You have a gorgeous body and here you go trying to perfect an already perfect body."

Jenna took the compliment with ease. She'd known Gunter since she started freelancing as an artist and she valued his opinion. "I know you think I don't eat enough. You're beginning to sound an awful lot like Dawn."

"I know, you women always zink you're fat or something. A man likes to have something to hold on to."

"OK," Jenna sighed, "You're sounding exactly like Dawn. For your information, I have gained three pounds in the last two weeks."

"Good, ve'll have to celebrate soon." Gunter ended the call.

Jenna placed the phone back in its cradle and continued her work. She wondered if Gunter would tell her who he was sending to her house. She knew the answer to that. No.

A ringing phone woke Zyrien later that evening. He opened his eyes from the best nap he had taken in a long time. But it was now after six in the evening. The phone rang again.

He yawned as he reached for his cordless phone. "Hello. Hey Angie, what's wrong? You in labor?"

His sister laughed at his nervous tone. "No, Zyrien. I just called to check on you, because I called you at work and your hyperactive assistant said you went home early. You rarely leave work before the sun goes down unless it's something important."

"I'm fine. Everything is fine. I just couldn't think at work," he confessed.

"Affairs of the heart, I take it."

"Maybe."

Angela huffed. "Why do you do this to me? You know that drives me nuts. Just spit it out."

Zyrien laughed at his sister's tone. She was an incurable romantic. She and her husband, Darrin, had met and married in the span of two weeks. That was five years ago and they were still acting like teenagers in heat.

"Zyrien Alexander Taylor, you'd better tell me," Angela threatened.

He knew he couldn't put her off. "All right. There's this woman at work. She's older than me," Zyrien began his story.

Angela listened as he continued his saga, before offering her opinion. "I hate to say I told you so, but I think this is what you need. She doesn't sound like those other women you've dated. I think she's gonna put you in your place."

"And just what is that supposed to mean?"

"You know you're dense. You're used to a certain kind of woman. The kind that let you do whatever and say nothing. This sister sounds like she does her own thing."

He already knew that. "Tell me something I don't know. What about today? How can I make it up to her?"

"Does she want you to make it up to her?"

Now that was a million-dollar question. And he only knew one way to find out. "Thanks for the advice, Ang, I'll talk to you later." He pushed the "End" button on the phone and hopped out of bed. He dressed quickly in a pair of knee-length shorts and a T-shirt. He shoved his feet into his favorite leather sandals and rushed downstairs.

He located his keys on the kitchen countertop and headed to the garage. Once inside his car, he extracted a piece of paper from the console. Jenna's address. Zyrien couldn't think of the last time he had used his position in the company to get information on a female. He was losing it and he hadn't even kissed her yet.

Chapter 4

He was crazy.

Or he was horny as hell.

That was the only explanation Zyrien could come up with on the spur of the moment. Here he was, all but stalking a temporary employee.

OK, maybe *stalking* wasn't the word he'd use. But that was just splitting hairs. Yes, Jenna was a temp and dating a temp was a strict no-no at the company. But something about the way she smiled at him and the sway of those slender hips in a tight skirt made him want to take the chance.

He parked his car in front of Jenna's house, not giving a moment's thought to how many infractions he'd committed just to obtain her address. The manager at the temp agency was a little surprised at his request, but she still gave him the information. After a few hints from the very expensive navigational system in the car, he had found her house easily enough.

A few things didn't add up about the mysterious temp. She'd been working at Duncaster and Finch for the last month. Unlike most temps, Jenna wasn't looking for a permanent position. The house was another piece to the puzzle. He would never have figured her for living in the trendy section of Dallas.

The house was cute in an artsy-fartsy way. The lawn was lush and green, something he would never have expected in the heat of a Texas summer. He couldn't imagine Jenna doing yard work. A woman that fine didn't do yard work. Then he noticed a small sign standing in the yard. LAWN MAINTAINED BY MITZI.

He checked his rearview mirror and noticed a black Porsche Cabrera parked behind him. A man of about twenty-five, ten years younger than Zyrien, got out of the car and ambled up the steps to the two-story house. What was this blond-haired man doing at Jenna's house?

Zyrien decided a little closer investigation was needed. He was just about to open the door when he stopped. What was he doing? He hated when people dropped by his house unannounced and now here he was doing exactly the same blasted thing. Was this woman really worth all this?

He watched as the front door opened and he smiled. Hell, yes, it was worth it. Jenna stood in the door in what he considered a pair of very well-worn, tight jeans. She also had on a cropped-top T-shirt, exposing most of her flat stomach.

For a second, he could have sworn she noticed him parked in front of her house without her permission. But she only invited the young man inside and closed the door, much to Zyrien's dismay.

Zyrien pondered his options for a few minutes and had almost talked himself into leaving until he noticed that Jenna and the young man were in a room that just happened to have the curtains open. He slid from behind the steering wheel of the car and decided to play detective.

He felt like a fool, crouching behind the large shrubbery, but it shielded him from view. Besides, Jenna should have closed the drapes if she didn't want anyone to see. *Yeah, that's it; make it her fault, Zyrien.* He chastised himself for being an even bigger idiot by stalking two people. He glanced inside the well-lighted room and gasped. "What is going on in there?"

He noticed a red velour chaise lounge, positioned in a

corner. Jenna walked around the room, stirring something in a large plastic container. Just what kind of kinky stuff was she doing with a guy almost twenty years her junior?

Zyrien stepped closer to the large window. This is what you get for invading her privacy, he reminded himself. He was just about to leave before one of her neighbors called the police when he caught sight of the young man. He was dressed in a bathrobe.

Zyrien's feet were now rooted to the ground. He watched in horror as the young man dropped the robe, revealing his nude body to Jenna, and casually took a seat on the chaise lounge!

That was more than Zyrien needed to see. He stomped to the front door and pounded on it like he owned the place. "Jenna, open this door right now!"

He didn't have to wait long before Jenna appeared. Her light brown skin was tinged with red. She was pissed.

Jenna stared at Zyrien as his nostrils flared with anger. She was just as mad as he was. Her model, Ian Brock, stood behind her, hastily tying the sash on the bathrobe, ready to step in and take charge of the situation, but Jenna could handle her own battles. Especially involving one very nosy young man who was invading her space at the moment. She hated that.

She held up her hand to stop Zyrien from stepping inside her house. "Just one minute, Zyrien. This is my house and I didn't invite you inside. I'm not breaking any of the stringent rules at work by painting a portrait at my house on my own time. What I do here is my own business and no one else's, including yours."

Zyrien nodded at Ian. "Who's your friend?"

"What did I just say?"

"Jenna," Zyrien pleaded. "I want to talk to you."

Jenna tried her best to contain her temper, but this was about all she could take in one evening. Zyrien had somehow found her address and tracked her down like she was on an episode of *America's Most Wanted* or that *Cops* show. "Whatever you have to say to me, Mr. Taylor, you can say it right here in front of Ian, who, by the way, is a paid model."

Zyrien sighed, a slow grin splitting his face as his body visibly relaxed in relief. "He's a model. A model for what?"

"Don't you try to make this about me," Jenna countered, knowing the old bait-and-switch routine when she heard it. "I could have you arrested. I didn't lurk around the windows like a common thief. That was you. You could have just asked me like a civilized person instead of invading my privacy."

"You saw me?"

"Does it matter?"

"Hell, yes, it matters."

Jenna knew the situation was going from bad to worse to there-had-better-be-a-punchline-at-the-end-of-this. She turned to Ian as he pressed against her back. "Ian, why don't you get dressed? I think that's all for tonight. We'll just start fresh tomorrow. I'm sure we won't have all these interruptions on a Saturday, right, Zyrien?"

Zyrien nodded, but was otherwise quiet.

Ian stood firm. "If you don't mind, I would like to hear why this man is lurking around your windows and spying on us. I won't leave you in a dangerous situation alone." He darted a nervous glance in Zyrien's direction. "I'd feel awful if something happened to you."

Jenna had two very stubborn men on her hands. Knowing the night would only get worse, she relented. "OK, Ian. Get dressed and we'll be in the living room."

That seemed to appease the man. He walked down the hall in the direction of the bathroom. Now, she had to deal with Zyrien. "OK, Mr. Taylor, why don't you come in, before all my neighbors think I'm having an orgy and want to participate?" She ushered him inside her house.

Zyrien had one chance to make up for all the things he'd

done wrong that evening. The list was only getting longer. He shouldn't have come to her house unannounced. He knew that, now. But at the time it had seemed like a grand idea.

He followed her into the room she called a living room, but he couldn't imagine how she could live in the room. Too many colors leaped out at him. Prosaic was his thing. He couldn't imagine relaxing in a room as busy as this one.

The oversized couch was red, blue, and green plaid, red being the dominant color. The chaise lounge was the deepest shade of red he'd ever seen in all his years, but it looked comfortable and able to accommodate Jenna's long legs. The coffee table was made out of oak, but it looked to have been refinished and now it had specks of red paint on it. He couldn't decide whether or not the paint spattering was intentional.

Zyrien liked neutral colors. That's why the walls in his house, his office, and the interior of his car were beige. Something nice and quiet. As he sat on the comfortable couch waiting for Jenna, Zyrien shook his head in wonder. Who knew she would be into bright, sassy colors?

"The colors are a little out there, huh?" Jenna sat on the edge of the chair almost laughing at Zyrien's expression.

"No," he lied. "It's just a little more than I'm used to."

She leaned back and grabbed a small pillow that had too many colors on it to count. "I like in-your-face things. I like bold colors. You know, something to get your blood pumping." She smiled, glancing around her living room as if seeing it for the first time.

It got his blood pumping all right, he mused, but knew he couldn't tell her that. "Why was that guy posing like that?"

"Why were you snooping outside of my house?"

"Don't change the subject."

She watched him for a long time. Her seductive brown eyes taking in his every scar and mole, and his five o'clock shadow. "I am an artist, Zyrien."

Well, he wasn't expecting that. "Is that your career path?"

"Usually."

"Why are you working at Duncaster and Finch, then?"

"Because I need the money."

He gazed around the living room. The house didn't look like it belonged to someone who needed money. "You could always sell this house."

She shook her head. "No. I love living here. I'm surrounded by the things I love."

Now that he had time to really look at her and the little he had learned about her, he could see that. "So why are you working at Duncaster and Finch? You should be creating."

"Buy a painting," she said. "Then I won't have to work."

Zyrien was about to comment when Ian entered the room. Ian took a seat on the couch at the opposite end from Zyrien.

"Has he explained why he was lurking outside? I could call my dad. He's the chief of police in Highland Park," Ian said, ignoring Zyrien's presence.

Jenna smiled. "No, Ian. Zyrien was just about to explain before he leaves."

Oh, so I'm leaving, huh? "Yes, Ian, I was concerned for Jenna's safety and I didn't know who you were. I'm sorry to intrude on your work time. So you won't have to bother your father. I'm sure the one crime they have in exclusive Highland Park this year will keep him very busy." He rose to leave, knowing he had indeed worn out his welcome.

"I'll walk you out, Zyrien," Jenna announced as she rose as well.

Zyrien had been around too many sistahs in his lifetime to know this wasn't over. Jenna was being polite for the sake of her model, nothing more, and nothing less. He nodded and headed for the front door. As he opened it, he heard Jenna whisper. "If you ever come to my house unannounced again, you're going to wish for Ian's dad to come arrest you. If I want your attention, I will let you know. Good night, Mr. Taylor."

Chapter 5

Faced with a closed door, Zyrien walked to his car with his heart in his hands. He had acted irrationally. There was no way around that. He was getting ready to do an about-face when his cell phone rang. His cousin and best friend, Lance Harris, was on the other end. "Hey, Lance." Zyrien tried to insert some life into his voice, but failed.

"Hey cuz, what's up? What's got you sounding like you just wrecked your ride? You didn't, did you?"

"Of course not," Zyrien said. "I'm just not feeling too good right now."

"I have the perfect solution. Let's go kick back a few beers at the Micro House and talk about it." The Micro House was a microbrewery that also doubled as a bar in downtown Dallas. It was also the newest place to hang out and be seen.

Zyrien needed something to boost his spirits and shake Jenna out of his brain. "All right. Just so happens I'm probably about ten minutes from there."

"What are you doing downtown? I know you're chained to your job and all, but this is too much," Lance said.

"Aw man, it ain't like that. Why is everybody trying to get all up in my business?" Exasperated, Zyrien took a deep breath. "If you must know, I was at a friend's house."

Lance laughed, turning down the blaring music in the background. "So you were at a female's house."

"Yeah."

"So bring her along. Is she legal? Can she buy her own brew?"

Zyrien knew his cousin was just being sarcastic. Lance and Jenna would get along great. "I know, I've dated a few women in their twenties who were financially challenged, but you're acting like they were underaged or something."

"No, cuz, it's just that last girl was nineteen with two babies, ready for you to become instant daddy. I'm glad you finally saw the light. She just wasn't good enough for you. So where were you?"

He really didn't want to rehash the horrible mistake he'd made that night. "Why don't you wait until we get to the Micro House? Then you can tell me how stupid I was."

"You've got a deal. See you in fifteen." Lance ended the call.

Zyrien slid behind the wheel of the car and headed for the Micro House.

Lance wasn't too hard to find, Zyrien realized, as he entered the bar. He was sitting at the bar with a glass of beer in front of him and a woman on either side of him. At forty, the former professional football star was still one of the biggest celebrities in Dallas.

Zyrien walked toward his cousin. He watched Lance say something to the ladies and they scampered off. "How does your wife stand it?" he asked, sitting on the bar stool next to Lance.

His cousin finished the last of his beer before he spoke. "Because Traci knows I'm coming home to her untouched. She attracts the guys, so it's a two-way street. It's called compromise, cuz. Now, what woman has you leaving her house this early?"

As much as he hated to admit it, Zyrien knew his cousin was a great sounding board for affairs of the heart. Lance was always the voice of reason. "Well, I met this woman at work."

"I already know how this is going to end. What is she? Twenty-one with three kids, baby daddy in jail?"

Zyrien grinned. Jenna was a complete turnaround from any women he'd ever dated. "Actually this woman is forty-two, no kids, and she's an artist."

Lance held up his hand in a cross formation. "Hold up, time-out. Did you say this chick is forty-two?"

"Yes, I did."

"So what's she working with?"

"You'll just have to wait and see, won't you? Provided I can get her to speak to me again."

Lance shook his empty glass at the bartender. "Make it two," he told the young girl. "Start at the beginning, Zyrien."

He did, and felt much better getting it off his chest. "I just don't know what to do now."

After Jenna slammed the door in Zyrien's face, she felt better, but only for a second. It just wasn't in her nature to be that mean, even if he had overstepped his boundaries and she had every right to be.

As she walked back into the living room where Ian waited patiently, she smiled. However misguided his passion was, at least Zyrien had some, she thought.

"What has you smiling like that? Surely not that short man who just left here." Ian stood and faced her. "Jenna, since your little friend has ruined the night, let's go have a brewski."

"I don't know, Ian. I really need to get to bed early. I'm going to the flea market in the morning and I want to get there bright and early to scope out the bargains."

Ian shook his head at her. "Not good enough. Come on, it's Friday night, we both deserve a little relaxation."

Jenna thought for a moment. He was right; after Zyrien's surprise visit, she could use some relaxation. But the kind of relaxation she had in mind didn't come in a bottle.

Later, as Jenna entered the crowded bar, she decided Ian was right. The building was larger than she'd imagined. She and Dawn would have to come here on girls' night. The atmosphere was just right for Dawn, she thought—plenty of guys to drool over her voluptuous form.

The Micro House was just the kind of place to kick back and relax. It was a four-story renovated warehouse. The two top floors were for the brewery, the bottom floor was the bar area, and the second floor was a dedicated gift shop.

It reminded Jenna of a trendy coffeehouse, mainly because of the couches in the middle of the room. There were also booths, tables, and a circular bar. The bar was crowded with men watching a baseball game or whatever sport was played in the summer. There had to be fifty guys seated around the bar and there were probably ten televisions. One man in particular stood out to Jenna more than the rest.

"Of all the bars in town," she murmured, ready to retreat from the bar before he saw her.

But Ian grabbed her by the waist. "Hey, the bar is this way." He grabbed her hand and led her to two vacant stools at the end of the bar. Unfortunately, they were in Zyrien's direct line of vision.

"That's her!" Lance blurted out a little too loud. Patrons around the bar glanced in the direction of Lance's pointing finger.

Zyrien almost regretted pointing Jenna out to his cousin when she and that idiot, Ian, walked into the bar arm in arm. "Yes, that's her. What do you think?"

"I think she's about three inches taller than you. How does that work logistically? If you know what I mean," Lance hinted.

"Why does it have to be about sex, man?"

Lance glanced across the bar and shook his head. "Man, she's hot. I can't believe she's over forty. That woman is gorgeous! Man, if I weren't in love with my wife, I would be over there knocking that guy out of the way and taking her out of here and making her my woman."

"OK, OK," Zyrien said trying to control his temper. "You can stop with all the playa commentary."

"Why you tripping? You act like you don't know what to do with a woman like that. Man, she ain't got no kids, no drama, her own place, and she's creative. I bet she's a freak in bed. That adventurous kind of woman who'll try just about anything. That spells a damn good catch in my book. And plus she looks like a million bucks. You're stupid for still sitting here."

Jenna tried to keep her eyes on Ian and his animated conversation about his career as a male model. She tried. Really, she was trying not to give in to her desire to sneak a peek at Zyrien. Finally, she pretended to wipe her mouth with a napkin while glancing across the room. She and Zyrien locked gazes. *Darn.*

"Jenna, are you even listening to me? I'm sitting here telling you about the biggest modeling gig of my twenty-five years and you are gazing across the bar at Tarzan."

"Tarzan?"

Ian shook his head. "You know, that fool that beats on his chest like he's king of the world, like he was beating on your front door. I'm at least four inches taller than him," he leaned toward Jenna, whispering, "in all directions." He winked at her.

"Ian!" Jenna laughed. "I can't believe you just said that." But she wasn't so dumb not to notice certain things. Like Ian constantly touching her, and being only a breath away from kissing her. Even with all that, Ian didn't jump-start her engine.

"Jenna, you're a beautiful woman. A man would be insane not to want you."

"Now, how about that beer I owe you?" She hoped he took the hint and changed the subject.

"You drink beer? Most women just drink wine."

"I do drink wine, but I love microbeers. My favorite is this brew called Fat Tire. It has a little kick to it."

"OK," Ian agreed. "I'll try one."

"Good," Jenna faced the bartender, smiling. She could order beers and still sneak a peek at Zyrien.

Which was what she did.

Zyrien stared at Jenna. She was actually laughing with Ian and touching him on the arm. Maybe they were lovers and maybe he was a fool.

"Zyrien, why don't you just go over there, knock that guy out of the chair and have a conversation with that woman and find out what the heck is going on?"

Zyrien finished his beer and signaled for another. "No. I do have some pride."

Lance laughed. "I can't tell. You're watching her. She's watching you. Sitting here doing nothing is just crazy."

Zyrien was about to remark when a woman approached Lance.

"Lance, it's nice to see you out without your wife."

Lance winked at Zyrien. "Hey Hannah, it's nice to see you. No, Traci isn't here tonight. This is my cousin Zyrien Taylor."

Zyrien didn't like this woman openly flirting with his married cousin. So what if she looked like a dead ringer for Julia Roberts? She spelled trouble with a capital *T*. She offered him her pale skinny hand. "Nice to meet you, Hannah. Where's your husband?"

Lance coughed, trying to cover his laugh. "Don't mind

my cousin. He's in a foul mood. Hey, why don't you do me a big favor?"

"Anything for you Lance, you know that."

"See that guy over there talking to the black woman across the bar?"

Hannah glanced across the bar. "Yes, I see her. What about her? Don't tell me you want her?"

"I'm happy and in love with my wife, you know that," Lance said. "I want you to distract the man, so my cuz here can make a little small talk with the woman. It would really help us out."

Hannah looked like she was really thinking about it, but Zyrien also noticed how she was looking at Lance. She would have walked through hell for him, if he asked her.

"OK, Lance. I'll go to the ladies' room first, then I'll make my move." She eased off the stool and headed away.

Zyrien shook his head in amazement. "Man, you got a lot of nerve. You know she wants you."

"Yeah, but she ain't going to get me," Lance said confidently. "Hey, she's going to take care of ol' boy, so you just be ready to make your move."

Zyrien sat at the bar waiting for his opportunity. Two beers later, he finally saw the moment he had been waiting for. Ian slid off the bar stool and headed for the men's room. Zyrien laughed as Hannah followed him.

Lance faced his cousin. "OK, man, do me proud." He nodded at Jenna. "Man, you know she's got it going on if she can down a beer like that. Personally, I think she's going to give you a run for your money."

Zyrien stood. "What does that mean?" But he already knew. Jenna wasn't like any woman he had ever dated. He was hooked already and they hadn't even kissed. Hell, they hadn't had a real date yet.

"You know what that means. When you do finally touch her, you will burst into flames. Go."

There was no point in arguing with his cousin, Zyrien knew, because Lance was absolutely correct. Zyrien walked through the maze of people, trying to get to Jenna. When he finally rounded the side of the bar, he noticed that a young man was seated in Ian's vacated seat.

He neared the couple. The guy was younger than Ian! He looked all of twenty-one. As he overheard the conversation, he knew from her tone of voice that she was annoyed.

"I told you, my boyfriend will be right back," she told him.

But the young man was persistent. "And I told you, I'm waiting until he gets back. I don't believe you have a boyfriend. I've been sitting here twenty minutes and he hasn't returned. If you were my woman, I wouldn't leave you alone for one second."

Zyrien said a quick thanks to Cupid and intervened. "Sorry it took so long, honey." He wrapped his arm around Jenna's shoulder, inhaling her fresh scent. Even in a crowded bar she smelled like paradise.

It took her a minute to register that Zyrien was rescuing her. "Oh, oh, that's all right. Baby, this is . . ." She smiled at the young man, "I'm sorry I didn't catch your name."

The young man looked absolutely floored. "Jared." He slid off the bar stool and motioned for Zyrien to sit down. "And I was just leaving." He stalked off.

Zyrien knew he had been taking a big chance, but it had worked. He glanced at Jenna, before they both started laughing. At least she wasn't pissed. He sat down facing her. "Well, I guess the painting session is over for the night?"

Jenna crossed her legs. "Yes, we thought we could both use a breather, so Ian wanted to come here." She glanced around the club. "He went to the bathroom a while ago. I wonder what happened to him?"

"Maybe the line is really long," he lied. Zyrien knew that Hannah probably had Ian cornered. "You know, I am really sorry about earlier."

Jenna waved him off. "Forget it."

"I wish I could, but my behavior was intolerable. I would like to make it up to you. How about dinner tomorrow night and then you can tell me all about your art career."

Jenna pondered the offer. "Does that include Ian as well?" She winked at him.

Zyrien knew she was messing with him. His answer would dictate whether he would actually have a date with her. "If you would like him to, he's more than welcome." He couldn't believe he had just offered to pay for a man's dinner. Especially a man he didn't really like.

Jenna finished the last of her beer and signaled the bartender. "Can I get you one?"

"If you give me an answer." Although he didn't approve of women buying his drinks, Zyrien gave in this time. He somehow knew that Jenna had her own rules in life and he would just have to learn to play along.

The bartender approached her. Jenna smiled. "We'll have two Fat Tires, please." The bartender nodded and left the couple.

Zyrien couldn't contain his apprehension. "Jenna, what are you ordering?"

"Trust me," was all she said.

Zyrien didn't like not being in control. It just wasn't in his nature. "If I trust you, what do I get?"

"Why, the biggest gift of all. I will let you take me out to dinner."

That perked him up immediately. She was actually willing to go out with him again, after all their misunderstandings and his showing up unannounced.

The bartender deposited their drinks on the counter and left before Zyrien could even think about paying. Jenna patted his hand. "It's OK, Zyrien, I'm running a bar tab," she explained. "Consider it a present."

"A present for what?"

"Getting rid of Ian." She picked up her glass of beer and

took a healthy swallow. "I just love this brew. Try it, you'll love it."

Zyrien did as she suggested. He hated to admit it, but the brew had just enough of a kick to put his mood in a much better place.

"I didn't get rid of Ian," Zyrien defended himself.

"Please," Jenna drawled. "I saw that Julia Roberts wannabe over there talking to you, then all of a sudden Ian disappears and here you are. I'm not a dunce. I can put two and two together. Tell your friend 'thanks.' Ian was starting to get to me."

Zyrien was shocked, to say the least. Had she really been watching him as intently as he was watching her? A man could only hope. He took another swallow of beer. "Man, this is some good stuff. What do you say to dinner tomorrow night?"

Jenna nodded, smiling, a sure sign she was getting ready to pull the rug from under him. "I'd have to say 'no' to tomorrow night."

Zyrien struggled to maintain a stoic face. He tried to act as if the words she had just uttered hadn't sent his heart straight to his stomach. "Oh, I understand." He really didn't, but he tried to put up a good front anyway.

Jenna caressed his hand gently. "No, you don't. You only heard what you wanted to hear. I said 'no' to tomorrow night, because I have to paint. I'm open to other suggestions."

When Zyrien could breathe again, he said plainly, "That's always good to know."

Chapter 6

Saturday afternoon, Jenna smiled at the portrait on her canvas. The sun streaming into her studio made for perfect lighting. She would have to thank Zyrien for the interruption last night. "OK, Ian, you can get dressed now." Jenna placed her palette of paints on the nearby table. "I can't believe I got so much work done. The portrait is coming along nicely."

She walked down the hall to give Ian some privacy. As she entered the kitchen to brew some Darjeeling tea, she pondered her next project. The phone rang, startling her back to reality.

"Did you go to the museum today? I took my nieces to the Dallas Museum of Art, but I didn't see you." As usual, Dawn didn't give her time to say "hello."

"I know, Dawn. I was so tired from last night that I slept until almost noon. Then Ian came over for our painting session and the day has gotten away from me."

"I thought you were going to paint last night. I was expecting you to tell me that you were halfway through it. What did you and the model get into last night? I thought models, artists, and writers were off your list of possible bed partners?" Dawn chuckled. "I always thought two artistic people needed to be together."

"Not in my case," Jenna answered. "Anyway, Ian and I didn't get into anything. He had just stripped his clothes off when Zyrien showed up unannounced, demanding to know what was going on."

Dawn cleared her throat. "Could you repeat that?"

"Yes, you heard me correctly. He showed up at my house last night and was snooping around like a thief or a stalker. You can just imagine what he thought when he saw Ian posing nude for me."

"Did he think you were running a stud service or what?"

"Pretty much," Jenna commented drily. "Then I had to put him in his place and kicked him out of my house."

"Then what happened? That doesn't sound very tiring," Dawn baited her friend as only Dawn could.

"Well, you know me and my temper," Jenna said. "After I told him about himself, he left. After that, I was just going chalk the night up to bad luck, but Ian persuaded me to go have a drink. We went to the Micro House."

"I hear that's a meat market. When can we go?"

Jenna laughed. "Dawn, you are so bad. I was thinking we could go for girls' night. Anyway, you'll never guess who was there."

"No."

"Zyrien was there with his cousin. You'll never guess who his cousin is."

"A relative of his, I would imagine," Dawn quipped.

"No, Miss Smarty-Pants, he's Lance Harris."

"The retired linebacker for the Dallas Cowboys," Dawn said, clearly in awe. "He's one of the few professional athletes who don't have some kind of scandal or baby mama drama attached to their name."

Jenna nodded. She'd forgotten Dawn was something of a sports nut. "You know he's married. After Zyrien and I buried the hatchet and actually made a date for next week, I was introduced to him. He's really a nice guy and he loves his wife.

He sports a huge, diamond-encrusted wedding band. It's hard to believe he and Zyrien are related. Lance is like six-four and Zyrien is not."

"Am I going to have to start calling you "Shallow Jenna"? This guy must like you to go all the trouble of stalking you," Dawn laughed. "What's a little height differential?"

"It doesn't matter, not really. OK. You know I have a thing about that."

Dawn muttered something undetectable under her breath. "That was years ago, Jenna, let it go."

But she couldn't. She tried, but she couldn't. "You know I was always the tallest girl in class. We were almost seniors in high school before the boys finally started catching up with me."

"Jenna, we were kids then. You know how cruel children can be to someone who's different."

"Yes, but you weren't the one they called all those horrible names." All through school she was known as "giraffe," and "she-giant," and "skyscraper" just because the boys hadn't reached their growth potential.

"Jenna, just because this guy is a little height-challenged, doesn't mean he's less of a person. That was junior high and high school. As you recall, at our twentieth class reunion four years ago, those same guys were trying to hit on you. So you see there is justice in this world."

She realized Dawn was right and she should forget the past and focus on her portrait. "OK Dawn, you're right. I'm really going to try to not think about those horrid years. So what if he's three inches shorter than me? I have a whole two days to get ready for our date."

"Two days. You're going out on an honest-to-goodness date during the week. He can't fix you breakfast in bed if you both have to go to work the next morning."

Jenna shook her head. "For a woman who has been married for five years, you sure do think about sex a lot."

"Well, you forget my husband is also five years younger than me and plays professional hockey."

"No, how could I forget that my best friend is married to one of the most popular players of the Dallas Stars? I bet half the women in Dallas are still mad at you for marrying Chad Brunner and taking him off the market."

"Speaking of, I think he just woke up for round two. Meet me for lunch tomorrow. Bye." Dawn ended the call.

Jenna placed the phone on the counter, laughing. It was off-season for Chad, meaning Dawn was taking advantage of her wifely rights. *Poor Chad,* Jenna mused. *I'll bet Dawn is wearing him out!*

Ian walked into the kitchen fully dressed in khaki shorts and a denim short-sleeved shirt. "Oh, I hope that's coffee. I need some caffeine. I have a date later and she might not like it if I fall asleep on her."

Jenna had a good idea who it was. After he went to the restroom at the bar last night, he only returned to tell Jenna he'd come get his car later. "Is it the brunette from last night?"

Ian grinned. "Yeah," he said. "Hannah is beautiful and smart. She's making me dinner tonight."

"Wow, that's great, Ian." Jenna poured him a cup of tea. "I know you wanted coffee, but this is better than nothing."

Ian nodded and took the cup of hot liquid. After he doctored it to his liking, he took a healthy sip. "Oh, this was just what I needed."

Tuesday night, Jenna sat on the couch waiting for Zyrien to pick her up for their official date. Initially she thought they would dine at the restaurant near work, but he insisted on picking her up at her house.

She was dressed in a light brown linen pantsuit and a pair of black flats. She opted not to wear the matching silk tank top under the jacket. Glancing at her watch again, she told herself to calm down. He wasn't late yet.

Ten minutes later, her doorbell rang. Jenna checked herself in the hall mirror before answering the door. Zyrien stood in her doorway dressed casually in khaki slacks and a polo shirt. He smiled at her.

"You look great, Jenna."

"Thank you, Zyrien. You look nice yourself. Come in." She waved him inside. "I just have to get my purse."

He nodded and headed for the living room while she went down the hall.

When she returned to the living room, Zyrien wasn't there. She walked to the room she considered her studio and there he was, admiring some of her work. "See anything you like?"

"I do now." He was actually flirting with her.

"I was speaking in terms of the picture. What do you think?"

Zyrien stared at the unfinished portrait of Ian. "Hard to believe this is that guy the other night. It looks like an old painting or something."

"It's a Renaissance-style painting."

"Is it sold already?" he asked, walking around the room and noticing some of the other portraits.

"Not yet. I'm hoping to put it in the Dallas Art Gallery when it's finished."

"Why?"

"If I can get it hung in a gallery, more people will see it. Hopefully, the director would ask for more work, or maybe give me a solo showing."

He nodded as if he understood. Which Jenna knew was probably not the case. Most noncreative people never quite understood the art process. "Ready?" was all he asked.

"Yes."

He grabbed her hand and they left the house. After he helped her into his car, they were off. Jenna decided not to worry about what they would talk about over dinner. What did she have in common with a man eight years her junior, anyway?

He headed for the West End, a popular tourist spot in Dallas, and home to the trendiest restaurants. They parked across the street from The Palm Restaurant, a five-star steakhouse, and the pride of Dallas.

Well, that was at least ten cool points, she mused. He led her across the street hand in hand. “Reservation for Taylor.”

The waiter nodded, and ran his chubby fingers over the clipboard. “Yes sir, right this way.”

After they were seated, Zyrien gazed across the table at her. “So, what do you think?” For some reason her opinion mattered very much.

“This is wonderful. Thank you.”

“You’re welcome. Now tell me about you.”

“What about me?” Jenna watched the waiter approach the table.

“May I take your drink orders?”

Zyrien motioned for her to order first. “I’ll have a glass of Kendall Jackson Chardonnay.” Zyrien added a bottle of imported beer and the waiter left the table.

“Tell me about your art?”

Jenna shrugged her shoulders. “I love to paint.”

“How did it start?”

Now that was a painful story. “Well, about fifteen years ago, my mother died of a heart attack. It was so sudden, I had a hard time dealing with it. I went to counseling and was told to find a hobby.”

“So you discovered art?” Zyrien asked, thinking he knew the whole story without hearing it.

“No. I discovered Gunter,” she said with a sly smile. “I met him at a counseling session for grief. He had just lost a lover to AIDS. We became friends instantly. He’s a world-renowned artist, but now he just paints when he wants to and mostly for fun.”

"So what does Gunter have to do with Jenna?"

"Everything," she answered, watching the waiter returning with their drinks. After he took their dinner order, he was gone again.

"Like what?"

"You don't give up, do you?"

"Don't change the subject."

She took a deep breath and began. "Like I said, I was having problems letting go and he helped me find a creative outlet for my frustration. I didn't know I could paint until I met him. I owe him my happiness."

Zyrien knew he wasn't getting any more information out of her. "OK."

Jenna took a sip of the wine. "What about Zyrien?"

"I work a lot." Boy, was that the understatement of the year.

She smiled at him, leaning back in her chair. "Oh, come on, you can do better than that. You're in management. Lie."

He tried his best not to crack a smile, but it was useless. "You're right. I can do better than that." He decided he would bait her just as she had him earlier.

"You were saying." She motioned with her hand for him to continue.

With a dramatic exhale, he continued. "I work a lot, spend time with my family. That's really important to me. Sundays, I spend at my parents'."

"Now was that so hard?"

Yes, actually, it was. He hated talking about himself. "What do you do when you're not creating a masterpiece, or working?"

"I go to museums, lectures, garage sales, and shopping."

He held back a retort that would no doubt send her temper soaring and send him straight to the doghouse. He opted for a more supportive statement, since he wanted to stay on her good side. "That sounds well-rounded."

"In other words, you probably think it's boring. But it's not.

You probably spend your time hanging with your buddies, or boyz." She grinned, taking another sip of wine.

"I told you, I spend a lot of time with my family. You'll find that I'm very mature for my age. Usually, Saturdays, if I'm free, I spend with my nieces, nephews, and a handful of cousins. Like last Saturday I borrowed my dad's SUV and took about ten kids to the bookstore for story time, then out to eat."

"You're very brave. I can't imagine being around that many children at once. I have one niece and she's twelve. And I don't see her very much. My niece lives in Washington State with her mother. My brother's on wife number two and they don't have any children."

He couldn't imagine not seeing someone from his family almost daily. Although he liked his solitude, he cherished the time he spent with the family. "When is the last time you saw your niece?"

She shrugged her shoulders. "I don't know—probably about three years ago. I talk to her once a month."

Zyrien nodded, noting the longing in her voice. He wanted that sassy attitude back. "So why are you here in Dallas?"

She actually smiled. "Dawn. And I was raised here, but Dawn, mostly."

"Dawn?"

"Yes, she's my best friend and my guiding light. We've been friends forever. She's married to Chad Brunner of the Dallas Stars."

"I bet you get some good seats." Zyrien took a long drink of beer.

"Sometimes. Usually, it's at the cost of dating one of his buddies."

Zyrien digested that sentence as he finished his drink. He hadn't meant to drink it that fast but he needed to keep his mouth occupied or he'd say something that would totally make her mad. "Well, I guess you won't be using any of his tickets this season," he declared.

She smiled at him. "I always use his tickets. Do you have any idea how much tickets behind the glass go for? There's no reason I can't use them." She gazed at him with a challenge in those brown eyes.

She definitely knew how to push his buttons.

After their dinner was placed before them, Zyrien continued their conversation. "I mean, if you really want to see a hockey game, we could go together, so no more dates."

"Zyrien, we are only on our first date. I do believe that must be a record in trying to control someone's life. But I have to let you in on a little secret."

"What?" He cut a large piece of the rare steak and put it in his mouth, watching her.

She took another bite of salad, then a tiny piece of meat, chewing slowly, savoring the flavor. She wiped her mouth, knowing that she had his attention. Jenna leaned across the table and he could see her cleavage quite well. "I'm uncontrollable. As long as you remember that, we'll get along just fine."

Zyrien coughed, and tried to avert his eyes from her cleavage but he couldn't. It was like looking at the eclipse. He knew he wasn't supposed to, but he couldn't tear his gaze away from the view.

He reached across the table, grabbing her hand and caressing it gently. He whispered in a low tone, "Just remember I don't like being told what I can't do and we'll get along even better."

Jenna swallowed hard, knowing all too well the look Zyrien had in his eyes. Desire. Lust. Maybe a little of both, she hoped. "We should finish our meal."

But Zyrien didn't remove his hand. "You don't feel it?"

Of course she did; she wasn't dead. "Feel what?" This was

going to be more difficult than the little fun she had originally envisioned.

"You know perfectly well what I mean." He finally removed his hand and resumed eating his meal. "But I'll play it your way. For now."

Where was Dawn when she needed her? Jenna shook off her nervousness and regained some of her confidence. They finished the meal in silence. She watched as he signed the credit card receipt and rose. "Ready?"

For what? "What?"

Zyrien smiled at her, reaching for her hand. "I think we need to take a walk before we head back to your place or you'll get me into trouble."

At least somebody has some brain cells, she thought. "That sounds like a good idea. I haven't been down here in a while."

He nodded, knowing she was babbling. He grabbed her hand and they walked outside into the hot Texas night. Jenna figured he would let her hand go once they were outside. He didn't.

They walked in silence, taking in the sights along the nearly deserted streets in the West End. Jenna diverted her mind from thinking how heated Zyrien's hand was and thought of her art project. She wanted to capture that heat on canvas.

"I demand equal time in your head, Jenna," Zyrien said.

"What are you talking about?"

He stopped walking and stood in front of her. He leaned toward her and kissed her gently on the lips. "I demand as much time as you give your art project. When you're with me, you're with me."

She smiled. Was he actually jealous of her career? Or was he trying to control her already? "I can't control the creative process. When an idea pops into my head, it's there and there's nothing I can do about it."

He pulled her closer to him, pressing her body against his.

"Well there's something *I* can do about it." He leaned toward her and kissed her gently on the mouth again.

Before he knew what happened, she placed her hands on either side of his face to bring his lips in kissing range. "Well here's what you should do about it." She kissed him hard, lips against lips.

"Jenna, what are you doing—?"

Jenna didn't answer him. She slipped her tongue past his lips and headed for his tonsils. She didn't stop until she felt him moan and his lower body finally getting into the picture. *That's more like it,* she thought. Slowly she ended the kiss. They stood locked in an embrace in the middle of the West End, panting like they had just won the Dallas Marathon.

Chapter 7

The next morning, Jenna entered her department, instantly noticing her coworker, Dezarae Rucker, standing by her desk with her back to Jenna. "Good morning, Dez, what's going on?" Dez turned and faced Jenna with a sly expression on her pecan-brown face. "I love that dress." It hugged Dez's petite frame, giving her trim hips volume.

Dez looked at her, smiling. She ran her hand over her dress. "I got it at Wal-Mart. But you should see what came for you." The petite woman stepped aside.

Jenna couldn't believe her eyes. Two dozen red roses sat in a crystal vase on her desk. "Oh my gosh!" She stepped closer to the flowers, dropping her purse on the floor with a thud. "How long have they been here?"

Dez tossed back her shoulder-length hair and shrugged her slender shoulders. "I got here at seven and they arrived shortly after that."

Jenna hoped they were from Zyrien, but didn't want Dez to know. Besides, it wouldn't look good with her being a temporary employee and him being a manager. It could mean the end of her job. "Who brought them in?"

"The receptionist," Dez answered. "Who did you think was going to bring them?"

Before Jenna could formulate a decent answer, Dez's phone began to ring. She knew it was Dez's husband. "I bet that's Dante making his morning call," Jenna teased.

Dez rolled her brown eyes toward the ceiling. "He's just calling to tell me he dropped the baby at day care. Like he has to report in or something. Just once I'd like him to say, 'Hey boo, I love you. Let's skip work and go get our groove on.'" She stomped the few steps to her desk to answer the phone.

Jenna opened the card, scanned it, and then laughed out loud. She read the card again. "Jenna, no one has affected me the way you do." It was signed,"Your next model."

"So who bought the temporary employee flowers?" an irritated female voice asked. "I hope it wasn't an employee?"

Jenna looked in the direction of that voice in confusion. She was about to answer, but Dez answered for her. "If you must know, Katonya, they're from her man. Not that it's any of your business, anyway."

Katonya narrowed her eyes at Jenna. "Maybe it's her lunch partner. I'd hate for the higher-ups to know who's been to the West End recently." She stalked away.

Jenna and Dez stared at each other for a moment before they burst out laughing. "That woman has been on my case since I started here. She gives me twice the work of anyone else."

"Don't worry about Ms. Thing," Dez told her. "She thinks her you-know-what don't stink. Anyway, she's always bragging about how she can get a man to do this and that for her. Well, she used to date Zyrien Taylor a few months ago until he broke it off. Turns out, she'd been seeing someone up here while she was dating him and he found out. Now she wants Zyrien back, but he don't want her and baby daddy is in jail for the third time."

Jenna shrugged. "That has nothing to do with me," Jenna lied. "I just wish she'd leave me the heck alone and let me do my job. I don't know why she's singled me out for torment.

There are several other temps in this department she could harass." She sat in her chair and turned on her computer.

Dez stood at Jenna's desk. "Oh, I think you know. But I can wait for you to share that reason." She walked to her desk.

Jenna ignored Dez's remark and signed on to her computer. She opened her e-mail program and giggled. She had five e-mails from Zyrien. Unfortunately, she also had five from Mr. Storm giving her more work. It was almost as if both he and Katonya had it in for her.

With a sigh, she started working on her assignment. She opened the spreadsheet labeled "Open Invoices." As usual, it was something her boss was supposed to have done. She keyed in the first invoice and noticed it had not been paid through the company's computerized accounting system. Great, she thought, it might have been paid manually, meaning a single check had been cut to pay the vendor. After a little investigation, she found out that was the case. Her boss had approved the payment himself, but failed to move the item to the "Paid" file.

She shook her head and started working on the next one. After about the fifteenth one, she got another e-mail. It was from Zyrien and he wanted to know why she hadn't responded to the other e-mails.

She decided to call him. "I want to thank you for the flowers," she whispered into the phone.

He muttered something under his breath. "We're not going to do this now. I have people in my office. I'll talk to you later, OK?" He ended the call.

Jenna hung up the phone, not knowing if she should be mad or not. Not wanting to give in to negative energy, she went back to work.

Zyrien grinned as he replaced the phone in its cradle. He had caught Jenna totally off guard with his brusque tone and for the first time in the last week, he felt in control of his world.

"So are we going to finish going over the notes for the

project or what?" Brenna spoke, interrupting his moment of triumph. "You have a production meeting with sales in an hour."

Zyrien snapped back to the present. "Actually, Brenna, get started on that and we'll meet this afternoon. I need to run some numbers before my meeting."

"Zyrien, something else is on your mind, and it's not this report that you're behind on. Would you like to talk about it?"

He looked across the mahogany desk at Brenna's expressive blue eyes and noted the caring look on her small face. "Thanks, Brenna, but it involves a member of your sex and you would probably take her side out of loyalty," he teased. "Just get those numbers I need and get back to me."

Brenna stood, and walked to the door. "Sure, Zyrien. Did you want me to check with Essential Temps as well, since that's the temporary firm we traditionally use?"

He shook his head. "No, we already know what their price margins are and their restrictions. See if the other companies allow their employees to work overtime or not."

Brenna watched him for a moment. "What about the full-time aspect? A lot of the Essential Temps don't work full-time hours *or* overtime."

"I know. That's the one thing in their favor. A lot of people working temporary don't want the added responsibility of mandatory overtime."

Brenna nodded, starting for the door. "You'd better call her back and apologize for your rude behavior. Or you'll be buying more than just a few dozen roses." She winked at him. "That was an internal ring, wasn't it?" She let herself out of his office.

Zyrien laughed as the door closed. And he thought he was being secretive. He definitely owed Jenna something, but an apology wasn't it. He leaned back in his chair, basking in his glory, when his phone rang again. It was a double ring, so he knew it wasn't Jenna. "Zyrien Taylor."

"Oh, I'm glad I caught you," Angie said. "I need a tiny favor."

Oh no, he thought. Why was his pregnant sister calling him? "Anything. What is it?"

"Can I bunk at your house tonight and maybe tomorrow?"

He took a deep breath. "What's wrong? You and Darrin finally have a fight?" He really couldn't afford to be distracted any more than he was already. "Don't tell me you guys waited five years into the marriage to start fighting."

Angie sniffed, and then the waterworks began. "He left me. He's been gone two days. I just didn't want to say anything to anyone. I guess it was my silly pride. Zyrien, what am I going to do?"

Zyrien tried to calm his sister through the phone. "Hey, baby girl, it's me. Tell me what happened." Zyrien took a deep breath and listened as his very pregnant sister attempted to tell him what happened to her very happy marriage.

"What do you mean, he said he was going to the store? This doesn't sound like Darrin. He's more responsible than that," Zyrien began stuffing papers into his briefcase.

Angie's cries finally slowed to a few hiccups. "It was because of the sonogram. The doctor said he thinks it might be twins. After that, Darrin kind of zoned out. He didn't say much on the way home and that night he slept in the guest room. But I haven't heard from or seen him since then. At first I thought the prospect of two children at once was it."

Zyrien tried to contain his anger as best he could. He liked his brother-in-law and this definitely seemed out of character for him, but he was sounding like a jerk. "Look, Ang, sit tight and I'll come get you."

He grabbed his briefcase and headed for the door. As soon as he shut his office door, he started reciting instructions to his assistant. "Brenna, I have a family emergency. Cancel my meeting and forward my calls to my voice mail. I'll check the messages later. Call me on my cell if there's a problem." He headed for the elevator, hoping that his brother-in-law would come to his senses quickly. The last thing his sister needed was to worry about the state of her marriage.

He didn't think about Jenna until he parked in front of his sister's two-story house. "Damn. She's going to skin me alive," Zyrien muttered as he took his cell phone out of his briefcase. He dialed the switchboard and asked for Jenna's extension.

He waited patiently for her to pick up the phone, but it went to her voice mail. He glanced at his gold watch, swearing loudly. Between meetings and trying to calm his sister, it was now Jenna's lunchtime.

He took a deep breath and slid out of the car. After he rang the doorbell twice, his heart began to race. Suppose the stress of a missing husband had been too much and Angie now needed medical attention? He jabbed the doorbell again. Finally a teary-eyed Angie opened the door.

"Any word?" Zyrien asked as he walked inside the house. He glanced around the living room. As usual, nothing was out of place. In his mind, he compared Jenna's colorful room to his sister's monochromatic house.

Angie blew her nose and rubbed her protruding stomach. "No, nothing. His cell phone is upstairs. His mother called this morning, and I finally had to tell her."

"What does she think?" He ushered his sister to the couch. "Does she have any idea where he is hiding?" Hiding was exactly what Darrin was doing, Zyrien thought.

Angie sat down and took a deep breath. "She can't believe he did something like this. Zyrien, you don't think he's found someone else and he's with her, do you?" Fresh tears streaked his sister's face.

He sat by his sister, cursing his brother-in-law for being such an idiot and running off without a word. "Angie, don't worry about that right now. I know that's not what you want to hear, but you don't need to make yourself sick."

"I think it's too late for that." She stood and headed for the nearest bathroom.

While his sister was emptying her stomach, he went to pack her overnight bag. When he returned, she was sitting on the couch. "Come on, sis, you'll see. It will all work out."

"But what if he doesn't come back?" She looked at him with those big brown eyes, breaking his heart.

He reached for her hand, helping her up. "Then we will handle it together as a family. You know we all love you, and whatever happens, we can handle it."

She wiped her eyes and headed toward the front door, with Zyrien on her heels. After they locked the house, Zyrien helped her into the car and they were gone.

Angie was too quiet. He would have given anything to hear her endless chatter about the state of his love life, but she sat in the passenger seat motionless and pale. Too pale. She looked like she was ready to blow chunks; not in his car, he hoped. "I think we should take you to the doctor. You don't look right to me."

"Zyrien, I feel fine." But she didn't look fine. Beads of sweat dotted her forehead and her breathing was very labored.

"Just humor me." He headed for the doctor's office.

He thought they would have to wait to see the doctor, but after they used a few well-placed words, like pregnant woman, husband gone missing, and stomach pain, she was rushed right in. Angie's doctor checked her over and prescribed bed rest.

As Zyrien got his sister settled in his guest bedroom, he broached the subject gently. "You know we're going to have to tell Mom."

She closed her eyes at the thought. "I know," she sighed. "Would you? I mean, I know I'm asking a lot, but I just can't go through it all over again. It was hard enough telling you."

Zyrien could only imagine how much his beloved sister was hurting. "Sure, baby. I'll fix you something to eat, too." He watched fresh tears trickle down her face as he closed the door. "Darrin better hope I don't find him first," Zyrien muttered as he walked downstairs.

After he finished discussing the situation with his parents, Zyrien prepared his sister some lunch. His parents were coming over later for dinner, and his mother was going to cook so he could get to work on his report.

But the most important thing right now was to keep his sister calm and out of the hospital. Which is what he reminded his mother that evening. "Mom, the main thing we need to do is keep Angie quiet and not fretting about that idiot. I'm sure he's just scared, but he's not seeing her right now, if he does show up here."

Arabella Taylor agreed. "Yes, I think that's best for now." She started preparing dinner. "Now, I'll stay here tonight so you can work."

Zyrien looked at her as Jenna's face popped into his brain. He never called her back. "Work! Jenna! Damn!" He was going to be under the doghouse.

"Zyrien Alexander Taylor, watch your mouth!" his mother scolded him.

"I'm sorry, Mom. I just remembered I need to call someone. She probably thinks I'm doing this not-calling business on purpose." He dashed off for the nearest phone. He quickly dialed Jenna's home number, since it was almost seven o'clock in the evening. But her answering machine told him she wasn't home. He realized she was either painting or she was out. Whichever it was, he couldn't talk to her.

Even with all that had transpired that day, he still wanted to hear her voice. He left a message for her to call him later.

"I hope this one doesn't have any children," his mother said as she set the table for dinner. "That last woman was just looking for a daddy for those horrible kids."

Zyrien smiled. Jenna was the direct opposite of any woman he'd ever dated. He usually dated younger women awestruck by his accomplishments, but Jenna didn't give a fig about what he had. “Well, actually, Jenna doesn’t have any children.” He couldn’t imagine Jenna with children. She had too much free spirit for discipline.

Bella smiled. “That’s good. How old is this girl?” She arranged three place settings on the table.

“Well actually, Jenna is a little older than me and she’s an artist.”

“How much older?”

“She’s forty-two,” Zyrien admitted, waiting for his mother to say that Jenna was too old for him.

“So she’s eight years older, good. She has some maturity about her.”

“Well, I wouldn’t go that far, Mom. She’s used to doing things her own way and our lifestyles are totally different. Her living room has so many colors in it, it gives me a headache just thinking about it. She drives a PT Cruiser, not a sensible car for a woman her age.” He left out the part about her painting nudes and him all but stalking her.

“You know opposites attract. I knew there was a woman out there who would put you in your place.”

“Well, that still has to be seen. There’s not a woman who can resist the Taylor charm. Besides, we’ve only had one real date and that was a battle in itself. I’m used to women putting me first. To Jenna, painting comes first.”

“Maybe she can paint me one day,” his mother said. “I would love to have a professional portrait done.”

“Mom, I’ve only been seeing her a little over a week. Provided we get past tonight, I think it’s a little early to be asking for a hookup. I don’t really think you’d want her painting you, anyway.”

“Why is that?” His mother sat at the table, facing her son.

“Mom, she paints nudes, mostly.”

Bella grinned. “Well, then I definitely want her to paint me. It can be a gift for your father. He always says I still look as good as the day we met.”

Zyrien shook his head. Why did his mother torture him so? The thought of his parents in an intimate situation always sent him to a bad place. “You have just overstepped the mother-son discussion line. Again. No talk about you and dad doing anything remotely connected with sex. That’s not natural.”

His mother grabbed a napkin, crumpled it up, and threw it at him. “You are such a prude!”

Chapter 8

OK, so he didn't call.

Jenna walked into her house, heading to the counter to check her phone messages. She'd just finished listening to a message from Dawn when the phone rang.

She walked to the nearest phone and looked at the caller ID display. Zyrien. As the phone rang incessantly, she finally picked it up, counted to ten, and said, "Hello."

"Jenna! My God, I've been worried about you," Zyrien said. "Are you OK?"

"Yes, Zyrien. Is there something you wanted?"

"Why the attitude?"

Jenna took a deep breath and walked to the living room. Something told her it was going to be a long conversation and she might as well get comfortable.

"Didn't you get the roses?" Zyrien asked impatiently.

"Yes, I got the roses," she said in a clipped voice.

He inhaled as if he was trying to contain his temper. "Jenna, I have had one incredible day. You wouldn't believe the things I've went through."

She heard the fatigue in his voice and wondered at it. "Why don't you try me?"

He hesitated. Then he took the one chance she gave him

and ruined it. "I'd rather not. It's personal and it involves my family."

Jenna saw the line he'd just drawn and grunted. "Well, don't worry, Zyrien. I wasn't trying to be nosy or anything. I was just offering a sympathetic ear. Good night."

Jenna replaced the phone on its charger, and headed to the kitchen. After getting some bottled water, she headed to her studio to study the painting. She had progressed a great deal and decided she could take the night off from painting.

Zyrien looked at the phone wondering where the hell Jenna could have gone in such a short span of time. "Man, I just don't get women," he muttered as he walked down the hall to check on his sister.

"Don't tell me, she didn't appreciate that 'it's personal' line?" his mother asked as she exited the hall bathroom.

"Mom, why are you listening at my door?"

"I wasn't listening. Your voice carries," his mother commented. "You know these new houses have thin walls. Zyrien, everyone has some kind of trouble, even you. I'm sure she would understand."

"But maybe I'm just not ready to put all my business in her court. I'd feel exposed and she'd used it against me."

His mother stared at him, shaking her head in disapproval. "Zyrien Alexander Taylor, I didn't raise you to be this unfeeling person."

He knew he probably should have told Jenna something and knew there would be hell to pay for this. "Mom, please. My main concern is Angie right now and finding that idiot husband of hers."

"Just don't forget about Jenna. No one likes feeling neglected."

Zyrien took a deep breath and sighed. "I know, Mom." He walked down the hall to his sister's room. He opened the door, peeked inside, and smiled. His sister was sound asleep on her side. Zyrien closed the door and went back to his room.

Once inside, he took a deep breath and looked at the pile of papers stacked on his nightstand. The report. He had planned to work on the report this afternoon, but between his sister, his mother, and Jenna, there just wasn't any time.

"No time like the present." He slid between his white cotton sheets, propped himself up in bed, and began reading the report.

But the numbers still didn't make any sense two hours later. The gibberish about the temporary workers' requirements wasn't making any sense. Who ever heard of guaranteed overtime? He rubbed his tired eyes, hoping it would help. It didn't. "Coffee," he said. He threw back the covers and walked downstairs to the kitchen.

"What are you doing up?" Angie asked, sitting at the table with a glass of milk and a sandwich in front of her.

"I could ask you the same thing," Zyrien shot back. He walked to the counter to make some coffee. "How are you feeling?" He stood against the counter waiting for the aroma of Hazelnut Delight to fill the room and silently inspecting his sister's features.

Angie took a deep breath, but it came out in a muffled sob. "OK." Another deep breath. "OK, that's not quite the truth. I couldn't sleep." She reached for a paper towel and wiped her eyes.

Zyrien sat beside her at the table. "Honey, I don't want you worrying about Darrin."

She shook her head. "It's not that."

"What is it?" He felt the thud of his heartbeat speed up. "Do you need to go to the hospital?" He mentally calculated how long it would to get there from north Dallas.

Angie smiled and rubbed her stomach. "You know for a minute I thought something was wrong, 'cause the last few hours I hadn't felt anything. So I got up and came to the kitchen to drink some milk. Then I felt it. A kick, then a turn. So I relaxed and decided to eat something." She gazed at her brother with those eyes that told him something else was bothering her.

"What is it, Ang?"

"I heard you earlier. I don't want to cause trouble between you and your new lady. I don't want to be the reason that something is wrong between you guys. I know our family can be overwhelming, especially when it seems we all turn to you for help at one time or another."

Why was everyone so concerned about him and Jenna? "Don't worry, Angie. Jenna is a little different and we just had our first official date last night, followed by our first official fight today, and it had nothing to do with you."

The next morning, Jenna arrived at her desk, hoping there were some flowers waiting for her today. Maybe Zyrien decided he was wrong and should have shared his family problems with her. Not. The only items on her desk were more files that she needed to complete.

"No, girl, no flowers today," Dez said. "I guess you didn't do a good job, huh?"

"I don't know what you're talking about, Dez." Jenna took her place at her desk and placed her purse in the drawer and locked it. She turned on her computer and opened her e-mail program. Just maybe, she thought. Her heart took a nosedive. No e-mail from Zyrien. She took a deep breath and grabbed the folders her wonderful lazy boss had placed on her desk.

An hour later her phone rang. It double-rang, signaling that it was an outside call. Jenna reached for the phone and took a deep breath. "Accounting, this is Jenna."

Dawn laughed. "Hey, I have some business in your building today. How about some lunch?"

"I thought we were going out for dinner tonight?" Jenna hoped Dawn wouldn't cancel on her. She really needed to talk to her friend.

"We are," Dawn said. "I just have some business in your building and thought we could have lunch somewhere. I want to hear the latest."

"Sorry, there's not much to tell," Jenna said, wishing she had more to tell her friend. "I'll see you at eleven." Jenna hung up the phone.

Two hours later, Dawn walked into the building of Duncaster and Finch, heading straight for the reception area. She approached the desk and spoke clearly. "I am here to speak with Kyle Storm."

The mature woman nodded and immediately dialed his extension. After a few short sentences, she nodded, then looked in Dawn's direction. "Mr. Storm said to meet him on the third floor, room 315." She handed Dawn the temporary security sticker and pointed to the elevators.

Dawn headed for the glass elevators. She stepped inside the empty car and punched the third button. The door slid closed. Before the car could jump to life, it automatically opened again. A muscular African-American man stepped inside the car, smiling.

"Sorry," he said, pushing the button for the seventh floor.

Dawn nodded, noting that his initials were on his button-down shirt: ZAT. Simple deductive reasoning told Dawn this was Jenna's man. He didn't look the way she had him pictured. He was a compact hunk of a man and looked like he took care of himself both physically and mentally. Dawn was expecting a nerd.

They rode the elevator in silence to the third floor. She stepped out and walked down the hall to the room. Kyle Storm was already in the room, waiting on her. His business casual dress differed greatly from Zyrien's. Kyle wore dress slacks and a plain button-down shirt. No initials, no tie, and his cologne didn't do a thing for her senses.

He stood and extended his hand to her. “Mrs. Castle, I’m glad you could make it. I was expecting your manager.”

Dawn took a seat across from the table. “I’m the manager of Harcourt’s Essential Temps, Mr. Storm.”

Kyle’s pale face had a sudden tint of red to it. “I didn’t mean to offend you or anything.”

He had expected someone a little paler, she thought. “You didn’t, Mr. Storm. What can Essential Temps do for you?” Or to you, she thought.

He leaned back in his chair, rolling a gold pen between his long fingers. “It’s about my temporary employee, Jenna Bradshaw.”

“What is it?”

Kyle rubbed his hairless chin. “How long is her assignment?”

“It is temp to perm,” Dawn said with a slight smile. *If this idiot only knew,* she mused. “Is there a problem with her work performance?”

“No,” he said.

“Has she been late?”

“No.”

“Is she the reason for this meeting?”

Kyle stood, and began pacing the length of the small room. Duncaster and Finch had been her biggest client for the last ten years and Dawn would hate to throw that away. “I just wondered—what are her qualifications to work here? Does she have a degree or something?”

Dawn gathered her strength, so she wouldn’t blow her top and lose one of her larger contracts. “If you’d like another worker in her place, just let me know. I have had several other managers ask for Jenna’s services when she’s done in your department,” Dawn lied.

He stopped pacing and stared at Dawn. “Really? You must be kidding.” He sat down in the chair next to Dawn. “I don’t have a problem with her work. In fact we’re thinking of offering her a permanent position. She's too quiet for my taste. I hardly ever see her talk to anyone and she doesn't take notes at the weekly departmental meetings."

But she always does your work, you slimebag, Dawn thought. Funny how that never came up in his conversation, but Dawn decided to make him sweat. "It has come to my attention that she has been doing someone else's work in addition to her own. Surely a man in your position would not let a temp take on more duties than a permanent employee." Dawn paused, letting the words soak through his thick brain. "I have instructed her to inform me anytime she has to do any extra work that is not her usual workload, since Duncaster and Finch is very stringent about the rules for the temporary employees. And I wouldn't want my relationship with this firm to be in jeopardy because someone is passing their work on to a temp."

Kyle nodded in understanding. "Of course, Mrs. Castle, I quite understand and will deal with the situation," he said in a defeated tone.

Dawn smiled and stood, gathering her briefcase and purse. After she had them situated, she extended her hand to Kyle. "It was a pleasure, Mr. Storm."

He nodded, hesitantly taking her hand. "I appreciate you coming here on such short notice."

"That's my job." Dawn left the room and headed for the elevator. She punched the "Down" button and pondered Kyle's questions. They weren't very work-related. Earlier on the phone he had made the meeting sound very critical and necessary, which it wasn't. Dawn had worked with people like Kyle Storm enough times in the last ten years to know he had a hidden agenda for this meeting. She just had to find out what it was.

The elevator arrived and she stepped inside. When she exited the lobby, she whipped out her cell phone and called Jenna. "Why don't we meet at the Italian restaurant?"

"Sure, no problem," Jenna said. "See you in fifteen minutes."

Dawn closed her phone and walked to her car. She was glad they were eating away from the office, since she didn't want Kyle to see her and Jenna together. Not that she had anything to hide, but she had to be careful. Her job was on the line.

Just as Jenna placed the phone back in its cradle, it rang again. A single ring. It could be Zyrien, she hoped, but knew in all probability it was her boss and tormentor, Kyle Storm. She picked up the phone and spoke in her most businesslike tone, "Accounting, this is Jenna."

"Well," Zyrien drawled, "hello, Jenna."

"Hi," she said, tossing a look over her shoulder, checking out whether Dez was in listening distance. She wasn't. "I hope your family is all right."

He took a deep breath. "Yeah, about that," he said quietly, "I really need to talk to you. How about lunch?"

"Sorry, I already have plans with Dawn," Jenna said honestly. *If he had been just a few hours earlier,* she mused.

"Of course," Zyrien said. "I would have asked earlier, but I had an emergency at home this morning, so I just got here."

"That same family issue, I take it."

"I want to tell you about it, but I don't want to do it here. How about dinner?"

Now she really was sorry. Damn girls' night. "I'm sorry. Dawn and I are going out to dinner."

"What is Dawn? Your new lover or what?"

"Look, don't get all stupid male on me. We had already made these plans. Her husband is out of town and she wants to talk."

Zyrien laughed. "OK, OK. That was over the line. I guess we could always have dinner tomorrow night." He took another deep breath. "That is, if you're not painting or something. How is the process going?"

Jenna smiled inwardly. "The process is going just fine, thank you." She softened her next words, "I should be done within a few weeks."

"So are we on for tomorrow night?" Zyrien asked.

"Unless you have another family crisis," Jenna remarked, instantly hating the words exiting her mouth. It made her sound jealous or selfish, she couldn't decide which one. "Sorry, that came out wrong."

"It's OK, Jenna. I know you didn't mean it the way it sounded. How about I pick you up about eight?"

"Sounds good." Jenna ended the call. She glanced at her watch and knew she was going to be late meeting Dawn if she didn't hurry. She grabbed her purse, waved good-bye to Dez, and headed for the elevator.

Once Jenna was inside the restaurant, Dawn waved at her from the bar. A man flanked her on either side. Jenna shook her head and walked toward her friend. "Dawn, what is with you and these guys?" Jenna asked, knowing the men would scurry at her next comment. "What about your husband, the big strong hockey player?"

The men nodded to her and left.

Dawn laughed. "I can't believe you did that. The cute one was going to buy our lunch."

"Now you of all people know I don't allow that."

"I know, but it was nice that he offered. Let's grab a table before they're all gone." She slid off the bar stool and they started walking to the food area, where they sat in a booth. Jenna didn't like the look on Dawn's light brown face. She had a mischievous smile that meant trouble ahead. Jenna took a deep breath and asked, "OK, what?"

Dawn made a production of unfolding her cloth napkin. She handled it like it was raw silk, or some other fragile fabric. Finally, she made eye contact with Jenna. "I had a meeting with your boss this morning."

Jenna smiled. "When is my last day?"

Dawn grinned. "That's the funny thing; he didn't complain about your work. He complained about the fact that you don't talk to the other employees."

"Figures. I don't talk to the other employees because they don't talk to me. And if I did talk to them, he would have said I was distracting them. So what happens now?"

Dawn reached for the menu and shrugged her shoulders. "Don't worry about him. He's got some kind of agenda going on. I just don't know what, or if it involves you."

"He and Katonya are always in his office with the door closed, when she's not giving me more work." She opened her menu, looking for the salad section. "And before you ask, yes I'm getting a salad, since we're eating out tonight."

Dawn held up her hand in mock surrender. "I wasn't going to say anything, at least about that."

"You know when you talk like that, my whole body tenses up. What do you mean?"

"I was just going to tell you that I saw your man this morning on the way to my meeting and wondered if you guys had talked this morning."

Jenna placed her menu on the table. "No, not really. He called me just as I was leaving for lunch and wanted to tell me about his family situation. I explained we had plans already, so we're having dinner tomorrow night."

The waiter came and took their orders. Jenna noticed as she recited her selection that the young man couldn't keep his eyes off Dawn's cleavage, which wasn't showing much, considering that she was wearing a suit. The waiter finally left after Dawn gave her choice twice. Jenna shook her head in wonder. "I just don't get it."

Dawn laughed. "I don't, either. Maybe he knows I'm married to Chad. You know what sports nuts guys can be. I bet

Zyrien loves to play basketball. Usually men of his stature love basketball."

"You mean short men have a Michael Jordan complex, don't you?"

Dawn shrugged. "Who knows? Now where are we eating tonight? Can I pick?"

Jenna watched as the waiter returned with their food. He departed much quicker this time. "I thought we could eat at Harry's, then maybe have a drink at the Micro House."

Dawn smacked her full lips loudly. "Oh, you know I just love Harry's Soul Food and I'm in the mood for good food." Just then her cell phone rang. "This should be Chad."

Jenna listened to the one-sided conversation and smiled as Dawn made loud smacking noises into the phone, then placed it back in her purse. "Well, I guess Chad misses you, huh?"

Dawn nodded, digging into her lunch. "Yes, he said his mother asked if I was pregnant yet."

"How is that going?" Jenna knew Dawn and Chad had been trying for the last two years for a baby, and, since Dawn was forty-two, they both knew time was running out.

"Can you believe that I'm actually tired of having sex?"

Jenna dropped her fork onto the table. "Dawn Castle Brunner, you are doing it again. No bedroom information."

Dawn waved the comment away. "Oh, lighten up."

Later that night, after pigging out on steak, baked potatoes, and salad, the women headed for the Micro House for a drink. They walked inside the bar and found that it wasn't as crowded as it had been the night Jenna came with Ian.

The women found two vacant seats at the bar and sat down. Jenna glanced around the room. No Zyrien. Not that she'd expected to see him, but it didn't hurt to hope. She did see a familiar face. "Oh my gosh, I can't believe he's here."

Dawn was too involved in the actions at the bar to answer

her friend with a logical sentence. She could only mumble something under her breath.

"Dawn, could you stop staring at that man across the bar and look at me?"

Dawn made a silly face at her. "You know my husband has left me. I need something to ease the pain," she said in mock sorrow.

"Yeah, right. Save that for someone who cares," Jenna shot back. "Your husband, who just happens to love you like crazy will be back in two days."

Dawn stuck her tongue out at her. "You're no fun. What are we drinking?"

"Well, I'm having a beer. Are you having your usual?" Jenna signaled for the bartender, smiling as he walked toward them.

"Yes, ma'am," the tall man said, wiping the area in front of Jenna and Dawn. "What can I get you beautiful women tonight?"

Dawn answered for them. "My friend will have a glass of your best microbrew, I believe it's called Fat Tire, and I will have a glass of white wine. Kendall Jackson."

The bartender nodded and quickly walked away. Jenna opened her purse and was about to retrieve her wallet when the bartender returned with their drinks. "From the gentleman." He nodded over his shoulder.

Jenna smiled and waved at Lance. "Tell him 'thank you.'" She watched as the bartender quickly retreated. "That's Zyrien's cousin, Lance Harris."

Dawn fanned herself. "Wow, he's still a hunk. Of course he can't hold a candle to Chad."

Jenna picked up her glass of beer and she saluted Dawn. "Here's to great friendships."

"Now that's a toast." Lance sat next to Jenna. "It's nice seeing you out. How was your date?" He grinned.

Dawn joined the conversation. "Hey, that's why we're here. So you can't find out before me."

Jenna took a deep breath. "Lance Harris, meet Dawn Castle Brunner, my best friend. Dawn, this is Zyrien's cousin, Lance."

Dawn extended her hand. "Nice to meet you. I must say the Cowboys haven't been the same since you retired."

Lance stared at Dawn. "Thank you. You a fan?"

Jenna choked on her beer. "She's only the biggest Dallas Cowboy fan in the state."

"Actually, I'm a bigger Stars fan than a Cowboy fan," Dawn added.

Lance took a drink of his beer. "This is your fault, Jenna. You got me drinking that Fat Tire brew now. This is good stuff." He glanced around the room as if he were looking for someone. "Why are you a hockey fan? I didn't think the sisters were into that sport. They're always saying it's too violent."

Jenna knew Dawn loved this part. She sat quietly and watched her best friend work her magic on Lance. Poor fool, Jenna mused; he hadn't even seen it coming.

Dawn took a small sip of wine, and placed her glass on the table. "I've only been a hockey fan for the last six years. My husband, Chad is the right wing for the Dallas Stars."

"I know there are a few brothers out there playing hockey. Although I'm not playing anymore, I try to keep up with trades and stuff. I didn't know Dallas had picked one up in the draft."

Dawn winked at Jenna. "I didn't say he was a brother. Chad is from Alberta, Canada. And is about as white as they come. You know, blond hair and blue eyes. He's been in the United States about fifteen years. I met him at a party about six years ago. We've been together ever since."

Lance was at a complete loss for words. He grabbed his glass of beer and chugged it down. After he finished, he only said one word. "Damn."

Chapter 9

Thursday evening, Zyrien stepped out of the shower just as the phone rang. He wrapped the towel around his waist as it rang a second time. He reached for it as it rang again. His mother would have answered the phone by now, but it continued to ring.

He punched the button and barked into the phone. "What?"

"Hey man, chill out," his brother Sean said. "I know this is date night and all, but I was just wondering if Darrin has showed his sorry face yet."

"No. Not yet. Hey, why don't you and Tiffany come visit Angie?"

"That's why I was calling. I just wanted to make sure she was feeling OK. You know how those pregnant women are, crying at everything in sight." Even though Sean was kidding, Zyrien knew his brother was concerned for their sister.

"She's pretty good, considering. Just don't upset her," Zyrien warned. "You know how you get sometimes. Not everyone gets your twisted sense of humor."

"Man, I didn't know I called my parents' house," he said sarcastically. "You know, you're starting to sound just like Dad. I'll talk to you later." Sean cut the connection.

Zyrien laughed, pushed the "End" button on the phone, and

threw it onto the bed. He glanced at the bedside clock. If he didn't hurry, he was going to be late for his date with Jenna.

He dressed in a shirt, shorts, and his favorite leather sandals. After he took one last look in the mirror, he headed downstairs. He walked into the living room, smiling at his sister as she lay on the couch watching a movie.

"How are you feeling? Are you sure you're going to be OK?"

She struggled to sit up. "Zyrien, I'm going to be fine. Mom is here. Although I told her I would be fine by myself."

Zyrien sat next to his sister. "If Mom needs to go home, I'll stay in. Besides, Sean and Tiffany may drop by later. Are you up for company?"

"Zyrien, you must go on this date. I feel fine." She smiled at her brother. "It's OK, Zyrien.

He patted his sister's hand. "I have some contacts at the hospitals and no one matching Darrin's description has wandered in, so he's still out there somewhere. Don't worry, Ang, everything will work out."

She nodded. "I'm not worried about Darrin. I have a feeling he's OK, wherever he is."

He hugged his sister and rose from the couch. "You're welcome to stay here as long as you need to. There's no rush about anything."

"You just go on your date and have a good time. And stop worrying about me and the babies."

"All right. I promise." Zyrien made that promise honestly. Jenna would require all his attention tonight. There wouldn't be room for Angie, the babies, or that idiot husband of hers.

He leaned down and kissed his sister on the forehead. "I'll see you later. I'll leave my cell on, just in case." He headed for the garage.

Jenna stood in front of her closet, not knowing what to wear. Zyrien told her it was a casual place, but that's where the problem started. It was June and the evening temperature still soared around eighty degrees. If she wore a short skirt, he would think she was trying to seduce him again. But if she wore slacks, it would definitely look like she wasn't trying all that hard to impress him.

She looked through her closet, hoping something would jump out at her. Finally something did. A floral print A-line dress that hugged her curves just enough and stopped right above her knees. She slipped on her high-heeled sandals and headed downstairs.

The doorbell rang and Jenna opened the door to a very casually dressed Zyrien. He wore cotton shorts and a matching shirt. She glanced down at his sandals. "When you say casual, you really mean casual, huh?"

"Definitely." He kissed her cheek, and then walked into her living room. "You might want to change your shoes."

"Why?" Jenna closed the door and followed him into the room. She had only spent the last hour getting dressed. "Where are we going?"

"To the barbecue joint, then bowling."

Jenna shook her head. "You'd better be kidding. That's not a date, buster."

"It is in my book. A date can be anything as long as both parties enjoy it. You seem to be a little laid-back. I thought it would be right up your street."

"I thought you wanted to talk. How can we do that at a barbecue place?"

Zyrien looked at her. "I take it you've never been to the barbecue joint? I think you look great, but they will think you're some stuck-up snob dressed like that."

She glanced down at her ensemble. She thought she looked pretty good. "Where is this place?"

"Oak Cliff," he said, referring to the predominantly black section of Dallas.

Jenna stood before him with hands on her hips. "Oak

Cliff," she repeated. "Why didn't you say so? I think I could wear this. But the bowling thing . . . I know if I walk in there with these shoes, the men will think I'm selling." She headed for the stairs. "I'll be right back."

She not only changed her shoes, she changed into cotton shorts and a sleeveless blouse that showed off a little of her flat stomach. When she walked back into the living room, Zyrien couldn't hide his satisfaction.

"You look great. I don't know about us going to the barbecue place now. Guys will be all over you."

"I'll just tell them to deal with you." Jenna reached for her purse on the table by the stairs.

Zyrien stood, nodding. "You know I could take them out, if they look at you wrong."

Jenna shook her head at him, not knowing if he was joking around or not. But she vowed she would find out soon.

They arrived at Tyrone's Bar-B-Que and Jenna couldn't believe her eyes. It was a barbecue place, but it was quiet and a hostess led them to their seats. After Jenna ordered a glass of wine and Zyrien ordered a beer, he asked her what she thought of the place.

"I think it's great. I'm intrigued."

He smiled as the waiter came back with their drink orders. "Well, Lance is one of the owners. He and a few ex-Cowboys wanted a nice barbecue place."

"Well, tell Lance, this is great."

After they gave their dinner orders, Zyrien leaned back in the leather chair. "Do you want to hear the good news or the bad news first?"

"I hate when people start a conversation with that phrase. Start with the good."

Zyrien coughed. "Well, the good news is that my pregnant sister is fine. She's expecting twins."

Jenna smiled. “That is good news. When is she due?”

The waiter interrupted their conversation with their dinner orders. After he placed a smoked chicken dinner in front of Jenna, and a baby back rib platter in front of Zyrien, he departed.

The aroma of the food momentarily diverted Zyrien’s attention. He quickly picked up one of the tender ribs and began eating before he realized Jenna was staring at him. “What?”

“You didn’t answer my question. When is your sister due?”

“Three months, around Labor Day.” He picked up another rib and quickly divested the bone of all the meat. He reached for the moist wipe and cleaned his hands. “Of course that’s just the good news.”

Was she going to have to pull the information from him physically? “OK, what’s the bad news?”

Zyrien took a long sip of beer before he answered. “Well, she’s going to be living with me for a while.” He glanced at her startled expression. “OK, why don’t I start at the beginning? Well, the day after our last date, my sister, Angie, called me asking if she could stay with me a few days.”

“I don’t see what is so bad about that,” Jenna commented, cutting her chicken into bite-sized pieces.

“Well, her husband, Darrin, went out a few days before and didn’t return home. She was starting to get worried.”

Jenna placed her knife on the table. “Oh my goodness. Did you call the police? He could be hurt or something.”

Zyrien shook his head. “No, Angie thinks he just ran scared when the doctor told them about the twins. I think he’s an idiot, putting his pregnant wife through all this. Anyway, after I picked her up, I took her to my house. My mom has been staying with me as well. My main concern is that Angie is OK, not worrying whether or not Darrin will come to his senses.”

She reached across the table and caressed his hand. “I guess me having an attitude wasn’t doing you any favors, huh? But what happens if Darrin doesn't show up? Are you going to hire a detective? Has she checked her messages since he's been gone?"

Zyrien couldn't control his heartbeat. Jenna was gently caressing his hand and her touch was slowly driving him mad. He concentrated on answering her questions. "Well, if Darrin doesn't show up soon, I am going to hire a detective to find his sorry ass, so my sister can divorce him. I believe in responsibility. If he wasn't ready for fatherhood, he should have been man enough to say so."

"But what about your sister?"

"What about her?"

"What if she forgives him and takes him back?"

"Then I would support her decision. I might not like it, but it's still her decision to make."

Jenna grinned at him, reaching for the knife to cut her chicken. "I think that's very mature. I don't know if the situation was reversed and it was my sister, I would react the same. I mean, yeah, I would hope for the best, but if he took his time coming back, I would make damn sure my sister didn't take him back."

Zyrien didn't want to spend his evening away from his family talking about his family. But he also wanted Jenna to know what was going on in his life. "So would you hire a hit man?"

She shook her head. "I don't have to. I can take care of that myself."

"Don't tell me you learned that in art class?" Zyrien laughed, polishing off another rib.

"Your eating habits are horrible. Anyway, Gunter bought me a lovely nine-millimeter for my birthday a few years back when I bought my house. You know, you really should eat a salad with all that meat," Jenna advised.

Zyrien glanced at Jenna's plate. It contained smoked chicken, a baked potato without the cheese, and a salad. His plate consisted of ribs and more ribs. "OK, I see your point about the veggies. You sound like my mom. But maybe you eat too many salads, so I'm balancing out the salad equation."

"Nice try, but no. Even those low-carb diets allow for some vegetables."

"OK. How about I order a really healthy dessert? You know, maybe a smoothie, or a sorbet?"

"Somehow I doubt they would have those here. This looks like a banana pudding, chocolate cake kind of place."

He loved surprising her. "Actually they do have smoothies here." He laughed as she looked at him doubtfully. "OK, it's more like fudge sundae, but I'm sure it's healthy."

Jenna didn't think she had the energy to bowl after such a good meal, but somehow she found the strength. Plus, Zyrien had made a wager. If she won, he would pose for her, if he won, she would have to teach him about art. It was a win-win for her.

Jenna tried not to gloat on the way to her house. She beat Zyrien by two pins: 160 versus 162. Her best game ever.

"You know, Zyrien, you don't have to keep your end of the bargain. You don't have to pose for me."

He picked up her hand and caressed it as he drove. "No, Jenna, the bet stays. My clothes are staying on."

She smiled at his eagerness. "How about this Saturday?"

"I'm really behind on my report. So it's going to have be the next Saturday."

"What kind of report?"

"I have this special report for the president of the company and it's due in about two weeks. With all the stuff that's been going on with my family, I haven't looked at it in a couple of days."

"Why did you ask me out tonight? This could have waited until Friday night. You should be working on the mystery report," she admonished him.

"I wanted to get this straight between us. I wanted to show you what you mean to me. Or I would like to."

A shiver of anticipation flowed through Jenna. "I think your plate is a little full right now, don't you?"

He turned onto her street. "Oh Jenna, you're like Jell-O. There's always room for Jell-O."

"Are you saying I jiggle when I walk? Maybe I need to work out more."

"No, baby. You look great when you walk. I think you're like Jell-O because you're flexible and do your own thang." He parked in front of her house and cut the engine.

"You weaseled out of that one."

He nodded, slid from behind the wheel, and walked to her side of the car. He opened her door and helped her out. They walked hand in hand to her front door.

Zyrien settled on her couch while Jenna went to make some coffee. By the time she returned, he was staring at his cell phone with a frown on his face.

"Is something wrong?" Jenna sat down beside him, placing the tray on the table in front of them.

He pulled her in his arms and kissed her gently on the lips. "I just called my house to check on Ang to see how she's doing, but no one answered the phone."

Jenna sat up and glanced at the clock on the wall. "It's after ten. Maybe she's sound asleep."

He shook his head. "No, my mom is there. I know Mom can't work the call-waiting option on the phone too well. I'll try back later."

Jenna nodded as she poured the coffee. She handed him a cup but he shook his head. "You want me bouncing off the walls tonight?"

She placed the cup on the table. "No, I just thought you wanted some."

He smiled at her. "What I want is already next to me." He pulled her to him. He kissed her again. His lips touched hers softly, tentatively, experiencing the softness of her lips. He teased her mouth open.

He nibbled her neck, easing her down on the couch. He moved on top of her. "Now this is what I've wanted all night."

Jenna grinned back at him. "Well I hope I don't disappoint."

"You could never do that." His hands began to caress her body. Hovering at her breasts, he squeezed them through her clothes. Jenna moaned, "Oh, yes."

Just then his phone rang. Without moving his position atop her body, he reached for the intruder. He looked at the display. "It's a strange number; maybe it's Darrin." He eased away from Jenna and sat up.

Jenna straightened her clothes and watched Zyrien as he took a deep breath and answered his cell phone. "Hello."

If his expression was any judge of how important the person on the other end of the phone was, Jenna assumed the president of the United States was on the phone.

Zyrien nodded. "I see. What room?"

Jenna scooted closer to Zyrien, grabbing his shaking hand, and leaned against him. Gentle lips kissed her forehead, making her heart flutter with anticipation.

He took a deep breath. "I'll be right there." He snapped the phone closed, kissed Jenna on the cheek, and rose. "Sorry, Jenna, I'm going to have to leave now. That was my mom. My sister started having cramps and they're at the emergency room at Medical Hills Hospital. I'll try to call you later." He headed for the front door and was gone before she could answer.

Chapter 10

The next morning, Jenna entered the building with the rest of the Duncaster and Finch employees. She had fifteen minutes before her official start time, so she darted into the cafeteria and bought a large cup of coffee before heading to the elevator.

As she waited with about a dozen people hoping to squeeze onto the same car, her boss approached her. "Hello, Ms. Bradshaw, I'm glad to see you on time today," Kyle Storm drawled.

As if she'd ever been late. Jenna smiled tightly at her excuse of a boss. "Yes, Mr. Storm." After her conversation with Dawn, Jenna decided not to give her boss any more ammunition against her. "Looking forward to another day of processing invoices."

He stared at her, no doubt trying to think of a retort to her sarcasm. Luckily, the elevator dinged and Jenna rushed to enter. Unfortunately, so did Kyle. He smiled as he eased himself into place beside Jenna. "Looks like we have a busy day ahead of us. You might have to stay late. You don't have a problem working overtime, do you?"

On a Friday night, Jenna mused. "Of course not. I just have to clear it with Ms. Castle first."

He muttered a curse under his breath, but was otherwise

quiet for the rest of the elevator ride. Jenna exited and headed straight for her desk. She greeted Dez as she sat down.

Dez was immediately at her desk. "You look like you didn't get any sleep. Anyone I know?" She laughed as she walked to the nearby file cabinet.

Jenna laughed, and took a gulp of coffee, hoping it would wake her. It didn't. "No, I just went to bed late." After Zyrien left, Jenna had waited up to hear about his sister. "How are things with Dante?"

Dez placed a folder on Jenna's desk. "The same. Boring. He doesn't know the meaning of spontaneous. Everything is always the same. Our routine never changes. Last night I tried to get him to watch a movie with me after the baby was asleep."

"And?"

"He said we could watch it on date night. He had paperwork to catch up on."

Jenna turned on her computer. "Well, that's something. I mean, at least he's willing to watch the movie."

Dez shook her head. "I know, so many women up here complain that their husbands don't want to do anything with them. At least Dante shares the responsibility of helping with the baby."

Jenna nodded. "So many women don't realize what they have until it's gone."

"Yes, they do," Dez replied. "I know Dante is a good man and they're hard to find. Don't think I'm letting him go just because of one little flaw." Dez returned to her desk.

Jenna instantly thought of Zyrien's flaws. He was definitely a workaholic. She also thought of the other side of Zyrien. The Zyrien who cared about his family, and who took his sister in when she needed it most and would support whatever decision she made.

In the distance she heard a phone ringing. Each time the phone rang it became louder. Finally, the noise registered: it was her phone. She picked it up and answered.

"I was beginning to wonder if you came in to work today. I would really like to take you on an honest-to-goodness date."

She smiled at the sound of Zyrien's baritone voice. It sounded so sexy, it sent a delicious shiver down her body, landing in the right place. "You did take me," she said softly, hoping not to be overheard.

"I mean a real one, with no distractions. My sister will be in the hospital for a few days, at least until her blood pressure is regulated. My mom is going to stay with her at the hospital."

"Wow, I guess that means I have to go out on a date with you, huh?"

He chuckled. "Yeah, pretty much."

Jenna giggled. "How about a home-cooked meal?"

"Sounds like a deal. I'll see you at eight." He ended the call.

Later, as Jenna was exiting the building, Kyle joined her in her trek to the parking lot. She wondered why he parked in the temporary employees' parking lot when the permanent parking was so much closer to the building. He was too skinny to claim he was doing it for the exercise. "What are you doing this weekend, Ms. Bradshaw?"

"I'm just cleaning my house, Mr. Storm. We're not working tomorrow, are we?"

He shook his head. "No. My son has a soccer game in north Dallas tomorrow. I was just wondering if your kids were in that league."

Jenna glanced at him. A slow red blush was slowly covering his face. "Well, actually Mr. Storm, I don't have any children."

"You were smart. Weldon is six years old and runs me ragged every weekend."

Jenna nodded. "Yes, I know the feeling. I may not have children, but I have friends who do." She neared her car and disarmed her alarm. “Usually after some time with their kids, I can understand why they’re always tired.”

Kyle didn’t answer her. He was too busy staring at her car. “Nice car. I really like those rims. I tried to talk my wife into letting me get some of those but she said ‘no.’ It caused our divorce.”

Jenna stared at him in disbelief. What kind of man would let a set of rims come between him and his wife? “I’m sorry, Mr. Storm.”

He chuckled. “Don’t think that was the only reason. It would take too long to tell you about it. Nice car.” He walked to his truck and left.

Jenna shook her head and slid behind the wheel of her car. “Well, that was extremely weird.” She started her car, powered on her cell phone, and left the parking lot.

She was calmly sitting in I-35 traffic when her phone rang. It was Dawn. Jenna giggled as her friend recounted her day with Chad.

“He surprised me by coming home early last night. One minute I was in bed asleep, the next thing I knew he was in bed with me and this is the first time I’ve gotten a breather. He’s taking a shower.”

“Wow, Dawn,” Jenna said. “That Chad sure has some stamina. All night and all day.”

“My man knows how to handle his business,” Dawn chuckled.

“Zyrien is coming over for dinner tonight. Any ideas?” Dawn was an expert in all things romantic, sexual, or just plain if you want to get your groove on.

“There’s only one place to go on a Friday night for gourmet dinner fixings,” Dawn said, sounding like a commercial. “Zippee’s. Get them to grill you some steaks or some salmon. Oh, I know, some grilled tuna steaks. Chad loves their food.”

“Chad loves anything you feed him.”

“You got that right, girl. Good luck.” Dawn ended the call.

Jenna headed to restaurant row in Dallas. Walnut Trail was one of the most popular streets in the city, due mostly to all the gourmet restaurants competing for the consumers' dollars. She pulled into Zippee's crowded parking lot and parked in the "to go" section. Although it was an expensive place, it was well worth the money.

She reached for a hand basket and explored the entrée counter. She studied the thick T-bone steaks, the salmon, and the swordfish fillets, before finally deciding on the steak. "Two T-bones," she said, smiling at the young man behind the counter.

"Yes ma'am. How do you want those cooked?"

Now that was a question she didn't have an answer for. If she ordered it too rare, it might gross him out. However, if she ordered it too done, he'd probably complain about it. Decisions, decisions. "How about medium well?"

He nodded and took two thick steaks out of the display case and put them on the grill. He turned back to the counter. "It'll be about twenty minutes, if you have some more shopping to do."

Jenna nodded and headed for the vegetable section of the small market. She picked out a large green salad for her and a smaller one for Zyrien. She also picked up some roasted corn, baked potatoes, cheesecake, and wine, then headed back to the meat counter.

She paid for her purchases and left the store. Confident with her food choices, she headed home.

Zyrien sat at his desk, not focusing on the report or anything his assistant was saying. His mind was on his sister. His mother had called earlier, reporting on his sister. Her blood pressure still hadn't stabilized. Zyrien wondered how long it would take for it to get back to normal.

"Zyrien?"

Hearing his name, he snapped back to the present. "I'm sorry, I'm not doing you any good today. I appreciate you staying late, but my mind is mush, Brenna. Go home to your husband and your baby." He rose from behind the desk. "I'm going home. I'll take the research you have and work on it this weekend."

Brenna shook her head at him. "You know you only have about two weeks to get that report ready and I rescheduled your production meeting for Monday." She stood, handing him the papers.

He smiled, opening his briefcase and stuffing the papers inside. "You know I thrive under pressure."

Brenna smiled. "I know. Good night." She left his office.

Zyrien glanced at his watch. He barely had time to stop by the hospital, get home, take a shower, and still get to Jenna's on time.

He made it to Jenna's with ten minutes to spare. Much to his surprise, Jenna was dressed in a slinky red dress that sent his hormones into overdrive. The dress caressed her curves and stopped just above her knees. She had on the same strappy sandals she'd had on the other night.

"Wow, you look great." He kissed her on the cheek, then gently on the lips. "I bought you a little something." He handed her a plastic sack with the local art store decal on it.

"You didn't have to bring me anything." Jenna looked at him with disbelief, but she opened the bag and shrieked. "Oh my gosh! I can't believe you bought these." She hugged him with a death grip, instantly turning him on. She planted kisses all over his face. "Thank you so much."

Zyrien chuckled as she finally led him in the living room. "I take it you like those paints. The guy at the store said those were the best ones most artists use."

"Yes, this is the right brand. I can't thank you enough. That's the art store where I buy my supplies."

Zyrien smiled, never divulging the fact that his youngest

brother picked up the paints and brushes for him. "I'm glad you like them."

She placed the bag on the table. "I'll use these when I paint you," she said.

"I don't have to get naked, do I?"

"You don't want to pose in the buff, huh? You know I have seen a nude man before. I thought you guys were always eager to show your body off to the public."

He leaned back against the couch. "Not this guy. I only do private showings."

She smiled at him, knowing exactly where this talking would lead them. And it was much too soon for that. "Well, I guess you'll be one of my few clothed portraits?"

He pulled her next to him. "You mean you actually do paint portraits like that?"

"Don't act so surprised," she said. "Come on, dinner's ready." She rose and walked to the dining room.

Zyrien followed her, loving the way the dress clung to her body as she walked. She motioned for him to sit down at the table and she went into the kitchen.

He admired the time she had taken setting the table. A bouquet of multicolored carnations laced with baby's breath and accented with daisies and other flowers made up the centerpiece. A bottle of Merlot sat on the table with a corkscrew by its side. He opened the bottle, poured some wine into the glasses, and waited for Jenna.

She returned with two plates. Each held a steak and a baked potato. She placed one in front of Zyrien and one at her place setting, and then she sat down. He noticed she had an array of vegetables on the table as well. Vegetables that he would never touch, he thought.

They toasted each other and began eating. Jenna glanced at him as he dug into the steak with gusto. "Do you like it?"

"Yes, this is great." He glanced at her, smiling. "You know this is just the way I like my steak."

Jenna nodded her thanks. "Have you checked on your sister today?" She cut her steak, waiting for his answer.

"Yes. I talked to Mom a few times during the day and I went by there after work. Her blood pressure is still high. The doctor won't release her until it's within range."

"What is it now?" Jenna wondered if Angie was worried about her marriage and that was what had caused her blood pressure to get out of control.

He shrugged. "I'm not sure. Mom said something about it being 160 over something. The doc wants it around 130. They got her on some kind of medicine that makes her drowsy. She was asleep when I visited her."

"When will she be released?"

"Probably not until next week, Monday at the earliest. That is, if her blood pressure goes down and she doesn't have any more cramps." He smiled at her. "I thought this night was about us?"

"It is," Jenna answered. She chopped her salad into small pieces as well. She noticed he was watching her. "What is it?"

He placed his knife down on the table. "I've just never seen anyone cut up all their food like that before. Is it a digestive thing?"

"Yes, it is."

He shrugged and resumed eating his steak. He had barely touched the potato, and, even less, the salad. "I know I need to eat more veggies." He picked up the fork and took a small bite of the spud. "Delicious." He did the same with the salad. "Mmm, good."

Jenna took a bite of her salad. "Patronizing me won't get you anywhere. You haven't touched any of the other veggies. I made broccoli and cheese, asparagus, and Brussels sprouts, and you didn't touch any of those."

"And I won't. Baby, I'm just not into that stuff."

"You should try to eat better. You'll live longer."

"Not if a car hits me, I won't."

"Touché." Jenna continued eating, thinking about his last comments. She had lost one parent to diabetes and another one to a heart attack. She had always vowed neither of those diseases would take her, and so far she had been successful. She was in great health, not without the help of a good diet and exercise. Most people thought she exercised to keep her figure trim, but that was only half the story. She did it to stay alive. Zyrien was saying something to her when she came back to reality. "What?"

"I was saying that I appreciate you looking out for me healthwise and all, but I do eat well on Sundays."

"Why on Sundays?"

"That's the day I spend with my family." He laughed. "You're doing it again. Trying to make this evening about my family. It's supposed to be about Zyrien and Jenna, no one else."

She nodded, suitably chastised. "OK, Mr. Taylor, what else do you want to do when we finish dinner? Rent a movie? Go for a walk in the park?"

He chewed on a piece of steak as he mulled his choices. He took a long drink of wine and thought some more. He wiped his mouth with the cloth napkin before he spoke. "Well, Jenna, I was thinking we could sit on the couch and make out like teenagers in heat." He smirked at her, daring her to accept his proposal.

Jenna smiled as she answered. "I was just about to suggest the same thing." The look of surprise on his face was worth every hot, burning kiss she would have to dish out.

Chapter 11

Saturday morning Jenna was awakened by an annoying noise. Someone was breathing in her ear and that someone was holding her in a death grip. And she was on the couch. How'd that happen?

She opened her eyes and laughed as the memories of the night flooded her mind. After dinner, she and Zyrien returned to the couch and had the hottest kissing war ever. Her last memory was Zyrien nibbling on her neck and telling her how soft she was. Now it was morning. She sat up and took inventory of her body. She still had on her dress and her underwear, and she wasn't wearing a bra to begin with, so she was still intact. She glanced down at Zyrien. His shirt was open and his slacks were unbuttoned.

Jenna stood and walked to the kitchen. She was measuring coffee when the phone rang. "It's barely seven in the morning and it's Saturday. Who on earth would be calling at this hour?" She reached for the phone as the coffee began to brew. "Hello."

"Jenna, how are you?"

"Hello, Gunter. I'm fine." She yawned, stretched her tired limbs, and thought about how nice a hot shower would feel right now.

"Look dahling, the reason I'm calling this early is because I finagled you an appointment with Greta Larson for lunch at Adolfo's at vone o'clock."

Jenna screamed with joy. Greta Larson was the head of new acquisitions at the Dallas Museum of Art. Adolfo's was a five-diamond restaurant in the middle of the art section of Dallas. If she could get Greta to display some of her work, that would be quite a feather in her cap and could actually open the door in getting into Maza's. "That's no problem, Gunter. Are you going to be there as well?"

"Yes, but you need to bring your portfolio vith you. And also some sketches of vat you're vorking on now. Unless it's finished," he said hopefully.

Jenna chastised herself for losing her focus on her project. It was nowhere near finished. It would take a week of intense concentration. "No, it's not finished yet. But I can bring my sketches along with my portfolio. See you at one." She hung up the phone took a deep breath. She was doing her victory dance in the middle of her kitchen when Zyrien appeared rubbing his eyes.

"What was all that racket?" He took a deep breath. "Is that coffee almost ready?"

"That racket, as you put it, was my jubilation. Gunter got me an appointment with Greta Larson."

Zyrien nodded. "And she is?"

"The acquisitions director for the Dallas Museum of Art. If she likes my paintings, she might put one of them in the new artists section."

He smiled at her. "Congratulations, baby."

"You have no idea what I'm talking about, do you?"

He didn't speak for a moment. "I know it's important to you, so it's important to me. I might not know what you're really talking about, but I will."

Jenna didn't know how to react to that statement. Perhaps they were just too different and there was no common ground.

But at least he was willing to learn about her craft. Somehow that separated him from the rest of the nonartist men she'd dated in the past. "Thank you, Zyrien." She stepped closer to him to kiss him good morning, but he backed away out of reach.

"No. Morning breath," he said, his hand covering his mouth. "You wouldn't happen to have an extra toothbrush?"

"Sure. Downstairs bathroom, there's a basket with toothbrushes, toothpaste, and mouthwash in it. How about I fix some breakfast while you're getting all prettified?" She grinned at him.

"Sounds like a deal." He left the kitchen.

Jenna walked to the refrigerator, thinking there was more to Zyrien Taylor than met the eye and now her curiosity was piqued.

When Zyrien returned, Jenna wasn't in the kitchen. He glanced around the large room and she was nowhere in sight. Then he heard the shower running upstairs. He ambled to the stove and lifted the lid on the fluffiest eggs he had ever seen. Another dish held bacon. He picked up a strip of bacon and popped it in his mouth as he walked to the coffeepot.

He was just about to start rummaging through the cabinets to look for some coffee cups, when he realized this wasn't his house. He decided the proper thing to do was to wait until Jenna returned. So he did.

When she returned, she was dressed in shorts and a T-shirt, her shoulder-length hair pulled back into a sloppy ponytail. She smiled at him as she entered the kitchen and began fixing plates of food. "Hope you're hungry," she said as she placed a plate of eggs, bacon, and toast in front of him.

"I'm always hungry," he teased, smiling at her. "Just not always for food."

Jenna placed a cup of coffee in front of him. "I thought we

agreed it was too soon for that." She sat down at the table with her mug of coffee.

"No, *you* said it was too soon. You drive me crazy all the time. My hormones haven't been this out of control in a long time. But I can wait, because when we do make love I want to give you my undivided attention." He picked up a forkful of eggs.

"I think we both have too much going on to think about it right now. You have your sister, and you need to finish your mystery report, and I have a very important meeting today," she said as she doctored her coffee.

He wanted to learn more about her craft. He knew the economy was starting to look up again and that would mean her art career would only get busier. Spare time would be a thing of the past and he would be left out in the cold.

Zyrien watched her as she ate. She only had two slices of bacon and one slice of toast. He had double the amount of everything. "What are you wearing to this appointment?" He nibbled on a piece of bacon waiting for her answer.

Jenna shrugged. "I usually stand in my closet and wait for something to jump out at me."

He would go nuts if he had no idea what he was wearing. Zyrien laid out his clothes for the week every Sunday night. His life required order. "I thought this was an important meeting and you're leaving something like that to chance?"

"She's looking at my portfolio, not whether I have on the correct color suit, Zyrien. This isn't like a business meeting. Artists are a different lot. We know when we should dress, you know, like a gallery showing, or one of those fancy parties at Maza's."

He opened his mouth to say something. He didn't know if he should apologize for insinuating she didn't know how to dress for an interview or ask what the heck Maza's was. Jenna answered as if reading his mind.

"Maza's is one of the most famous art museums in the

country. Getting into the Dallas Museum of Art would be great, but if I could get into Maza's, that would be the end-all. That would be like you getting to be partner."

He nodded. Glad she brought the art business down to a term he could understand. "I know you'll do great today. Why don't we meet later and you can tell me all about it?"

Jenna smiled at him. "I can't. I will probably be with Gunter the rest of the afternoon. And, depending on the results of today's lunch, it will probably dictate what I'll be doing tonight."

Well, he was firmly put in his place. And he didn't like it one bit. "Why don't you call me when you can?" He held his temper in check by glancing at his wristwatch. "I'd better get going. I need to get home, shower, change, and head over to the hospital."

"I understand. Please let me know how your sister is doing. I'll try to call after my meeting." She looked at the wall clock in the kitchen, and stood. "I hate to kick you out, but I need to start getting ready for my appointment."

"I know. You have to meditate or something before you get ready, right?" He stood and walked to the living room.

Jenna was right behind him. "No. I don't meditate. Gunter does. And you forgot something this morning."

Zyrien patted his pockets. Keys in front, wallet in back pocket. What could he have forgotten? He turned and looked at Jenna in confusion. His heart thumped louder as she walked up to him, grabbed him by his shirt collar, and kissed him.

"There. That's better. Have a nice day." She straightened his clothes and walked to the front door.

Zyrien stood rooted in the very spot. He couldn't move. Not with the kiss he had just received from Jenna. Every nerve, every hormone was telling him he needed to stay and make love to her right now. But he couldn't. It wouldn't be fair to either of them.

"Zyrien," Jenna called.

When he could move again, he noticed absently that she was at her front door, holding it open, a very blatant invitation to leave. "Oh yeah, I was leaving." He walked to the door and faced her. "I had a great time, Jenna. Good luck today. I know you'll show that Greta lady how good you are." He kissed her softly on the lips. "I owe you one," he said licking his lips, and then he was gone.

Jenna took a deep breath and closed her front door. She ran upstairs and stood in the middle of her closet, searching through her clothes for something to wear. Then she saw it. A blue Anne Klein suit. It flattered her figure and she had the perfect two-inch stilettos to wear with it.

A few hours later, Jenna walked into Adolfo's and glanced around for Gunter. Instantly she spotted his distinctive salt-and-pepper hair. He was dressed in one of his trademark Armani suits. She walked to the table, confident she could do this. Gunter stood and greeted her.

"Jenna, dahling, I'm glad you could make it." He kissed her on both cheeks before introducing her. "Greta, zis is Jenna Bradshaw, your next new artist."

Jenna extended a hand to the pale, thin woman. Greta accepted Jenna's, but the woman's hand felt cool, much like her appearance. Her dark suit looked about two sizes too big. Her black hair was pulled back in an efficient bun. "It's nice to meet you, Mrs. Larson."

Greta looked Jenna up and down before answering. "Gunter has sung your praises for the last few days. I'm sure you won't let him down." She took a sip of her wine. "Please sit."

Jenna nodded, not sure who was supposed to pick up the conversation now. As usual, Gunter rose to the occasion and charmed Greta—out of a little gallery space, Jenna hoped.

"Don't worry, Greta, I have been Jenna's mentor for quite

some time and vouldn't steer you wrong. She has some vonderful sketches of her latest painting."

Greta glanced in Jenna's direction, making her feel compelled to say something. "Yes, Mrs. Larson, I'm not quite finished with the painting itself, but, as Gunter mentioned, I do have a pencil sketch of the finished product." She passed an 11 x 16 sheet of rice paper to Greta.

Greta took the paper in her skinny hands and studied it carefully. "Yes, it does look nice. This is a color portrait, yes."

"Of course," Jenna answered.

Greta inspected the drawing. "Live model? Gunter tells me you don't use live models often. Is there a reason?"

Was she calling Jenna cheap? She mostly did nudes—why would she need models? "I like to use my imagination. I used a live model on this one and several of the portraits in my portfolio."

Greta smiled. "You answered that one very diplomatically. Just because I'm not an artist doesn't mean I don't understand the artist mentality."

"I don't understand." Jenna glanced sideways at Gunter until he looked in Jenna's direction. She discreetly held her mouth open in astonishment, silently asking if this woman was for real.

"Why don't we order lunch and you can tell me about your career?" Greta nodded for the waiter and quickly he appeared to take their orders.

Somehow, Jenna was able to eat her salmon salad and maintain a civil conversation with Greta. Having chalked the meeting up to experience and vowing to make sure she finished her project before presenting it to another museum director. She hoped Greta wouldn't smear her name too badly.

Gunter cleared his throat, bringing Jenna out of her sulk. She made eye contact with him, silently apologizing for letting her mind wander. But Gunter was smiling at her, and so was Mrs. Larson. Had she missed something important?

"Jenna, Greta asked, "when you could possibly be finished with the portrait."

Jenna took a drink of mineral water as she tried to gather her thoughts. "I could be finished within two weeks," she answered. Provided she didn't have a date. That was a bridge she would cross later.

Greta nodded and consulted her Palm Pilot. After she tapped on the display screen a few times with the metal stylus, she nodded. "How about three weeks? I'm having a women's showing then. I will need at least three paintings from you. Will that be possible? They can be any format you choose. Pencil, charcoal, or paint. I will have to approve them, of course."

Jenna nodded. "Of course. As I said before, I can have the portraits to you within two weeks. That would give me a week, just in case you don't like the ones I submit to you."

Greta smiled. "Good. I'm very excited to be working with you. The sketches look very sensual, almost bordering on erotic."

Jenna never thought of her paintings that way. She just worked from her imagination and instinct. If something didn't feel right, she didn't paint it. "Why thank you, Mrs. Larson."

"I told you to call me 'Greta.' You will these next two weeks. I will need updates, so I will call often."

Nothing would deter Jenna from making this opportunity happen, not even Zyrien Taylor. No matter how well he kissed.

That afternoon, Zyrien walked into his sister's hospital room, surprised to see her sitting up and talking to their mother. Angie was smiling and looking almost like her old cheerful self.

He was glad he had stopped at the florist and picked up some yellow roses, her favorite. "Hey, it's about time you decided to wake up." He walked to the bed and kissed his sister on the cheek. "You look good. How do you feel?" He handed her the bouquet and greeted his mother.

Angie yawned, admiring the flowers. "I feel better. I don't know what happened. The last thing I remember was laughing at something Sean said about the boys. Then I had a sharp pain, and I woke up here, with Mom watching me."

Zyrien nodded, not wanting to alarm Angie any more than was necessary. "It's OK, you're fine now." He took a deep breath. "Ang, I need to ask you something and I don't want you to get upset."

"Ask."

"Have you checked your answering machine lately?"

She didn't blink, didn't shed one tear. "Yes. Every day since I left home. I didn't check it yesterday, since I was in the hospital."

"Would you mind if I checked it?"

"No, I don't mind." She took a deep breath. "You'll need the access code. It's 1229."

Zyrien laughed. He should have guessed it would be something easy for Darrin to remember. It was Darrin's birth date, because he was memory-challenged. Zyrien nodded, making a mental note of the number to check the messages later.

Angie watched him. "How was your date?"

"It was good." Zyrien couldn't hide his smile. "Actually, we talked about you." Jenna had surprised him by being concerned about his family.

"I haven't seen that cow-eyed look in a long time," Angie giggled. "It's nice to know that playas fall hard too."

Zyrien shrugged and dialed his sister's home number. He waited for the prompts, punched in the access code, and listened to the messages. There were fifteen of them. He glanced at his sister as she watched him. "Is fifteen an excessive number of messages?"

Angie's brown eyes couldn't contain her shock. "Yes, usually there might be one or two. Everyone knew I was at your house."

Zyrien nodded. "Except for Darrin." He listened to the messages as the machine ticked them off one by one. The first one was Darrin dated yesterday. The next one was a few hours later, then two hours, then every hour. Zyrien listened as his brother-in-law spoke: "Hey baby, it's me. I'm OK. I just need some space to think. I know this is a bad time to say this, but I don't think I'm ready to be a father. I'm at my cousin's in Houston. You know, Eric. Here's the number, please call me." After Darrin rattled off the number, he disconnected.

Zyrien was furious at his brother-in-law for being inconsiderate and putting his sister in the hospital. "Hey, I'll be right back."

Angie stared at him. "Where are you going? Are you going to tell me what the messages were?"

Zyrien nodded. "Yes, as soon as I get back. I just remembered something I need to take care of." He stood and headed for the door, ready to give Darrin a piece of his mind.

Jenna and Gunter walked to her car in silence. They were both too happy and too giddy to speak and break the spell. Finally they reached the car and she disarmed the alarm. She glanced at him and they both laughed uncontrollably.

"I thought I blew it," Jenna admitted. "I thought she hated me and didn't want to take the chance on my nudes."

Gunter grabbed her by the shoulders. "You're a magnificent artist and don't you forget it. You'll be painting full-time again before you know it. That voman was rubbing my leg under the table. She was trying to feel me up until she realized it was useless."

Jenna gasped. "You mean she didn't know?" She thought it was common knowledge in the artists' community.

Gunter laughed. "You vere in a zone ven she leaned over and asked me point-blank if I vas gay."

"And she still wanted me." Knowing there was no way she was going to get Gunter in her bed, she had still wanted Jenna.

Gunter nodded. "You're good and it's your time. Now, how are you going to meet that deadline you have imposed on yourself vith a full-time job and a new love?"

"I'm going to get to work on it this weekend, starting tonight." She opened her car door and threw her purse and portfolio on the passenger seat.

"No, you go out and celebrate vith your new man. You start on the painting tomorrow. Because for the next two weeks you vill be working your skinny fingers to the bone. So you make the most of tonight." He winked at her.

"Gunter, Zyrien and I are just friends. That's all." Lie. "I'll stay focused and finish ahead of deadline."

He nodded. "That's my girl." He kissed her on the forehead. "I vill call you tomorrow."

Jenna nodded. Tears of happiness fell down her face. "I won't let you down, Gunter."

"You never have, dahling." He blew her a kiss and walked to the Mercedes that was parked a few cars down from Jenna.

She watched him drive away before she screamed in joy. She called Dawn and told her the good news. Luckily Dawn and Chad were taking a breather from a love marathon and the women could talk.

"What did Zyrien say?" Dawn asked. "I think it's great, and Chad and I will take you out to dinner tomorrow night."

"It will have to be in two weeks. I can't do anything until that painting is done."

"OK, girl. Just let me know when." Dawn disconnected.

Jenna took a deep breath. She couldn't believe it. She would have three paintings hanging in the Dallas Museum of

Art. Her chance was before her and nothing was going to deter her.

Zyrien waited until he was in the confines of his car before he called Darrin. He dialed the number and waited for it to connect. "Stay calm," he reminded himself. "Stay calm. You'll do no one any good if you're so mad you start yelling at him. Hear his side of the story first, and then yell at him," Zyrien muttered.

Someone finally answered on the third ring. Unfortunately, it was a young woman. "Who the hell are you?" The question slipped from Zyrien's mouth before he realized it.

But the woman was calm. "I'm Yvonne, Eric's wife. Whom am I speaking to?"

"I'm sorry, Yvonne," Zyrien said sincerely. "I wasn't expecting a female to answer the phone. I'm Zyrien, Darrin's brother-in-law. Could I speak to him?"

"Thank goodness. He's been going nuts these past few days. He's been trying to call his wife and she won't talk to him."

"Well, he should have tried my house, my parents, his parents, or the hospital where she's been the last few days. Could you put him on the phone, please?"

Yvonne gasped at Zyrien's tone. "Oh dear. I told him to quit hiding." She put the phone down. Zyrien could hear her yelling for Darrin. Soon he came on the line.

"Zyrien?"

Zyrien tried to calm his temper. "What the hell are you doing? Do you have any idea what you have done to Angie?"

"Zyrien, man, I'm scared. Twins. That's two of everything and we're teachers," Darrin whined.

"Yeah, and right now your wife is in the hospital fighting for her life," Zyrien spat. "Darrin, I don't get you. You've been married for over five years. I know you guys talked about starting a family. Why didn't you say something?"

"I don't know."

Zyrien yelled into the phone. "That's not a good enough answer, you freaking waste of space!" Zyrien pressed the "End" button and slid out of the car.

As he stomped back into the hospital, Zyrien realized it was a good thing Jenna was going to be busy all day; it would probably take that long to straighten things out.

His cell phone rang as he entered the lobby. He looked down at the display. Jenna.

He realized he was in too surly a mood for anyone, especially her. Besides, it was against hospital rules. She was probably calling to tell him about how great she was at the meeting and how she couldn't see him for months instead of just two weeks. He switched his phone to vibrate.

Chapter 12

Jenna paced in front of her portrait of Ian sprawled sensuously across the canvas. His blue eyes stared back at her, daring her to enjoy her good luck. But those eyes wouldn't stop her good feeling. This was a reason to celebrate.

She dressed in a slinky white silk blouse that not only showed off her flat stomach but also complemented her honey-brown skin. *Skirt or jeans?* she asked herself. She finally decided on a pair of worn Ralph Lauren jeans and a pair of sling-back three-inch heels.

Jenna grabbed her purse and headed to the garage. With her favorite song cranked up to the loudest setting on her Bose stereo system, she headed for the Micro House.

Later that evening, Zyrien just wanted a drink. He had been at the hospital practically all day and the walls were closing in. He had tried returning Jenna's call from earlier in the day, but she wasn't at home. Maybe she was still with this Gunter person, he hoped.

"Zyrien," his sister said from her hospital bed, rubbing her stomach. "I say this with nothing but love in my heart."

"What is it, Ang? Do you need something?" He rose, ready to go find whatever food his sister wanted.

She nodded. "What I need is for you to go home and maybe go out or something. Dad is coming up for night duty. I'll be just fine."

"I seem to remember you uttering those words the other night and you ended up here." Zyrien hoped he never had to relive that night again.

Angie shook her head. "But this time I'm already here. So why don't you call Jenna and go out tonight?"

"She had a big meeting today and I can't catch up with her to see how it went yet." He did need a breather. "I'll call Lance and see if Traci will let him out tonight."

Angie nodded her approval. "Good night, Zyrien."

He knew when he was licked and said good night to his sister. He left the hospital and headed home.

Two hours later, Lance picked him up for a boys' night out. They headed for the Micro House. Once at the lively bar, Zyrien sat zoning out until he heard Lance laughing.

"Man, you're like some whipped guy. Just sitting here playing in your beer, moping over Jenna. Why didn't you call her?" Lance asked, finishing his glass of beer.

"I did. She wasn't home. She had a meeting today with some art chick and she tried to call me once, but I had just talked to Darrin and I was in a mood," Zyrien said, draining the last of his beer.

Lance signaled the bartender for another round. As he glanced around the bar, he noticed a group of men hovering around a woman at the end of the bar. He nudged Zyrien. "Hey, I think you need to go to the men's room."

Zyrien looked at his cousin as if he had lost his mind. Zyrien laughed, "Man, you might need to go back to regular beer and leave that micro stuff alone. You're nuts. I do not have to go the men's room. My bladder is fine, thank you."

Lance nudged him again. "I think you really need to go. There's something you have to see."

Zyrien knew if he wanted his cousin to shut up, he would just have to go to the restroom. He slid off the bar stool and headed for the men's room, until someone caught his eye. A woman with shoulder-length hair was talking to a young man and she looked a lot like Jenna, he thought. At closer inspection, he realized that beautiful woman *was* Jenna. This was why she didn't return his phone calls. She was entertaining, he thought furiously.

He stalked over to where she sat, surrounded by a group of men who were probably half her age. She had a glass of beer in front of her and was about to take a sip when she noticed him.

"Zyrien!" Jenna rose and hugged him. "I tried to call you earlier."

She felt soft and warm. Zyrien's hands couldn't resist caressing her slim body, letting his hands rest lightly on her backside. He hoped the men would take the territorial hint and leave peacefully.

The men moaned and quickly dispersed, leaving the couple alone. Jenna grinned and picked up her glass of beer. She motioned for him to follow her to a vacant table.

After they were seated, Jenna stared at him. He had a strange look on his face. "I'm glad you're here. That must mean your sister is better."

"She's doing OK. Dad is sitting with her tonight. She told me I needed to go out tonight. I tried to call you at home, but I didn't get an answer."

"I called you earlier, to tell you about my meeting. It went great. I'm still jazzed about it."

He smiled. "I told you you were going to knock her socks off. Women never listen to me," he teased.

"She was impressed with my sketches. She's giving me

some gallery space and I'm going to be in the showing in three weeks." She still couldn't believe it.

He reached across the table and grabbed her hand. "That's great, baby." But his expression didn't indicate that he was thrilled. He looked indifferent. His mind was elsewhere.

"Zyrien, what is it? Is it Angie?"

He shrugged. "Not really. I checked Ang's answering machine. Darrin had called fifteen times since yesterday. One of those times he left a phone number. So I called him."

Jenna knew the bond between Zyrien and his siblings was a tight one. He was very protective of his pregnant sister, and was very upset with his brother-in-law. Jenna could only imagine the verbiage he had used. "What happened?"

"You think you know me, don't you?" He laughed one of those evil laughs that made Jenna's skin crawl. "I told him what I thought of him. What I'd really like to do is against the law. And right now Darrin isn't worth doing time in big house."

"What did he say?" Jenna caressed his hand, hoping that eased some of the tension of his ordeal.

"He had the nerve to say he didn't think he was ready for fatherhood."

Jenna could imagine what Zyrien had said. Thank goodness he'd only called. "Zyrien, I know this is a terrible time for you."

He nodded. "I'm depressing you with my family saga. I just feel so helpless about Angie. The only person who could make the situation better just declared he's not ready for fatherhood."

Jenna glanced at him, wondering what words would make him feel better. She realized there were none. "You've been at the hospital all day. I'm sure you're running on empty. You've yawned twice since we sat down. Maybe you should go home and get some rest," she suggested.

He nodded, agreeing with her. "I came with Lance." He glanced across the bar, spotting his cousin. Lance nodded at him and lifted his glass of beer to him in a mock toast. "He says 'hi,'" Zyrien laughed. "Would you mind taking me home?"

"Is this another trick hatched by Lance?" She glanced in the direction of the bar and noticed Lance was leaving the bar. "Where's he going?"

"Home."

An hour later, Jenna parked in front of Zyrien's house. This was her first view of his home and she was quite impressed. The house looked exactly like a house Zyrien would have. It was a two-story house, and all his rooms were probably white, she guessed. Everything was probably in its place and not a splash of color in the entire house.

"Why don't you come in for a while?" Zyrien offered casually.

Curiosity was killing her; who knew when she'd get another chance to view the monochromatic home? It would be at least a few weeks while she finished her project. "Sure." She opened her car door and slid from behind the wheel.

He met her as she rounded the car and grabbed her hand. "I should warn you that it's not like your place." He kissed her softly.

She let his tongue slide easily into her mouth, enjoying the sensation of his body pressed against hers.

He led her inside the house. "For the record," he started as he walked to the living room, "I like the fact that you're taller than me. It turns me on." He motioned for her to sit down on the beige sofa.

She sat down, taking in all the neutral-hued furniture. It was just as she feared. Monochromatic. Her living room popped with color. This room whispered. As she sat down, she rubbed her neck. "My neck feels stiff. Probably 'cause I was so tense at the meeting."

He wiggled his fingers, smiling. "Well, why didn't you say so? I can give you a massage to relieve some of that pain."

After the day she'd had, a massage sounded wonderful. "We are talking about a fully clothed massage, correct?"

He gave a dramatic eye roll toward his vaulted ceiling. "If we must."

Jenna scooted to the end of the sofa. "How's this? Is this enough space?"

He gave her that sexy grin again, meaning he was up to no good. "There's not enough space on the sofa. Actually, the floor would work better."

Jenna groaned at the thought of lying on his carpeted floor. "I know this is going to sound like a total come-on, but why not your bed? I'm sure you'll be a perfect gentleman and not take advantage of me, right?"

"The bed would work better," he said, not mentioning anything about being a perfect gentleman.

Which worked fine with Jenna. She stood and faced him. "Take me to your bedroom, Mr. Taylor." She held out her hand, smiling.

"Finally, the words I've been waiting to hear." He took her hand and led her upstairs.

"My God, Zyrien, that feels wonderful. Don't stop," Jenna moaned. "Those hands should be registered as seductive weapons."

Zyrien smiled down at Jenna's naked back. With a slight suggestion, he'd convinced her the massage would have a better effect if he could use some of the massage oils he just happened to have in his bathroom.

He was speechless when he laid eyes on her emerging from the bathroom wrapped in a sheet. She winked at him as she lay facedown on his king-sized bed. He was supposed to be seducing her, but somehow she had turned the tables on him once again.

Jenna moaned and wiggled her body as he rubbed her back.

Each time she moved, the sheet that covered her from her lower back down eased farther down her body. Her body was tight skin stretched over bone and just enough muscle to be sexy. Each time the sheet moved, Zyrien had to take a deep breath and steady his shaky hand.

"Zyrien?"

Her voice snapped him out of his zone. "Yes, Jenna."

"Why did you stop the massage? Are you finished?"

He didn't realize he had stopped. His hands were still on her back. He had just stopped moving them. "Sorry, I was giving you time to catch up with me," he teased.

"I think you're the one needs a breather," she joked. "Now that you have slicked me down with oil, can I take a shower?"

Zyrien was stunned. Was she for real? Why was she pushing him to the limit and beyond? "Of course, baby. Need me to come in and wash your back for you? You know, just to make sure you get all the oil off your beautiful body."

"No, I can manage." She sat up carefully, made sure the sheet was gathered around her body, and walked to the bathroom. When he heard the door close and the shower running, he fell back on the bed and moaned. He had definitely lost the battle.

Jenna woke the next morning refreshed. That massage Zyrien gave her had really relaxed her muscles and now she could focus on her artwork. She made her traditional breakfast of eggs and bacon, toast and coffee. Weekend breakfasts were the one meal she didn't skimp on.

After she finished breakfast, she walked to the studio. The phone rang just as she reached for her paints. She picked up, wondering who would have the nerve to call her when she had just warned everybody not to call her for two weeks.

"Were you really serious about the three weeks?" Zyrien asked, his baritone voice thick with sleep.

Jenna looked at her wall clock and mentally cursed. It was barely after seven in the morning. "Yes, I was very serious. What are you doing up so early?"

"I couldn't sleep. You had my hormones in overdrive last night. I was too frustrated to sleep. It will be your fault when I fall asleep in church today."

"You won't fall asleep," Jenna said. "That's not your style." She stared at her project, surmising what needed to be done. Talking with Zyrien wasn't on that list. "I hate to say this, but I really need to get busy."

"So you can't talk to me?" Zyrien asked in a clipped voice. "What was that last night?"

"Last night was a massage. You were trying to seduce me into making love with you, even though you knew how important this is to me."

Zyrien inhaled. "So I can't see you again until this is over. For three weeks?"

Jenna tried to contain her temper. "Zyrien, I explained this to you last night. I have to have the portrait done. Plus, I have to get two other portraits ready as well. Now I know you would like for me to direct all my energy into my project because you know this is what I want to do, right?" Jenna smiled as she waited half a heartbeat for him to answer before she retorted, "Besides, you have to complete your report."

"Of course," he answered. "Call me when you get a chance." He disconnected.

Jenna pushed the "Off" button on her cordless phone and placed it on the table, smiling. There was more than one way to skin Zyrien Taylor.

She hoped he wouldn't call her again until she finished her project or she would definitely have to start screening her calls. She slipped on her smock, which had more colors smeared on it than were in a large Crayola crayon box. She turned on the stereo and began working on her masterpiece.

As she finished the background, she started working on

Ian's perfect nude body. She smiled as the portrait began to take shape. She realized two things quickly. She was going to need Ian to sit for her one more time for some touch-up work. And her mind was on Zyrien, where it shouldn't be.

Later that morning, Zyrien decided to forego church and see his sister in the hospital. As he entered the quiet room, he saw a familiar face and his temper immediately soared. Darrin was sitting in the chair next to the bed. Angie was asleep.

As sound registered in the room, Darrin turned and stood too quickly. The flowers he was holding tumbled out of his hands and hit the floor. "Hey, bro," Darrin drawled. He extended his hand.

Zyrien didn't take it. Instead he opted for a nod of acknowledgment. "Where's Dad?"

"He said he was going to get some coffee." He looked sheepishly at Zyrien. "I want to thank you for making me come to my senses."

"It was a conversation that shouldn't have occurred," Zyrien said. "No one should have to tell you what your responsibility is." He glanced at her sister. "Does she know you're here?"

Darrin shook his head. "No, she's been asleep. Her skin looks really pale. Is she OK?"

Zyrien looked at his brother-in-law in disbelief. He wanted to hit Darrin, but he was on his best behavior. "Yes, Darrin, she's fine. Her blood pressure was elevated, you know, with everything that has been going on lately." He glanced directly at his brother-in-law.

Angie's voice interrupted the exchange between the two men. "Darrin, what are you doing here?"

She struggled to sit up. Both Zyrien and Darrin immediately went to her aid. She waved off both men and propped the pillows behind her.

Darrin watched his wife. "I'm sorry, baby. I messed up. I knew I shouldn't have run like that, but it hit me all at once. Two of everything."

Angie, to her credit, didn't flinch. She sat there calmly watching Darrin struggle for some kind of explanation. She caressed her bulging belly as she spoke. "You could have just talked about what you were feeling and we could have worked through this together as a married couple, but you chose to run to your cousin. I don't have the option of running."

Darrin opened his mouth to speak, but Angie held up her hand. "You know, I don't even care why you were scared. It doesn't matter."

Darrin plopped down in the chair. "Baby, you know I love you and wouldn't hurt you for anything."

"What do you call going out for some milk and not returning for days?" She took a deep breath. "You know, I don't want to do this right now. According to the doctor, I'm getting out tomorrow and I'll discuss it then."

Darrin smiled. "OK, baby, we'll talk about it when we get home tomorrow. I knew you would understand."

She shook her head. "No, Darrin, you don't understand. I'm not going home," Angie told her husband. "At least not our home."

Zyrien couldn't stop smiling. His sister knew this idiot needed to be taught a lesson in responsibility. "You can stay at my house as long as you want," Zyrien said.

"No, I'm going home to Mom's," she announced to the room. "I need space to think."

Darrin gasped. "Angie, I don't understand. I came back. Why do you need to think about anything?"

She stared at her husband. "Darrin, I don't trust you anymore. How do I know you won't run scared when the twins are born? When they get sick? We're supposed to be a team, Darrin. I feel like I'm all alone."

Zyrien almost felt sorry for Darrin. He also knew his sister was right. Trust had been broken and would have to be rebuilt. But how?

Darrin grabbed her hand. "Angie, you know I was just scared. I'm here with you now. I did call and tell you where I was," he pointed out.

Angie eased her hand out of his. "Why didn't you call Mom? Zyrien? You should have realized that I wasn't home after about the tenth call. You should have known that I was either at Mom's or Zyrien's." Angie grimaced and rubbed her tummy. "You didn't call there 'cause you didn't really want to talk to me."

Darrin took a deep breath. "What do I have to do to gain your trust? Is that even a possibility?"

Angie looked at him. "I guess that would depend on you. I'm not coming home until I feel I can trust you again."

"So what do I have to do?"

"Show me that you're ready for the twins."

Darrin threw his hands up in surrender. "All right, you win. I will show you that I can be trustworthy again." He stood and glanced at Zyrien. "I do want to be with you, Angie. Can I see you at your parents'?"

She nodded. "Give me a little time to think about it. I'll call you and let you know if I want to see you."

"It will be like I'm dating my pregnant wife," Darrin whined.

Angie smiled. "You are."

Chapter 13

Three weeks later, Jenna stepped back from her painting and experienced a moment of jubilation. Her portrait of Ian was hanging on the wall in the Dallas Museum of Art. She couldn't stop smiling.

"Get zat smile off your face," Gunter said, walking up beside her. "It looks vonderful, dahling." He wrapped his arm around her waist and kissed her on the cheek. "So does the other artwork. See, three veeks of intense concentration and you completed your goal."

Jenna nodded, taking in Gunter's black tuxedo. "You look great. Big date?"

His head bobbed up and down. "Yes. You." He looked her up and down. "I vore this for you. I hope you vore that for me." He nodded at her strapless black tea-length gown.

"Of course," she lied. She hoped Zyrien would show up and end their three-week hiatus.

"Jenna, I didn't think you vould lie to me. We both know you vore that clingy thing for your man. He's going to have a lot of competition tonight. Just vait until the masses get here." He kissed her hand. "This is your time to shine. Make the best of it."

Jenna nodded, watching Gunter inspect the other displays.

She still had another hour before the showing was scheduled to begin. She felt as nervous as a bride.

"Hello, Jenna," Greta Larson spoke. "You've done a wonderful job. Just like I knew you would."

"Thank you, Greta," Jenna mumbled, not quite sure how to take the woman's compliment. She took in Greta's black suit. "I appreciate you giving me this opportunity."

"Your artwork speaks for itself," said Greta. She took a step closer to Jenna. "Could we meet for lunch next weekend? I would like to discuss another showing. You know, maybe a one-woman show or something to that effect."

Jenna's heart fluttered. "Sure, Greta. Next Saturday would be fine."

Greta spoke in a stage whisper. "You know I hear the art director from Maza's may be in attendance tonight."

Jenna gasped. "Really?" If she could secure a display in any of Maza's five galleries, she would be ecstatic. "I'll be on my toes." She smiled as Greta left the display area.

Jenna headed for the lounge area to get in a little quiet time before guests started arriving. As she sat on the leather couch, she chanted a prayer. *A little extra help never hurt,* she thought.

Zyrien dressed in his best suit. He knew the drought with Jenna was nearing an end. These last three weeks tested his strength as a man, a manager, and a human being. Every time he saw Jenna in the hall at work he thought he'd explode. Nighttime was no better; the dreams he had would have made Jenna blush.

After he slipped on his favorite pair of Kenneth Cole shoes, he headed out the door. As he drove to the Dallas Museum of Art, his cell phone rang. He grappled for the phone, hoping that it wasn't another family crisis. "Hello," he breathed.

"Quit worrying," Angie said. "Darrin is on his way over. We're going to the movies with Sean and Tiffany."

"Angie, you know I believe Darrin should be taught a lesson, but don't you think it's going a little too far? I mean, in the last few weeks, he's taken you out to dinner, to the movies, to plays, and you even made him suffer through watching those childbirth videos."

"No, I don't think I've gone too far," Angela huffed. "Besides, he volunteered to watch them with me and Mom."

"You're enjoying this, aren't you?" Zyrien pulled into the museum parking lot. "Hey, I gotta go. I'm here at Jenna's showing. You be nice to Darrin."

"Hey, I'm letting him see me, aren't I? I know he loves me, but it's time for him to grow up and face his responsibilities. That is, if he wants to."

"You know he does. Wish me luck."

Angie chuckled. "I guess I should tell you that Mom and Dad are on their way to her showing, too."

He muttered a curse. "Why?"

"Mom wants to see her work, and she thought it would be nice to show her some support."

"Only my parents would show up and try to ruin my game. Man, they should be at home like parents are supposed to be," Zyrien complained.

"You know you don't mean that. Besides, I'm glad you're finally going to get you some. And I won't even tell you what I heard our parents doing last night."

"I don't want to know. Good night." Zyrien pushed the "End" button on the phone as the valet approached his car. He slipped out of his car, handed the key to the young man, took the plastic card, and headed into the museum.

He made a silent promise that he would be on his best behavior. He was offered a glass of champagne and directed to the third floor. This night was all about Jenna, not the report on which he did so well he received a pat on the back from the higher-ups, not about his sister torturing his brother-in-law. It was all about Jenna Bradshaw. And in the morning, he hoped it would be all about them over breakfast.

He walked into the large room, unprepared for the vision of beauty before him. Jenna wore a strapless dress that hugged every curve of her body, and her shoulder-length hair hung in a mass of curls that fell just below her shoulders. Ten or twelve men stood transfixed as Jenna explained her painting to them. The companions of those men looked a little put out. Zyrien laughed. That was Jenna and she was his.

He made his way closer to her, fuming as a very tall gentleman took her in his arms and gave a her kiss. Then Jenna kissed him back! As she hugged the man, she noticed Zyrien and had the nerve to wave him over.

But like a fool, he walked toward her. He had no choice. His brain told his legs not to move, but his heart was the ruling factor. He walked right into her arms and hugged her.

"Zyrien, I'm so glad you could make it." She hugged him again. "This is one of my dearest friends, Clark Riniski, also a fellow artist," Jenna boasted proudly.

Zyrien offered his hand to the man. "Nice to meet you." Zyrien thought his name sounded very familiar, but couldn't think where. Then it hit him. The bus. "Your stuff is on the city buses, right? I remember now. The city wanted a different image, so they chose you from about twenty local artists. It was in the business section of the *Dallas Morning News*," he explained to Jenna.

Clark nodded. His shoulder-length dark hair shook with the motion. "Yes, Jenna will be on next year's buses."

Zyrien looked shocked. "What?"

"Oh yeah, they couldn't decide between Jenna and me. So I got this year's and she has next year's. She's just too modest to tell people. She's one of those who believe talking about it before it happens jinxes it."

Zyrien couldn't believe it. "Well, I think that's something

she should have mentioned." He winked at Jenna. "Remind me to scold you later for not sharing."

"Of course. I'm going to count on it," she whispered, grabbing his hand. "You know your parents are here? You could have told me they were coming. They introduced themselves to me a little while ago. Your mom is a hoot. She volunteered to pose for me."

Zyrien shook his head. "Oh, no. I thought she was kidding about that. Or at least, I had hoped she was kidding."

Jenna leaned down and kissed him. "To see that look of embarrassment on your face, it's worth it. I might even take her up on it."

"Baby, you don't understand what my mom is asking."

Jenna nodded. "Your father explained exactly what he wanted."

Much later, after her show had ended, Jenna drove home, ready for part two of the evening. She parked her car in the garage and walked inside the house, waiting anxiously for Zyrien to arrive. They'd decided to forego going out to celebrate and eat something at Jenna's. But food wasn't the only thing they had on their minds.

"Where is that man?" Jenna wondered, returning from the kitchen with a bottle of champagne and two glasses.

She lit the candles on the dining room table as the doorbell rang. It rang again as she surveyed her work of setting the table. She opened the front door before it rang a third time. "I supposed this means you're upset I took so long," Zyrien said and kissed her on the cheek.

Jenna led him to the couch and they sat down. She poured the champagne as she spoke. "No, I'm not upset. This is a free country. You can drive as slow as you want."

"I do have a good excuse for being late." He kissed her gently on the lips. "And it was well worth the time."

"Really?" Jenna picked up the champagne flute and took a sip. "I'm waiting."

"Well, I know today probably wiped you out and I had wanted to surprise you with dinner already prepared."

"I don't see a sack or smell any wonderful food," Jenna said.

Zyrien laughed. "You don't cut me any slack, do you?"

"You're here, aren't you?" Jenna asked. "Please continue your story."

"Well, before I was interrupted, I was about to tell you why I didn't have the food with me."

"OK, I'll bite," Jenna said drily.

"They're at least an hour behind on orders, but since it's near here, they'll deliver it. Since we have some time to kill, I thought we'd chat."

OK, that got her. "Chat?" She'd figured he'd want to spend the time in bed, but he wanted to talk.

He took her hand in his, looking deeply into her eyes. "Jenna, I know you think I'm just a boy toy. Although we haven't actually played yet; but I want you to know that I'm totally serious about you. Just because I'm younger than you doesn't mean I care for you any less than a man your age."

"Zyrien," Jenna started, "you don't have to seduce me. And I won't hold you to anything you might say in the heat of the moment."

"Dammit, Jenna. I'm being up front with you and you're treating me like some mentally challenged teenager who's trying to hit it."

"I never used those words, Zyrien. But you're right, I'm not taking you seriously and you want to know why?"

He nodded.

This had to be good if she wanted the evening to continue on its true course to the bedroom. "Because I didn't want you interfering with my comeback. I haven't sold a painting in almost a year. That's where my focus is."

He shook his head. "I can't say I like being second in your heart, but I understand about your focus. I know I won't always be second. But in your quest for your comeback, I'm there for you."

It was more than she could have hoped for. Most nonartists didn't understand, but at least he supported her. "Thank you, Zyrien." She kissed him softly on the lips. "I never wanted anything as badly as I want to be a successful artist."

Zyrien sighed. "I know. My youngest brother, Sean, is an art major and he explained the creative process to me. Jenna, all I'm asking you is to let me in."

He was asking a lot. A lot more than she was ready to give, but she had to meet him at least halfway. "OK, Zyrien, I can try. Right now I can't make any promises more than that."

"Thanks, baby."

The food arrived shortly after their talk. Jenna went upstairs to change while Zyrien took care of the food. Then she returned to the living room outfitted in one of her favorite lounging dresses. The blue sleeveless cotton dress molded her hips and stopped just above her knees. Zyrien had set the table, lit the candles, and unpacked the food.

"Where's the jazz music playing softly in the background? That's all that's missing," she said, entering the room.

Zyrien walked to her. "I wasn't trying to use props to seduce you. I don't need props," he teased. He wrapped her in his arms. "All I need is right here." He kissed her gently on the lips.

Jenna was getting lost in the promises his lips were making. She wanted more. She wrapped her arms around him, bringing him against her chest and loving the feel of the contact. She needed more. "Zyrien," she whispered against his lips. She tasted his lips, savoring the taste of heat and desire before slipping her tongue inside his mouth.

"You mean . . . " He pulled her close to his body after she gave her nod of approval. He kissed her with a force that awakened every erotic nerve in her body. His body was hard muscle moving against her. There was no turning back, only moving forward. Blowing out the candles, she reached for his hand as she led him upstairs.

They entered her bedroom. Jenna smiled and Zyrien was taken aback. She looked at her room as if seeing it through his eyes. Zyrien's house was one color, neutral. Maybe there were too many colors for the average person, she mused.

"I went a little crazy with the colors," Jenna admitted.

"It looks good," Zyrien said slowly. "It just takes a little getting used to." He sat down on the bed and ran his hand over the purple satin down comforter. "I don't think I've ever seen a comforter quite this color before." He patted the space beside him. "Why don't you sit here?"

Jenna obliged. She sat on the bed, waiting for him to make the next move. But he didn't. He seemed content to hold her hand. She leaned to kiss him, but he shook his head.

"This is one time I'm taking charge, Jenna. Right now I just want to hold your hand."

She knew she had to wait. "What do you mean? Are you implying that I'm bossy?"

Zyrien forced himself to take it slow. He had been waiting for this moment for over a month. Actually, he'd been waiting for this moment from the first time he saw her over two months ago. He wanted to draw out the feeling of ecstasy as long as possible. He eased Jenna down on the bed, caressing her every curve and fumbling for the zipper on her dress.

"It's on the side," Jenna said between kisses. She was unbuttoning his shirt in a rapid, sure motion.

His silk shirt hung open and Jenna rubbed her hands over his smooth chest. Her soft lips kissed his chest and moved down his body, while her hands removed his shirt. She was driving him out of his mind and he still hadn't found the damn zipper.

Jenna grunted and sat up. "Here, I'll do it." She stood and reached for the side of her dress, expertly unzipping it. She let the dress pool around her bare feet and stood before him in a black strapless bra and a black lace thong.

"Well, I hope I meet with your approval, Zyrien."

He gulped the air and swallowed hard before he could answer. Never in all his dreams did he imagine she looked that good. Oh, he had an idea when he gave her that massage, but the idea paled against the full reality. "You are beautiful, baby." He kissed her flat stomach.

Jenna shivered at the sensation of his lips on her body. "I believe you're next, Mr. Taylor." She leaned closer to him. "Or I could do it for you."

"Why don't you?" He reclined on the bed, enjoying her playful nature. She hovered over him and struggled with his belt buckle. He didn't know if she was doing it on purpose or not. It only stoked his fire for her and his massive erection. He thought he'd explode before she got his slacks off.

When he was left in just his silk boxer shorts, Jenna smiled. "Is that for me?" She grinned, caressing his erection.

Not able to stand one more touch of her gentle artist's hands, he pulled her down on top of him and rolled over her until she was under him.

He kissed her neck, throat, and collarbone. He pulled her strapless bra down with his teeth, freeing her breasts. He rolled her dark nipple with his tongue before taking it in his mouth.

Jenna moaned and wiggled under him. "Not yet," he said against her breast. Her hands caressed up and down his back, attempting to get even closer to him as he moved to the other breast.

"Oh my God. Zyrien," Jenna gasped, throwing the purple satin pillows on the floor. "I need you. Now," she growled.

He knew he'd have to hurry, because he wouldn't last much longer, either. *Condom,* he thought. He eased off her to retrieve his protection, but Jenna had a gold packet in one hand and was pulling back the covers with the other.

Zyrien was all man, Jenna mused. She sat up and pulled the strapless bra off and slipped out of her thong while Zyrien covered himself with the condom. Jenna leaned to kiss him. "You have a nice body, Zyrien."

He didn't answer. Instead he kissed her, easing on top of her. His tongue deep inside her mouth was mating with hers, making her more anxious by the second. She didn't know how much more she could take. His hands caressed her breasts before feeling their way around her body. He gently nudged her legs apart with his knee.

His kisses left a trail of fire from her lips down to her tummy. Jenna's hands massaged Zyrien's scalp as he dared to kiss the area where the fire was the hottest.

He tasted her as if she were a fine wine. She needed to be sipped, swirled, and gently sucked before he invaded her with his tongue. Jenna's world suddenly turned upside down. She gasped, trying to catch her breath and hold on to the feeling taking over her body. She grabbed the bedsheet as he tasted her fully. Sensation of something glorious was speeding through her body as breathing became something she forgot how to do. The climax thundered through her body as she screamed his name.

Zyrien hovered over her as she tried to catch her breath. Her chest heaved up and down with spent pleasure. She ran a hand over Zyrien's flat stomach, but he grabbed her hand and shook his head. "Oh, no. We're not done yet, baby." He leaned down and kissed her on the neck and entered her body with one quick surge forward. "Oh Jenna," he said. "God, you feel good."

She closed her eyes, enjoying the sensation of being perfectly content. He pulled out and Jenna opened her mouth to complain, but then he surged farther inside her. Immediately she wrapped her legs around him, making sure he wasn't going anywhere anytime soon.

He lay against her, crushing his body to hers and kissing her neck, driving her positively wild. As he moved against her, she tried to delay another orgasm fighting its way through her body. She gritted her teeth, willing her body to hold on just a few more strokes, wanting to enjoy the feeling of completion with Zyrien.

Her body couldn't last one more thrust.

Jenna grabbed Zyrien's shoulder, riding out the intense pleasure. As her body calmed down from the most wonderful orgasm she'd ever had, she felt Zyrien finally giving in to the sensations and heard him scream her name before collapsing on the bed next to her, resting his head on her chest.

"That was spectacular, baby." He struggled to catch his breath. "I don't think I can move."

"Good. 'Cause I got some plans for you." Jenna stroked his back, her hands gradually making their way to his butt. She squeezed gently.

"Oh no, baby. Not now," Zyrien muttered against her breast, creating a delicious shiver in her.

Jenna's hands caressed his body. "We have all night, Zyrien." She stared at him as he stared at her.

"We sure do, baby." His beautiful hazel eyes drifted closed and soon he was asleep.

Jenna watched him sleep, his arms around her, quickly following him to slumber land.

Chapter 14

Jenna woke the next morning bright and early. Feeling energized from the previous night's activities with Zyrien, she decided to fix breakfast. After she showered and dressed, she headed downstairs and found uneaten food from the night before.

She made omelets with green peppers, onions, mushrooms, and cheese. The phone rang as she measured the coffee for the maker. She answered it on the second ring, instantly laughing as she recognized the caller.

"Well, how was he?" Dawn asked.

Jenna gasped at Dawn's frankness. "How was your flight? I wish you and Chad could have been there last night. How's his grandmother?" They'd had to miss Jenna's showing because Chad's grandmother had gotten pneumonia.

"Fine," Dawn answered. "That woman is going to outlive everybody. Turns out it's the flu." Dawn paused. "OK, I know Mr. Stud had to be good, if you're not willing to report on his shortcomings." Dawn chuckled. "I take it you did the deed."

"You have been around too many hockey players." Jenna knew she hadn't answered her friend's question and had no intention of doing so. "I'll tell you all about it when you get back." Jenna knew Dawn was impatient about affairs of the heart and not knowing would drive her nuts.

"Please, just one little detail," Dawn begged. "Chad is in the shower. You know his grandmother is full-blooded French. So his mother is making the breakfast of a thousand fat grams. Thank goodness he's been working it off me."

Jenna smiled, remembering the night before. Zyrien satisfied her in a way she didn't think was possible for her anymore. It had been ages since she'd had an orgasm and she'd had two with Zyrien in one night. "You know, I actually broke out in a sweat."

"I can't wait to meet this guy," Dawn mumbled. "When we get back, we'll have dinner."

Jenna heard footsteps on the stairs. "He's up. I'll talk to you later. Love to Chad." Jenna placed the phone on the charger and plastered a smile on her face.

Zyrien walked into the kitchen, barely making eye contact with her. He was dressed in his shirt and slacks from the evening before, but he was barefoot. He glanced around the kitchen. "Good morning, baby." He walked to her and kissed her.

"Good morning." Jenna hugged and kissed him. "Now sit down. I've been slaving over a hot stove all morning to make this." She noticed him looking around again. "The coffee mugs are in the third cabinet to your right."

He reached into the cabinet pulling two mugs off the shelf. "How did you know what I was looking for?" He closed the door.

Jenna smiled as she walked to the table with a plate in her hand. "First of all, I've been working at Duncaster and Finch for over two months and I've known you for almost as long. I always see you with a cup of coffee in your hand in the mornings."

"What's the second reason?" He poured coffee into two cups and took them to the small table. "I know you. There has to be a second reason."

She smirked at him. "You don't look like a morning person. You need some kind of stimulant to get you going or you'll be grouchy. I don't like grouchy." She finished bringing all the food items to the table. "Now sit down."

He walked to her chair, motioning for her to sit down. "After you, Ms. Bradshaw."

Jenna sat down in her chair, grinning like a schoolgirl as he brushed his lips against her cheek before pushing her chair closer to the table. "Thank you."

After a quick glance at each other, they gave thanks and began to eat. She watched Zyrien dig into the omelet with gusto.

"This is good, Jenna." He took another bite. "Being that we're sharing breakfast, I want to ask you something." He took a sip of coffee.

Jenna's hand shook at the gentle statement. He said it so calmly that she wondered at it. "Shoot."

He took another bite. "Why are you working at Duncaster if you have been appointed to paint the buses? I mean, I know that's got to be some serious cash they're going to pay you. So why work at a job you don't like instead of doing what you love?"

"Painting the buses, as you put it, doesn't start for another nine months. I have to make it until then. No, I don't like accounting, but it pays the bills for now. Working in accounting is all I know besides painting. When one fails, I fall back on the other." She took a sip of coffee, proud of her short answer. The long answer would have taken far too long to tell him and he probably wouldn't understand her need always to have a backup plan.

"So are you going to quit when the bus thing starts?"

She shrugged. "I don't know. I like the work. I mean when I leave work, I leave work. I don't have to bring anything home but me." She knew she was going to quit, but wasn't ready to share that information with Zyrien.

"Yeah, I remember those days. Sometimes, I really miss them. But other days I thrive on the demands of my job. I really like being in charge of something. I guess that comes from being the oldest of eight and always having to worry about the others."

She already knew that. The few dates they had managed to have, someone from his family was always calling. She thought it was wonderful to have that many people concerned about him. It showed how close Zyrien and his siblings actually were. She heard him clear his throat. "What is it?"

He laughed as he picked up his plate. "I was asking if there were any more omelets or if I could make one. But you went into Jenna-land and didn't answer me."

"Sorry. There's more on the stove." Jenna looked down at her plate. It was still over half-full. She glanced at his taut stomach. Where did he put all the food he ate?

Zyrien walked to the stove, refilled his plate, and returned to his seat. "What are you thinking about? I mean, I know it's not me," he chided.

Jenna picked at her omelet. "Stuff. You know, thoughts that just jump into your head from nowhere. I was thinking about my family and the fact that I really don't have one. All I really have is my brother and he's in Austin. We had kind of drifted apart, but the last few years we've bridged the gap by keeping in better contact. I just feel like we've lost something we'll never get back. I guess the Fourth of July holiday has just got me thinking."

He nodded as if he understood. "You probably didn't believe me when I told you a day of being with my family and I'm craving solitude," Zyrien said, attempting to lighten her mood. He glanced at his watch. "Since you treated me to the best night of my life and a delicious breakfast, how about I treat you to lunch?"

"That's sounds pretty good." Jenna knew if they didn't get

out of the house, they would soon be back upstairs on their way to paradise in her bed.

He took a long sip of coffee. "Great, we can go by my house and I can change clothes, then we'll swing by my parents'."

Jenna choked on the bacon. "Did you say your parents?"

"Yes. Is there a problem? You talked to them last night."

"I know I did. It's just that I wasn't expecting to see them so soon. This should be interesting."

Jenna watched the scenery as Zyrien drove to his parents' home in DeSoto, a suburb of Dallas. As he turned onto Knightsbridge Court, she noticed one house that looked to be having a party and mentioned it to Zyrien. He laughed.

"That's my parents' house. The driveway looks like that every Sunday. Mom likes to have everyone over for Sunday dinner."

Please, she hoped, not today. She didn't want to eat with his entire family. "We're not staying for lunch, are we?"

He hesitated. "Well, Mom is kind of expecting us. I called this morning to tell her I wasn't coming to church today."

"Oh no. You missed church because of me?"

He reached over and patted her hand. "I didn't miss it because of you. It's OK. My mom is not going to call you the devil or anything like that. She didn't go, either. So there."

She took a deep breath. "OK. I just have this thing about karma. There's good and bad. I don't need any bad karma right now."

He parked in front of the large two-story house, leaned over, and kissed Jenna on the cheek. "Don't worry, they're harmless. Plus, Mom already likes you 'cause you paint. She loves that artsy stuff." He slid from behind the wheel and walked to her side of the car and helped her out.

Jenna was glad she'd opted to change into something

comfortable. She wore a simple cotton skirt set with low-heel sandals. She glanced at Zyrien's cotton walking shorts, happy that he was dressed as casually, his T-shirt emphasizing how physically fit he was. Biceps bulged at the sleeves of the shirt. "You look nice, Zyrien."

"Right back at you, babe." He grabbed her hand and led her to the house. He twisted the knob, opened the door, and pulled her inside.

Jenna was shocked at the interior of his parents' home. Where Zyrien's house was monotone in color, his parents went wild with colors all over the house. The large living room was a peach color. Two women with babies sat on a blue couch. A big-screen TV dominated a corner in the room. A beige recliner sat in perfect alignment with the TV. Probably his father's, she mused.

"Hey, where's Mom?" Zyrien asked the women. "Jenna, these two couch hogs are two of my sisters, Natasha and Bailey. Guys, this is Jenna."

Natasha had a pecan complexion. She smiled at Jenna and nodded at Zyrien. "Nice to meet you, Jenna. Mom said you had a showing last night. I'm sorry we missed it. Zyrien neglected to inform us." She darted her eyes at her brother.

"That's perfectly all right," Jenna assured Natasha. "My pictures will be hanging in the museum for three months. The next time I have a showing I will give more notice. Even my friend and her husband missed it."

Natasha stood with a small baby in her arms. "This is Braeden, the latest addition to the family. He's eleven months old and has just mastered walking."

Jenna made cooing sounds to the baby and to her shock he reached out for her. But Jenna made no move to take him. Natasha nodded her approval. "It's OK, Jenna."

"I'm just not around children much. It's been ages since I held one. I don't want to hurt him or anything."

Natasha snorted. “Are you kidding? Boys are indestructible. At least the ones in this family are.”

Finally, Jenna took the chubby little baby. His complexion was a lighter brown than his mother’s. He had eyes like Zyrien. Little Braeden reached for Jenna’s hair and pulled. “Ow!”

Zyrien laughed. “Oops, forgot to warn you about that. He’s notorious for hair pulling. That’s why Tasha cut all her hair off.” He motioned at his sister’s very short, layered cut. “She said she’d let it grow back when he started walking.”

Jenna handed the toddler back to his mother. Zyrien led her to the kitchen. “I’m sure Mom is cooking her heart out in here.”

His mother was in the kitchen, putting the finishing touches on a green salad in a gigantic bowl. “It’s nice seeing you again, Mrs. Taylor.” To Zyrien, she whispered, “Exactly how many people are eating here today?”

“And I told you last night to call me ‘Bella.’ One of my daughters and her family is in Houston this weekend. So that’s four less and Angie is upstairs, so maybe sixteen.”

Jenna’s mouth hung open in amazement. “And you do this every Sunday?”

Bella nodded, a broad smile on her face. “When I was growing up, my family was large, but we’re so distant from one another. We rarely got together for anything unless it was a funeral. I promised myself when I had my family, I wouldn’t let that happen. So far so good. I see my kids at least once a week.”

Jenna understood. Although she and her brother had begun to bridge the chasm in their relationship, there was nothing like a large family. Zyrien led her outside to where his father, James, and three brothers, Sean, Carson, and Jason, were gathered around the grill. Zyrien’s two brothers-in-law, David and Jacob, were watching five children ranging in ages from five to ten as they played near the patio.

Jenna sat next to Zyrien at the extralarge dining table. True to Bella's word, there were sixteen people in attendance, between the adults, the children, and the toddlers. Jenna gazed at Zyrien as he joked with his brothers. She could barely hear herself think with all the chatter. It was wonderful.

"Jenna," Bella broke into her thoughts, "I was just telling my daughters about the picture we want you to paint of me. The girls think it sounds great. My stick-in-the-mud sons are not on board with the idea."

Jenna didn't want to turn a simple portrait into a boys-versus-girls battle. "Bella, why don't you come to my house one day? You can look at some of my other portraits and you can see if that's what you really want," Jenna hedged.

Bella perked up. "Oh, that will be great. Since tomorrow is the Fourth of July, why not tomorrow? I'll treat you to lunch."

"Oh, that's not necessary. I love to show my artwork."

Later, Jenna relaxed on Zyrien's couch. "You know, your mother is coming over tomorrow." She took a deep breath as he kissed her neck.

"You'll be back in plenty of time," he said against her neck. "My sisters thought you were the bomb." He rained kisses on her cheek, her ear, and her collarbone.

Jenna gasped. "Oh, really." She kissed him when his lips neared hers.

"You know what your kisses do to me." He kissed her softly, then the kiss went from zero to fifty in about two seconds.

When their lips parted, they were both panting for air. "Wow, have you been saving that up or what?" Jenna asked.

He kissed her again. "You know what else I've been saving up all day?"

Jenna smiled at him. "I can only guess." She leaned closer and kissed him.

Zyrien moaned and stood, grabbing her hands. He led her

toward the stairs. He muttered something unrepeatable when Jenna stopped at the bottom stair. "What is it?"

Jenna stared at him. "I haven't been properly asked for an evening of passion. What kind of woman do you think I am?" She smiled, planting a wet kiss on his lips.

Any other time, he would have retorted with some kind of barb, but not this time. He was too far gone. "Jenna, baby, I really need you." He stepped closer to her and hugged her, rubbing his body against hers.

Jenna felt the heat transfer from his body to hers, igniting a forest fire of passion. She kissed him urgently. "OK, that works."

Zyrien laughed. "You like doing that to me, don't you?" He didn't give her time to answer. "You're definitely going to pay for that." He led her to his bedroom.

Jenna sat on the bed. "Can I give you a massage?"

"Not this time, baby." He joined her on the bed. "Right now I just want us to have some quiet time. I bet being around all my family today, you could use that?" He took off his shoes and lay down on the bed. He motioned for her to join him.

Jenna thought he had a caring family. "Honestly, I'm not used to being around so many people. Artists are a solitary lot. As long as I'm creating, I could go days without human contact." She took off her shoes and snuggled up to Zyrien, resting her head on his chest.

He caressed her hair. "Well, Ms. Bradshaw, you'll have to create with me nearby."

Jenna was silent, not knowing exactly how to respond. She did the next best thing. She kissed him, telling him with her lips what her mouth refused to say.

He quickly relieved her of her blouse, throwing it on the floor. Jenna sat up and pointed at his T-shirt. "Take it off."

He complied. Then he took off his shorts and boxers, standing nude before her, looking very sexy. Jenna patted the space beside her.

If Jenna thought he would feel uncomfortable under her intense inspection of his body, she was quite wrong. As her kisses moved down his muscular body, he only moaned her name. He laughed as she reached his flat stomach, and held his breath as she moved lower. As he realized where she was headed, he pulled her back up so that they were face-to-face.

"Not yet." He kissed her as she straddled him. "How about taking off the rest?" He pointed at her skirt.

"Make me."

He did.

Chapter 15

Jenna prepared for Zyrien's mother's visit to her house. Everything was in its proper place. She showered and dressed in an aqua sundress with big sunflowers painted all over it. The dress stopped well above her knees, but it was one of her favorites. She'd painted the sunflowers on it herself.

She was slipping into her favorite sandals when she heard her doorbell. She walked downstairs and peeked at her living room, making sure everything was in place for Bella. Jenna had a cheese snack tray, a bottle of wine, and some dainty cookies on the table. Once satisfied, she went to open the front door.

Bella Taylor had her own sense of style. She was dressed in a cotton sundress. She also had all of Zyrien's sisters with her. The five women smiled at Jenna.

"I hope you don't mind the girls joining us," Bella asked. "The boys came over to voice their dissent over the painting. So Angie and I just had to get out of there. Before you knew it, the Suburban was full of women."

Jenna waved them inside. "Of course not. The more the merrier. What would you like to do first? I have some wine and cheese in the living room. Or would you like to see the paintings first?"

"Paintings!" the women yelled in unison.

Jenna nodded and led them to her art gallery. She opened the door and they walked in. The women gasped in awe. Bella was instantly impressed. "Yes, I want a nude portrait." She glanced at one of the paintings of Dawn.

She walked closer to the picture. Dawn was sprawled on a lounge but she wasn't exactly nude. She was dressed in a sheer, floor-length peignoir. Bella stared at the picture and soon the others were looking at it as well.

"That is a beautiful picture, Jenna. Who is she?" Angie asked.

"That's my best friend, Dawn. She posed for that the night before she married Chad. This is about five years old. Dawn made me promise I would never hang it in a gallery."

"Why?" Bella stood transfixed by the painting. "I would have thought she'd want the public to see it."

"Well, for a while she and Chad had it at their house, but so many of Chad's teammates came over and saw it, a fight usually followed."

"Is Chad some kind of athlete?" Angie asked.

"Oh, yeah. He's the right-winger for the Dallas Stars. Dawn is five years older than he is. Actually, I'm having dinner with them tonight."

The Taylor women exchanged glances with each other.

"What is it?" Jenna walked into the adjoining room to get her proudest piece of work.

Jenna carried the covered canvas painting into the room. "Oh, that. He knows I already have plans. Surely he wouldn't expect me to change my plans at the last minute. I won't." She leaned the portrait against the wall before uncovering it. "I would like to show you something, but you can't tell Zyrien about it or he'd have a cow."

The women nodded and Jenna uncovered it. The women gasped. It was a picture of Jenna in her birthday suit, sitting sideways in a red leather chair, her long legs hanging over one side and head back in total abandon. She held a martini glass in one hand and she was smiling.

"Zyrien would kill whoever painted this," Angie stated. "I mean it's a gorgeous painting, but I know my brother. He'd definitely lose it."

Bella stared at the painting. "This is beautiful. Why do you have it hidden?"

Jenna shrugged. "I don't know. I guess the same reason most beauticians hate to do their own hair. It just doesn't seem right to have my own picture hanging in my studio."

Bella nodded. "I know, but it's so pretty. Yeah, my son would have a fit."

"I have had offers for it. A friend of mine painted it about six years ago, and it's in his portfolio. A company wanted to buy all the rights to it, but I refused. I didn't want it just showing up anywhere."

"That's my girl, stand your ground." Bella took a deep breath. "And I want my portrait just as my husband wants it."

Jenna smiled. "My schedule is really tight right now. It's going to be a few months before I can do any preliminary sketches of you."

"OK, Jenna. I'm at your disposal," Bella grinned.

Jenna couldn't help smiling. "I think it'll be fun. As I told Zyrien, I won't charge you."

But Bella wouldn't hear of it. "Oh no. I will pay you, because that's time you could be using for another painting."

Now a little bartering was in order. Jenna put her arm around Bella's shoulder. "How about we make a deal? Show me how you made that delicious chicken yesterday."

"Honey, you got yourself a deal. How about we celebrate? Let's go out to eat." Bella led the way down the hall.

Later, Jenna waved as Bella peeled out of her driveway. She had the Suburban doing about fifty in a thirty-milean-hour zone. Lunch with the Taylor women was more than she had expected. She'd anticipated that they would all shout Zyrien's praises during the meal, but instead they all warned what a workaholic he was.

That was no surprise to Jenna. He couldn't have gotten to management level at such a young age without giving up something. She'd lived that life once and had no intention of ever going back. That was before she discovered art and how relaxing it was.

She walked into her studio and returned her painting to the closet. She glanced at her watch, noticing that she had a few hours before she had to meet Chad and Dawn for dinner. Perfect time for a nap.

She had just closed her eyes when her phone rang. "Good grief, I just wanted a little nap," she mumbled, reaching for the phone. To her surprise, it was her brother.

"Hey, sis," Ansel Bradshaw crooned. "How is the Fourth going? I tried to call you earlier, but I guess you were out."

Jenna sat up, not believing her brother was actually on the phone. Usually she was the one who initiated the calls. "Yeah, Ansel, I was out. How are you? Funny thing you calling, I've been thinking about you a lot this week."

He laughed. "Well, I guess we've been thinking about each other, huh? I was thinking about coming for a visit."

"Really," Jenna squealed. "It would be wonderful to see you. I know we don't talk to each other nearly enough. I want to change that. I want to get to know your wife, too." She had only met her sister-in-law a few times over the course of her brother's marriage.

Ansel became quiet. "Well, about that. You don't have to worry. We're separated."

Jenna's heart sank. "Oh Ansel, I'm sorry. What happened? You guys have been married for over five years."

"We were only really happy for two. The last few years our careers have taken us in different directions." He took a deep breath. “I didn’t call to bring you down. Only to give you my new phone number. The cell is the same.”

“Well, whenever you want to visit will be fine. Just let me know,” Jenna said.

“Thanks, sis. You know this is my second marriage gone bad. I’m beginning to wonder if there’s such a thing as happiness.”

Jenna instantly thought of Bella and James Taylor. They were the picture of longevity in a marriage. “Yes, there is. You just haven’t met her yet.”

“You sound pretty peppy. Who are you seeing? Is he an artist?”

“He’s not. He’s the opposite of every man I’ve dated.”

Ansel chuckled. “Let’s see. If my memory is correct, that means he’s black, a businessman, and a tight-ass.”

Jenna began to chuckle as well. “You’re three for three, little brother. Call me with your travel plans.”

Zyrien watched as his mom parked the Suburban in the garage late that afternoon. He decided that, since his mother and sisters had occupied Jenna’s afternoon, he could do a little snooping. Was he actually going to pump them for information? Yes. Yes, he was.

He made it to the truck just as Angie opened the door. “Hey,” he smiled at his pregnant sister as she struggled out of the passenger seat. “I just realized that Darrin wasn’t here today. What gives?”

She smoothed her maternity top, rubbing her extralarge stomach. “I told him I needed a breather. He was smothering me. He wasn’t this attentive to me when we were dating.”

Zyrien knew his brother-in-law deserved whatever Angie doled out. But he also knew that Darrin was doing whatever Angie wanted to get back in her good graces.

“I told him,” Angie stated, “that we’re having a family day.”

"He's part of the family, Ang." Zyrien reached in the back seat of the Suburban and grabbed the doggie bags from the restaurant. "Man, I guess you guys had a nice lunch, huh?"

His mother answered as Angie waddled into the house. "Yes, we did. After Jenna showed us her pictures. She's an excellent artist, by the way. We went to Javier's. You should have seen how much Angie put away. I know tonight isn't going to be fun. Those enchiladas are going to take their revenge."

Zyrien laughed. In the last month, Angie had developed a craving for Mexican food and it always fought back. Apparently the babies didn't love Mexican food as much as their mother did.

He hadn't planned on meeting Dawn and her husband, but what Jenna wants, Jenna gets. She convinced him to join her, Dawn, and her husband for dinner. And Zyrien wanted to stay on her good side for as long as possible. So he agreed.

After Jenna and Zyrien joined Dawn and her husband at the table at Ramon's, a quaint Italian restaurant in North Dallas, Zyrien totally understood Lance's words.

Dawn was beautiful. Not the knock-your-socks-off beauty that Jenna had, but the quiet beauty that snuck up on you. She had a voluptuous body compared to Jenna's slender frame, with straight black hair that stopped just above her shoulders. She had big brown eyes, and a mouth that hadn't stopped moving since he and Jenna joined them.

Chad never had a chance. After introductions were made, he simply watched Dawn with the awe of a man truly in love with his wife. In contrast to Dawn, he was white. A little fact that Jenna had neglected to mention to Zyrien, who had wondered what brother would have been playing hockey in Texas. Now he knew. Chad had blond hair and blue eyes, but, contrary to the hockey-player stereotype, he had all his teeth, and was dressed in a suit.

Zyrien listened as the three chatted about something he would have thought was a private matter between Dawn and Chad.

"How's the baby-making project going?" Jenna asked, looking over the menu.

Chad laughed. "She's wearing me out. I told Dawn I'm going to need a week to recuperate from our little time in Canada."

Dawn giggled. "Oh baby, you're the one who insisted on that midnight session in your parents' hot tub." She kissed Chad on his cheek. Zyrien found himself laughing at Chad's discomfort as he turned a deep shade of red.

Dawn turned her attention to Zyrien. "Well, Zyrien, from that smile on Jenna's face and your presence here, I bet you're not so bad yourself."

Zyrien dropped the water glass he was holding. He was too stunned at Dawn's comment to realize that water had spilled all over the front of his shirt.

"Zyrien!" Jenna called. She was dabbing the water from his shirt. "You have to excuse Dawn. Her brain doesn't have a filter." She smiled at him. "We're used to her, so pretty much nothing shocks us anymore. You'll get used to it."

He snatched the napkin from Jenna's hand. "I can do it," he gritted through his teeth. He noticed her hurt expression. "It's OK, Jenna." He caressed her hand. "Really, baby. It's OK." Jenna cleared her throat and stared at Dawn. Dawn stared back at her, then stuck out her tongue at Jenna.

Finally, Dawn looked in Zyrien's direction. "I apologize if my little comment rubbed you the wrong way. I just call it like I see it."

He shrugged, willing himself to stay calm. "Hey, my mom is a lot worse than you. So bring it."

Dawn sat up and rubbed her hands together. "We're going to get along just fine as long as you understand one thing."

Zyrien nodded. "And that is what?"

Dawn nodded at Jenna. "This is my best friend in this world. You hurt her, you hurt me. You hurt me, you hurt Chad. Do I need to explain any further?"

"Not to me," Zyrien answered.

Dawn smiled. "Good. Now let's get down to business."

Zyrien thought he'd been a good sport, but now he decided he could do a little prodding. Ever since they sat down at the table he thought he had seen Dawn somewhere but couldn't place her. But now he had. "I saw you in the Duncaster and Finch building some time ago, didn't I?"

Dawn darted a glance in Jenna's direction. "Maybe. I'm in a lot of buildings," she said vaguely.

He closed his eyes, calling that memory back to the surface. "We were on the elevator together. You got off on the third floor."

Dawn was impressed. "Wow, how do you remember things like that?"

He hated to admit his memory association. "Well, it was the day after my sister left her husband and moved into my house. The reason I remember you was because you reminded me of my sister when she was happy. I would have done anything to get her to smile like you were smiling."

"Now Dawn, I know you and your best friend have discussed it, but I'll explain for Chad's sake. My sister Angie is now staying at my parents'. She's making Darrin, that's my brother-in-law, jump through some serious hoops. My mom thinks it's hilarious, I think she's going overboard. I guess it's a woman thing, but Ang is happy for now, and that makes me happy."

"I was expecting to hear a short joke," Zyrien said as he drove to Jenna's house. "You made Dawn sound like she was going to have a machine gun of insults for me, but she's just like Mom. Says whatever is on her mind and it's up to you deal with it or not. I like her," Zyrien admitted.

Jenna faced him in the small interior of his car. “Really?” He reached over the console and grabbed Jenna’s hand, caressing it in her lap.

“Yes, she’s a handful, but it seems Chad has her in check. A couple of times I noticed him giving her the eye and she quickly changed the subject.”

She laughed. “Yes, Chad is the only one who can do that.”

Zyrien smiled. “It’s nice to know there’s actually a man who can shut Dawn up.”

Chapter 16

Tuesday morning, Jenna walked into the building trying hard not to smile. The weekend had been glorious. She felt her career was back on track and she could actually see the end to the temp job situation.

She wore brown cotton trousers, a lightweight matching sweater, and black stilettos. The shoes were a result of a shopping expedition with Zyrien's mother.

After getting some coffee, she headed for the elevators. She was thirty minutes early for work, so there was no line at the elevator, thank goodness. She did spot one face she wished she didn't have to look at so early in the morning. Kyle Storm, her boss. He noticed her and walked to her.

"Good morning, Jenna. How's that lovely car of yours?"

"Fine, Mr. Storm." Why was he being so nice to her all of a sudden?

He looked her up and down, and then cleared his throat. "I have a special assignment I need to discuss with you. Why don't we meet in my office, say around nine?"

Jenna knew he wasn't supposed to give her any more special assignments, but he didn't know that. "Sure thing. Should I call Ms. Castle before or after the meeting? She instructed me to tell her anytime I had any special assignments."

Kyle's pale face actually became paler. He muttered something under his breath. "Oh, yeah. Why don't we save that call for after the meeting?"

Jenna nodded. Luckily, the elevator sounded its arrival and Jenna hurried inside. Kyle didn't enter the car, mumbling something about getting coffee.

Her joy was short-lived. Katonya moved next to her as the car jumped to life. "Looks like you had a good weekend, Jenna. I found some overdue invoices in your file and I put them on your desk this morning. I need those processed as soon as possible. Let me know when you have done your job."

"Sure, Ms. Washington." Jenna knew there was no way that she'd left any invoices unpaid. More than likely it was something Katonya or Kyle hadn't done. Jenna couldn't wait until those two people were history. The elevator doors opened and Jenna went to her desk, but stopped in her tracks at the picture before her.

Dez sat at her desk wiping her eyes with toilet tissue. In fact her entire desk was covered with wads of tissue. Jenna placed her purse and cup of coffee on her desk and went to her friend. "Dez, what is it? Is something wrong with the baby?"

Dez shook her head. "No, Dante Jr. is fine," she whispered. "Dante and I had a fight last night and it lasted all night." She grabbed another wad of tissues.

"Why don't we talk down the hall?" Jenna didn't want the entire department to hear Dez's marital woes, especially Katonya.

Dez took a deep breath. "Won't you get in trouble for not being at your desk?"

Jenna shrugged. "You let me worry about that. Come on." She motioned for Dez to follow her down the hall. She spoke in a voice only Dez could hear. "Besides, we don't want Katonya to hear all your business, do we?" She winked at her friend.

Dez attempted to dry her eyes as she laughed. "No, I sure

don't. The next thing I know, that heifer will be e-mailing everybody telling them I was crying at my desk and she had to do my work." She rose from her desk and followed Jenna.

Once seated in the small conference room, Dez poured out her heart to Jenna. "I wanted to take the baby to the fireworks displays in the city park last night. Dante thought there would be too many people there and was mad because we hadn't discussed it. I told him I didn't think that needed a discussion. It was just fireworks, Jenna! It wasn't like the baby was going to light them. We were just going to watch them."

Jenna was confused. "I don't see how that escalated to an all-night fight."

Fresh tears poured down Dez's brown face. "I'm getting to that part, Jenna," she answered in a clipped voice. "If I had to do it all over again, I would have just kept my mouth shut."

Jenna felt her friend's pain. But she didn't regret any disagreement she had with Zyrien. They'd always come to a compromise. "What did you say?"

"After, he started talking all pompous to me—you know he has a degree in engineering," she added in a proud tone. "I'm very lucky. Dante is a good man." She noticed Jenna's exasperation. "OK, I'll get back to the story. After, I asked him why he couldn't do anything spontaneously. Why did we have to have an agenda for everything we do? Even when we have sex, it's been planned out already."

"What else?"

Dez took another deep breath. "He said the only spontaneous thing he ever did was marry me and sometimes he regretted it."

Jenna's mouth hung open. How could a man say something so evil? "I'm sorry, Dez. What did you do?"

"At first I was going to go to my mom's, you know, just to clear my head. But I remembered that she and my stepfather were going to Vegas for the holiday and I didn't have a key to their house. They just moved into a condo in north Dallas," she explained to Jenna. "Then I was going to call my sister, but Dante yanked the phone out of my hand and told me I wasn't going to run to my no-account siblings because we were going to get this straight. I was actually scared of my husband. He's usually Mr. Calm, Mr. Order, but he was out of control. I was actually scared he was going to hit me."

"What are you going to do?" Jenna wanted to help her friend, although she didn't have any idea of how she was supposed to go about it.

"I don't know," Dez said. "This morning, he tried to apologize for what he said last night. But I just want this fight to be over and for us to go back to where we were with him not being spontaneous."

"Is that fear talking?"

Dez shook her head. "No, I'm not afraid to be alone. I just don't want Dante Jr. to grow up without his father."

Jenna pondered her thoughts. She didn't know Dez all that well and she might be putting her nose in where it didn't belong. But what else was new? She considered Dez to be her friend. "Look, Dez. I understand about being afraid. But I think you're shortchanging yourself. You're a beautiful, smart woman and any man would be proud to be with you. Dante is taking you for granted. He thinks you'll always be there. He's treating you like that old pair of comfortable stilettos in the back of your closet."

"You think I'm right?"

"I think you stand your ground. No man wants someone he can control. So what if Dante likes everything planned out to the ninth degree? I say surprise his behind and you'll see, he'll be glad you did."

"Is that how you hooked Zyrien Taylor?" Dez rose from her chair.

"I don't know what you're talking about."

Dez walked to the door and turned back to Jenna before she

opened the door. "Why do you think Katonya glares at you all the time? She wants Zyrien back, and in the worst way."

Jenna rose and neared her friend. "I didn't realize she was watching me that hard. I mean, usually in the ladies' room she stares at me when I'm washing my hands and she's always telling me what I did wrong."

"Oh, you better watch your back. She and Mr. Storm are tight, if you know what I mean. Rumor has it they're hitting the sheets." Dez laughed. "Katonya only knows how to do one thing. And it's gotten her pretty far up the corporate ladder."

"Oh my," Jenna whispered. She also made a mental note to make sure Zyrien didn't eat lunch with her anymore. No use making her life at Duncaster any harder than it had to be, especially with Katonya riding her already. "Let's get back to our desks before she reports both of us to Mr. Storm."

Zyrien arrived just a few minutes before his nine o'clock meeting. He had intended on getting to work early and calling Jenna, but he'd overslept. Something he never did.

Jenna was working her way into his heart.

"Zyrien, do you have the finished report?" his boss asked him, snapping him out of his Jenna fantasy.

"Yes, Mr. Duncaster. My assistant is making copies for all the executives." He stood to see what was keeping Brenna when she opened the door with bound copies of the project.

Mr. Duncaster watched as Brenna handed a copy to each of the members at the table. "Thank you, Brenna." He dismissed her with a smile.

Brenna nodded at Zyrien and exited the room. Zyrien took control of the meeting. "As you can see, the report details the cost of taking over the accounting for the government contracts. To do that, we would have to increase the manpower in the accounts payable, receivable, and the auditing departments."

Mr. Duncaster riffled through the thick booklet, stopping at the graphs Zyrien had created. "It says here that Essential Temps is one of the more expensive contracts. What if we went with a lower-price temp agency?"

Zyrien instantly thought of Dawn. "Well, Essential has the higher price tag because their temps are all degreed professionals. You get what you pay for."

"You wouldn't be favoring one temp agency over another, would you?"

Zyrien shook his head. "You asked about using a cheaper agency and I told you honestly. You want stellar workers at minimum-wage pay."

"But is it feasible?"

He nodded. "Yes, it's feasible. Pull out all temps and hire less qualified ones; it will require some training. Lower quality means less productivity. You know they'll need a window of time to get acquainted with our accounting software."

Mr. Duncaster grunted. "Time is one thing we don't have. So Essential Temps has us by the you-know-what?"

"No, they don't. It's a matter of what we want to do. If we're willing to cut all those temps and hire the cheaper ones, are we willing to lose a month to training and risk a high turnover rate with less qualified people?" Zyrien knew they weren't, but wanted them to realize how idiotic it would be to fire all the temps who were already doing the job. "And while those temps are training, are we willing to pay the temps we have now?"

Mr. Duncaster's facial expression took a turn for the worse. "You're telling me we would actually be paying two different temp companies, if we want to cut the Essential temps out?"

Zyrien tried to hide his triumphant smile. "Yes, sir, that's what I have been trying to tell you for the last few weeks. I've crunched the numbers and no matter how you want to look at it, if we want to cut the temps, we're going to pay through the nose."

The other participants in the meeting all looked toward Mr.

Duncaster for a reaction. He thumbed through the pages; pondering the information Zyrien had just given him. "Well, what about when the work starts coming in? Are they going to be able to handle the volume of work?"

"Some of the departments will have to be realigned to compensate for the workload, but it looks like the conversion should go smoothly."

Zyrien saw the puzzled looked on the executives' faces and explained. "A conversion will be necessary due to the stringent security and compliance with requirements the government will need in place."

"Oh," Mr. Duncaster breathed. "I thought it was something on our end."

"No, the government will want a meeting before all this starts taking place. They meet with all the accounting firms in contention for the contract," said Zyrien. He hoped he would not have to go, but knew he was the most likely candidate. After all, it was his report.

"Fine, just keep us informed," Mr. Duncaster said as he rose from his chair at the head of the oval-shaped table. "Great job, Zyrien." He left the room.

Zyrien sat in the quiet of the conference room, satisfied. At least Jenna would get to keep her job. She and all the rest of the temps would have jobs for now.

A few hours later, Jenna sat alone at a table in the cafeteria. She had promised Dez an idea to help her get her marriage back on track. Jenna took out her trusty pad and began sketching an idea, something she did when she was thinking.

"Hey, can I join you?" Zyrien sat down before she could refuse.

Jenna smiled at him. "You know, maybe you shouldn't be seen eating with me. I don't want to get into trouble."

He smiled at her as he picked up his sandwich to take a bite. "You had a run-in with Katonya."

"A little skirmish," she admitted. "But I don't want any more trouble. I can take care of myself, but I don't want her to take it out on Dez or something, since we're friends." She didn't want to elaborate on Dez's marital woes.

"You let me worry about Katonya," Zyrien said. "If she does anything to you out of line, let me know. Technically, she falls under my jurisdiction and I can still put her in her place."

Jenna nodded, knowing this wasn't the end of her dealing with the ex. She went back to her sketching.

"What are you doing?"

Jenna shrugged. "Just thinking."

"About me, I hope." He took another bite and a big gulp of soda. "Hey, how about dinner tonight?"

She would have liked nothing more, but she had a meeting this weekend to get ready for. "I can't. I have a meeting with Greta—you know, the curator at the Dallas Museum of Art—this weekend. She's interested in letting me do a one-woman show around Labor Day. I need to get my portfolio in order."

"So I'm taking the backseat again."

"Zyrien, you know everything I have done has been leading up to me getting more gallery space. Why does it have to be about you?"

He threw his napkin on the table. "It doesn't have to be about me. I would just like to see you. Why can't I come over and help you pick out portraits?"

Well, at least he was showing a little interest. But was it truly interest in her career or was it the need not to be alone? "I don't think so. I usually do that with Gunter," she lied. "He's coming over tonight."

"Oh, it's like that."

Jenna stared at the little boy Zyrien had become. "Yes, it's like that. You know I'm trying to get my career back on track. Do I come between you and your work?"

He stared at her. "All the time. I used to be able to put together a report in a couple of hours. Now it takes me days to get focused, 'cause you keep sneaking into my brain."

It was almost as good as "I love you," or at least, "I care for you and it was not just sex," she mused. She figured that was about as good as she was going to get from Zyrien Taylor. "Well, it's nice to know you have that focusing problem, too. That's why Gunter is coming to help me. I don't know which pictures should be included."

He gave her a big, broad smile for her trouble. "If we weren't in such a public place, I'd give you a big ol' kiss."

Two days later, Jenna watched Dez prepare to leave for lunch with her husband. "Are you sure you have everything?"

"Yes, I'm picking up lunch, then we're meeting in the park. You were so right, Jenna. Once I told him what I was feeling about him and our marriage, he was open to change. This is his first attempt. The only thing he knows is that we're having a picnic in the park. He doesn't know about the hotel room." She had reserved a room at a hotel nearby just in case their lunch ran long.

Jenna smiled at her. "I know things will turn out great. Nothing like a change in the routine to put a spark in the relationship," Jenna chimed. She grinned as she remembered one time a spark almost engulfed her in flames of passion.

Dez walked to Jenna's desk. "I know you, Jenna Bradshaw. What is that smile for?"

Jenna shook her head, not wanting to plant any more ideas in the young woman's head. "Nothing, girl. Go on and rock Dante's world. Don't forget to call me if you want me to pick up Dante Jr. for you."

"I appreciate the offer, Jenna. But I know you don't have children and would be making a great sacrifice to keep him and I couldn't ask you to do that. Dante isn't that good." She waved "bye" to Jenna and left.

Well, at least they're on the road to recovery, Jenna thought of Dez and Dante. She returned her attention to the work Mr. Storm had so politely given her earlier that morning. She was interrupted before she could process her first invoice.

"Ms. Bradshaw," Katonya drawled in a nasty tone, "there's some unpaid invoices on Dez's desk. Could you make sure they are processed?"

"Of course, Ms. Washington." Jenna rolled her eyes as Katonya sashayed her way back to her desk. Jenna knew there were no such invoices and went back to work.

Or at least that was her plan. Her phone rang about thirty minutes later. After she spoke the official greeting, she recognized Zyrien's voice.

"How about dinner tonight? Before you say no, I was thinking something quick. I would just like to see your face and maybe touch you," he said gently.

Jenna was about to answer where he could touch her when Katonya appeared at her desk again. Jenna pretended it was a business call. "That will be fine. Why don't you call me on my cell with the estimate on my car? I get off work at five."

It took Zyrien a few momentss to catch up to her, but then he just laughed and said, "Tell Katonya I said 'whaz up.'" He disconnected.

Katonya looked down at Jenna, sneering. "Don't tell me something is wrong with your PT Cruiser? I didn't think a woman your age would drive that kind of car. A sedan would be more suitable. Maybe a minivan?"

"Well, as you know, I don't have to please anyone but me. So I like my car. I don't need all that space for children since I don't have any, and I haven't been married." That ought to teach her to mess with grown folks, Jenna mused as Katonya stomped back to her desk.

After work, Jenna walked to her car, thankful she'd made

it through the afternoon without another verbal skirmish with Katonya. Thankfully, Mr. Storm kept her busy and away from Jenna. As Jenna made the trek to the temporary employees' parking lot, she noticed that her car was leaning to one side. *Please don't be a flat tire,* she prayed.

But it *was* a flat tire. Jenna sighed and reached for her cell phone. She dialed roadside assistance and a young woman named Tiesha told her it would be about forty-five minutes before someone would be there. "That's fine. I'll be waiting," Jenna said, ending the call.

She took a deep breath and made another call.

"Hey," Zyrien said.

"Hey. I might be a little late," Jenna said.

"I'm pulling up to the restaurant now. Where are you?"

"At work."

Zyrien laughed. "Did Katonya make you work late? Really, where are you?"

"I'm at work. I had a flat tire. I'm waiting on roadside assistance to get here."

All the laughter immediately went out of Zyrien's voice. "Why didn't you call me? I could have changed it for you."

"And have half the temps see a manager changing my flat? No, thank you. Besides, that's why I pay for the service."

"But baby, that's what I'm here for. That's what a relationship is about. We're supposed to be there for each other."

What a conversation to have now! "We're in a relationship?"

Zyrien muttered something under his breath. "Not yet, but it isn't for lack of trying on my side. As much as I tried to fight it, you're in my heart, Jenna Bradshaw. How many men do you know would just sit at home because their woman was too busy to see them? I'm working around your schedule, not mine."

She had two ways to retort to his declaration. Brushing off his comments would only infuriate him, or she could have declared how she really felt.

"Zyrien, I feel—" she started, when she noticed the wrecker pulling into the parking lot. "Hey, roadside assistance is here. See you in a few minutes." She ended the call before admitting she loved him.

The young man hopped out of the wrecker. "You Ms. Bradshaw?" he asked, looking at his clipboard. At her nod, he continued his task. "I need to see your ID and your roadside assistance card."

Jenna reached inside the console and retrieved the cards for him. He inspected them, then got to work. As he changed the tire, he admired the rims on the car.

"Nice rims. This your son's car?"

"No, this is my car," Jenna said proudly. "Of course that was before I knew every rapper, athlete, and entertainer had these rims on their car, too."

"If you ever want to get rid of them, let me know. I have a PT, too."

"Thanks, but no. I like them," Jenna stated. Every young man who came near her car always wanted to buy those rims and each time her answer was the same. No.

About twenty minutes later, Jenna saw a familiar black BMW enter the parking lot. "Oh, no," she whispered.

"What's wrong, ma'am?" He looked up at Jenna from his squatting position on the ground.

Jenna shook her head at him. "Nothing, just the arrival of a moron."

Zyrien parked his car next to Jenna's. He slid from behind the wheel, not dressed in the suit she'd assumed he'd be wearing, but a polo shirt, slacks, and casual shoes. He smiled as walked to her.

"What are you doing here?" Jenna asked, for lack of anything else to say.

"You were in distress, so I came to save you." He put his arms around her waist, pulling her close to his body.

The young man looked up and smiled. "Zyrien Taylor.

Man, I haven't seen you since you were dating. . . ." the man let the sentence drift off into that sacred man zone. "I mean, I haven't seen you in a while."

Zyrien cleared his throat. "Yeah, it's been a minute. Jenna, this is Brandon Hill. He's my cousin," Zyrien explained.

Jenna nodded. So that was how Zyrien knew the mechanic. She watched the men do the brother handshake thing and Brandon resumed putting the tire back on the car.

Zyrien kissed her on the cheek. "You didn't finish the conversation. I know Jason is almost done with your car, so why don't we go to your place and continue it?"

Jenna knew she had stuck her foot in her mouth and now he wanted a confession. "Why not your place?"

He smiled and wrapped her closer to his body. "Because I don't have a big-time meeting in two days with the art curator. And Angie let it slip about some painting of you in your birthday suit I just have to see."

Jenna gasped. "I don't know what you're talking about."

"Oh, please. I overheard her and Mom talking about how great it looked. By the time they realized I was listening, it was too late to recant."

She wanted to do something to wipe that smirk off his face. She kissed him with all the heat of the Texas sun in summer. As she felt Zyrien's tongue fight hers for control, Jenna pulled back.

Zyrien moaned, leaned his head against her neck, and let out a curse. "You did that on purpose."

Duh. "Of course I did. That was for eavesdropping."

Chapter 17

Saturday, Jenna walked into the Dallas Museum of Art, heading straight for the reception desk. A young woman greeted her with a generic smile.

"Hello, how can I help you?"

Jenna adjusted the large portfolio case in her left hand. She fished Greta's card out of her shoulder bag and handed it to the receptionist. "I have an appointment with Mrs. Larson. My name is Jenna Bradshaw."

The woman smiled instantly. "You painted that nude hunk on the sofa," she acknowledged. "I love that picture." She cleared her throat. "Is he a friend of yours?"

Jenna smiled. "He's an acquaintance. Would you like me to relay a message?"

The woman actually blushed. Her tanned skinned grew redder by the minute. "Oh no. He's very handsome." She reached for the phone and pulled it to her ear. After a few minutes, she replaced the phone in its cradle and looked in Jenna's direction. "Mrs. Larson said to meet her on the fourth floor. That's where the administrative offices are. In room 455. She'll be there momentarily."

Jenna thanked the woman. After taking the elevator to the fourth floor, she entered the room. The door opened inward and there stood Greta Larson, dressed in a sleek black suit. "Jenna, I'm so glad you could make it." She motioned her inside the large office.

After Jenna took a seat in one of the two leather chairs opposite the mahogany desk, she set her leather portfolio case in the second chair. "Thank you, Mrs. Larson. I appreciate this opportunity."

Greta smiled, almost all her white teeth showing. "I thought you were going to call me 'Greta.'"

Jenna, surely not wanting to upset the women who held the key to her comeback, nodded her head. "Of course, Greta," Jenna said.

Greta grinned. "Good. Now that that's over, we can get down to business. I want to schedule you in a one-woman show.

"Yes, Jenna, you heard correctly. I know you're ready for a one-woman show. It would put your name back into the artists' community and before you know it, you will have offers for more paintings."

That had been Jenna's dream ten years ago. And over the years, she had been doing OK, but she hadn't had this kind of offer, ever. This was her chance. "When?"

Greta clasped her hands together. "I was thinking about Labor Day weekend. I know you have a day job and that's a holiday. The official opening would be Saturday and your paintings would hang in the gallery until the New Year."

Tears of happiness flowed down Jenna's face. She couldn't believe it. She was actually going to get her shot at a comeback. Not really a comeback, she mused, since she wasn't exactly on top to begin with, but close enough. She wiped her face with the back of her hand.

"Here," Greta offered a Kleenex. "I know just how you feel."

Jenna took the tissue and wiped her face. She probably looked a holy mess. "You don't know how much this means to me," she said.

Greta nodded. "When I got this job, I cried too. I'm sure those are happy tears, right?"

"Definitely."

Greta sighed. "Now that we have that settled. I will need about twelve paintings, different sizes and mediums. In about a week or ten days, could you give me some idea of what you're going to use in the showing? If you have some stills of the artwork, that would be great. I can get some publicity ready. We only have about seven weeks to get ready. So the sooner you can get me the sketches, the better."

This was where being focused came in. She always had her pictures photographed when she finished her work. "I can get you stills by Monday. I just need to go through what I have to see what I would like to present to you."

Greta snapped her fingers. "I know this is going to put some pressure on you and you don't have to do it, but how about a fresh painting? Since your nudes are your trademark, why not do a new one?"

Jenna had plenty of nudes. She had nothing new besides the picture of Ian, but she had been tossing an idea around in her head. "Well, I think I might be able to work on that one. Can I get back to you on that?"

"Of course. If it doesn't fit in the timetable, I understand." She stood. "Would you like to see your gallery space?"

Jenna gasped. Greta's question was like asking a new mother if she'd like to see her baby. "Yes, I'd love to see it." She rose and grabbed her portfolio.

"You can leave your case in here. I'll lock my office."

Jenna nodded and placed it gently in the chair. "Thank you, Greta."

They took the elevator to the second floor. Jenna walked around in amazement, gazing at all the gorgeous paintings on the walls. Was she good enough for her nudes to hang on the wall in throwing distance of Picasso, Renoir, Matisse, or Monet?

"Jenna, here's where your pictures will be hanging," Greta

told her. "I thought it would liven the Impressionists up to have a young kid on the block."

Jenna laughed. At forty-two she would have never considered herself a young kid, but in this case she had to agree with Greta.

The room was large and a moment of inspiration hit her. She had the perfect idea for a new picture. The new project would serve two purposes: it would mark Jenna's comeback and give Dez back her confidence. "I think I can get you that new nude. I have to double-check with the model, but I think it can be done."

Greta sighed. "That's great, Jenna. I knew you could do it."

Jenna took a deep breath. It was finally her time. She knew she could do it, too.

Zyrien sat at his mother's kitchen table checking his cell phone display for the tenth time. Maybe his battery was down and his phone couldn't ring. Jenna's meeting was at one o'clock. It was now almost three-thirty. What could be taking her so long to call?

"Zyrien," his mother called from the patio. "How long are you going to sit at the table watching the food? Why don't you bring the steaks outside, so your father can start grilling?"

He suddenly remembered what he was supposed to do. He had been given the chore of bringing the steaks outside. Where was his brain?

"Zyrien!" she called again.

"Okay, Mom. I'm on my way." He grabbed the tray of meat and carried it to his father. "Sorry, Dad, I got distracted."

"I know you're worried about Jenna. It's only been a few hours. Maybe her meeting ran long? You should have offered to accompany her," his mother said from her chair under the awning protecting her from the hot Texas sun.

"Mom, that's like her accompanying me to a very important meeting. No way. I just thought maybe my batteries were down or something."

"Well, don't forget to tell her to come to our house for dinner," Bella reminded her son.

It had been his mother's great idea to have the family over to celebrate Jenna's meeting. Zyrien had wanted something for just him and Jenna, but his mother was not to be outdone, so they were grilling steaks and waiting for Jenna to arrive.

"I know." He hated the way he was acting, but nothing could be done about it. "You know I completed my project at work last week, got a pat on the back from the higher-ups, and you didn't have me over me for a steak dinner. I'm only your son," he teased his mother. "One of four, I might add."

She rose and walked toward her son. "You're in management; this is different. Jenna is an artist."

Zyrien held up his hands in defeat. "I'm not even going to ask you to explain your rationale," Zyrien said.

His mother put her hands on her slender hips. "Well, how about this one: she doesn't have any family here and she's a fabulous artist."

Zyrien conceded defeat. "All right, Mom." He hugged his mother. "I love you for doing this."

Jenna sat in the comfort of her car three and a half hours after her meeting with Greta had started. She glanced around the empty parking lot to make sure she didn't have any witnesses and let out the loudest scream.

She picked up her cell phone and called Zyrien. She dialed his home number first, and hung up when she heard his voice mail engage. She dialed his mother's number. "Hi Bella. This is Jenna."

"Honey, I'd know your voice anywhere. I think someone here has been dying to talk to you."

"Good. I'm just dying to tell him my news."

Bella laughed. "You can tell me."

Jenna knew better than to tell his mother before telling Zyrien. He'd kill her. She laughed, imagining his crestfallen face. "I think I'd better talk to Zyrien first."

"Yes, you know my son. I'll get him. He just went back in the house. We're having a cookout in your honor. I just know things went well. So come over as quick as you can. The kids should be here by the time you get here."

Jenna was going to cry at Zyrien's mother's simple gesture. "Thank you, Bella. You really didn't have to. I appreciate the thought." She couldn't remember the last time anyone gave a cookout in her honor. It was a gesture of love.

"Jenna, you're part of this family. You're the first woman my son has gone wild over and I know you're a good person. Besides, I like you, too."

Jenna tried to hold back her tears, but it was useless. "Thank you, Bella. I'll be over as soon as I change clothes." She ended the call before she realized she hadn't talked to Zyrien.

He called back before she could dial a single digit. She sniffed and answered the phone.

"Baby, what's wrong?"

She smiled at the nervous tone in his voice. "Nothing is wrong. I'm just happy."

"How did your meeting go? I know you aced it, right?"

"Can we talk about this later?" She was starting to get a headache with all the crying she'd done in the last few hours.

"No, I want to talk about this now," Zyrien demanded. "You call and talk to Mom and not to me."

"Zyrien, I just need a moment, OK?" she pleaded.

Something in her voice made him instantly forget about the tantrum he wanted to throw. "Baby, I'm sorry. I just was feeling . . . you know," he said softly. "I guess I was feeling a little left out."

"It wasn't intentional, Zyrien. I have just had one of the

biggest days of my life and I just need for you to understand how emotional this is for me."

He took a deep breath. He had intended to give her grief for not telling him first, not to make her cry on the phone. In the few months he'd had known her, he couldn't recall her crying. He didn't like it. It made him want to hit something in frustration.

He listened to her gentle sobs through the phone, wishing he was there with her. "Jenna," he said softly. "Tell me what the lady said." He was beginning to fear that all hadn't gone well with the art director.

"That's not why I was crying. Greta wants me to have a one-woman show Labor Day weekend."

"Then what has you all upset?"

"Your mother."

"What?"

"She told me you guys are having a cookout for me. I guess it just got to me." The sniffles cranked up to real tears again. "I just thought that was a lovely gesture and no one has ever done something that nice for me."

Women. He would never understand women. His mother loved to host cookouts, but he wouldn't dare tell Jenna that, especially not with her blubbering like she was. "You're worth it, baby. You want me to pick you up?"

"Yes, Zyrien, please."

"OK, I'll pick you up in an hour. Is that enough time?"

"Yes," she whispered. "I love you." She ended the call.

Zyrien smiled as he snapped his phone closed. Then reality hit. "Did Jenna just say she loved me?" No one heard him ask this monumental question because he was sitting at the table alone. He realized that she had. "Damn. She did it to me again. She said it first."

Chapter 18

"Jenna, are you sure you're OK? You don't look so good," Zyrien said. They were waiting for Jenna's stomach to settle down before they sat down to the celebration dinner.

She didn't feel good, either. After he picked her up, they'd headed directly for his parents' house. At first the emotions of the day caught up to her and she cried a river. Zyrien, not knowing exactly what to do, brought her a glass of wine to calm her nerves and that was where all her troubles started.

"I guess that lunch didn't agree with me." She could feel her stomach fighting with her head, reminding her of the error of her ways. "I was so excited about the museum, then the stuff with your mom, I forgot about eating."

Zyrien sat in the chair next to her. "Baby, you just don't look well. Why don't you go upstairs and lie down? I'll come get you when everything is ready."

Jenna held a wet paper towel against her forehead. "A nap isn't going to help my stomach. How about some crackers or something."

Zyrien jumped out of the chair, heading into the house. "Sure, babe. I'll ask Mom what can settle your stomach."

Jenna laughed, and then let out a moan. She really shouldn't have had that glass of wine.

"I don't think I've ever seen that boy move that fast," his father chuckled, joining Jenna at the table.

"My stomach is just a little upset, James. Zyrien went to get some crackers. I'm hoping it'll settle enough to eat."

"Good," he said.

Zyrien soon returned with a tray of crackers, assorted breads, and a glass of milk. He placed it before her. "Mom said the milk would help settle your stomach."

Jenna picked up the glass and that was totally the wrong thing to do at that time. She dropped the glass and headed for the house, making a beeline for the nearest bathroom.

Zyrien jumped up, ready to follow Jenna, but his father grabbed his hand. "Let her alone for a minute, son. She might not want you to see her like that."

"But Dad, she's sick and it's my fault. I gave her the wine."

His father wouldn't let go of his hand. "Zyrien, you have the weakest stomach of anyone I've ever seen. You'll be throwing up right beside her."

He knew that, but he had to go to her. "I know, but I have to. I love her, Dad." He headed into the house.

He ran past his mother and his sisters as they pointed upstairs. Zyrien took the stairs two at a time and headed to the first bathroom he found and burst inside. Jenna was hovering over the toilet.

He reached into the medicine cabinet looking for the pink miracle liquid he knew his mother kept stocked like it was a fine wine. He opened the bottle and set it on the counter. He also located a new toothbrush and toothpaste, and grabbed a hand towel out of the linen closet.

Jenna had finally stopped vomiting and was now sitting on the edge of the oval-shaped bathtub, breathing very hard. "Thanks, Zyrien. You haven't left out anything." She nodded at the neatly arranged items on the counter.

He handed her the pink wonder liquid. "I'm the upchuck

king in this family." He helped her to stand. "You want me to stay in here with you?"

Jenna took a teaspoon of medicine, then drank some water. "What will your family think of you being in here with me?"

"Doesn't matter what they think. It matters what you need. If you need me to stay, I'll do that. I was just trying to give you some space."

She smiled at him as she opened the toothpaste. "As much as I would like for you to stay, I don't want you watching me brush my teeth. Get out."

He blew her a kiss and left the bathroom. "I don't believe you guys," he said to his four sisters. "Can Jenna and I have a few minutes of privacy? She's not feeling well."

Angie grinned at her brother as she started walking to her room. "Oh, Zyrien, it's just that we've never seen you like this over a woman. I mean, you don't have the strongest constitution when it comes to stuff like that."

"Nieces and nephews," he muttered. He followed his sister to her room. "Hey, Ang, I need a favor."

Angie stopped walking. "You need a favor? That's rich. You never need anything."

"What's that supposed to mean?" Zyrien was offended.

Angie rubbed her tummy, opening the door to her room. "I mean, you're the person everyone in the family runs to for help. I called you when Darrin took off, Sean calls you when he and Tiffany have a fight, and I won't even talk about Bailey and Natasha. You're our go-to man. It's seems strange you need assistance for anything."

"Well, actually this is for Jenna. I wanted to invite her friend Dawn and her husband Chad to the cookout. I don't have her number and I was thinking maybe you could ask your friend Mandy, if she could get their number."

Angie walked to her bed and plopped down. "First of all, her name is not Mandy. You guys call her that because you think she's a man-hater, but she's not. Her name is Megan

Wright. Second of all, you don't have to go to all that trouble. I have Dawn's cell number. Jenna gave it to me. Dawn's brother is an attorney and I was going to call her, but hadn't got around to it yet."

It was way easier than he could have expected. He hugged his sister. "Angie, you're always full of surprises. Could you call her and tell her about the cookout? Jenna might overhear me and I want it to be a surprise."

Angie smiled. "You're such a romantic."

"That has to be our secret," Zyrien said. "Speaking of, is Darrin coming over?" He noticed his brother-in-law's presence less and less around his parents' home. "Are you guys still working it out?"

"He is. I'm not. I don't feel like I can trust him anymore. I told him I was filing for legal separation. Of course, he asked for one more chance."

"And?" The one thing Zyrien had dreaded looked like it was coming to fruition. He didn't want his sister to be the second marriage casualty in their family, with his brother Carson being the first. But how could she stay married, if she couldn't trust her husband to stay by her side when the going got tough?

"I told him that I had to think about it. I'd rather raise the kids alone than be with someone I can't really rely on. What happens when some other problem arises? I want to know he's going to be there no matter what. Like what you have with Jenna. You just stood in the bathroom and didn't leave her side until she told you to get out."

"So you guys were listening at the door," he realized. "I thought I heard someone snickering on the other side of the bathroom door."

Angie reclined on the bed, pulling the comforter over her body. "We were just making sure you didn't get sick and embarrass your manly self."

He smiled. "Are you feeling OK?"

"Yes, just exhausted. I'm carrying twins, you know."

She did look tired. "Angie, if you need to talk about anything, you know I won't judge you. I can be objective."

She reached out and touched her brother's hand. "Zyrien, it's OK. I've been up most of the day helping Mom get ready for this shindig. I just need a little energy nap. I usually take one every day about this time."

Zyrien cleared his throat. Jenna was right, as usual. Angie had to come to her own decision about ending her marriage. There were things he just could not control.

Hours later, Jenna didn't think her life could get much better. Zyrien's parents had gone far beyond a casual cookout. They had ribs, steak, hamburgers, and hot dogs.

Then she was surprised when Dawn and Chad walked into the backyard, carrying a large box. Dawn walked to her friend and hugged her. "Congratulations, Jenna." She handed the box to Jenna.

Bella walked over to the couple and introduced herself and everyone else to Jenna's friends. They were soon sitting in front of Jenna.

"I'm so glad you could come," Jenna said. "But tell me how you knew."

Dawn picked up the glass of wine. "Ask your man. Angie called us."

Jenna remembered giving Angie the number on the Fourth of July. "Very good, Zyrien. I'm shocked."

Zyrien's brown skin actually reddened. "It wasn't nothing. I know you guys are tight and she wouldn't want to miss this moment."

Jenna leaned and kissed him. "Thank you, baby." She kissed him again and the kiss became more intense as he joined in. That was until they remembered they had an audience. She immediately broke off the kiss. "I'm sorry."

Bella and James laughed. "Hey, nothing to be sorry for,"

James said. "There's nothing wrong with being in love, is there, son?" He kissed his wife.

A few days later, Jenna sat across from Dez at a table in the cafeteria. "I have a confession," Jenna said quietly, "but I'm going to need your help." It was time to confess about her profession to her friend.

Dez gazed across the table at Jenna. "What is it? Are you finally going to tell me about Zyrien?" The women were enjoying their break together in the cafeteria.

"I don't know what you're talking about," Jenna lied. "I'm confessing about my other career." She took a deep breath and spoke. "I'm an artist. I do paintings." She just neglected to mention that she painted mostly nudes.

Dez's eyes danced with amusement. "I thought you seemed like one of those artsy kinds of people. You're always so laid-back. Even when Katonya is in your face about something stupid, you never lose your temper or curse her out. I always see you sketching in that little notebook of yours and you talk about karma. I had to go home and look that word up, I want you to know."

"I didn't realize you noticed me doing that. Anyway, I have the opportunity to have a one-woman show at the Dallas Museum of Art in September and I would like to you pose for a picture."

"Me? Are you sure? I mean, I'm not a supermodel. I'm short and still have baby fat from Dante Jr.," she objected.

That was the main reason Jenna wanted to paint Dez—because she wasn't a supermodel; she was real. "I think you look great, Dez, but there is something else I need to tell you."

"You mean my picture would hang in the Dallas Museum of Art? That would be awesome."

"Dez, before you agree to this, you should look at the pictures in my portfolio. I do mostly nudes."

Dez gasped. "You want all my stuff hanging out like that? Dante would have a fit, then divorce me, and take the baby. I don't know, Jenna. I thought I was going to be dressed."

"OK, I understand. But still come over and look at my pictures. Maybe we can come up with something that will let you stay married and I can still paint a portrait."

Dez agreed and Jenna gave her the address to her house. "Why don't you bring Dante?"

Jenna had just returned to her desk when her phone rang. She knew exactly who it was. "Accounting, this is Jenna Bradshaw."

"Hello," Zyrien said, "I thought we could have had our break together, but you went with Dezarae Rucker."

Jenna smiled. "How do you know what I did for break?"

Zyrien chuckled. "I have my sources. Besides, Katonya made sure I knew that you were on break with a permanent employee. She wanted me to call Dawn and report you for fraternizing with an employee."

Jenna sighed. That woman was going to be the death of her temp career yet. "So now she doesn't want me talking to anyone on my break. Why am I her concern?"

It was Zyrien's turn to sigh. "Why don't we talk about it tonight?"

They didn't have anything to talk about, at least not on the subject of Katonya. Jenna already knew that Katonya and Zyrien had dated. It didn't take a rocket scientist to figure out why she disliked Jenna so vehemently. But still, it was nice for Zyrien to know he didn't call all the shots. "I can't. Dez and Dante are coming over tonight to look at my portraits. I'm considering painting her for the one-woman show."

Zyrien gasped. "Not in the nude."

"We're discussing it. I don't know if she'll want to do it. So she and Dante are coming to check out my pictures."

"So what about me?"

"I'll have to see you tomorrow. This is business." Jenna ended the call.

Later that evening, Jenna showed Dez and Dante around her small studio. Dante didn't look like any of the pictures Dez had of him. He was tall compared to Dez, but was still an inch or two shorter than Jenna. His pecan-brown skin was smooth, his black hair cut very short and professional. He didn't look like he had a spontaneous bone in his body.

She initially thought Dante would be screaming a fit, but he just looked at the portraits. Nodding at them and asking questions about the models, what motivated her to paint that way, and what kind of paints she used.

"Exactly what would Dez be wearing?" He glanced at his wife, smiling at her.

"Well, that will depend on Dez. Whatever she feels comfortable in. I principally paint nudes for display, but have done some with clothes. Dante, I want both you and Dez to realize this will be hanging in the Dallas Museum of Art for at least three months."

Dante walked to his wife and hugged her. He kissed her, rocking back and forth. "Honey, it's up to you. Whatever you decide, I'm behind you."

Jenna guessed that in Dante's very organized world this was his version of a man's ultimate fantasy. Instead of him having sex with two women, his wife would be on display for all to see.

Dez looked up at her husband. "Are you sure? What do you want?"

"I want what you want," Dante said.

"Me, too."

Jenna was getting a sugar rush from all that sweet talk between Dez and Dante. She hoped Zyrien never talked to her like that. OK, that was a lie. Jenna wanted Zyrien to talk to her exactly like that, kisses included.

"Why don't you guys sleep on it tonight? Then Dez can

give me her answer tomorrow. Meanwhile, I'll work on some sketch ideas," Jenna suggested. She hoped the smile she noticed on Dante's face was his approval.

Dez answered for them. "Jenna, I can give you my answer now."

Jenna didn't want to put too much stock in that smile spreading across Dez's face. "What's your decision?

"I'll do it."

Jenna hugged her friend. "Thank you, very much. I'll only need you a few nights to pose for the picture. Maybe for about two hours a night for three nights."

"Are you sure that's enough time?" Dez asked as Dante kissed her forehead.

"Why don't we go to the living room and I can explain the painting process to you guys?" Jenna led them to the living room and they took a seat.

She continued. "First I sketch out my idea. Which I will probably do tonight. Then, when you pose, I will do a final sketch, and after that I just let my fingers do their thing. If there's any touch-ups to be done, I'll call you back in a few weeks. The painting should be done within a month."

Dante held his wife's hand. "Can we see it before it goes to the museum?"

"Of course. It's not going on velvet or anything distasteful. I have some pictures hanging in the museum already in the women's exhibit if you want to see how a picture would look in the gallery."

Dez spoke up. "There's no need, Jenna. Whatever you want me to do is OK. I trust your judgment."

Jenna knew it was a milestone to get Dez to agree to baring her body for all the art world to see. But when Dante leaned over and kissed his wife on the mouth, Jenna knew she had his approval.

Chapter 19

Friday evening, Jenna buzzed around her studio making sure everything was in place for her first sketching session with Dez. She had wine to calm her co-worker's jittery nerves, and jazz music played softly in the background. A little Charlie Parker always soothed her after a bad day at work.

After she was satisfied, she awaited Dez's arrival. She had invited Dante to the session, but he declined. "I'd better not," he said. "I want to be surprised."

He would definitely get his wish, Jenna mused, imagining Dante Rucker's expression when he saw his wife's nude body on a 30" x 60" canvas. The doorbell brought Jenna back to the present. She opened the door and let Dez inside, leading her down the hall to the studio.

"There's no rush, Dez." Jenna motioned for her friend to sit on the couch.

Dez nodded. "Can I have a glass of wine?" She was dressed in shorts and a tank top, not looking anywhere near her age of thirty.

Jenna settled on her seat behind the easel. "Sure, help yourself. Models usually like something to relax them."

Dez slid off the sofa and poured a glass of white wine. Instead of sipping the wine, she finished the glass in one quick swallow and replaced the glass on the tray. She must have realized Jenna was watching her. "I'm sorry, girl. I just needed something to chase the fright away."

Jenna laughed, instantly approving of anything to get the portrait started. She really didn't have time for a day of stage fright. "No problem."

"So what do I do now?" Dez asked, walking back to the seat. "Do I strip here?"

"No. There's a changing room down the hall. There's also a terry-cloth robe hanging on the door. I'm working on your time schedule, Dez. If you're not ready to disrobe, I can bounce some of my ideas off you to see what you think."

Dez's brown eyes became large. "You mean you want my advice?"

"Of course. You're a very important part of the process," Jenna told her friend. "I value your opinions. Remember, you gave me the heads-up on Katonya."

Dez laughed. "Yeah, me and Ms. Thang have never gotten along. When I first started working there, and she noticed the picture I have of Dante on my desk, she started asking me all sorts of questions about him. Where did he work? What was his job title? Stuff like that. One day he met me for lunch and Katonya saw him in the lobby," she stopped speaking, obviously remembering something funny, because she had the silliest grin on her small face. "She had the nerve to give Dante her phone number. You know I had to tell her about herself after he told me."

"What did she say?" Jenna set a sketch pad on the easel. "I mean, you caught her with her hand in the cookie jar, so to speak. What excuse could she possibly give you?" Jenna hoped the casual conversation would relax her friend.

Dez rose, heading for the doorway. "She said she didn't realize he was my Dante. Even so, he wears a wedding band; she still shouldn't approach someone else's husband. So I politely told her that if I caught her anywhere near my Dante I would show her what a pissed-off black female could do and it wouldn't be pretty."

Jenna giggled. "I can't imagine you even uttering those words."

"You should have seen her face. Ever since then, she rarely talks to me. If she thinks she can get over on you, then she'll pick on you."

"Don't I know it. She called Zyrien, I mean, Mr. Taylor, and told him you and I had break together."

Dez walked over to Jenna. "Girl, you know I know. I've seen him checking you out in the elevator, down the hall, and he always just happens to be by the elevator when you leave for the day. You don't have to worry. I'm not going to tell anyone you and Zyrien are kickin' it. Personally, I think you're good for his ego."

Jenna couldn't help asking. "What do you mean?"

"Well, I've been at Duncaster and Finch three years and in those three years, Zyrien has had his share of women. But you're different. You don't run behind him and I see how he looks at you when the other managers talk to you."

Jenna didn't get a chance to ask Dez how Zyrien looked at her, because Dez picked this moment to get her courage. She walked down the hall and quickly returned in nothing but the white terry-cloth robe.

"OK, I'm ready." She stood in the middle of the room, glancing around nervously. "Zyrien isn't one of those drop-in brothers, is he?"

Jenna's mind immediately went back to the first time Zyrien came to her house unannounced. "No. He usually calls before he drives over here."

Dez nodded, taking in the information. "Good, 'cause I don't want him seeing me in the buff like this. It's hard enough that you have to see me, since we work together. But you're an artist, so it's all right."

Jenna smiled at her friend. It always amazed her that so

many people didn't mind an artist seeing them in their birthday suit. "Are you sure you and Dante are OK with it hanging in the museum for all to see?"

Dez started untying the sash on the robe. "Yes, I want to do something spectacular and since I'm married to Dante, this is about as wild as I can go. How many women can say their picture is hanging in the museum?"

Zyrien sat on his couch glancing at the TV, but staring at the cordless phone on the table in front of him. He wanted to call Jenna, but knew she was sketching for her next showing and he couldn't disturb her. Not if he wanted to keep on living, anyway.

He was just considering calling Lance to go for a beer or something to occupy his time when his doorbell rang. Maybe Lance had read his mind, he thought, as he opened the front door. But it wasn't Lance.

Katonya Washington stood in his doorway, dressed in what could only be described as painted-on jeans. Her blouse was unbuttoned, showing off much of her cleavage, and short enough to show off her flat stomach.

"Katonya, what on earth are you doing here?" He didn't motion for her to come inside. If he did that, it would only lead to trouble and misunderstandings.

"Why don't you let me inside your house and I could tell you." She smiled at him. "I have been in your house before. And, may I add, your bed, as well."

He couldn't deny her statement. That was another time in his life, a time he wished he could forget, since meeting Jenna.

"Things have changed."

"So, she has you like that, huh?" Katonya's tone was short and accusing.

"What are you talking about?" Zyrien stared at her, thinking of how he could get rid of her. "What are you doing on this side of town, anyway?"

"I know you are seeing Jenna Bradshaw, the temp. You know that's against the rules. I don't know what you see in her. Kyle doesn't like her. He says she's always writing in some tablet and hardly talks to him."

Zyrien laughed. "Well, I see you and your boss are pretty cozy, but that's your MO, isn't it? And I know about him calling the temp agency on her, too. Was that on your behalf?"

She had the nerve to look insulted. "What if it was?

"That's not very professional, especially for Kyle Storm. I can't believe he's using his position as regional accounts manager to try something like that. So are you sleeping with him?"

"Why? Do you care?"

"No."

"Zee, why don't you give us another chance? Jenna is too old for you. You need someone who can give you children. She'll have you acting tired like her old behind. You know, with her being over forty, I can't believe she took that temp job. It just goes to show you she doesn't have much going on upstairs."

Zyrien grasped the doorknob tightly so his hand wouldn't somehow find Katonya's face and slap her into another time dimension. His father would kill him for even thinking about raising his hand in anger at a female. "Look, why don't you keep Jenna's name out of your mouth and we'll get along just fine?"

Katonya gasped. "I see she got you like that. Where's Jenna, anyway? There's no way I would have let you sit at home alone."

"Yeah, you'd have me at the mall buying stuff for your kids and you. Where's your other boyfriend? How's he dealing with you kickin' it with your boss?"

"He's dealing just fine." Translation: Baby daddy was back in jail.

"Girl, when are you going to dump that loser? You and those kids deserve more." The kids did, anyway.

"We deserve you," Katonya said in a quiet voice.

A few months ago, Zyrien probably would have jumped at the chance to be with her, but now he knew there was more to life than buying someone's affections. "And I deserve Jenna."

Her mouth hung open at his statement. "What are you saying?"

Zyrien took a deep breath. "I'm saying I don't want to go back with you. Not now. Not ever." He closed the door, leaving her on his doorstep in astonishment.

He took a deep breath. He knew he shouldn't have admitted to seeing Jenna. Katonya could make his life miserable at work and threaten the reputation he'd worked so hard to achieve. He finally heard her stomp away from his front door.

After he heard Katonya's car rumble down the street, he knew what he had to do. It was breaking the rules of not calling while she was creating, but this was important. Jenna would kill him, but both their jobs hung in the balance. He had to warn her about Katonya, who had a mean streak. He wanted Jenna to be prepared.

Zyrien pulled up in front of Jenna's house and noticed something strange. The blinds in her studio were closed. Usually when she painted, the blinds stayed open. He knew she always babbled something about natural light versus fluorescent. He was going to have to start paying more attention to the artistic side of Jenna Bradshaw.

As he approached the house, he had an awful thought. What if it were Ian posing nude for her again? She had been very secretive about who she was sketching. He knew she wanted something earthy or real. Something he really didn't understand. He stopped cold as another thought hit him. What if it was his mother?

He ran to her front door and banged on it with his fist. If his mother was in there, someone had a lot of explaining to do.

The door swung open. "Zyrien, what are you doing here?"

He ignored her question and stalked past her, heading down the hall to her studio. "Who is the mystery model, Jenna?" He continued walking as she continued calling his name. "It had better not be my momma in there!"

"Zyrien, don't you dare open that door!"

"Who's in here?"

Jenna caught up with him as he grasped the doorknob, and attempted to block his entry. Zyrien couldn't contain his anger any longer and moved her hand out of the way. "Why have you been so mysterious about this? If we're together, we need full disclosure." He opened the door and walked into the studio and got the shock of his life.

Dezarae Rucker stood before him in her birthday suit. Zyrien was too shocked to move. All he could do was cover his eyes and mutter, "I'm sorry."

Dezarae shrieked and ran out of the room.

"Shit," Zyrien muttered.

"My sentiments exactly." Jenna grabbed the bathrobe. "I'll deal with you later." She went down the hall, breathing in and out slowly, trying to get a rein on her temper. She had to have a calm face when she faced Dez, because she knew Dez was going to be hysterical.

As she approached the bathroom, she could hear Dez crying through the door. She also heard her talking, apparently on her cell phone, and most likely she was talking to her husband. "Dez, it's Jenna." She tried the handle, but the bathroom door was locked. "Can I come in?"

Sniff. "Is Zyrien still here?"

"Yes, he is. Would you like me to send him home?"

Sniff. Sniff. "He saw me naked, Jenna." Sniff. Sniff. "He's going to tell everyone."

Jenna shook her head. Talk about an evening going totally

wrong. "I'll be right back." Jenna marched back to the studio where Zyrien was still in the same spot she left him in. "Zyrien, you're going to have to leave. But before you go, you're going to need to apologize to Dez for bursting in on her like that."

He nodded, knowing better than to counter Jenna in the mood she was in. "What about you?"

"I'm not your problem right now. Later, yes. Right now, I need for you to assure Dez that you're sorry and you aren't going to tell everyone at work you saw her nude."

He gasped. "Jenna, you know I wouldn't tell anyone."

Zyrien did look like he was just as embarrassed as Dez was, but this wasn't about him. This was about him not respecting her work. "I know you wouldn't, but she doesn't. So go apologize, then leave."

Without another word, he headed down the hall. Jenna sat on the couch, not believing what a jerk he had been. He didn't respect her privacy for crap.

Ten minutes later he returned. "I am sorry, Jenna. I know I shouldn't have disrespected you like that. I had no idea who you were sketching and it was driving me crazy. Then Katonya showed up at my house tonight, attempting to seduce me. I just kind of lost it."

Jenna was too upset for Dez to be worried about Zyrien's ex. "I just need for you to leave right now."

"OK. Can I call you later?" He looked at her with those sad hazel eyes. "I'd like to explain. I'll do whatever it takes to make this up to you."

"I'll call you," Jenna said, not hiding the hurt she felt. She didn't head down the hall until she heard the familiar noise of Zyrien's car leaving her neighborhood and the havoc he'd just caused.

"Dez, it's OK. Zyrien is gone. You can come out now," Jenna called from the hallway. "I promise you will be laughing about this in a few months."

Dez didn't respond.

Jenna leaned against the door, not knowing exactly what to do. She just wished Dez would come out of the bathroom, so they could at least talk about it face-to-face. "Dez, I'm going to make some tea. Come into the kitchen so we can talk about this." Jenna headed for the kitchen.

Almost an hour later, Dez walked into the kitchen. She was still dressed in the bathrobe. Her round brown face was puffy from crying. She sat at the table in silence. Jenna placed some tea and sandwiches in front of her.

"Dez, I can't apologize enough. I know words are not what will make you feel better. Especially when I know how hard it was for you to pose nude in the first place." She took a deep breath. "If you don't want to model for me anymore, I understand."

Dez reached for one of the hand-painted mugs and poured the tea. "Well, I talked to Dante about it, and he made me realize something."

It wasn't an affirmation or denial, but maybe that was a good sign, Jenna hoped. "What was it?"

Dez added three teaspoons of sugar, then milk, to her tea. She took a sip and looked at Jenna. "He said I need to get used to people seeing me nude, since the picture will be hanging in the museum." Her lips curved upward ever so slightly in a smile.

"So you still want to model?"

She nodded. "At first, I wanted to just run away. Quit my job, like Dante has wanted me to do for the last two years, and hide under a rock. I was so embarrassed Zyrien saw me like that. But like you say, it will just take time for me to get over that."

Jenna was so excited that her project was saved! She had to keep her hands busy. She poured a cup of tea and sipped. "I will make sure that Zyrien doesn't interrupt us again. I will enlist the help of his mother and sisters, if it becomes necessary."

Dez gasped. "They're gonna help you like that? Dante's family doesn't even offer to babysit for me and we're married."

Jenna nodded. "Between you and me, Zyrien's mom wants me to paint her nude. A present for his father," Jenna explained. "Every time the subject is discussed, Zyrien gets sick to his stomach."

Dez laughed for the first time since Zyrien had stormed into the studio hours earlier. "I knew he had a weak stomach. Wimp. Last year, his assistant was pregnant. She got really sick and Zyrien lost his lunch trying to help her."

Jenna tried to stifle her laughter, but failed. "He has his moments. I don't know what got up his butt today, but I'm sure I'll find out." She reached across the table and grabbed Dez's tiny hand. "I'm glad you're OK with this. You don't know how much this means to me."

Dez grinned back at her. "Sure, I do. This means you'll be leaving Duncaster soon and painting full-time. You'll get to live your dream, Jenna."

"What about you, Dezarae? What's your dream?"

She pulled her hand away from Jenna's and leaned back in the chair. She shrugged. "I don't know. I mean, I know there's more to life than working at Duncaster, but I like having my own money. I wish I knew what I was good at."

Jenna knew that feeling. The wondering where her life was going. She'd had it every day before she discovered art. She had always felt like she was missing something in her life. "I know how you feel. Maybe there's a way to find out what you're good at. I stumbled into art totally by accident. I met Gunter—he's my mentor—at a grief counseling meeting and the rest is history."

Dez shook her head in disbelief. "I love your attitude. I bet you don't have a bad day, do you?"

"Not anymore. Life is too short for bad days."

Chapter 20

Saturday morning, Jenna woke to the phone ringing on her bedside table. She didn't want to open her eyes, let alone face the day. But the phone wouldn't quit ringing.

"Hello," she mumbled. "It's Saturday and it's early. Make it fast."

Zyrien laughed. "You didn't call me back. How did Dezarae do after I left?"

Jenna grunted. "It's too early for this. Why don't I call you back?" She placed the pillow over her face, blocking out the sunlight.

"Because the last time you said you'd call me back, you didn't. How did it go after I left? You know, I feel really bad about that."

Good, he should feel really bad, she thought. "Zyrien, after some tea and conversation, Dez did fine. We tossed around ideas and I started the prelim sketch that you interrupted."

She heard his noncommittal "Hmmm."

"You know, if this is boring to you, why did you ask me?"

"Baby, you know I'm behind whatever you do, but I need to know if Dez is OK."

Well, at least he was concerned about what he had done.

"She's fine. I'm sure she'll avoid you like the plague for a while, until she feels a little more comfortable with posing nude."

Zyrien sighed. "You know if I could take back that incident, I would. I was thinking about sending her some flowers or something. What do you think?"

Jenna thought it was a nice gesture. "I think it's a great idea. Her husband might think otherwise. He was the one who convinced her to keep going with the portrait."

"Oh, maybe I'll think of something else. I'm having lunch with Angie later today. Maybe she can give me some ideas."

"How's Angie? Is she still thinking about a divorce? What's Darrin's reaction to this?"

He took a deep breath. "Jenna, I can't believe you went there. You're worse than Mom asking me a million questions at once." He took a deep breath. "Well, I think she's confused right now. She loves Darrin, but she doesn't think he'll be a reliable father. But he's really trying," Zyrien said in his brother-in-law's defense. "He knows he messed up, and he's trying to make it right. I just don't know if he can."

"Is that enough? I know she has every right to wonder if he'll take off again when the going gets rough."

"Look, baby, I didn't call to talk about anyone but you and that's the one person we haven't talked about. How about dinner tonight?"

"My choice of restaurant?" Jenna queried him.

"Of course."

"OK, there's a showing of Clark's work tonight in Fort Worth and there's a restaurant right across the street that has the best Mexican food in town," Jenna suggested. Since Zyrien was eating crow, she might as well make it worth her while.

"Isn't that your artist friend?"

"Yes, is that a problem for you?" Jenna challenged him.

"No. Am I out of the doghouse?"

Jenna smiled, wishing she could see the look on Zyrien's face when she said, "No. You still have to pose for me."

Dead silence on the other end of the phone. Then he cleared his throat. "Jenna, I don't know about that."

"Zyrien, you have a nice body. Show it off. And you do owe me for bursting in on my session with Dez."

"Yeah, you're right. I do owe you. All right, when do you want me?"

She needed a little diversion. Seeing Zyrien in the nude might just do the trick. "How about after breakfast? I'll be done in plenty of time for you to have lunch with Angie."

"OK baby, as long as no one else sees the picture but you."

"Sure, honey." Jenna giggled as she crossed her fingers.

A few hours later, Zyrien parked in front of Jenna's house, ready to do her bidding for being an insensitive jerk. He glanced to the passenger seat of his car, which held two dozen red roses, a medium-sized canvas bag of paints, brushes, and a new palette for Jenna. He grabbed the items and headed for the front door.

He had expected Jenna to be dressed in her usual painting attire, tight jeans and a T-shirt. Like everything in his relationship with her, nothing went as he planned. Jenna opened the door dressed in a pair of linen Capri slacks and a cropped top, showing off her flat stomach, and no shoes. *She did that on purpose,* he thought. Just to drive him nuts, and it was working.

"Hey, baby." He leaned to kiss on her the lips, but Jenna turned so he could only kiss her on the cheek, which he did. He'd take whatever he could get at this point. He handed her the roses and the sack. "I bought a little peace offering."

She took the sack, but not before reading him the riot act about presents. "Zyrien, how many times do I have to tell you? Presents are not the way to a woman's heart. Presents only mean that you're not really sorry, you just want peace or is it a piece?" She winked at him and let him inside the house.

She was playing with him, but he deserved it. So he'd take it like a man. "Jenna, I'm really sorry about yesterday. It just drives me crazy thinking of you looking at some other man in the buff."

"Well, you need to get over it," she said. "This is my career and painting nudes is a big part of it. So unless you plan on posing for me each time, deal with it."

He knew there was so much more at stake than just him bursting in on her yesterday. "Jenna, I know this is what you love to do and you know I'm behind you 100 percent, right?"

Jenna sat down on the sofa. "But you don't respect what I do."

He sat beside her, not believing the conversation they were having. "I respect you." Then he realized this was about the day before. "Yesterday wasn't about me disrespecting you. It was about me being jealous. I know art has a place in the world. I just wish you didn't always paint nudes."

She laughed. "I don't just paint nudes; I paint other things, too. You've seen them," she pointed out. "Nudes are just the thing that makes me money right now. I have a picture of Dawn and she has clothes on."

"What do I have to do to show you that I respect your art career?" Zyrien waited while she took his question into consideration.

She shrugged, then an evil smile crossed her lips, making Zyrien want to get up and run of out her house. Whatever she was about to say was not going to be pleasant for him. "I want you to sit outside with me."

Zyrien sat in one of the lounges and glanced around her backyard. "I never realized you had a backyard. This is really nice."

She looked at her yard as if seeing it for the first time. Her rose garden was her neighbor's pride and joy. Mitzi Klume loved planting flowers and had a green thumb. She took pity on Jenna's nonhorticultural background and took over the cultivation of her entire yard.

"Thank you, Zyrien."

He looked her over and laughed. "I know you didn't do this."

"How?"

He grinned. "I know you, Jenna Bradshaw. Those roses I sent you the first time didn't last two days. That's how I know. Plus Mitzi has a sign in your front yard."

"OK, so you think you know me." She watched him take deep breaths and she had a brainstorm.

Zyrien closed his eyes and finally relaxed in the chair. "You know, this is nice. I never sit outside in my backyard. This is relaxing."

Jenna agreed. She quietly reached for the sketch pad and pencil that she kept by the chair at all times, and started to sketch Zyrien in a relaxed pose. Something that didn't happen too often. He was always worrying about something, or someone. He needed someone to worry about him. Was that her? Was she ready to give up a part of herself and become part of his monochromatic world?

As she continued sketching, she realized she was willing, but she wasn't ready or able. She had a few things in her own life that needed to be settled first. Like her career, for one. Would he support her in her quest to be a successful artist?

"Hey, what are you doing?" Zyrien struggled up from the lounge and walked to her. "You were drawing me with my mouth hanging open like that?"

She turned the sketch pad over so he couldn't look at it any more. "Zyrien, you were relaxed. Your mouth wasn't hanging open that wide, anyway."

Later that evening, Zyrien and Jenna were seated at Del Marco's, a Mexican restaurant in the heart of Fort Worth's art district. Jenna was dressed in a strapless short number that made Zyrien's temperature soar upward, along with parts of his body.

The waiter approached the table and took their order. Zyrien noticed that instead of the waiter standing near him and taking the orders, the young man hovered near Jenna. Was he really staring down her dress in front of him? Zyrien cleared his throat and said in his most threatening tone, "If I thought you were staring down my lady's cleavage, I would be talking to your manager."

The waiter hurriedly left the table.

Jenna laughed as if Zyrien had just told a joke. "Zyrien, you're overreacting. He wasn't looking down my dress. Well, no more than usual."

Zyrien shook his head. Jenna made the young man's leering at her cleavage sound like the most natural thing outside of breathing. How was he ever going to fit into her carefree world? This was going to be a long night.

At the Spotted Leopard, a small gallery across from the restaurant, Zyrien decided that it was indeed going to be one of the longest nights of his short relationship with Jenna.

As soon as they entered the room, Jenna was surrounded by her artistic friends, who seemed to be primarily men. Zyrien stood in a corner and watched with simmering anger. One man in particular made Zyrien's territorial side emerge when he took Jenna in his arms and gave her a kiss on the mouth. Jenna was momentarily taken aback, but recovered quickly. Zyrien hurriedly strode over to the couple. He put his arm around Jenna's waist and glared at the taller man. "Everything OK, baby?"

"Of course, Zyrien. Clark was congratulating me on my upcoming show. He just got a little carried away," she explained.

Clark cleared his throat. "Yes, I wasn't aware you were Jenna's escort. I mean, she's wearing the dress."

Zyrien knew there was a story behind the dress and it would probably only infuriate him more. "I'm sure Jenna will tell me all about it later tonight. Please excuse us." He led Jenna away from the annoying artist.

They found a secluded corner before she spoke. "Zyrien, let me explain."

He shook his head. If she explained about that blasted dress that he shouldn't have let her wear in the first place, he would be tearing the place apart with his bare hands. "Not necessary. Let's just forget about it, OK?"

Jenna caressed his face with her hand. "I know this is not your kind of evening, but it's really important to me. A lot of my friends are here. Thank you for coming." She leaned down and kissed him.

Zyrien was ready to get lost in the softness of her full lips, when he remembered they were in a public place. He pulled away regretfully. "You just hold my place for later."

"You've got a deal."

Zyrien inspected the paintings as Jenna mingled with her friends. Every once in a while he looked for Jenna and smiled when he spotted her looking at him. Instead of feeling he had the upper hand in the relationship, which he clearly didn't, it made him feel content, happy, and loved. Three things that meant trouble for Zyrien Alexander Taylor.

Chapter 21

Sunday afternoon, Jenna met Dawn for brunch. She waited for her friend in the lobby area of Donatello's, Dawn's favorite Italian restaurant. Jenna had to admit the food was outstanding. This was the one place she abandoned her diet regimen.

Her cell phone rang, attracting the attention of all the other patrons waiting for a table. It rang again before she was able to silence it. She took a deep breath, knowing it was Zyrien calling and she'd need all her patience to deal with him.

"Zyrien, you know this is girl time," Jenna chastised her current love.

"This isn't Zyrien," Ansel said. "It's your brother, Ansel Langston Bradshaw."

Jenna laughed. "I'm sorry, Ansel. I thought you were someone else."

Ansel grunted. "Yeah, sounds like."

Jenna ignored her brother's sarcasm and asked, "How are things going?" She also knew her brother called her maybe once a week and they had already talked earlier in the week. Something must be up.

"They're going," Ansel said ruefully. "There was a reason I called. I wondering if you could stand a houseguest for a few weeks."

"Boy," Jenna chastised her younger brother. "You know you don't have to call me. Just show up. That's what I'd do. When are you coming?" She also knew she had an art obligation to Greta. "The only reason I ask," she reassured her brother, "is that I have a portrait due and I have to get it done. So you may be on your own for a little bit while I finish."

"I'm glad to hear your artwork is back on track. I know punchin' a clock isn't your thing. How's the new guy? Have you broken him in yet?"

"Actually, he reminds me of you," Jenna responded. "He's always trying to be so serious all the time. Well, you know that isn't going to last long with me."

"Doesn't he know how many men have fallen before him?" Ansel's laughter was becoming contagious. "Just don't hurt him too bad, Jenna. He didn't know he was dating the queen of free spirit."

Jenna laughed as well. "You know, he went with me to Clark's showing last night. He did pretty well for a nonartist."

Ansel's laughter finally quieted. "Thanks, Jenna. You were exactly what I needed. I was feeling sorry for myself, but I knew five minutes on the phone with you and I'd forget every problem I've ever had."

"What's wrong, Ans?"

"Just feeling like a loser. I can't even hold on to a wife," he admitted.

"You can't hold on to someone who isn't right for you. You just haven't met her yet," Jenna reminded her brother.

"OK, Ms. Ray of Sunshine, I'm going to hold you to that." He paused. "Don't tell me it's girls' day out and you're waiting for the infamous Dawn Castle Brunner, terror of all men in the universe?"

Jenna couldn't keep the smile off her face. "Will you ever let that go? That was twenty years ago and you were a bratty teenager."

Ansel grunted. "She slapped me in front of all my friends," he complained. "I was so turned on."

"You were sixteen then. A good gust of wind turned you on," Jenna teased. "To answer your question—yes, I'm waiting on Dawn."

"I don't see how poor Chad can deal with her. Talk to you soon." He ended the call.

Jenna shook her head and closed her phone. "Ansel isn't ever going to get over that," Jenna mumbled.

"Get over what?" Dawn sat down beside her. For once, Dawn wasn't all dolled up. She was dressed in beige Capri pants, a white blouse, no makeup, and her hair was pulled back into a sloppy ponytail.

"I was just talking to Ansel. He's still mad at you, by the way." Jenna assessed her friend's pale face. "What's wrong with you?"

Dawn bowed her head and whispered. "Would you mind if we didn't eat here today?"

Jenna turned and faced her friend. "Of course, I don't mind. But you better tell me what's going on with you."

Dawn took a deep breath. "Well, you know Chad and I have been trying to get pregnant for the last three years with no luck."

"Yes, Dawn," Jenna chimed.

"Well, a few days ago, I realized I missed my period last month. I mean, there's been so much going on with his parents, his grandmother, and my parents, I guess it just slipped my mind."

Tears sprang from Jenna's eyes. She couldn't wipe them away fast enough. "Do you think?"

"I don't want to tell Chad. I don't want to get his hopes up. So I figured we could get a pregnancy test and go to your house." Dawn looked at her with those big brown eyes that had made many a man threaten to leave his wife.

"Of course, we can get a test."

* * *

Three hours later, Jenna sat consoling a crying Dawn. The test was negative and, to make matters worse, on her last trip to the bathroom, Dawn started her period.

"I can't believe this," Dawn said between heart-wrenching sobs. "We do it almost every night. When I have a fever. When I don't. Whether we're in the mood or not. Why can't I get pregnant?"

"Maybe that's it, Dawn," Jenna said carefully. "Maybe you guys should refrain from sex for a while."

Dawn dried her eyes. "Jenna, I'm married to a hockey player, remember?"

"I know you're married to Chad. Have you thought about a fertility specialist?"

Dawn sniffed. "Well, for one, Chad would never go to a fertility doctor and neither would I. It's like looking online for a date. There's a certain stigma of failure attached to it." She blew her nose. "I'm hungry. Why don't we go to the Micro House and have a drink? I'm starving and I'm dying for some hot wings."

Jenna hugged her friend. "Sure we can go. Dawn, I know when the time is right, you and Chad will get pregnant."

Dawn stood and reached for her purse. "You sound like Mom. I told her I missed my period last month and she told me I wasn't pregnant. Damn, I hate it when she's right."

Jenna nodded. Dawn and her mother were too much alike to get along for too long. But sometimes it did seem like Justine Castle had a special gift. Jenna grabbed her oversized shoulder bag and led Dawn to the garage.

After they were settled in Jenna's car, a thought occurred to her. "Did your mother say when you'd get pregnant?" Jenna pressed the button for the garage door to open.

Dawn rummaged through Jenna's CD collection. "She told me that I would, but a life-changing moment would happen first." She looked up from Jenna's console. "When are you going to get some real music? This big band stuff is so awful. Could you at least listen to jazz?"

Jenna knew Dawn was just trying to occupy her mind by complaining about her eclectic taste in music. "Every time you ride in my car, you complain about the music. I've been listening to big band for the last ten years. It helps my creative flow."

Dawn sucked in a breath. "You're gifted, Jenna. You were meant to be an artist. Sometimes destiny is a little slow in showing you your place in the universe, but it always gets there."

"Now that sounded like my friend Dawn, and I could say right back at you." She put the car in reverse and slowly backed out of the garage.

After Jenna made sure the garage door was secure, the women set off for the Micro House.

Zyrien moped around his house for most of the afternoon. He was trying not to act like a jealous man by going to the restaurant and spying on Jenna and Dawn. But he knew spying wouldn't be the smartest thing to do, considering he was already in the doghouse. He did the next best thing. He called Lance and invited him to their favorite watering hole, the Micro House.

"Sure, cuz. Jenna must be otherwise occupied?" Lance chided Zyrien.

"What makes you say that?"

"For one, if she wasn't occupied, you would be with her. And if she's anything like my wife, they have girls' day out or some other nonsense. You know a day of doing girlie stuff and running men into the ground."

Zyrien was glad to know he wasn't the only man alone on a Sunday afternoon. "Man, how do you deal with it? It's not like she has a lot of free time 'cause she has a portrait due next month, but she's not even spending it with me." As soon as the words left his mouth, Zyrien realized he was whining. "Oh man, now I sound like one of those whipped men."

Lance laughed. "That's because you are. See ya in an hour." He ended the call.

Zyrien shook his head at his cousin's comments, threw his cordless phone on his unmade bed, and walked to his closet. After selecting a pair of shorts and a shirt, he got dressed, ready to prove to Lance—or at least to himself—that he wasn't whipped. But one look in his oversized mirror told him that he was.

As Jenna and Dawn walked into the Micro House, they headed for a booth instead of their usual bar stools. Dawn had cheered up considerably and was ready to eat food.

"Please tell me that you're not eating diet food today?" Dawn pleaded. "We're celebrating, remember?" Dawn reached for the giant laminated menu. "I'm feeling the need for some buffalo wings and nachos."

"All right, Dawn," Jenna said. "This is a celebration, so no tears, either." The waiter approached their table and took their drink order. Jenna and Dawn both ordered glasses of wine.

"What, no beer?" Dawn quizzed her friend.

Jenna shrugged. "No, I'm feeling mellow."

Dawn nodded, smiling. She was looking in the direction of the entrance. "Did you tell Zyrien we were coming here?"

"No. He knows today is our day." She watched as the waiter returned with their drinks and took their food order. "Why do you ask?"

Dawn took a sip of wine and grinned at Jenna. "Because he and his sexy cousin just walked in the door."

* * *

Lance nudged Zyrien. "Say, isn't that Jenna's buddy over there? Weren't they having girls' day or something? Man, if she sees you here, it's going to look like you don't trust her."

Zyrien was already in enough trouble with Jenna without her thinking he was stalking her again. "Man, we need to get out of here." He pulled his cousin toward the exit door. The last thing he needed was for Jenna to see him.

But Lance was too slow. By the time the men could get through the maze of people, Dawn was tapping Zyrien on the shoulder.

"You can run, but you can't hide." Dawn laughed. "Come and sit with us." Dawn walked back to the table, leaving the men to follow her, or not.

"Man, she didn't ask," Lance said. "She told us. What's up with her?"

Zyrien laughed. "That's Dawn. She won't give you many options, if any. Come on." Zyrien headed for the table. When he arrived at the table, he thought Dawn was going to move so he could sit by Jenna. Wrong. Dawn slid in next to Jenna.

"Look who I found," Dawn teased.

Jenna looked at him with a bright smile. "Hey, Zyrien. I see you have your accomplice with you." She nodded at Lance.

"Yeah, you too." He and Lance sat across from the women.

Dawn piped in, "We're celebrating."

"What?" Zyrien signaled for the waiter, who took his and Lance's order. "I mean, what are you celebrating?"

"Girls' day out," Jenna said.

Zyrien looked from Dawn to Jenna. He knew something bigger was going on between the women, but now was not the time. He switched topics and turned his attention to his cousin. If he didn't know better, he'd swear Lance was drooling over Dawn. "You know Dawn is the manager for Essential Temps, that upscale temp agency our company uses."

Lance smiled at Dawn. "Really, we were thinking about getting an accountant for our business. I'm part owner in Tyrone's BBQ," he explained. "Maybe I should call you."

Dawn smiled and rummaged through her purse. "Here's my card. I'd be happy to send you somebody."

Lance smiled at her. "Thank you, I'll call you next week after I talk to the other partners."

Dawn nodded, just as her cell phone rang. "Hey baby," she said into the phone, and rising from her seat at the same time. She walked to a quiet corner to talk to her husband.

Jenna grinned at Lance. "Thank you, Lance."

"Actually, baby, that was me," Zyrien pointed out. "What do I get for bringing up Dawn's job?"

Jenna leaned across the table and kissed him. "That." She took her seat again. "And there's plenty more where that came from." She winked at him.

Zyrien couldn't believe what just happened. Jenna kissed him in front of Lance. He'd never live that down. But on the other hand, he reminded himself, it was a good kiss. He licked his lips and smiled. "Can I get another one?"

Before Jenna could answer, Lance did. "Why don't you guys just go get a room?" Lance started laughing. "It's like being around horny teenagers," he complained. "I can't wait until Dawn gets back to the table for some sanity."

"Boy, are you backing the wrong horse," Zyrien muttered. If Lance was expecting sanity from Dawn, he had a rude awakening ahead.

Chapter 22

Sunday evening, Jenna woke to the noise of Zyrien snoring in her ear. She giggled as his hands began roaming her body. But she had had a moment of inspiration and had to act on it.

As she slipped from the bed, she heard him moan in frustration. "Baby, where you going? I was just getting, you know, good."

Jenna tied the bathrobe securely around her nude body, knowing that by "good" he actually meant "hard." "I know baby, but I've got to work on this while it's fresh in my mind. Why don't you work on getting really *good* and I'll reward you."

He sat up, looking like a sex god in the middle of her bed. "I'll be waiting," he said with a wink.

Jenna blew him a kiss from the doorway. She walked downstairs and grabbed the cordless phone form the kitchen counter. She punched Dawn's phone number and waited for her to pick up. Chad's voice greeted her on the second ring.

"Hi, Chad. Is Dawn up?"

He laughed. "No, she's sleeping off the effects of some cramp medication. She was hurting earlier."

A very bad thought occurred to Jenna. Dawn had drunk about three glasses of wine. That, plus some medication would definitely not do Dawn any favors. "Chad, are you sure she's OK?"

Chad grumbled, "I know about the pregnancy test and it being negative. Dawn came home blubbering something about failing me again. By the time I finally understood what was going on, she was beyond consolation."

Jenna brought her hand to her mouth. Poor Dawn. Poor Chad. "I'm sorry, Chad. I know how much you guys want a baby," Jenna said ruefully.

"Well, it doesn't matter to me, but thanks to her mother, Dawn thinks we have to procreate to be happy," Chad informed her. "I think we're happy without a baby."

"Yes, you guys are happy," Jenna agreed. "I know it will happen. Just make sure she doesn't take too many pills. She did drink quite a bit last night."

"I checked on her earlier, she's fine."

Jenna breathed a sigh of relief. "That's good, Chad. Tell her to call me later." Jenna ended the call.

Satisfied for the moment, Jenna made some coffee. After she had a steaming hot cup of coffee, she headed to her studio. She turned on her stereo and soon Charlie Parker was serenading her as she took out her sketch pad and some charcoal pencils.

She squeezed her eyes shut, calling up the images that had inspired her earlier that morning when Zyrien was feeling her up. What a choice to have to make: work or sex. Unfortunately, her practical side chose for her. That was why she was sitting behind her easel instead of being in bed with Zyrien.

The images weren't far away. She visualized Dezarae sitting on a sofa. Her hair sprinkled over one shoulder and the other one bare. In her vision, Jenna saw her co-worker in stilettos, something Dez never wore to work. Jenna started sketching, her fingers flying over the rice paper in a rush of excitement.

In a matter of two hours, Jenna had four preliminary

sketches of Dez in different poses. She decided she'd let Dez pick one. Suddenly another vision pushed its way into Jenna's mind. The picture was vivid. It felt so real. Dawn was reclining on the couch showing her protruding belly.

Jenna dropped her pencils. Was that just her imagination gone wild? Of course, she reminded herself. But she hoped it was a sign for the future.

Zyrien felt Jenna when she slid back into bed a few hours later. He opened his eyes and turned to face her. "I hope your work was productive." He kissed her.

Jenna nodded, her eyes tearing up. "Yes, you might say too productive." She moved closer to him.

"What do you mean?"

She took a deep breath. "Being an artist, sometimes too many images come to me at one time."

"Is that what happened this evening?" He wiped her tears away.

She sniffed. "Yes."

"Was it a certain image?" Zyrien wasn't quite sure what he needed to do. So he pretended their pillow talk was a business meeting and Jenna was a potential client.

"Yes. I visualized Dawn pregnant," she said quietly.

"Isn't that a good sign?" He wanted Jenna to smile, say something smart, anything but her solemn, teary face.

"I don't know, but it looked so real. She was wearing a pink peignoir and her stomach was huge, like she was carrying twins. I just don't want it be a bad omen and I caused it by imagining it."

Zyrien drew her into her arms. "Baby, you have nothing to do with Dawn. You're her girl. You just have to be there for her and Chad." Zyrien cleared his throat. "I mean, we have to be there for Dawn and Chad."

Jenna's eyes flashed in recognition as the words sank in.

"Really, Zyrien? Do you really mean that? Or do you just want to have sex?" She moved a centimeter away.

"Baby, you know that ain't true. I just want to see you smile. I think I'd do just about anything to see you happy. I love you, baby." He leaned forward to kiss her.

She moved away from his kiss. "Not so fast," she warned.

"What?"

"I love you, too." She all but jumped on top of his more than ready body.

Zyrien reached for the condom in the nightstand. "Wait, baby," he gasped, but he knew it was too late. He was already inside of her and nothing but God coming down out of the heavens could make him stop. "Oh, man." He threw the unopened condom package in the air. Jenna giggled and kissed him.

For the first time in his life, Zyrien threw caution to the wind and would just have to wait to see if it threw anything back.

A few hours later, Jenna had showered and dressed and was now fixing a very late dinner. When Zyrien woke, he was going to be surprised to find out that she was frying pork chops for their meal. She just wouldn't tell him she was frying them in extra-virgin olive oil or how healthy it was. That would ruin everything.

By the time Zyrien made it downstairs, dinner was on the table and Jenna was on the phone. Dawn had finally returned her call.

"Jenna, I appreciate the concern, but I'm OK. My honey and I had a long talk and I've come to realize that the world won't end if I don't have a baby. I'm married to a wonderful man who loves me. A lot of women don't have that."

Jenna was stunned, but relieved. "You're right, Dawn. All that matters is that you and Chad love each other." Jenna ended the call, deciding not to tell her friend about her vision.

Jenna set the phone down and watched Zyrien as he sat at the table. "How do you feel?" He looked cute and sleepy.

He yawned. "Tired. I guess you wore me out." He speared a pork chop with his fork. "I didn't think you ate fried foods, as a rule," he said.

Jenna reached for the salad bowl. "Rules are made to be broken. I felt like something special, since you were so outstanding."

He cleared his throat. "About that."

Jenna shook her head. She knew what he was about to say. They hadn't used any protection; she didn't want him to feel guilty. "It's OK, Zyrien. I'm at a good point in the month. We're OK."

He smiled. "You know nothing would make me prouder than to get you pregnant, but I would prefer doing it in the traditional manner."

Jenna nodded. "Me too."

They smiled at each other and started eating. Jenna noticed that Zyrien had piled two pork chops and a scant amount of veggies on his plate. Well, it was more vegetables than he would have eaten a few months ago, she thought. She smiled for the little victory it was.

Monday evening, Jenna paced her living room as Dez carefully inspected the sketches. She was picking out the pose she liked best before she disrobed. Thirty minutes later, Dez held up her choice.

"I like this one." She handed Jenna the sketch. "I think Dante will approve of this one. I think I'll look very sexy." She shook her head. "Dante is going to pop an artery."

Jenna laughed. "Well, I don't want that. It would be nice to see him astonished or surprised." She looked at the sketch of Dez and grinned. "I think this might just do it."

Dez snapped her fingers. "OK, let's do this." She walked down the hall to change out of her clothes.

Jenna headed for the studio and waited for Dez. She assembled the canvas and paints. She took out her favorite brushes and pie plate. She assembled the colors as Dez walked in.

"Why are you playing with that glass pie plate? You making Zyrien something special?" Dez walked into the room in the terry-cloth bathrobe. She sat down on the red velvet chaise lounge, watching Jenna.

Jenna laughed. Most of her art friends thought she was crazy for using the clear glass pie plate for her palette instead of one of the more traditional or expensive ones. But through experience, she found the pie plate worked better. "I started using this a few years ago and I liked it."

Dez stood and took off the bathrobe, revealing her short nude body. She didn't have the stilettos on, but that was a minor detail Jenna could add later. She couldn't wait until the picture was finished. Dante Rucker would definitely pop a gasket when he saw his wife in such a seductive pose.

The next day, Zyrien walked into the meeting, not expecting it to last long. He wanted to talk to Jenna and had planned his timing perfectly so that no one would suspect he was fraternizing with a temporary employee. He would definitely be glad when that stupid little rule was gone.

But as he listened to Mr. Duncaster speak, his heart began to sink with each word. His schedule was about to change. Again.

Avery Duncaster cleared his throat and looked directly at Zyrien. "I've just been on the phone with Washington and there's been a hiccup with the proposal, Zyrien. You're going to need to go up there and straighten out those boys." He held up his large hand to stall Zyrien's complaining. "Now, I know you worked really hard on this project, but they're having some problems about the software."

Zyrien instantly became defensive. "What kind of problems?" That contract proposal had all but consumed his life. "I worked out every single detail of the software implementation, including the training of our employees with the damn software they are so concerned about!"

Duncaster looked at Zyrien with sympathy in those blue eyes. "I know you did. You did outstanding work and no one is doubting your abilities. As a personal favor to the firm, please just go to DC and stroke their egos so we can get the contract finalized, and we'll be at your mercy."

Zyrien mulled over the request—or, more precisely, the demand. He could go to DC, firm up the deal, and have a feather in his cap, for just a few days of schmoozing with the government big boys.

"I'll have Brenna book me on a plane tonight. I have to tie up some loose ends on my other duties," he explained. The main loose end was the woman he was in love with.

Mr. Duncaster nodded approvingly. "That's great. I'll give you the contact info after the meeting. I know you'll do Duncaster and Finch Accounting proud." He stood, signaling that the meeting was over.

Zyrien gathered his pad and pen and hurriedly left the office. He tried to imagine Jenna's response to his out-of-town trip. Would she be happy for the free time or mad because it sounded like he was trying to get away from her? He noticed his assistant by the elevator. "Brenna, when you get back to your desk, I need you to book me on a flight for DC this evening."

Brenna's blue eyes expanded with shock, then understanding. "Of course. Have you told," she glanced around to see who was listening, "you-know-who yet?"

He smiled, knowing that he'd been busted. "I've no idea what you're talking about." He winked at her and continued to his office. Once in the solitude of his office he let his guard down. He didn't want to go. Especially since he didn't know how long this nonsense was going to take. The government boys needed someone to hold their hand, assuring them that they had made the right decision.

He dialed Jenna's four-digit extension and waited for her to pick up.

"Accounting, this is Jenna," she announced in her sexy voice.

"Hi, it's me," he said in a low voice. "I need to talk to you, now."

"Who is this?" she asked.

"Baby, don't play with me. I'm not in the mood."

"I'm sorry, you must have the wrong extension. I don't speak with moody people. May I put you through to Ms. Washington's extension?" Jenna was teasing him.

"OK, I'm sorry. But I really do need to talk to you. My assistant is away from her desk; you could come up right now."

"My boss wouldn't approve of such a transaction, sir. May I suggest an alternate arrangement?" she said in a very business-like tone.

Zyrien understood Jenna-speak fluently. Someone must be too close for comfort. "OK, I'll meet you across the street for lunch."

"I hear Jason's Deli has a wonderful salad bar."

"OK. This is the last time you're getting your way," Zyrien scolded her, knowing his threat was a lie.

Jenna laughed. "Twelve o'clock." She ended the call.

Zyrien shook his head and replaced the phone in its cradle. What was it about her that just drove him nuts? Was it the need to have her way? Or goading him at just the right time to make him realize he was being a jerk?

He sighed. Whatever it was, he wanted more of it in his life and would do just about anything to achieve that goal.

* * *

He met her as promised at Jason's Deli. She was dressed in a brown suit that did her body proud. She was sitting on the bench along with two men, one on each side of her. Once she spotted Zyrien at the entrance she jumped up to meet him. He couldn't help but notice the men's appreciative glances at her backside.

"Hey baby," she said, kissing him lightly on the lips. "Those two nice gentlemen kept me company while I was waiting for you." She nodded at the men now leaving the restaurant.

Zyrien looked at her incredulously. "You mean the two men who are now leaving?"

Jenna nodded, pulling him to the slowly moving line to order their food. "Yes. They were just being nice. Let it go," she chided him. "Besides, I told them I was meeting my man."

Well, that made him feel a little better. He held her hand as they perused the menu. "What are you having?"

"I'm having the salad. I told you they have an excellent salad bar. Besides, tonight, Dez and I are going to eat Chinese food after our session."

"How's that coming?"

Jenna smiled proudly. "Great. I might be finished early."

He smiled. "That's great, baby." He watched as the mature woman took their order.

They walked to the counter and he shook his head as Jenna reached for her wallet. "No, this is a date."

"No it's not. This is lunch," Jenna countered.

"I said 'no.'"

Jenna stared at him for a minute. "Well, it sounds like someone had his Wheaties this morning." She smiled and grabbed their drink glasses while he handed the clerk his credit card.

After they settled at a table and the young waitress delivered their order, Zyrien finally began to enjoy the meal. He watched Jenna meticulously chop up the vegetables in her salad into tiny pieces. After she had it to her liking, she poured two dollops of dressing on her salad. He took a bite of beef barbecue sandwich.

"OK, what is so important that you had to see me?" Jenna took a bite of salad.

Zyrien chewed slowly. Maybe if he chewed slow enough she would forget what she asked. He chewed slower, until Jenna's brown eyes stared at him like laser pointers. He swallowed, cleared his throat, and grabbed her hand. "OK, Jenna, it's like this," he explained. "I have to go out of town on business. I have to leave tonight. I'm not sure how long I'll be gone. Probably no more than a couple of days," he promised.

Jenna extracted her hand from his. "Is that all? You had me going for a minute there. I didn't know what to think."

Zyrien stared at her. "You're not upset?" He would be having a screaming fit, if she had told him this scenario.

"Zyrien, you're the national accounts manager. It's logical for you to have to go out of town on occasion. Besides, this couldn't have happened at a better time." She took another bite of salad.

Zyrien pushed his plate away from him. "Explain."

Jenna sighed dramatically. "I'm on a deadline and we probably couldn't see each other this week anyway, so it's kind of good you're having to go on this business trip," she teased. "I trust you." Her face became suddenly very serious. "But if I call you and some young thing answers the phone, you're going to be sorry. Real sorry."

He didn't doubt her words for one minute.

Chapter 23

"I can't believe Zyrien went out of town," Dez said through clenched lips. She couldn't open her mouth fully, since Jenna was concentrating on painting the details of her face and had already lectured her once about moving.

Jenna concentrated on the portrait. She couldn't afford to let her attention waver; even the small details such as Dez's full, pouty lips had to be precise. "He left last night and he doesn't know how long he'll be in DC. I'm hoping it's at least until the weekend." She'd have a chance to catch up on some much-needed sleep, as well as her painting.

"You know you miss him," Dez teased. "It's funny watching him watch you at work. To the untrained eye," Dez clarified for her friend, "it seems like he's just staring into space. But I know better. Every time Mr. Storm comes near you, Zyrien watches him. It's uncanny how Zyrien always just happens to be in the vicinity."

"Maybe he's visiting Katonya." Jenna knew it wasn't true.

"No, she's chasing him and makes no secret about anyone knowing it. I think it's sad. She should channel that energy into those bad children she has."

Jenna gazed at Dez as she lounged on the couch. The portrait was coming along wonderfully. With any luck she'd finish before Zyrien returned. "Those children aren't Zyrien's, are they?" She knew they weren't, but one could never be too sure.

"No, baby daddy is in and out of jail. I don't know why she wastes time being with him."

Jenna nodded. She often wondered why women always ended up with the same type of man. In the past, she often dated fellow artists and usually the relationship didn't work out. There was something to be said about opposites. Dante and Dez were direct opposites, so were Dawn and Chad, and Zyrien was the total opposite of her.

"Jenna," Dez called, laughing.

Jenna realized she was in a daydreaming zone. A place she couldn't afford to be with a deadline looming over her head. "I'm sorry, Dez. Did you say something?"

Dez chuckled. "Yes, I was telling you your phone was ringing. Maybe it's Zyrien," she chimed.

Jenna could now hear the phone. "It's probably my friend Dawn. Her husband is getting ready to go to hockey training camp."

The look on Dez's face was priceless. "I didn't know there were brothers playing on the Dallas Stars."

Jenna shook her head. "They aren't. Dawn is married to Chad Brunner."

"I've seen him on the commercials. He makes me want to go to a hockey game just to see if he's really as fine as he looks on TV." She glanced at Jenna. "Is he?"

Jenna decided to let the machine pick up the phone. "He's nice looking, but I've known Chad for over six years. He's like a brother to me."

Dez shook her head. "Just wait 'til I tell Dante you know Chad Brunner. He loves hockey."

Jenna couldn't imagine uptight Dante Rucker liking anything as violent and fast-paced as hockey. "I'm sure Chad will be at the showing. You guys can meet him."

Dez's face split into a wide grin. "Thank you, Jenna. Dante

is trying to talk me into letting him and his brother, Jamaal, buy season tickets. He almost had me until I found out he wanted those really expensive seats behind the players."

Jenna knew exactly which area Dez was talking about. That was where she usually sat with Dawn. "I'll ask Chad if he can get him some tickets. Everyone should sit behind the glass at least once. It's awesome." Jenna wiped the excess paint from her brushes, then put them in cleaning solution. "OK, Dez, that's it for tonight."

While Dez was putting on her clothes, Jenna decided to check the message. After she transferred the brushes to a container so they could dry, she headed down the hall to the phone. She thought it was Zyrien, but she was surprised to hear her brother's baritone voice.

"Hey, Jenna."

Jenna strained to hear the message, but couldn't make out any more of his garbled conversation. Ansel must have been at a bar, a club, or some other extremely noisy place. She could only make out a couple of words. "Need, change, see you." The line went dead.

She replayed the message several times, but she couldn't make out any other words. Dez emerged dressed in jeans and a T-shirt.

"So, was it Zyrien?" Dez reached for her purse and slung it over her shoulder.

"No, it was my brother. He left a cryptic message, so I'll try to call him later." Jenna yawned and stretched. Her body was exhausted. "I think I'm going to bed early tonight."

Her doorbell rang. Jenna and Dez exchanged glances. "Didn't you drive here?" Jenna thought maybe Dante was playing the jealous husband.

Dez nodded. "Yeah, you don't think Zyrien punked out of the meeting and came back early?"

"You know Zyrien is business first, everything else second. We have that in common," Jenna laughed. "You know, business before pleasure." The women shared a laugh and Jenna amended her statement. "Well, most of the time, anyway." She walked to the door, looked through the peephole, and gasped, "Oh my God."

"What is it, Jenna?" Dez asked in a hushed voice. "Want me to call the po-pos?"

Jenna shook her head and opened her front door. She hugged her brother as if he had just come back from the Gulf War. He was dressed in slacks and a tailored shirt, looking like a male model. "Ansel, why didn't you tell me you were coming? What are you doing here? Are you all right? What's wrong?"

Ansel laughed and released his sister. "Damn, girl, it's good to see you." He glanced around the room. "I'll answer your questions, but first I must introduce myself to this young lady." He extended his large hand to Dez. "I'm Ansel Bradshaw."

Dez was momentarily speechless. She darted a glance at Jenna. "This is your brother?"

Jenna knew what Dez wanted to say. Just like every other woman who met Ansel Langston Bradshaw, Dez was taken with his good looks and Southern manners. "Yes, Dez, this is my younger brother, who was supposed to tell me when he was coming, so I could adjust my schedule, so we'd have time to visit."

Dez grinned, her big brown eyes still on Ansel. "I'm Dezarae Rucker. Jenna is painting me," she said proudly. Then she turned her attention to Jenna. "Why don't you take tomorrow off? I know you're a temp and all, but the workload is light right now and it would probably be the best time. It's not like you want to be permanent, anyway. Just think how pissed Katonya will be." Dez laughed.

Jenna mulled the thought over in her mind. She could spend the day with her brother and in the evening she could paint Dez. "You know, that sounds good. I'll call Dawn tonight."

Dez looked at her with a puzzled look. "Why do you have to get permission from Dawn?"

"Along with being my best friend, Dawn is also the manager of Harcourt's Essential Temps."

"But I know Chad makes good money. Why is she working?" Dez asked in an incredulous tone. "I know Chad must be making bank with all those sponsors and stuff."

"Dawn loves her job." Jenna knew only one thing would keep Dawn Castle Brunner from working and that would be the one thing she couldn't have. A baby.

Dez shook her head, bid them good night, and headed for the front door, but Ansel stopped her.

"Dez, I'll walk you to your car." He left no room for either woman to argue with him. He opened the door for her and motioned for her to precede him outside.

"That boy," Jenna mused. She knew something was on his mind and it must be big for him to leave Austin. She waited for him on the sofa.

A few minutes later, Ansel entered the house with a suitcase. He sat the bag by the stairs and walked into the living room. "I guess you want to know why I flew up tonight without so much as a warning?" He plopped down on the couch and let out a tired breath.

"If you want to talk about it." She so hoped he did.

Ansel grinned. "Yeah, like you don't want to know all the sordid details."

Jenna wanted to know, but not at the expense of her brother's emotional well-being. "Look Ans, why don't you get a good night's sleep and we can talk tomorrow. I have to call Dawn." Jenna rose. "Come on, I'll show you where you'll be sleeping." Jenna was happy to have her brother sleeping under her roof. For some reason, it gave her a sense of family.

Zyrien didn't make it back to his hotel room until well after midnight. This was supposed to be a simple business trip. He was just in DC to stroke some government egos, not get drunk his first night in town.

But one drink soon turned into three, four, five, and so on. He wasn't in any condition to speak with Jenna and not start a fight or sound like a pathetic, lovesick teenager. As he fell into bed, he decided he'd call her in the morning.

The next day, he was blessed with a ten-minute break between meetings. He had to meet the committee chairman for lunch. He dialed Jenna's work number and was more than surprised when he didn't hear her soft voice.

"Accounting, this is Dezarae, how may I help you?"

Why couldn't it be anyone else answering Jenna's phone?, Zyrien thought. He'd even settle for Katonya. Ever since walking in on Dez, Zyrien had avoided her at work like the plague. "Hey, Dez, it's Zyrien. Did I misdial or something?"

"No, you didn't," she said curtly.

Was she still upset about him bursting in on her? "Look Dez, I'm sorry about the other week. Where's Jenna?"

"Jenna's phone was forwarded to me, in case there were any vendor calls that came in."

She was deliberately not answering his questions. "Dezarae, please. Where's Jenna?"

"She's not here today. She took the day off."

"Why?"

"I'm not sure. Why don't you call her at home? She should be there," Dez said.

Zyrien didn't like the insolence in her tone, but didn't have the time or energy to deal with her. He thanked her and ended the call.

What could have been wrong? Zyrien walked down the halls of the Capitol building. He reached the appropriations committee door and took a deep breath.

"Hello, Mr. Taylor," the receptionist greeted him with a smile.

"Hello, I'm here to see Mr. Phillips." He sat in a chair and placed his briefcase on the floor.

"He's in a meeting," she explained. "It'll be a few minutes."

Zyrien nodded and took out his cell phone. "I'll just step outside and make a quick phone call."

The mature woman nodded. "I'll come get you the minute he finishes up his meeting."

Zyrien walked into the hall, punching numbers as he paced. He listened as Jenna's phone rang and rang. It finally went to voice mail, but he didn't leave a message. He tried her cell phone with the same luck and he didn't leave a message. What could be wrong? Maybe she just needed some time for the portrait.

But he had to know for himself what was going on. Who could he call? He needed someone who wouldn't run and tell his family he was insanely jealous. Lance! Lance would do him a big favor and he would keep it on the down low. He punched out the number and hoped his cousin would answer.

"What's up, Zyrien?"

Zyrien heard the unmistakable sounds of a restaurant in the background. "I need a favor."

Lance snickered. "Done."

In all his life, his cousin had never agreed to anything so fast. Usually it took a conversation about how it could benefit Lance. But this time Lance was almost rushing him off the phone. Zyrien couldn't imagine why, and couldn't dedicate any time to it. He explained the situation to Lance. "So I need you to go check and make sure she's OK."

Lance mumbled something, laughed, and then came back on the line. "She's fine, Zyrien. Just catching up on her painting."

"How can you be so sure? All I'm asking you to do is to go check on her. You know, when you were playing football and you wanted me to check on your wife, I did it without any hesitation." Zyrien hated bringing up old news, but he needed to know about Jenna or it would slowly drive him nuts. He couldn't afford any distractions, especially if it was just Jenna taking the day off.

Lance sighed. "I know because Dawn just talked to her earlier and that's what she told Dawn."

"How do you know that?"

"Because Dawn and I are having lunch."

Chapter 24

Zyrien looked at his phone as the display read: "call ended." Something wasn't right in the city of Dallas. Why was Lance having lunch with Dawn? He knew Dawn had placed the new bookkeeper at the restaurant, but that was a few weeks ago. There was no practical reason why two people married to two other people would be having lunch together.

He redialed his cousin. This time Lance was not as jovial as just a few minutes before. "What?" he barked through the phone. "I thought you were on a business trip. Why aren't you conducting any?"

"Because my married cousin is having lunch with my girlfriend's married best friend."

"How about you relax," Lance said. "It's nothing, man."

Zyrien knew it was something and Jenna would probably hit the roof when she found out. He noticed the receptionist glancing in his direction. She waved at him, beckoning him inside the office. Zyrien sighed. So many problems, so little time. "Look Lance, I gotta go. This discussion isn't over." He ended the call.

He took a deep breath and walked down the hall to the chairperson's office, ready for some major ego stroking.

Wilbert Crate, chairperson for the budgeting committee, greeted Zyrien with a hearty handshake.

"How about we grab some lunch across the street and we can talk?" He headed out of his office as if Zyrien had already agreed.

Soon they entered the Bull Pen, a local hangout for the employees of the Capitol building. After he and Wilbert took their seats, the other members of the budgeting committee soon joined them.

Zyrien's mind kept floating back to his conversation with Lance, even as introductions were made. Shaking hands and getting slapped on the back was not his idea of fun, but he did it for his job and his future. He would worry about Lance later.

Zyrien struggled to concentrate on the questions the men threw at him. For every scenario they could come up with, he had a practical response.

"What happens if the system has been compromised? Would our accounting information still be secured?" Wilbert asked as he ordered his fourth martini. "I mean, say some computer geek breaks through your company's firewall; important government information would be there for the taking."

Zyrien took a sip of his mineral water before he spoke. He learned the night before that he couldn't keep up with these professional drinkers. So today he stayed with nonalcoholic drinks. "Wilbert, your concerns are valid. Duncaster and Finch has procured the finest firewall protection to prevent such a disaster. I might add that one of the requirements for Duncaster and Finch securing the contract was that the government would use their own firewall protection as well. So in the event a computer hacker could get through one firewall, they would be less likely to get through two."

"Well, you got me there. I don't know much about a firewall, virus, or any of that other computer crap." Wilburt lifted his glass to Zyrien.

Zyrien lifted his glass to the gentlemen at the table. If he could survive the next few days with these men, he'd definitely get confirmation on the contract, his life would return to normal, and he could focus his energy on Jenna and the rest of his job.

Jenna stared across the breakfast table at her brother. He had been so quiet all morning and she did her best not to pry. But now it was past lunchtime and he hadn't uttered a word about his sudden trip to Dallas. He just stared into space. It was time for big sister Jenna to start asking the hard questions.

"Ansel, I've been really good and not asked, but now I have to know. Is everything OK?"

He took a bite of his sandwich and chewed slowly. He pointed to his mouth.

She knew what he was doing. Whenever he didn't want to talk about something he just shut down. "Don't play that 'my mouth is full' routine with me. You know I will just sit here and wait until you don't have a mouth full of food to hear what you have to say." She leaned back in her chair and folded her arms across her chest. "I could always call Dawn. I know she could make you talk."

He swallowed. "All right, anything but Dawn coming over and torturing me."

Jenna reached across the table and patted his hand. "You know you can talk to me, Ansel. I know we haven't been as close as we should over the years and that's my fault. I was so busy trying to keep my art career afloat, I didn't get to know you and wife number two."

Ansel shook his head. "You didn't miss much. I guess I thought I should be married, but it was trouble from the start."

"It doesn't matter. Look at it this way. At least you and . . ." Jenna couldn't remember her sister-in-law's name.

"Monica," Ansel supplied for his sister. "Don't worry,

Jenna. Like I said, you didn't miss much. Everything was about her and her career. She works for the Attorney General."

"So what happened?"

"Well, she had gotten a promotion at the AG office. I was happy for her. It was what she's wanted since I've known her. She wanted to be head legal counsel and nothing would stop her, including me."

Jenna instantly understood. "A single attorney had a better chance for advancement than a married one."

He made the motion of a gun with his thumb and forefinger. "You just won the daily jackpot," he said drily.

Jenna remained silent and searched for reassuring words, but couldn't find any.

"It's OK, Jenna. I know I wasn't the best husband. I don't want you thinking she's this awful woman who picked her career over me." He hesitated for a moment. "Wait, that's what she did. Why am I defending her?"

"Because you're hurting. It's going to be fine, Ansel. You'll get through the divorce proceedings and you'll be just fine."

He looked at her sheepishly. "Actually, that was really the reason I came up unexpectedly. When I got home yesterday, a letter from some lawyer told me Monica wanted to start divorce proceedings as quickly as possible. She was offering me fifty grand."

Jenna gasped. "Fifty thousand dollars so you wouldn't fight the divorce. What about the house?"

"Well, when we married, she had just bought a house. So I sold mine and moved in with her. I just went along with it. The house was in her name only. We really didn't have any ties to each other. She didn't want kids, pets, or anything that would deter her from her job."

"And you stayed married to her for how many years?" Jenna couldn't hide her amazement.

"Five years." He smiled at his sister. "Not every woman

knows they can have both a career and a marriage. I wish Monica could have been more like you."

She was shocked at her brother's comment. "Thank you, Ansel. I think Zyrien is like you."

Ansel leaned back in his chair. "Oh yeah, Mr. Wonderful. So tell."

Jenna smiled. She was almost bursting at the seams to tell him, but didn't want to throw her relationship with Zyrien in her brother's face. "Well, he's not like any man I've ever dated. His family is amazing. He's the oldest of eight children."

"That's a lot of people. So is he a mama's boy, being the oldest?"

"Hardly," Jenna said. "It seems like everyone in his family comes to him with their problems." Jenna quickly explained the latest crisis in Zyrien's family. "His sister is about seven months pregnant and separated from her husband."

Ansel let out an expletive that shocked Jenna. "How could any man leave his wife at such a critical time? I don't blame Zyrien. I would have wanted that guy's ass on a platter."

"Well, everything is fine now. I think Angie is considering divorce, but Darrin, that's her husband, is begging her to take him back."

Ansel played with the saltshaker. "Do you think she'd take him back after he did all that?"

"No, I don't think she will. I also think she's confused."

Ansel smiled at Jenna. "I think someone has become an honorary member of Zyrien's family and you love it."

She couldn't deny it. She loved the time she spent with Zyrien's family. It made her treasure the solitude more. "Yes, I do. They're all very nice. Maybe you'll meet them while you're visiting," she said. "His mother wants to pose for a portrait."

Ansel's smile faded. "Please tell me you're kidding. What is she? Like sixty-five or something?" He made a disgusted sound.

"First of all," Jenna said, "quit being a prude. Second, Bella looks great and she's only fifty-two. Zyrien is eight years my junior."

"Well, hell, I definitely have to meet this guy," Ansel said on a laugh.

Jenna threw her napkin at her brother in an attempt to wipe that grin off his face.

Jenna couldn't enjoy her moment of triumph long. Her doorbell rang. "Now who could that be?" She asked no one in particular. Maybe Zyrien had wrapped his business up and wanted to surprise her.

She opened her front door to a tearful Dawn, dressed in a tan linen suit.

"Dawn, what's wrong?" Jenna stepped aside as Dawn stomped past her, heading for the living room. Jenna had no choice but to follow her friend. Ansel also joined the women.

Dawn stared at Ansel. "Hey, Ans, it's good seeing you. It's been a while since you've been to Dallas." She took a deep breath. "Ans, do you mind? Girl talk."

Ansel put his hand over his heart. "No sarcasm. Dawn, I thought you loved me."

Dawn wiped her eyes with the back of her hand. "You're getting a freebie today. I'm sure I'll have plenty of opportunities to make up for it, right?"

Ansel rose from his seat. "Yes, you're right, as usual. I'll be here a while. I'm not leaving because you told me to, but because I'm going to take a nap. So don't get a big head." He left the women and headed upstairs.

Jenna laughed at her brother's retreating figure. "Just one day, I would love to see you two talk like normal human beings."

"This *is* normal," Dawn insisted. "Ansel keeps me on my toes."

Jenna watched Dawn fidget with her purse. She took the purse out of Dawn's lap, looking her directly in the eyes.

"OK, Dawn, what brings you by when you're supposed to be at work?"

"Well, I had a business lunch and he wanted to meet downtown."

Jenna handed Dawn a Kleenex as the tears tumbled down her face. "Dawn, what are you not telling me?"

Dawn wiped her face and took a deep breath. "Jenna, you know we've been through so much together, I want to thank you for being there for me."

"Dawn," Jenna prodded. "Tell me something."

"I had lunch with Lance Harris—you know, Zyrien's cousin. He wanted me to get him a temp for the barbecue place."

Jenna nodded. "Yes, you placed someone there two weeks ago. So why are you having lunch with him now? Is he dissatisfied with the person you placed there?"

Dawn shook her head. "No, actually the guys at the restaurant like her and are ready to make her permanent."

"OK, Dawn," Jenna said in her calmest voice. "We can sit here all day and dance around the real issue that has you here in my house crying or you could tell me what the hell is going on!"

Dawn gasped at her. "Man, Zyrien is out of town for just a few days and you're already having a fit. Are you frustrated already? You didn't have that 'you're going out of town sex' before he left?"

"Zyrien and I are not the topic of discussion, Dawn."

"All right. I had lunch with Lance today and things got out of hand."

That had Jenna's attention. "Start from the beginning."

Dawn nodded. "It started a few weeks ago when I placed Ginger Hughes at the restaurant. Lance called to tell me how great she was working out."

Jenna nodded. "Sounds harmless."

"The next day, he asked me to lunch to celebrate Ginger. So

I went. We had the best time. We talked about everything—sports, stocks, and the fact that neither of us has kids."

"So how was it out of hand? It just sounds harmless. Men and women can be friends without having sex."

"That was the first lunch. Then we had lunch three times last week. I told him the Stars had started training camp and Chad was working out every night. So one night we had dinner."

Jenna could see exactly where this was leading and neither of them deserved that. "Dawn, this will only lead to trouble," Jenna warned. "Harmless or not."

"I know," Dawn admitted. "That's why I told him that I couldn't have lunch today. I explained that I felt like I was cheating on Chad and I loved him too much for that. But he showed up at my office and the general manager was there, so of course he used it to his advantage. He pretended he was unhappy with Ginger and threatened to terminate the contract, so the general manager insisted I go and soothe his ruffled feathers."

Jenna couldn't believe Lance was being so underhanded. "So you were forced into lunch with him."

"I didn't tell you about after," Dawn whispered.

"What?"

She took a deep breath, blew her nose, and whispered. "When we got back to the office, he was helping me out of his car and he rubbed against me. At first I thought it was an accident and didn't say anything. But I reached inside my purse to get my phone to call Chad, and he did it again, and this time he pinned me against the car. Jenna, I swear I never gave him any reason to do that. I mean, I do a little harmless flirting, but I'd never purposely get a man aroused like that."

"I know you wouldn't, Dawn, and I know you love Chad and you wouldn't do anything to hurt him. Lance was taking advantage of the situation. What on earth would make him think that you'd even entertain the idea of an extramarital fling?"

Dawn wiped her face, shrugging her shoulders. "I don't know. He kept saying Chad wasn't man enough for me."

"Why would it be his concern, even if it were true?" Jenna was every bit as confused as Dawn by Lance's behavior. "What happened after that?"

Dawn inhaled and told her the rest of the details. "After that, I didn't care what he said or what he told my boss. Usually I try to please the client at any cost, but the cost just got too high. I walked inside, ready to quit my job, and told my boss what happened."

"That's great, Dawn. I'm very proud of you for standing your ground. What did your boss say? Do you still have a job?"

"Yes. She was very understanding and said she'd assigned Lance's account to another office, so he has no excuse to call me."

"Wow, Dawn that's great. At least you won't have to have any contact with that idiot anymore. I can't believe he did something so crass. Wait until I get my hands on him," Jenna promised. "He's going to hate the day he ever tried to feel you up."

Chapter 25

Zyrien excused himself from the table of loud, boisterous politicians and looked around for a quiet corner. Jenna was probably fuming by now, since they hadn't spoken since he left. He hoped she would be in a forgiving mood.

He dialed her home number and waited patiently for her to pick up, but she didn't. After the fifth ring, her voice mail kicked in. He tried her cell. Same business. Finally, he looked at his watch and swore under his breath. "Dezarae." He knew that when Jenna was painting, that was all her world focused on. He would have to try her later. But why hadn't she called him? He'd been gone just over a day and not one word.

Calm down, he told himself. Don't look for a fire when there was no need. He thought of another way to get the same information. "Hey Mom, how is everything going?"

"Fine, Zyrien. You'll never guess who's here." His mother didn't exactly sound right.

He sighed. "Is Darrin over there? I thought he and Ang agreed to give each other space."

His mother laughed. "That boy is no fool. But he's not the one visiting. Jenna, Dezarae, and Ansel are visiting. I invited them over to celebrate. That Ansel is very attractive. I can see why Jenna is so proud of him."

"Who is Ansel?" Zyrien never heard this name before and why was he at his mother's house? Jenna wouldn't dare bring another man into his mother's house. He was just about to ask the question again when the chairman beckoned him back to the table. He couldn't tell the man who held the contract approval in his hand to wait, so he told his mother good-bye, and shoved the cell phone back in his pocket.

That night he had two people to straighten out. His woman and his cousin.

Hours later, Zyrien finally freed himself of the committee and now had some unfinished business to take care of. He first called Lance, hoping it would be a short conversation. He dialed his cousin's cell phone. As soon as Lance answered the phone, he knew. "What did you do to Dawn?"

Lance signed. "Ah man, it wasn't nuthin'. You act like she's your woman or something."

"Look, the last thing I need is for you to try those tired playa moves on Dawn. You know she's happily married and you're trying to get another notch. You've been acting pretty good these last few years and your wife is happy with you, don't screw it up."

"I didn't screw anything up," Lance protested. "Look, I just got off the phone with your woman, so I'm guessing Dawn blabbed. Jenna wants to have lunch so we can talk."

Zyrien didn't like the sound of that, either. Jenna wanting to meet with Lance alone only meant the situation was worse than Zyrien could have imagined in his wildest dreams. "Why don't you tell me what happened?"

Without his usual playa monologue, Lance told his story of meeting Dawn for lunch and even coercing her into going with him earlier that day. "My libido got the best of me."

"That's no excuse. Why would you do that?"

Lance sighed. "'Cause of her husband."

Zyrien rubbed his forehead with his fingers. Why can't there just be a simple solution to a problem? Why was he in a family of nuts? And now he had dragged Jenna and Dawn into his family's mess. "What does Chad have to do with anything? I didn't think you had even met him."

"I didn't have to meet him. Aunt Bella went on and on about how attractive he was, and how he was doting on Dawn. I guess I was jealous." Lance swore under his breath. "It's going to sound really stupid to you, but it was a brother thing. Knowing that Dawn was married to Chad was eating away at my nerves. She's a beautiful woman and I just lost it."

Finally Zyrien could see the whole ugly picture. "I can't believe you're a racist like that. I see women of every color under the rainbow approach you, and in the old days, you didn't turn any of them down. So don't try to start playing the race card now." Zyrien stopped speaking, because he was very near shouting at the man he considered his best friend. "Look, you do need to apologize to Dawn privately, because that was a sneaky and low-down thing to do. We'll finish the discussion when I return to Dallas." Zyrien ended the call.

He sat on the bed in his hotel room and shook his head in disbelief. He dialed Jenna's home number, hoping he could talk some sense into his stubborn woman. It was past ten, so Dez wouldn't be there and then there was the issue of the mysterious Ansel person. What kind of name was that, anyway?

He listened as the phone rang. On the third ring, she finally picked up. With great relief in his heart, he spoke. "Hey, baby. Heard there's been a problem with Lance." But the voice that answered him wasn't Jenna's, nor Dez's, nor Dawn's, for that matter. It was a decidedly male voice and he was laughing at him.

"No, man. I'm not your baby. She's actually in the shower. Would you like to talk to her now? Or would you like her to call you later?"

What else could go wrong? "Neither." He hung up the phone. Now what?

* * *

Jenna walked downstairs tying her robe hastily. “Was that Zyrien?”

Ansel looked up at her, smiling. “Yeah, he thinks I’m your man.”

“You are,” Jenna chided.

Ansel shrugged. “You know what I mean. A strange man is answering his woman’s phone. I fully expect him to come screaming through that door any minute now.” Ansel walked toward the living room. “Hey, *Seinfeld* is getting ready to come on. You still watch?” He sat down on the couch, grabbed the remote, and clicked the button, bringing the TV to life.

“Of course I still watch.” She glanced at the red neon clock above the fireplace. “I just have time to throw on my Betty Boop nightshirt and I’ll be right back.” She walked to the stairs.

Ansel nodded. “Aren’t you going to try Zyrien? He sounded a little upset.”

“Which is why I’ll talk to him tomorrow,” Jenna said smiling, knowing she had to explain. “He gets a little jealous and I can’t remember if I ever called you by your name or not. So he probably does think something stupid right now. So it’s good to let him stew in his own juice for a while.” She hurried upstairs to change.

While she was upstairs, she also called Dawn. Thank goodness Dawn and Chad were making out and she couldn’t talk long. After agreeing to talk in the morning, the women hung up. When Jenna returned to the living room, her brother had popped some popcorn and it was waiting for her on the coffee table. Unfortunately for her, it was loaded with butter. He also had put out two glasses of soda. Jenna didn’t normally eat this late, but she also didn’t normally have her brother visiting, so she thought it was worth any weight she might gain.

* * *

The next day, Jenna met Lance at a sandwich shop near her house. He was already there and waiting. Jenna walked straight to the table and sat down. "Hello, Lance. Thank you for not making this more difficult than it already is."

He nodded at her. "Let's just get this over with, so I can get back to the restaurant."

"That wasn't your concern yesterday." Jenna stared at him. "I liked you, Lance. I thought you were a nice guy, not like so many athletes out there abusing their celebrity status. But here you are acting just like the rest of them."

He had the nerve to look like he was a victim. "I'm human, Jenna. All she had to say was 'no.'"

"She did say 'no.' She didn't want to have lunch with you yesterday and she told you why. But you showed up at her job and forced her to have lunch with you."

"I didn't think she meant 'no.' Women always say 'no,' but they really mean—"

"'No,'" Jenna finished for him. "Besides the small fact that you're married and so is Dawn—why would you do such a thing?"

He shrugged. "Look, I know I was wrong. Let's just leave it at that. I'll apologize to her the first chance I get."

Jenna shook her head. "That is not what this is about, Lance. I want to make sure you understand what you've done to my friend. You caused a very confident women to doubt herself, when she has nothing to be sorry or feel guilty for."

Lance toyed with the saltshaker. He rolled the miniature Corona beer bottle in his large hand. "Most women consider it flattering to have a man like me pay attention to them. Don't tell me she's not used to that. Guys are always checking her out."

Jenna nodded. "Those men also know when she says 'no,' she means 'no.' As with any woman," Jenna added. "Dawn has been my best friend since junior high and since Zyrien and I are dating, I know there's going to be times when we're all together."

"I will apologize. I overstepped the line and I'm sorry. You have no idea how sorry. I had to hear the riot act from Zyrien last night. This doesn't have to go past us, right? I mean, you don't have to tell Bella or anyone in the family?"

"They won't hear it from me or Dawn, but I can't speak for Zyrien. I trust you won't say anything to Chad?"

Lance glared at her. "Hell, no. I don't have anything to say to him. Not now, not ever."

Jenna wasn't so much shocked at his words, but at the emotion in his voice. "You don't like Chad, do you? You've never met him. He's good to Dawn."

Lance stood, signaling the conversation was over. "Look Jenna, I like you. You're good for Zyrien. I do not have to like Chad. He's not what Dawn needs."

"What does Dawn need?" Jenna asked sarcastically.

"A black man." He left the shop.

Jenna shook her head. "Idiot."

The next evening, Ansel was actually whistling as he flipped steaks on the indoor electric grill on the kitchen counter. He was either in a happy place or it was the effect of the second glass of wine. Jenna watched her brother as he joked with Dawn.

Dawn had finally put the episode with Lance behind her. She sat at the table chopping vegetables for the salad. "Just you wait until Chad gets his hands on you."

Ansel drained his glass. "Oh, no. You're not sending in the Canadians, are you?"

Dawn laughed. "What are you, chicken? Chad only tops you by three inches and probably fifty pounds. Sounds like a fair fight to me," she said. "How much longer for those steaks?"

Ansel used the fork to spear one of the rib-eye steaks. He

held it up. Juice cascaded down to the grill, creating a not-so-wonderful smell in the kitchen. "I don't think they're ready yet. Maybe ten or fifteen minutes."

Dawn pushed the salad bowl away. "That smells awful. Jenna, can you finish for me? I-I-I bathroom," Dawn mumbled through the fingers covering her mouth. She stood abruptly, knocking the chair over, and headed out of the room.

Jenna and Ansel looked at each other. "Probably just the stress of the last few days," she reasoned. She started chopping the vegetables.

Ansel shrugged his broad shoulders. "She looked kind of funny earlier, but I just figured it was something to do with that mess with Zyrien's cousin. Speaking of, you should call him."

Jenna shook her head. "I'll call him later tonight. He's probably out drinking with his college buddies, or at some strip club with the politicians."

"Your mouth is going to get you in a lot of trouble one of these days, Jenna Lynette Bradshaw," Ansel admonished his older sister.

"It already has. His name is Zyrien Alexander Taylor."

"He probably gets turned on when you talk all sassy to him, doesn't he?" He placed the steaks on a plate. "I mean, a woman with a little bite to her is always exciting."

Jenna never thought of herself as having a bite. She always thought she was just doing her thing. If people didn't like it, they could leave. "Thank you, Ansel. I think. I'm sure Zyrien will read me the riot act for not calling."

He walked to the table with the plate of meat. "You think that's wise? If it were me, I would have wondered why my woman hadn't called."

Jenna grunted. "Well, he's in DC on business. It's something very important concerning some big government contract."

"Well, then, I wouldn't call him, either," Ansel said sarcastically. "In fact, if I were you, I would cut him off completely."

"Are you nuts?" Jenna stood and walked to the counter.

She put three baking potatoes into the microwave and set the timer. "That's hurting me, too. It only works if he suffers," she said with a smile.

"That's my girl." He glanced around the room. "Hey, you think Dawn fell in the toilet?"

"No, she's probably talking to Chad on the phone or something." She headed out of the kitchen. "I'll check on her just to make sure."

Jenna walked to the bathroom and she heard her best friend throwing up and groaning simultaneously. "Dawn, are you OK? You've been in there for quite a while. I have the pink stuff in the cabinet."

Dawn groaned. "I—I—oh no." She started all over again.

Jenna hated feeling so helpless. She leaned against the door listening to Dawn's retching and painful noises. Jenna went to the kitchen to search for something to settle Dawn's stomach. As she searched her cabinets for the fat-free crackers, a strange thought occurred to her. She laughed. "No way." She giggled again.

Ansel came up behind her. "How's Dawn?"

Jenna grabbed the box and held them close to her chest. "She's going to be just fine. Will you do me a favor?"

Dawn was crying. Jenna was crying. Even Ansel had tears of happiness trickling down his face. The trio sat on the couch in Jenna's living room. Dawn's wish had finally come true. She was pregnant.

Dawn held the stick in the air. "I think I'm going to frame it. Chad will be so surprised."

Jenna wiped her eyes. "Will you make sure you go to the doctor as soon as possible to confirm it? I bet Chad will be floored."

Dawn smiled. Her brown eyes glistening with tears gave

her a very vulnerable look. "I just can't believe it. How did you know?"

Jenna snickered. "Dawn, when is the last time you missed a meal?"

She actually looked humbled. "Oh yeah, that's right." She snapped her fingers. "You know, I threw up yesterday, too. I just thought it was because I realized Lance was trying to put the moves on me. I'm glad it was because Chad knocked me up."

"Dawn!" Jenna admonished her friend. "You're awful."

Dawn leaned and hugged Jenna. "And you're the best friend I've ever had."

"I don't care what you have to do," Zyrien growled at the petite redhead behind the counter. "You get me on the next plane to Dallas. Nonstop." He was trying very hard not to lose it in the Washington-Dulles airport. The last thing he wanted was Homeland Security drawing their guns on him.

"Yes sir, Mr. Taylor. The next flight won't leave for at least three hours and will put you in Dallas around six Saturday morning," the ticket agent said. "That's the best we can do."

It wasn't good enough, but what else could he do? Throw a fit and go to jail? "All right."

She seemed relieved that he could be placated so quickly. "Thank you, Mr. Taylor. Please let me know how I can help you any further."

He nodded, handed her his credit card, and put his luggage on the scale. He didn't even care if he went over the weight limit of fifty pounds. He would see Jenna in a couple of hours and he hoped his world would be right very soon.

After he was settled in the waiting area, he tried Jenna's house again, and again a very male voice answered the phone. But this time Zyrien couldn't make out anything the man said. It sounded like a party. Now she was having a party!

Zyrien leaned back in the seat and decided just to forget about it for now. What could he do, anyway?

By the time he landed in Dallas and retrieved his car, he was so grouchy, no one deserved to see him in that mood. It was just past seven in the morning. Against all his better judgment, he headed to Jenna's.

He parked in front of her house. Nothing looked different, he thought. He rang the doorbell and waited. And waited. He rang the doorbell again.

He was getting ready to start banging on the door when he heard her padding to the front door. When the door opened, Zyrien's heart fell to his stomach. A very tall African-American man stood in the doorway in his boxer shorts and nothing else.

Zyrien glanced at the number on the house, just to make sure before he accused the stranger of stealing his woman. "Is Jenna here?"

The man smiled instantly. "Yeah, she's here. Who are you?"

Zyrien cleared his throat. The guy was well over six feet. Zyrien didn't think he could take him, but if it came down to it, he would try. "I think the bigger question is: what the hell are you doing here?"

Before things could get really ugly, Jenna appeared at the door, tying the sash on her bathrobe. She smiled at him instantly. "Zyrien, you're back early."

He stared at her. No, "how was your trip?" or "I missed you." Nothing. She stood there looking like a goddess to his tired eyes. "Is that a problem for you?"

Finally, the large man stepped aside so Zyrien could enter the house. Jenna grabbed his hand and led him to the living room. "No, it's not a problem. You met my brother, Ansel?"

Zyrien sat down on the couch. "Not officially." He extended his hand. "Sorry about earlier," he grumbled.

Ansel took his hand. "No problem. If you can deal with

Jenna and Dawn, then I'm glad to meet you. Not many men can say that," Ansel said.

Zyrien suddenly felt silly for all the misgivings he had had all week. "Jenna didn't mention you were coming for a visit," Zyrien hinted, wanting to know how long he'd been in town and being too embarrassed to ask.

Ansel smiled. "You know us Bradshaws. We act first, think about the consequences later. I showed up a couple days ago. Don't know exactly how long I'll be staying. Marital discord."

It must be the season for that, Zyrien thought, instantly thinking of his sister. "I understand. Welcome to Dallas."

Ansel rose from the love seat across from the couple. "I was born here, but thanks anyway. I'm going to shower," he announced. "Nice meeting you, Zyrien." He walked upstairs.

"Same here," Zyrien called after him. After he was sure Jenna's brother was safely upstairs, he moved closer to Jenna. He pulled her in his arms and kissed her. "I missed you like crazy," he whispered against her lips.

Jenna caressed his head as she deepened the kiss. "Me too. You get everything taken care of?"

He nodded. Fighting the need to take her upstairs to her bedroom. Not a good impression to make on her brother. His fingers started traveling and untied to the sash on her robe. "Baby, I want you so bad, but there's a lot we need to talk about first." He playfully bit her bottom lip, savoring the flavor of her toothpaste.

Jenna pulled back, smiling at him. Teasing him with those soft hands. "Good thing Ansel is upstairs, huh? You look a little tired, Zyrien. I want you rested up, so there will be no excuses about you being too tired to fulfill your duties." He grabbed his hand. "Come on, you can keep me company while I make breakfast."

Zyrien followed her like a zombie. In the highly aroused state he was in at the moment, he would have followed those hips into the pits of hell.

Chapter 26

Jenna busied herself making breakfast, knowing Zyrien was watching her every move. She decided on omelets, bacon, and toast. "I think after breakfast you should go home and get some rest. I'd say you could stay here, but your mom and Angie are coming over later."

Zyrien poured a cup of coffee. "Why are they coming here?"

Jenna turned from her cooking and faced him. "You don't really want to know, do you?"

He tried to look innocent, but apparently decided against it. "No. No, I don't. This is not about that portrait, is it?"

"What do you think?" She turned and resumed her cooking. "Of course it's about the portrait. She wants to see how Dez's portrait is coming along, since I'm almost done." Jenna decided a little teasing was in order, just to make sure he was still awake. "But I told Bella you could probably describe it better since you've actually seen Dez in the buff."

He looked up from his coffee cup. "Not even funny. You know that was an accident. Why you wanna bring that up now?"

Jenna began making the omelets. She poured the first mixture in the skillet. "Because the next time I tell you not to go into my studio, you'll listen."

"You got that right. I learned my lesson." He rose from his seat and walked to her, hugging her from behind. "Hey, I'm going to head home and get some rest. Don't let Mom and Angie talk you into a mother-daughter portrait." He kissed her on the cheek. "I'll call you later."

Jenna took the last omelet out of the skillet. "Hold it, Zyrien Taylor." She took the skillet off the burner. "Don't you think you're leaving my house without kissing me properly."

He stopped walking and turned around, facing her. "Baby, all you had to do was ask." He covered the distance between them as fast as he could. He pulled her into his arms and kissed her thoroughly. "How was that, Ms. Bradshaw?"

"I don't know. I think I need another one to make sure you're doing it right." She kissed his lower lip.

"I could always go to McDonald's for breakfast," Ansel drawled, walking into the kitchen. He took a seat at the table, eyeing Jenna's culinary efforts. "I knew I smelled eggs."

Jenna kissed Zyrien again, ignoring her brother's catcalls and whistles. She wondered how far would Zyrien go in front of an audience. Nothing like pushing the envelope, she thought. She teased his lips apart with little resistance.

Apparently all his concentration had headed south. She felt his erection pressed against her. "Feels like someone already had their Wheaties."

"We just missed you, that's all," Zyrien teased. He kissed her gently on the lips and backed away. "I'd better go." He walked out of the kitchen.

Ansel tried his best not to laugh. His best wasn't good enough at the moment, Jenna thought. At least he waited until the alarm signaled that the front door had been opened and closed before he started laughing hysterically. "I don't think I've seen action like that since I was a teenager. No wonder you keep him around."

* * *

"Jenna, this painting is gorgeous," Bella said a few hours later. Bella and Angie had arrived as scheduled to look over the painting. "But then, again, everything you touch seems beautiful. I can't wait until you paint me." Zyrien's mother smiled at her.

"Thank you, Bella. I've had a good time painting Dez. She's going to be shocked when I tell her it's almost finished. I just need to do a few more touches and then glaze it. Then I can relax until September." Jenna tilted her head and inspected the painting closely, looking for any imperfection in the portrait. She sighed with relief when she couldn't find any.

"Have you heard from my wayward son? He's only called me once since he's been away and that's not like him."

Jenna knew Zyrien was close to his family, but surely Bella wasn't upset that he hadn't called. "Actually, Bella, he got back this morning. We had kind of a mix-up with Ansel being here. He should be home sleeping right now."

Bella nodded. "Good. I keep telling him he can't be worried about us so much. He needs to live his life. Looks like he's finally listening to me."

"Yes, he showed up this morning. Ansel opened the door wearing only his boxer shorts and that's where the morning got a little sticky." Jenna snorted. "You should have seen Zyrien. He was fuming. It was really funny."

Angie joined in the laughter. "Yeah, I can just see Zyrien trying to be all tough and Ansel easily tops him by at least five inches." She groaned. "I thought we were going out to eat. The kids are hungry," she said, rubbing her stomach.

Jenna didn't want to ask. It was possible, she thought. Angie looked even larger than she had just a few days before. "Are you OK, Angie?"

"I know what you're thinking," Angie remarked. "It's OK, Jenna, you can ask me. I won't start crying, promise. Yes, I've gained four pounds since Thursday. I woke up and waddled to the bathroom, and screamed bloody murder. Mom says it's normal, since I really hadn't gained a whole lot of weight, and I'm carrying twins."

Jenna observed Angie. She wasn't much taller than Zyrien and although she looked every bit pregnant, she didn't look like she was carrying twins, let alone at twenty-eight weeks. "You look wonderful, Angie. I would never guess you're carrying twins."

"That's not what your brother just said."

Jenna frowned. "Did he insult you? Ansel is known for being blunt," she said, hoping he hadn't said anything harsh to her.

"Funny," Ansel drawled, joining the women in the studio. "I'd say that about you, Jenna." He looked at the picture, obviously shocked at the image before him. "This is Dez? Wow, it doesn't even look like her! She looks hot in this picture."

"That's because she doesn't have any clothes on." Jenna smiled in satisfaction. If she could elicit this kind of reaction from her brother, she was on the right track.

Ansel shook his head. "No, it's not. The picture looks sensual. I don't even think of her as being nude. I think of her as just looking beautiful in the picture. She reminds me of Venus."

Jenna tilted her head to one side. She supposed he was right. "You mean Venus Diaz, your college sweetheart?"

"Yes. Don't you think so? Smooth brown skin, flowing black hair cascading down her shoulder, a rounded stomach just ready to bear all those Bradshaw offspring."

Angie sighed dreamily. "That was beautiful. What happened to Venus?"

Ansel took a deep breath. "She went back to the Dominican Republic after college. We still keep in touch from time to time. She's married now with four kids and is a college professor there."

After a few moments of silence, Bella picked up the conversation. "I thought we were going out to eat?"

Jenna nodded. Food would probably help them all. She knew it would definitely help her mood and probably Ansel's as well. "Yes, Bella. I just need to get my purse," she said, heading for the door. "I'll be right back."

"OK," Bella replied, "We can go in the Suburban, to make sure Angie has enough room."

Jenna laughed as she headed upstairs and retrieved her purse, making sure she had her cell phone with her. Just in case Zyrien called. By the time she made it back downstairs, they were all waiting for her outside. She locked the door and they were off.

She sat in the back seat with her brother. "Ans, are you OK eating with a bunch of women?"

"As long as one of those women isn't Dawn, I'll be OK."

Bella looked at Ansel in the rearview mirror. "What's wrong with Dawn? I really like her. That husband of hers is a hunk."

"Nothing is wrong with Dawn," Ansel clarified. "It's just that, after the other day, I don't think I can look at her and not start blubbering like a woman."

Jenna was touched that it meant so much to Ansel, but knew Bella and Angie were clueless. "Dawn just found out she's pregnant the other day and we were lucky enough to be there. It was a very emotional moment." Jenna got misty-eyed just thinking about it.

Bella nodded. "I can imagine. Tell her congratulations for me. How did Chad take the news?"

"Pretty well," Jenna answered. "They're on their way to Hawaii for a week."

"That's so romantic," Angie said with wistful desire. "I wish that could have happened for me. You know, something totally unexpected, but appreciated."

"Well," Jenna admitted, "Dawn had been hinting at the trip for about three months now. Her forty-third birthday is next month.

So they're just celebrating her birthday early," Jenna said, not wanting Angie to feel like she missed something important.

Angie wiped a tear away. "It's still awesome."

Jenna had to admit, if to no one other than herself, that it was awesome.

After he woke up from his nap, refreshed, and relieved that Jenna hadn't kicked him to the curb, Zyrien knew he had unfinished business with Lance. He called his cousin and they made arrangements to meet at the nearby sports bar for a late lunch.

Zyrien pulled on a polo shirt and shorts, his favorite tennis shoes, and headed out the door. When he arrived at the sports bar, Lance's Lincoln Navigator was already there.

He didn't really want to have this conversation, but for anyone to go forward from this fiasco, they would have to talk. Zyrien slid from behind the wheel of his car and headed inside.

The reason Lance liked The Pit was that no one would bother him here. It was housed in a strip mall in north Dallas, and no one ever would have guessed that most of the Dallas Cowboys hung out at this small restaurant. Lance waved at Zyrien from the back booth. Zyrien squared his shoulders and prepared for battle. He walked to the booth and took a seat.

"Hey," they said in unison, both feeling the awkardness of the moment.

"Look, man, I know this is going to be hard, so let me go first," Zyrien said. "I don't know what has gotten into you lately, Lance. I thought all your womanizing days were over. You have to apologize to Dawn and Jenna."

"Man, save all that talk. I tried to talk to Dawn yesterday, but she wouldn't answer her cell. I wouldn't dare call her house. As soon as I can get her alone, I will."

Zyrien wanted this over with. He pulled out his cell phone and dialed Jenna's number. After the third ring, she picked up.

"Hello."

"Hey, baby," Zyrien said. "Hey, I'm with Lance and he needs to talk to Dawn."

Jenna's tone instantly bristled at the mention of Lance's name. "He should apologize to her," Jenna said tightly. "That rat."

"Baby," Zyrien cautioned, "we can talk about it later. I just want to make sure he talks to Dawn."

"Well, I'd love more than anything to be there when he does apologize, but it will have to be next week. Dawn and Chad are vacationing in Hawaii. They left this morning."

"I thought they just went on vacation or something?"

Jenna gasped. "Oh, I forgot to tell you. Dawn's pregnant. Just about two weeks, as far as we can tell."

Zyrien stared at Lance as Jenna continued her babbling. Zyrien learned that Chad had taken his wife to Hawaii to celebrate the addition to their family. "That's great, baby. Where are you?"

"We're at the restaurant."

"I can tell," Zyrien teased. He could hear loud voices in the background. "I can barely hear you. Who's the designated driver?"

"Quit being such an old man," Jenna teased. "Ansel had a few beers, but your mom is driving."

"All right. How about dinner later?" He didn't really want to have dinner. He wanted to have Jenna.

"You don't really mean that, do you?"

Busted. "I would just like to spend some time with you. You know it's been more than a few days."

Jenna laughed seductively. "Why don't we talk about it later?"

Zyrien opened his mouth to respond, but he was too late. Jenna had already disconnected.

"So where's Dawn, so I can get this over with?" Lance played with his empty beer bottle. "Man, I wish I'd never tried anything."

"Actually, she's in Hawaii, so you're off the hook for a little while."

Lance shrugged. "So we cool?"

Zyrien honestly didn't know. It was a complex situation, but he didn't have the energy to deal with Lance at the moment. After all, this man was his best friend. Wasn't everyone allowed a mistake? But Lance had made his share of mistakes. Luckily he picked the wrong person this time or the situation could have easily escalated into something awful and deadly. "I can't speak for Jenna or Dawn. But as for me, yeah, man, we cool."

A few hours later, Zyrien prepared dinner for Jenna. He was dressed in jeans and his favorite Howard University T-shirt. He fixed all her favorites: grilled chicken, baked potatoes, salad, and cheesecake. OK, the cheesecake was *his* favorite, but a little temptation never hurt.

As the doorbell rang, Zyrien lit the candles on the table and went to answer the door. To his horror, not only was Jenna at the door, but so was Ansel. They were both smiling at him. Zyrien had the funny feeling he'd been played. "Hey, baby." He kissed Jenna on the lips. "Hey, Ansel," he said sheepishly. He couldn't ask the man to leave, so he'd just have to grin and bear it.

Ansel laughed boisterously. "Don't worry, Zyrien. I'm not staying. I just drove Jenna over here. I'm on the way to your mom's house for dinner."

Zyrien couldn't hide his relief. "No offense, Ansel, but I'm glad you're not staying. Do you know the way to my parents'? It's pretty far."

Ansel nodded. "I've been there twice since I've been here. Plus Angie is with me, so I won't get lost, and I'm great with directions."

Zyrien opened his front door and, sure enough, there was Angie sitting in the passenger seat of Jenna's PT Cruiser. She waved at her brother. Zyrien waved back, shaking his head. "Why didn't she come in?"

Jenna laughed. "She would have ruined our joke."

Zyrien smiled. He was getting used to being the victim with the Bradshaw siblings. "You're going to have to pay for that later," he told Jenna.

"I hope so," Jenna teased.

Ansel cleared his throat. "That's my cue to leave. See you guys tomorrow." He kissed Jenna on the cheek and left.

After they heard Jenna's car rumble down the street, Zyrien took her in his arms and kissed her. "You don't know how much I missed you."

Jenna eased out of his arms and stepped back from him. "Why don't you show me?" She grabbed his arms and they headed upstairs to his bedroom. They had some time to make up for.

"You definitely won't get an argument from me," Zyrien drawled. "About the Lance and Dawn fiasco," he started his saga, but Jenna stopped walking and covered his lips with her fingers.

"No, not right now. We can talk about that later. Right now it's just Zyrien, Jenna, your bed, and a box of condoms."

Chapter 27

Jenna laughed as Zyrien nuzzled her neck after a very heated lovemaking session. "Are you taking some vitamins or something?" She rolled over on her back so she could look into those dreamy hazel eyes. She had missed him so much.

"No baby, I was just saving it for you." He eased on top of her. "With all that's been going on this week, I just wanted to show you how much you mean to me." He kissed her deeply. "How long is your brother going to be here?" His kisses moved past her neck and he gently bit the area above her collarbone.

"I don't know how long Ansel will be here. I'm just happy he's visiting." Jenna's hands roamed his naked body freely. She missed their time together. She laughed as her hand reached his erection. He moaned against the nape of her neck, sending a delicious shiver down her body.

Zyrien kissed her again. "Are you ready for another wild ride?"

Jenna grinned at him. "So are you bringing a friend?"

He reached for the box of condoms inside her bedside table. He retrieved a gold packet and waved it front of her face. "This is all the help I need." He kissed her, nudging her lips apart.

As their kiss deepened, Zyrien slipped inside her. Who would have thought they'd already made love three times? Apparently they both had lost time to make up for. "Jenna, you feel so good," he whispered against her ear.

Jenna gasped as he filled her. "I should send you away more often, if you have this kind of energy." For once, Jenna didn't think she would be able to keep up with a man eight years her junior, as he increased his stride. But she was definitely going to try.

The next time Jenna awoke, Zyrien was gone from the bed. She rose from the bed on slightly wobbly legs and headed for the shower.

When she finished, she sat on the bed, drying her body with one of Zyrien's oversized bath towels. He walked into the room with a tray of food.

"I thought you might be hungry." He placed the tray on the nightstand. "I mean, since you wore me out. I really didn't think you had it in you." He smiled at her, enjoying watching her slip on one of his T-shirts and a pair of his boxers. "You look really sexy in my clothes," he said. "I'm about ten seconds from stripping them off you."

Jenna laughed. "No, you're not. You have reached your sexual quota for the week, Mr. Taylor. Now feed me." Jenna sat on the bed and pointed at the tray.

He looked at the tray. He looked at Jenna. He looked at the tray again. "Come on, baby, just once more."

He looked adorable. "No. I want to eat dinner or breakfast, depending on the time," Jenna told her lover. She winked at him. "Then we'll talk."

"So Lance was just feeling jealous that Dawn was married to Chad?" Jenna asked, relaxing against Zyrien's spent body in his king-sized bed. She had just granted his wish and now they were both exhausted.

He yawned, pulling her closer to his body. "Yeah, I told him he has to apologize to both of you for doing something so stupid."

Jenna had figured it was the green-eyed monster fueling Lance's slimy motives. "I told Dawn as much. She had convinced herself that she'd done something to warrant Lance's advances. It took me a while to convince her that she was the victim."

"I'm just glad nothing of any true consequence happened. Lance used to be a dog before he married Traci. It was nothing for him to be dating five or six women at the same time."

Jenna grunted. "That's not a dog; he's a male whore."

"He's still my cousin. Lance and me been tight a lot of years. I was best man at his wedding," Zyrien said in defense of his philandering cousin.

Jenna turned and faced him. "I didn't say you're anything like Lance. I'm saying that Lance used those women back in his days." She kissed him with a loud smack. "But, if you're thinking about living in Lance's player shoes, you just let me know."

His fingers twirled a strand of Jenna's hair. "Baby, my mama didn't raise a fool. I know the real thing when I see her."

Jenna stared at him in disbelief. "You think I'm the real thing?"

Over the next few weeks, Jenna didn't think her life could get much sweeter than it already was. She had completed Dez's portrait for her showing, which was a month away, and her brother was still visiting and finally healing from his disastrous second marriage.

Ansel insisted he wasn't getting married again, but she knew that if the right woman came along he would change his mind. Too bad she didn't have any single friends.

Saturday afternoon she waited for Zyrien to pick her up for

a date at the Fort Worth Museum of Art. Ansel was in his usual position of lying on her couch watching TV. Jenna thought it was time for him to start going out. She blocked his line of vision, so he had to look at her. "Ansel, don't think I don't enjoy your company, but when are you going to start doing something besides lying on the couch?"

"I'm fine, Jenna." He tried to look past her, but she blocked his attempt.

"I know you are. But I want you to be happy," she said, taking a seat on the corner of her coffee table and looking down at him. "Don't you have any hobbies or something?"

Ansel sat the TV remote on the table. "I see this is going to be one of those talks, isn't it?" He took a deep breath and sat up, facing his older sister. "Jenna, I'm fine. I'm not lonely and I'm not depressed. I won't take my life by my own hand the minute you walk out the door on your date with Zyrien."

Jenna shrugged. "I just want you to be happy."

"I *am* happy. I took a leave from work to decide what I want to do and where I want to live. I've also decided to take the settlement from Monica. I probably should leave Austin, too, but I haven't made that call yet." He glanced at his sister. "You just have a good time with the Zee man."

Jenna grimaced. "He hates being called that. I heard some girl at work refer to him like that, and I couldn't even begin to repeat the words he used."

"For a little fellow, he's a little out there."

Jenna laughed. "He reminds me of you." She stood and modeled her outfit for her brother. "What do you think?"

"I like it."

Zyrien watched Jenna as she explained each painting at the museum in Fort Worth. He didn't think he'd like a place full of the different genres of art or what someone else considered art. He looked at a display of what had to be melted bicycle parts mixed with someone's tool set; he didn't call this art.

Jenna leaned closer to him and whispered. "I know what you're thinking. That melted scrap iron is worth a million dollars."

She has to be lying, he thought. She was just joking. She had to be. "A million bucks! You must be kidding."

Jenna assured him that she wasn't. She pointed to the small card stating the very fact.

Zyrien shook his head in amazement. "Baby, your stuff must be worth a mint."

She shook his head. "This is abstract. I like painting real people. This is left up to your own interpretation. What do you see?"

"Junk," he answered honestly.

"OK, forget about it being worth a million dollars. What do you see?"

Zyrien tried to concentrate. He really did. "Sorry, I still see junk."

She shook her head. "OK, maybe abstract is not for you."

"Now I agree with that." He grabbed her hand, wanting to get out of the museum. "How about some dinner?"

Jenna nodded. "I would love some fajitas."

An hour later, Zyrien watched in amazement as Jenna, the healthy eater, ate three beef and shrimp fajitas. Inhaled would have been a better word. "Would you like some more beef?"

"Are you offering?" She smiled at him, taking a long drink of beer.

"I was referring to your plate." He nodded to the empty dish before her. "But hey, I'm game if you are."

"I thought you said beef, not a shrimp," she teased. "I think I'd rather have dessert, anyway."

Zyrien smiled. "You know you're going to have to pay for that. Shrimp. I'll show you a shrimp," he shot back. Zyrien's cell phone rang. He looked at the display and sighed. It was his parents' number. He hoped there would be no crisis tonight. "Mom, most likely," he told Jenna, putting the phone to his ear.

"Zyrien, is Angie with you?"

Zyrien shook his head, hoping to clear his mind. Maybe it was the beer, he thought. "Mom, what are you talking about? Angie should be at home with you, unless she's out with Darrin."

"Well, that is normally the theory. But your father and I had gone out to dinner. Angie didn't want to go, so she stayed home. Anyway, when we got home about an hour ago, she wasn't there. I thought maybe Darrin came over and they went for a drive or something. But Darrin just rang the doorbell and Angie isn't here." Bella sighed.

His mother was beginning to get hysterical. Zyrien glanced at Jenna, and signaled for the check. "We're going to have to go to my mom's. Something strange is going on at the house," he said. To his mother, he said, "Mom, I'm on my way. Did you call her friends? Was there some kind of note?"

Bella sniffed. "No. Nothing. The house was locked like normal and nothing is missing. What could have happened to her?"

"Mom, don't worry. I'm sure there's a logical explanation." He ended the call and took a deep breath. *Maybe one of her girlfriends came and took her somewhere*, he hoped with all his heart.

The waiter approached the table and handed Jenna a credit card receipt. "Thank you, ma'am." He glanced at Zyrien, then left the table.

Zyrien knew his brain was working in slow motion, but he would have remembered the waiter bringing the bill. He watched Jenna scribble her name on the small slip of paper, and, for some reason, he felt a little piece of his manhood slipping away. "What are you doing paying, Jenna? You know I hate that. This is a date; the man is supposed to pay."

She dismissed his statement, placing the receipt on the plastic tray. "You were busy talking to your mother. I was just trying to help speed things along. I know we need to get going. Do you really want to sit here and wait or do you want to get going?"

Practical. He hated when she was practical and made more sense than he could. "OK, I'm sorry." He rose from his seat and reached for her hand. "Ready?"

Jenna took his hand and rose. "Yes. You can bring me up to speed in the car."

And that was exactly what he did. "This isn't like Angie. Usually she'll leave a note if she's leaving the house with Darrin."

"Maybe Darrin came by and they went for a ride or something?"

"No, that's what's got Mom all crazy. Darrin just showed up to see Ang."

The silence in the car stretched slowly into madness before Jenna's cell phone rang.

Zyrien looked at her as he sped through the streets of Dallas. "I hope that's Angie calling you."

Jenna shook her head. "No, it's Ansel. Probably wondering what time I'm coming home," Jenna said. "I'll tell him to meet us at your parents'"

"Sounds like a great idea," Zyrien commented.

"Hi, Ansel."

"Jenna, I don't know what to do," he said on the rush. "They took her and won't let me see her."

"Ansel," Jenna said, "Calm down. They won't let you see who?"

Her brother took a deep breath. "Angie called me about two hours ago. She was having some bad stomach cramps or something girlie. Her parents were out, she knew you guys were on a date, and she tried most of her other brothers and sisters, and couldn't get anybody. So she called me. I took her to the hospital and they won't let me see her."

Jenna's heart skipped a beat. "What hospital?"

She heard muffled voices, then Ansel came back on the

line. "We're at City View Hospital, ten minutes from her parents' house. What should I do? This woman won't let me see her, because I'm not a relative or the father. I hate HIPAA," he grumbled.

"I know. We'll be there in twenty minutes. Sit tight." She ended the call and turned to Zyrien. "I have good news."

He looked at her. "What and why did you tell Ansel we were on our way to your house?"

"Because Angie had called him earlier and he took her to the hospital. They're at City View."

He took a deep breath. "Why did she call him?"

"She couldn't get anyone else. What's wrong with my brother taking her?"

"Nothing is wrong with that. I know Ansel has only been here a month. How did he know where the hospital was? What if something critical happened and there's no one to sit with Angie?"

"Zyrien, things happen that you can't control. I'm thankful that he was able to take your pregnant sister to the hospital."

He turned onto the street where the hospital was located. "Baby, you know I like Ansel, but this is my sister we're talking about. He doesn't know his way around town."

Jenna didn't allow herself to dwell on his statement, knowing he was upset about his sister. She'd read him the riot act later. "For your information, Mr. Taylor, both Ansel and I were born and raised right here in Dallas. Plus, I know my brother can read a street sign that says 'hospital.' It's not like he had to trek all the way across Dallas; the damn hospital is only a few minutes' ride from your parents."

They finished the ride in silence. By the time they arrived at the waiting room, Zyrien's family had also made it. Bella greeted them and motioned for Jenna to sit next to her. "Ansel called us," Bella explained. "I was so thankful he was there for her. I shudder when I think what could have happened."

Jenna caressed Bella's hand, reassuring her the best she

could. "It's all right, Bella. Ansel got her to the hospital and I'm sure she'll be OK." Jenna glanced in Zyrien's direction before asking, "Where is Ansel?"

"Oh, he's in talking to Angie. After I gave that little intern a piece of my mind for not letting Ansel in the room, he let Ansel have a few minutes. The nerve," Bella spat. "He only brought her to the hospital in the first place."

"Where's Darrin?" Jenna thought it was odd the father wasn't in attendance.

"Well, when he found out that Angie called Ansel instead of him, he took off. She's going to have her hands full trying to make this up to Darrin."

Jenna didn't think Angie would try very hard. "Was he very upset?"

Bella shrugged. "Yes, but I think she doesn't trust him and needed someone she could depend on. That's why she called your brother."

Just then Ansel walked into the waiting room, happy to see his sister after such an ordeal. "Hey, sis."

Jenna stood and hugged her brother. "Hey, you. I'm very proud of you."

Ansel looked at her, then at Zyrien, noting that he was across the room, rather than at Jenna's side. "I hope you guys didn't fight about this."

"Of course we did," Jenna whispered, so Bella's mothering ears couldn't hear.

Ansel stepped back from his sister. "Are you guys OK? I don't want to cause trouble between you guys."

"Stop worrying. He's just upset and said some things he shouldn't. After I see Angie, we can go home."

Ansel knew better than to put his nose into Jenna and Zyrien's relationship by suggesting that she speak to him before they left. He nodded and took a seat. "I'll be right here."

* * *

Later that night, Jenna settled in her bed and reflected on the evening. The ride home with Ansel was more eye-opening than she would have believed. Since his arrival in Dallas, Ansel hadn't shown any interest in dating; now she knew why. While Jenna was at work, Ansel and Angie had reluctantly become friends. It all started with Bella needing to go out and not wanting to leave Angie alone, so she'd enlist Ansel to babysit, so to speak. Not wanting to alarm anyone, they kept the arrangement to themselves.

Ansel assured Jenna he and Angie were just friends. A sounding board for bad marriages. Ansel confided in his sister that Angie was more hurt by the dissolution of her marriage than she let on. He told his sister of the many times Angie would cry for hours and all he could do was hold her.

Everyone needed a friend like that. Someone who wouldn't care if you blubbered into the next millennium. "That's great, Ansel. Please remember she's a married woman. And a married pregnant woman at that."

He smiled at his sister. "I know. In a kind of perverse way, it was good to hear someone else's troubles. It made mine seem pretty small."

Jenna agreed with him and headed for bed. Now, as she lay in bed, staring at the ceiling, her fight with Zyrien seemed like just a small bump in the road. She wasn't really mad at him, but knew he needed time alone with his family. She knew he didn't see it the same way.

Once Angie's condition was stabilized, everything would fall into place. Zyrien would realize he'd overreacted and beg his queen's forgiveness, Darrin would finally start acting like a father-to-be, and her younger brother would find what he was looking for.

Chapter 28

Angie's hospital stay lasted only a few days. She was dismissed with strict rules. If she wanted to attend Jenna's showing in four weeks, she had to stay in bed. No exceptions.

Ansel and Jenna were among her first visitors. Jenna planned their trip strategically so that she wouldn't bump into Zyrien. So far so good.

Ansel brought Angie flowers, and Jenna brought her a few books to help her pass the time. Angie sat up in her bed, propped against a mound of pillows. She was dressed in an extralarge Dallas Mavericks T-shirt as her nightshirt. Grabbing some Kleenexes, she turned to Jenna. "I'm sorry you and Zyrien are fighting. I didn't mean to start a fight. For the record, I told him to quit being an ass and apologize." Angie blew her nose.

Ansel reassured his new friend, "Don't worry, Angie. He'll realize Jenna is about as stubborn as he is. It's going to be a real contest of wills to see who gives in first." He handed her the roses. "These are for you."

Angie sniffed and reached for the flowers. "Thank you, Ansel. I really appreciate you taking me to the hospital. You were there when I really needed it."

He patted Angie's leg. "Don't you worry about a thing.

Remember, you have to stay calm. If you need anything, don't hesitate to call me." He rose and left the room.

Angie looked at the tall retreating figure. "He's been so nice. I don't see why anyone would divorce him," she said wistfully.

"I could say the same about you," Jenna said. "I have to admit, I think my brother is very special."

Angie nodded. "I know. Our timing seems horrible, doesn't it? Well, at least I got a great new friend out of all this. I don't know what I would have done if he hadn't taken me to the hospital."

Jenna didn't, either, but didn't want to think about that. Negative energy, she reminded herself, don't let negative energy into your life. She wasn't about to give negative energy the chance to flourish. "I hate to rush, Ang, but I'd better scoot before your brother gets here."

Angie nodded and slid down in bed, preparing for a nap. "Yeah, he can be a jerk when he knows he's wrong. If he does anything else, he's going to max out his credit cards trying to make it up to you."

Jenna stood and kissed Angie on her cheek. "Take care. I'll see you in a few days."

Angie nodded. "Call me."

Jenna agreed and left the room. She walked downstairs to say good-bye to Bella and to collect Ansel, so they could leave before Zyrien made his nightly appearance.

She almost made it.

Zyrien entered his childhood home as quietly as possible. He wanted to get Jenna alone and finally apologize. But in a family of seven siblings, six nieces and nephews, two parents, and who-knows-how-many cousins in the house, that was impossible. As soon as he hit the door, his mother pulled him aside and into the kitchen for some privacy.

"Zyrien, Jenna and Ansel are here. Don't make a scene," his mother told him. "You know you're completely wrong."

Zyrien loosened his tie and sat at the kitchen table. The day had been horrible and even worse because he couldn't talk to Jenna. "I know, Mom. I planned to straighten it out before she leaves."

His mother was fixing his sister's dinner. She placed a plate heaping with baked chicken, baked potatoes, steamed broccoli, and a salad on a tray. She poured a glass of milk and added it to the ultrahealthy meal.

"Don't you look at me like that, Zyrien. Angie has to eat healthy. I know I wasn't big on making you kids eat right when you were young, but now I'm thinking about my grandbabies. I want them to get here as healthy as possible."

Zyrien didn't argue with his mother. He had to find Jenna. He left the kitchen without another word. As he made his way to the living room, he saw her. She was dressed in the same blue suit he'd seen her in earlier that day. The short skirt only made him remember what was under the skirt. He guessed she was wearing a color-coordinated thong and matching bra.

He shook his head, trying to clear those lusty thoughts. He walked with purpose toward her. When he reached his destination, he whispered in her ear, "Can I talk to you outside?"

Jenna stared at him as if he had three heads. "No, you may not. Ansel and I were just leaving."

"Jenna, please."

She and Ansel headed for the front door. Zyrien felt like he was in an obstacle course, dodging siblings, sidestepping nieces and nephews, but he caught up with Jenna as she reached the front door. He grabbed her by her arm, not giving her any room to object, and dragged her into his father's office.

Jenna watched with amazement as she was gently shoved into a leather chair. Zyrien sat next to her in the matching chair. "Now, we're going to talk about last week. Yeah, I know I said some things to you I shouldn't have and I'm sorry for that. I can only claim insanity."

She didn't answer him.

He continued speaking. "Jenna, you know I love you. I wouldn't do anything to hurt your feelings. You know that. You're my number one priority."

Still, she was quiet.

What did he have to do to get her to speak? "Will you either tell me that you forgive me or to get lost? Give me something?"

That made her smile. "You're forgiven," she said calmly. "But if we do this again, you're going to be sorry."

"I already am."

It took Jenna two weeks to convince Zyrien that he'd apologized enough. For the last fourteen days, he had brought paints, brushes, a new easel, a new smock, flowers, and he even presented her with a weekend getaway scheduled for the weekend after her showing at the gallery.

It also took Jenna two weeks to convince him she wasn't upset with him. So when she told him she was having dinner with Dawn on Friday night, he took it personally. But it didn't change Jenna's plans; she met Dawn at the Bistro as arranged. Chad was out of town, seeing his grandparents before the hockey season started. Dawn elected not to accompany him, since he was coming back in two days. Plus, her doctor strictly forbade any traveling, due to the pregnancy.

Jenna met Dawn at the restaurant. Jenna walked to the table, shaking her head at her friend. The three men scattered when Jenna cleared her throat and took a seat.

"You know, with Chad being a daddy-to-be, I'd think he'd forbid you to go out alone," Jenna said. She unfolded the napkin and placed it on her lap.

Dawn took a sip of water. "He did. He said I could only go out with you. Since I'm pregnant, I didn't want to have any secrets between us, so I told him about Lance. He was upset."

Jenna knew exactly how jealous Chad was and had had the misfortune to see his wrath in person only once. The episode resulted in a five-thousand-dollar fine from the National Hockey League and two missed games, plus his teammate went to the hospital with a broken jaw and two cracked ribs. "You know I'm not crazy about violence, but it would have been worth it to see Chad scare the crap out of Lance."

Dawn smiled. "Well, Ms. Bradshaw, this is your lucky day. I just happen to have a present for you. It's a DVD of my man confronting Lance. Before you start thinking I set Lance up, it happened purely by accident."

"I bet."

"Really," Dawn said laughing. "Chad was home and we were filming. He wants to film me every month while I'm pregnant," she explained to Jenna. "Anyway, Lance came to the house to apologize, not knowing Chad was there, and all hell broke loose. Luckily, Lance backed down from the dueling with pistols thing."

"Please tell me you're kidding."

"Of course I'm kidding. Chad was mad, but he's not crazy. Anyway, after that Chad and I had the best sex ever."

Jenna shook her head. "I guess things are back to normal with you guys."

"Pretty much." Dawn opened her menu and began looking at her dinner choices. "If it's a girl, I'm going to name her after you. Do you mind?"

Jenna was speechless.

Dawn laughed. "Say something. Yes or no?"

Jenna opened her mouth, but nothing came out. Finally she forced herself to speak. "Dawn, you've waited so long for this, are you sure?"

"You've been my best friend and we've been through a lot together. I would be proud to have a daughter named Jenna. Maybe she'll be an artist, just like her godmother," Dawn said.

Jenna gasped. "You're naming your daughter after me, and I'm going to be a godmother?" She reached for her napkin and wiped her eyes.

Dawn had tears in her eyes too. "I told Chad you were going to tear up over this. He owes me a massage."

"You guys are too much." Jenna swatted at her friend. "I'd be honored on both counts."

While Jenna was enjoying her night out with Dawn, Zyrien used the time to visit with his family, namely Angie. It was time for some tough talk. He entered her room, surprised to see her working on her laptop computer.

He took a seat at the end of her bed. "Hey, how's it going?" She was dressed in an oversized Dallas Stars hockey T-shirt this time. "Where did you get all those T-shirts?"

Angie folded the computer closed and set it aside. "Well, Dawn and Chad gave me this one, Ansel gave me the basketball one, and Sean gave me the football one."

"Why?" He felt left out and didn't know why.

"Because I told Jenna how roomy the shirts were and how I couldn't fit into my nightshirt anymore. Why?"

Zyrien shrugged. "Why didn't you tell me?"

She smiled at him. "Zyrien, are you jealous?"

"No."

"Yes, you are. You've done so much for me, I was trying to give you a break. I don't want Jenna thinking we can't survive one day without you."

"She doesn't think that. I just feel like I missed something important. Have I?"

"Only me gaining weight. Now what brings you by? I know Jenna is out with Dawn, so is this a pity visit, or a 'I'm bored' visit?"

Zyrien was sunk and he knew it. "OK, I wanted to talk to you about Darrin."

Angie took a deep breath. "What about him? I haven't seen him in a couple of weeks."

"What are you going to do about him? Are you actually thinking of raising two babies on your own?"

"Yes. I don't want the babies wondering if this is the day daddy can't handle life any more and takes off. They're better off not knowing that side of their father."

Zyrien nodded. It made sense. Darrin couldn't be depended upon for being responsible and he melted under pressure. Angie had made a sensible, logical choice. "I'm behind you whatever you decide. You know that. I want to know how you are dealing with all this. You're due in less than a month and you're legally separated from your husband. What about school?"

"I'm taking the year off. I already called my boss and explained the situation. I told Darrin that after I have the babies I would be filing for divorce, unless a miracle happens."

"What about Angie? I want you to tell me what's in your heart. I know you're hurting. Don't keep all that hurt locked up inside you. It won't be good for the babies."

She nodded, fighting back tears. She sucked in some air and the tears began to fall. "I thought we would be together forever, Zyrien. We were so well suited. We both have our master's in education, and love racquetball. I guess the signs were always there, I just chose to ignore them. He's run off before," she admitted. "When I found out I was pregnant, he was gone for a few days."

"Damn." Zyrien scooted closer to his sister, drawing her into his arms, and he listened to her cry. He rocked and comforted her until the mass of tears subsided. "Angie, you don't have to hide anything from me. Not ever."

She withdrew from his embrace. "I know. Ansel said the same thing. But I was embarrassed." She reached for a Kleenex on her bedside table. "And before you ask me something embarrassing, Ansel and I are just friends."

"I know. Jenna told me." He watched his sister dab her eyes, then blow her nose.

"Darrin accused me of cheating with Ansel. I'm about to give birth to twins and this idiot accused me of cheating." Angie shook her head. "Men. I just don't understand them. I mean, I'm the one carrying the heavy load and he's whining because I didn't call him first. If he had been any kind of man, he'd have been here in the first place. He was over two hours late. He was supposed to keep me company while Mom and Dad were out."

Another fact no one in the family knew. Good thing or else Darrin would be a dead man, if anyone had known.

Friday morning, Zyrien sat behind his desk reviewing his notes for the upcoming meeting. The contract was set and all the government had to do was send the managers down to train on Duncaster's part of the software and they were home free.

The notes fell from his hand as he enjoyed an intense fantasy starring him, Jenna, and a hot tub. It was something about that sassy mouth, her iron will, and her creative genius, that just drove him nuts and had him as horny as a teenager.

"Zyrien, your board meeting is in ten minutes," Brenna called from his open door. "You know you can't be late. Mr. Duncaster will pitch such a fit."

He snapped out of his daydream, startled to find Brenna smiling at him. She was babbling something about a meeting. What meeting? "Brenna, what are you talking about?"

She walked farther into the office. "You have a board meeting in exactly . . ." she looked down at her watch, . . . "eight minutes. You need to take the software manual with you. The government big boys are coming to learn our software next week. Remember?"

How could he forget his biggest accomplishment to date? He nodded at his assistant. "Yes, Brenna. I remember." He picked up the papers and headed out of his office. "If I get any calls, please let them know I'm in a meeting and will call as soon as I get out."

Brenna nodded, instantly knowing he was talking in office code. “I’ll tell her.”

Zyrien laughed, and walked to the elevators. After pushing the button for the special car that led to the boardroom, he got ready for what he hoped was the last meeting about the conversion. He now understood why the government wasted so much money. They were always having meetings.

He entered the boardroom with a few minutes to spare. He took his seat and waited with the rest of the executives of the company.

Fifteen minutes later, Mr. Duncaster entered the room, followed by his secretary. He was dressed impeccably, as always, in a signature blue pinstriped suit. “Gentlemen,” he said, taking his seat at the head of the table. “Pardon my tardiness. I was on the phone with DC. Damn politicians are always nervous about something.”

That didn’t sit well with Zyrien. He had scheduled everything perfectly. Training the DC guys next week, followed by Jenna’s showing on Saturday and surprising Jenna with a trip for the following weekend.

“Zyrien.”

“Zyrien!”

He dropped the pen he was holding. “Sorry, sir. I was thinking about the upcoming training modules.”

Avery Duncaster didn’t buy that for one minute. “Well, I was just informing everyone of the itinerary for the DC boys next week. Do you have any questions?”

He’d feel better if he knew what exactly was going on. “No, sir.”

Duncaster rose, causing every one else to stand, showing a measure of respect. “Well, if you do, let me know. The itinerary needs to be followed as closely as possible.” He left the room.

Zyrien nodded, watching the others file out of the room, one by one. He noticed a stack of papers in the middle of the table. He reached for one and read it. It was the itinerary for the next week. He stuck it in with the rest of his papers and went back to his office.

It was then that he noticed the schedule for the following week. The trainees didn't get there until Tuesday and training was to conclude on Saturday, culminating with a dinner including Zyrien, his bosses, and the management team from DC. He read it again. Saturday! Jenna would skin him alive if he missed her showing.

"Oh, no," Zyrien moaned, rubbing his forehead. "I'm in so much trouble."

"What's wrong?" Brenna walked inside his office and closed the door. "She did call and I told her you'd call back," she said in a stage whisper.

Zyrien looked up at his assistant. "Thank you, Brenna. Especially for not blowing my cover." He took a deep breath.

"OK, what is it? Can I help?"

"Not unless you can clone me by next Saturday."

Brenna took a seat. "Sounds like someone has too much on their plate. Didn't you tell Mr. Duncaster you had a previous engagement on Saturday?"

"How do you know about Saturday?"

"Because I e-mailed it to you yesterday, and this morning. I placed a printout on your desk, because I knew you wouldn't open those e-mails."

He just wasn't paying attention. "Well, I guess I was preoccupied."

"Yes, I just bet you were," Brenna smirked. "But I remember what being in love is like. What are you going to tell Jenna?"

Zyrien darted a glance at Brenna. It was one thing for her to know about Jenna, and not speak her name, but when she actually called Jenna by her name, it reminded him how much he was breaking the rules by dating a temp. "I have no idea."

* * *

Katonya sat in her car with only one real choice. Well, she had two, but one was actually doable. Since discovering her pregnancy a month ago, she tried to find the courage to tell her lover, but instead of feeling joy, as she thought he would, he told her to get rid of it.

But she couldn't do that, either. So Zyrien was her only solution to the problem. She knew he'd do right by her even if it wasn't his baby. She just had to make him think it was.

She watched as the last of the employees left the building. He was always working late, she mused. Kyle ran out of the building at precisely five. Zyrien stayed until at least seven every night.

He walked out of the building talking on his cell phone. To that old woman, no doubt. Jenna was too old for him. But that was a problem that would be dealt with soon. Katonya had tried her best to get her fired, but she was too efficient at her job.

She parked next to Zyrien's BMW. She'd always liked riding in the car, with its leather interior. It was the life she should have had, if she hadn't been listening to Kyle. She might get fired in the process, but she was going to make sure Kyle got his. She was so deep in thought, she jumped at the sound of Zyrien tapping her window. She let her window down.

"What are doing here, Katonya? Didn't I tell you it was over?"

She knew he'd be mad and she was correct. "Save that for later. I got a problem and you're going to help me."

He leaned against his car. "What?"

She ran this through her brain several ways. With Zyrien, there was no such thing as subtlety. "Zee, I'm pregnant and it's yours."

"What?" He spat out. "There's no way that's my baby. I haven't been with you in four months. You're telling me you're four months pregnant?"

She hadn't thought about the dates. She was actually only

eight weeks, but for her plan to work she had to lie. "Yes, I am. Remember that last time?"

"I remember you telling me you needed three hundred dollars when I got ready to leave. I also know that's not my baby. I used a condom with you every single time. I don't take chances."

"Oh, it's yours. So what are you going to do?"

He looked at her. "I want a DNA test. Then we'll talk." He got in his car and left.

Zyrien waited until he was safely away from work before he pulled over and did something he hadn't done in a long time. He cried. How could that woman ruin his life, just as he found true happiness with Jenna?

After he calmed down, things started to make a little sense. One thing he knew for sure: he had used a condom. Jenna was the first woman since his teenage years with whom he hadn't used a condom. Why would Katonya wait until now to say anything? Something wasn't sitting right and he was going to find out what it was.

If Jenna found out about this, she would definitely kick him to the curb. How could she understand? He knew he wouldn't, if the situation was reversed. How could he work this out? Unfortunately, Lance was no longer an option. He couldn't go to his parents or his siblings. In short, Zyrien had no one to turn to.

"Zyrien, what's wrong?" Jenna asked as they snuggled on her couch a few days later. "You've been preoccupied all evening. Is something wrong with the report? Is Katonya threatening to tell about us again?"

He smiled ruefully. "No, baby. I just got something on my mind and I need to work it out."

"You can talk to me," Jenna said. "You know I won't judge you."

"Yes. I know that, Jenna. But this is something I have to do alone and without everyone all up in my business."

"Oh." Jenna rose and walked to the front door. "Why don't you go home and work it out all alone?" She opened the front door.

"Jenna, you don't understand. This is something I've really got to think about."

"Well, you got to leave here. You obviously don't trust me or think I'm good enough to share your problems with."

"Baby, you don't understand."

"No, I don't, but you're not letting me, either. So good night, Mr. Taylor."

He stood, and walked to the door. "Jenna, I promise you'll understand soon." He kissed her cheek and left without another word.

Jenna closed the door and walked upstairs. She wondered what was troubling Zyrien and why he didn't want to share with her. When was he going to be able to share with her? He was so used to being in charge of everyone else's lives, was he incapable of sharing?

Wednesday afternoon, Katonya sat in Kyle's office waiting. Being stood up would be a better word. He was supposed to meet her to discuss the baby. She knew better.

"Katonya, Kyle asked me to tell you that he had an emergency and to give this to you." Brenna handed her an envelope.

Feeling like the biggest fool this side of the moon, Katonya thanked the small woman, took the envelope, and left the office.

She noticed Jenna and Zyrien discussing something very heatedly near the elevator. Jenna shrugged her shoulders and stomped away. Zyrien watched Jenna until she turned the corner leading to the invoicing department.

"I hope it wasn't anything I did," Katonya said. She rubbed her stomach. "You know we should talk."

"Is that a conversation for three?"

Did he know her secret? Had he figured out the baby wasn't his? Had he figured out who the actual father was?

"No, it won't be a conversation for three. Unless you count our baby."

He grabbed her by her arm. "Speaking of, where's the sonogram? I want to see it. When are you going to the doctor again? I want to go."

"No, I don't want you there."

"Why not? You afraid that I'll find out that you're not sixteen weeks along?"

Her mouth dropped open.

"Yes, you'd better be sure before you point a paternity finger at me." He walked to his office without another word.

Katonya felt her heart racing. She wasn't going to be able to pull this off. Maybe Kyle was right. She already had two kids. What on earth would she do with another child?

Zyrien had to confess to Jenna. He didn't want all this to hit the fan and her not know what the heck was going on. She'd kill him for not telling her, but what would she really do? He went to her house ready to tell all, but her house was dark.

He sat in his car thinking, wondering, and hoping the situation would right itself soon. He doubted Katonya was as far along as she professed to be.

The garage door opened and Jenna's car pulled inside. She and Ansel got out of the car. They were both wearing exercise clothes. Where Ansel's clothes were loose and comfortable, Jenna's clothes were too tight for his taste. She was wearing a skimpy top.

Without another thought, he got out of the car and hurried toward her. "Jenna, what the hell are you wearing?"

Ansel walked inside the house without greeting him. Jenna took a deep breath and walked toward him. "I'm wearing what I always wear to work out. If you have an objection to it, tough."

He hadn't come to fight with her. He wanted to tell her about Katonya and the trouble brewing. But what was he going to say: maybe it's mine, maybe not? He had to wait until he was sure. No use striking a match to lighter fluid. "I'm sorry, Jenna. I just lost it."

She looked at him. "Do you have everything worked out yet?"

"Not yet, but it's getting there. I didn't come to talk about that, I came to see you and talk about your day."

"Well Zyrien, since this thing has you preoccupied, work it out. When you're with me, you're with me." She walked inside the house.

Zyrien stood there dumbfounded. He remembered telling her those very same words when they started dating and now she was throwing those very words back at him. He was going to have to fix this mess with Katonya and fast.

Jenna sat at her desk Friday afternoon, counting the seconds until it was time to go home. She glanced at the clock on the computer and she still had thirty minutes to go.

Things with Zyrien had hit a snag, but she couldn't let that bother her now. The showing was just a week away. She had to focus her energy on that. Not that Zyrien was going through some sort of crisis and chose not to include her in his troubles.

She noticed Katonya walking to her desk, no doubt ready to give her more work. She was correct.

"Jenna, those invoices weren't paid correctly. Research these and see how they were paid," she said.

Jenna waited for the familiar sound of a stack of papers

being dropped on her desk. But instead she heard Katonya groan in pain. She finally looked at the younger woman and immediately hopped out of her seat. “Here, why don’t you sit down?” Katonya looked like she was ready to be sick all over everything.

Katonya sat down and let out a tired breath. “Thanks, Jenna. I guess I was tired or something. Must have been the effects of yesterday, maybe it’s a bad reaction to the medication.”

“Want me to call the nurse?”

“No, I don’t. Nothing she could do anyway,” Katonya panted. “I just have to get through it.”

Jenna didn’t want to pry, given her tenuous relationship with Katonya, but if an ambulance was needed, she wouldn’t hesitate to call one. “What happened yesterday?”

She leaned back in the chair, trying to catch her breath. “If you must know, I had a procedure yesterday, if you know what I mean.” She nodded at Jenna.

Jenna knew that was code for an abortion. The rumors were true. Katonya had been pregnant. “I’m sorry.” Jenna knew she could never take a life, even if that meant giving up art.

“Me too, but the father wasn’t willing to help. I didn’t really have a choice.”

Jenna felt her eyes tearing up. God help her; she’d never be in that predicament. “He wanted the, you know?”

Some of the color was coming back to Katonya’s face. “He demanded it.”

Jenna shook her head. “Men. Sometimes they’re such a waste of space.”

Katonya laughed, and then caught her side in pain. “Oh, my God. The pain is killing me. Did you have water on your desk? I must have spilled it because I feel something dripping on my leg.”

Jenna shook her head. “It’s you, Katonya. You’re bleeding.” She reached for the phone and dialed the emergency number.

Katonya threw her head back. “Jenna, page Zyrien.”

"Zyrien?"

"Yes! Now!"

Against her better judgment, Jenna did as Katonya asked. She sat in Dez's empty chair and waited for someone to get there. A few minutes later, Zyrien appeared.

He briefly glanced at Jenna, but went to Katonya. Horrified, Jenna watched as her man comforted his ex-girlfriend. "Zyrien, what's going on?"

He darted a glance in her direction. Again, he focused his attention on Katonya. "It's going to be fine, baby."

Katonya grabbed Zyrien's hand. "Will you go with me?"

He looked at Jenna again, but returned his attention to Katonya. "Yes."

Jenna didn't have time to properly digest what the hell was going on, because the emergency team was busy working on Katonya. As she watched them take a barely conscious Katonya away, Zyrien's eyes met hers.

"Later," was all he said and followed the stretcher out without a backward glance.

Crazy, insane thoughts whirled through Jenna's brain. She felt her eyes filling with tears. How could he betray her like this? She had to get out of this place and quick. She grabbed her purse and left, not caring one second if she got fired or not.

Once at home, she told her brother the events of the day. She felt better sharing her feelings with someone. Maybe a man would know what the heck was going on.

"Sorry, sis. I don't know what's up Zyrien's ass. I thought he was totally into you. I can't understand why he would hide all this. If she's not pregnant, why not just step up to the plate and tell you? Why not just break up if he had gone back together with her?"

Jenna grabbed a tissue and blew her nose. "I don't know. You know, Ans, I'm not one of those clingy women. He could have just said he wanted her back. I might not have liked it, but I would have dealt with it."

Ansel hugged his sister. “This doesn’t sound like Zyrien. He’s like Mr. Responsibility; I can’t see him making her get an abortion, either. I think we’re missing part of the puzzle.”

“Well, I guess we’ll never know.”

“I can’t see Zyrien giving up without a fight,” Ansel said. “And I know you ain’t trying to hear that right now. But this is coming from a twice-divorced man: there’s probably a logical explanation for everything. Even his escorting his ex-girlfriend to the hospital.”

Jenna didn’t see how that was possible.

After moping around most of the weekend, Jenna decided she was just going to sleep in. Sundays were made for relaxing, she thought, sleepily. But a persistent phone wouldn’t let her revel in her misery. It kept ringing, demanding that she pick it up. She reached for the phone and mumbled “hello.”

“Good morning, sleepyhead,” Gunter said, cheerfully. “I’ve got some good news for you.”

Jenna struggled to sit up. “What is it? Is it something about the showing next week?”

Gunter laughed. “No, dear. I was contacted by Pierson Grant, the millionaire; he vants to buy the portrait of Ian.”

Jenna placed a hand on her heart, hoping to calm it down and that it wouldn’t pop out of her chest. “H-how much did he want to pay for it?”

Gunter laughed. “He offered twenty-five thousand and vants to commission another for upvard of a hundred.”

“What did you say?”

“Vell, since I’m your mentor, I asked him vat kind of portrait he was talking about. He vants one with him and his wife in the buff, very tasteful, of course. A Renaissance painting. And due to his hectic schedule, you vould need to fly to him.”

Jenna couldn’t believe any of this. Could she actually quit that job sooner than she expected to? “But Gunter, I have to work. I’d have to meet them and see what they wanted. What if I can’t do it?”

"Nonsense, I know you can. He's sending his private jet for you this afternoon. He lives in Portland, Oregon, you know. A limo vill pick you up in about six hours. So, missy, I suggest you pack a bag and get ready."

"But what about my showing?"

"Honey, don't worry. I explained to him that you just needed prelim sketches of him and his wife to get started. He'll give you half of your—vatever you're asking—vhen you get there. You can get back here by Thursday and we can do a valk-through for the showing on Friday and you'll have all day Saturday to make any changes. How's that?"

Gunter had thought of everything, she mused. Maybe she did need to put some miles between her and Zyrien for now. Plus, she would have the means to quit her job now. Dawn would probably kill her if she didn't take the chance she'd been waiting on. There was only one answer.

"OK, Gunter, it's a deal. I need something in writing."

"FedEx should be arriving at your door before noon." He disconnected.

Jenna took a deep breath. Then another one. A loud piercing yell filled the room. She immediately called Dawn and told her the news.

"Oh my God, Jenna, you have to take this chance. Don't worry about work. I'll find someone else to fill your spot."

"But what about my boss, Kyle?"

"Oh, a little birdie told me that, since his relationship with Katonya has come to light, he's no longer the regional accounts manager." She laughed. "When are you leaving?"

"What did you say about Kyle and Katonya?"

"Oh honey, I thought you knew or I would have told you. My contact at Duncaster called me with the news. Katonya was pregnant, but it wasn't Zyrien's, like she had everyone believing. She was only two months along and it was Kyle Storm's baby. They were having an affair, but he didn't want the baby. So he paid for her to have an abortion. The rest is history. When are you leaving?"

"A limo is coming for me this afternoon," Jenna answered, her mind still whirling around what Dawn just told her.

"Great, we can celebrate. Right after I throw up." She ended the call.

Chapter 29

Two hours later, Dawn entered Jenna's house, munching on some crackers, and speaking on her cell phone. "Yes, Chad, I threw up twice this morning. I'm fine. When are you going to be home?"

Jenna laughed at her friend. She knew exactly why Dawn was anxious for her husband's return. Jenna closed the door and followed Dawn into the living room, listening to the one-sided conversation.

"I miss you. I'll see you Monday. Blow me a kiss when they interview you after you guys kick the Redwings' ass." She folded the tiny phone and placed it in her purse.

Jenna thought Dawn looked more serene than she had in years and told her friend so.

"It's this hormone thing. I'm only eight weeks and those hormones are all over the place. One minute I'm the happiest woman in the world, the next I'm sobbing about how fat I'm going to get and the fact that Chad is in Detroit and won't be home for two more days. Then I'm always feeling horny. Just you wait, Jenna, you'll see."

Jenna shook her head. "Unless I can get that way by thinking about it, it's not going to happen."

"I'm sorry, Jenna. It clearly slipped my mind. Blame your

godchild. Speaking of, have you talked to Zyrien lately?" Dawn winced. "Sorry, is that subject off-limits right now?"

Jenna didn't want Dawn to feel bad. "It's OK. Anyway, I'm not going to have time to think about Zyrien Taylor, considering I'm going to be painting two nude people. Who knows what kind of poses they're going to want?"

Dawn shook her head. "Are you excited about painting the Grants? You know, all he has to do is tell a few of his bazillionaire friends and you'd be set for life."

"Yeah."

"It's Zyrien, isn't it?"

"Yes, it is."

"Jenna, you can't focus on that right now. You need to focus on that fat one hundred thousand dollars you are about to collect for doing what you love to do. If it's time for you and Zyrien to be together, then it will happen."

As Dawn's words soaked in, Jenna agreed. "You're right, as usual. Come on and help me finish packing."

Dawn nodded and followed her upstairs to her bedroom.

Zyrien didn't want to wake up. But he had responsibilities and he had to get things right with Jenna. How could one misunderstanding snowball out of control like it had? Once he was sure Katonya was OK, he left the hospital to explain the entire story to Jenna, but it was too late. She found out the hard way that Katonya had been pregnant. Talk about a web of deceit.

He hadn't meant to keep it from Jenna, but he knew she wouldn't understand and would never speak to him again. He was correct on all counts. Jenna refused to speak to him, wouldn't return his calls, and had somehow turned his own family against him. He had no idea how he was going to fix this mess.

He dragged out of bed and let the hot water of the shower

beat some sense into him. First of all, he had those idiots from DC to deal with. With Jenna, he'd just have to camp out at her desk until she spoke to him. It might bring their relationship to light, and it would cost him the job he'd been chasing all these years, but he had to think about his future.

No job was worth losing Jenna in the process. He'd thought the rule was stupid anyway. And he'd tell Mr. Duncaster so as soon as he handed in his resignation.

"What do you mean, Jenna Bradshaw isn't available for work anymore?" Zyrien all but screamed into the phone to the assistant manager at Harcourt's Essential Temps later that morning. "Where's Dawn?"

The woman with the soft voice at the other end of the phone shuffled papers on her desk, irritating Zyrien that much more. "Mr. Taylor, per Mrs. Castle, Jenna resigned her position this weekend."

"Where's Dawn?"

"Mrs. Castle is out of the office this morning. Is something wrong with the new replacement?"

Zyrien reined in his temper. None of this was this woman's fault. He thought Jenna went a little overboard by quitting her job. Never in a million years would he have thought she'd bolt.

"Mr. Taylor."

"Sorry, I just wasn't aware. Please ask Mrs. Castle to call me at her convenience."

"Certainly. Is there anything else I can help you with?"

Sure, bring Jenna back to me, he thought. "No, that's it. Thanks." He replaced the phone and rubbed his forehead with his hand. Now what?

"You know, I would check with her friend."

Zyrien raised his head at the familiar voice. Brenna. "You're too smart for your own good."

She smiled at him. "I know. You should pay me more." She took a deep breath. "I'd heard she quit this morning. You know the invoicing department is buzzing with the knowledge that you accompanied Katonya to the hospital Friday. You didn't earn a lot of cool points by not telling Jenna the havoc Katonya was causing you. Kyle has also been replaced by Joan Bryant this morning."

"Good riddance to bad rubbish," Zyrien said. "That prick deserved way more than a demotion. And now look, Katonya's lying in the hospital and Jenna won't speak to me."

"Zyrien, I know you probably don't want to hear this, especially from me, but I do know how you feel. I've had a miscarriage, so I know what it feels like to lose a child," Brenna said.

He stared at Brenna. Her pale face was becoming blurrier by the second. "No, you don't know." He stood and paced his office. "Katonya was pregnant, but the baby wasn't mine. She didn't have a miscarriage. She had an abortion."

"That was about the time you guys were hot and heavy," Brenna reminded him.

"She was also hot and heavy with Kyle, hence his abrupt departure."

"So that explains it," Brenna said.

"What?"

"About two months ago, I was delivering some papers to Kyle, but Katonya was in his office. Kyle was livid about something. He said 'I don't how you do, get rid of the mistake.' She ran out of his office."

He nodded. That jibed with Katonya's hospital-bed confession yesterday. It was Kyle's baby she killed, not his. "Thanks, Brenna."

Ten minutes later, he sat across from a very quiet Dez. Against every bit of good sense, he decided to talk to Jenna's friend anyway. He pulled her into a conference room for a quick chat.

"Mr. Taylor, I do need to get back to my job."

OK, she probably spoke to Jenna at some point this weekend, he mused. "Where's Jenna? Why did she quit?"

"I don't know." She rose from her seat. "Was that it?"

"No, it's not. The longer you take to tell me, the longer I'll keep you in here. So you can tell me, get back to your job, and we can all be happy."

She studied him for a long minute before she spoke, "It has to be about you, doesn't it?" She sat down. "You want Jenna and will do anything to get her back. Why couldn't you just say that you'd gotten Katonya pregnant in the first place instead of trying to play this crazy mind game with Jenna? That's what I don't get about you, Mr. Taylor. You seem like a brother that would step up to the plate and take your responsibilities seriously, but you're just like the rest of these guys."

Zyrien sat very patiently and listened. Dez had every right to berate him as she did. That was because she didn't have all the facts. But now he was going to set the record straight. "I'm not the father of Katonya's baby. You can believe me or not, I don't care. But I'm not putting her business on the street like that. You're right. All I want right now is to talk to Jenna. I'm desperate enough right now and I don't care what I have to do to get the information, but understand this, I will get it."

Dez gave a dramatic sigh and took a seat. "She went to Oregon."

"Oregon? What the hell? Why is she there?"

"You'll have to ask her," Dez said. "She didn't give me all the details."

He shook his head in defeat. That was the best he was going to get for now and he would have to make it work in his favor. He rose and walked to the door. "Thanks, Dezarae." He left the room without another word.

Five days later, Jenna was flying back to Dallas, ready to face the world. "Ms. Bradshaw, we should be landing in about fifteen minutes. A car will be waiting to take you home," the pilot announced.

"Thank you, Carl." Jenna fastened her seat belt and braced herself for the landing. She glanced around at the leather interior of the private jet, loving every decadent thing there was about being the only passenger on a six-passenger plane.

After she exited the plane, she noticed the limo and the driver waiting beside it. She felt like a celebrity. She doubted she could ever go back to flying coach.

She approached the limo and slid inside. The last five days had been a dream to her.

The Grant mansion had been luxurious and had servants galore. There was even a young woman at Jenna's beck and call. If Jenna looked like she needed something, it was that young woman's job to get it and get it quickly.

When Jenna arrived home, it seemed unusually quiet. Ansel had returned to Austin to tie up loose ends. He was moving back to Dallas to be near Jenna. She was happy about that. He was supposed to be back by Saturday in time for her show. She'd been given a second chance with her brother and this time they were going to stay in touch. It wouldn't be hard this time, since he was going to live with her for a little while. At least she had that.

"Your vork looks vonderful, Jenna." Gunter said as he walked around the large room. Some of her best work was displayed for all to see. "I especially like the vone of Dezarae. She looks regal. Like a, how you say, a Nubian queen. I can't believe her husband is not having a fit."

Jenna glanced at the picture of Dez, glad she had followed her instinct and given it a Renaissance look. "I think her husband is more proud of the picture than jealous. It might be different tomorrow night when he realizes how many men will be looking at it."

Gunter, dressed in a blue Armani suit, smiled at his protégée. "I think I've cornered the proud department. I'm very proud of you, Jenna." He hugged her. "How about some lunch and I've got some more good news for you."

Jenna wiped her eyes. "What?"

"I just received confirmation that the art director from Maza's Art Gallery will be in attendance. So I want to see smiles on that gorgeous face." He grabbed her hand and led her out of the museum.

Once outside, Gunter faced her. "I feel like something loaded with pasta, marinara sauce, and mozzarella cheese. How about you?"

Jenna nodded. Tomorrow was going to be perfect. Just perfect. Just without Zyrien. "I think Italian sounds fine."

Saturday evening, Zyrien sat at the table in Donatello's, with the training team for the software Duncaster and Finch had purchased for the transition, and two members of the committee. Howard Clark, lead trainer from Chambers Software of Boston, rambled on and on about how his company's software would put Duncaster and Finch on the map.

"What I'd like to do, Mr. Taylor," he said in that upper-crust Boston voice, "is to arrange for one of the financial magazines to do a little 'how they're doing' thing on you guys in a few months. It would be a win-win situation for both sides. We could both get free press and we will both profit from that by generating new business."

Zyrien took a deep breath. He should have opted out of this dinner. He should be supporting his lady love and telling her how sorry he was, instead of listening to this idiot think of more ways to generate more sales. "First of all, Howard, this is a government contract. Any publicity has to go through the channels. It's not up to me or Duncaster and Finch, for that matter. It's up to the committee." He nodded to the two men at their table. Bill Anderson and Max Tucker smiled in acknowledgment. "Those are the guys you need to kiss up to, not me."

Bill, assistant to the chairman, cleared his throat. "Actually, it's not my ass, either. The chairman makes all decisions of that nature, and he didn't make the trip to Texas." He smiled at Howard. "I personally think it's a great idea, but it doesn't stop at me. Although . . . Old Howard looks like his lips could do my sixty-year-old ass justice."

The men laughed—everyone except Howard, who looked a little upset at being the *butt* of the joke.

Howard coughed. "Why didn't the chairman attend?"

Max spoke this time. "Mr. Chairman doesn't travel much. He leaves that part of the job to us. We give him all our input from meetings like these and he makes his decisions based on that."

That gave Howard a glimmer of hope. He took a sip of his imported wine. "Since you like the idea, what are the chances of him giving me the go-ahead on the magazine coverage?"

"That will probably be shot down," Bill admitted.

Zyrien smiled. Howard was a great sales rep. Persistent as hell. He would probably go back to Boston and tell his boss, Terrance Chambers, that there was hope of getting magazine coverage. Bill and Max never said "no." They didn't say "yes" either, but a firm "maybe" had closed many a deal, Zyrien mused.

He wondered how Jenna's showing was going. He knew everyone in his family was attending, including a pregnant Angie, and even Darrin. His mother had read him the riot act earlier for not telling anyone about his problems with Katonya. In fact, his ears were still ringing.

He heard the men discussing the latest political mishap in Washington in very loud voices. He rose and threw his linen napkin on the table. All discussion stopped.

"Gentlemen, excuse me. I have another appointment. Have a safe journey home."

A look of pure insult crossed Howard's face. "Another appointment? Duncaster assured us of your cooperation," Howard bellowed.

"I have done everything humanly possible to ensure a safe transition. I've sat with you most of the week, answered all your questions, but now you're on my time. I have a gallery showing to attend."

He left the men sitting at the table in amazement. Zyrien might not have a job come Monday morning, but he hoped he'd have Jenna back.

Jenna walked around the showing, completely and utterly shocked at the number of people milling around her exhibits. Dressed in her best "schmoozing dress," she answered questions from her guests.

Of course, the scene-stealer was the picture of Dez relaxing on Jenna's favorite settee. Dante stood next to his wife, all smiles and adoration. Jenna couldn't have been prouder of Dez if Dez had painted the picture herself.

"Dez, you look gorgeous," Jenna admired the clingy dress she wore. "I'm glad you're showing off your figure rather than hiding it behind loose-fitting clothing."

Dez nodded, her microbraids hanging loose about her shoulders. "I have you to thank for that. You gave me my self-esteem back." Dez wiped away a tear. "After the baby, I just didn't feel sexy, but looking at this portrait, I feel very sexy."

Jenna hugged her friend. "You're going to make me cry," Jenna whined, "and that's not allowed." She hugged her friend again.

To Jenna's surprise, a very relaxed Dante did something spontaneously. He hugged her. "Thank you, Jenna. I'd forgotten how much I loved this woman and how beautiful she is." He planted a wet, noisy kiss on her cheek.

A tear escaped Jenna's eyes. "I told you no crying." She wiped her eyes. "Now go mingle before I start blubbering like the emotionally stressed woman that I am."

Jenna had barely taken two steps when Ansel appeared,

dressed in a black tux. He kissed his sister and hugged her. "I'm so proud of you, big sis. Your dream came true."

"Almost," Jenna whispered. "Almost."

"Hey, don't worry about Zyrien. To quote someone wise, maybe he's not the one for you."

"I know, but it doesn't hurt any less," Jenna said. And to add to that hurt, Zyrien's parents and his seven siblings and their appropriate partners entered the room. Bella walked to Jenna and embraced her in a tight hug.

"Jenna, this looks wonderful," Bella said, then whispered, "my son is an idiot."

Jenna nodded. "You won't get an argument from me on either count."

Bella also hugged Ansel, then whispered, "Darrin's here."

"I know," Ansel said. "Ang called me the other day to warn me. Don't worry, Bella. Angie and I are friends only. Darrin's her husband. I understand my place on the food chain."

Jenna wasn't expecting such an honest answer from her brother. She also knew there was more than just friendship between Ansel and Angie, but there wasn't much she could do about it. Timing was everything. She touched her brother's jacket-covered arm. "I'm sorry, Ans."

He smiled. He actually smiled. "Don't worry. I'm a big boy." He hugged her and said only loud enough for Jenna to hear, "But thanks for loving me enough to care."

This evening was going to cost her many tears, Jenna mused as she tried to fight more from surfacing. "Could you get me a glass of champagne?" She motioned toward the bar.

Ansel nodded and took off. Jenna noticed Angie waddling in with Darrin on her heels, playing the role of a father-to be. Angie didn't look well, but Jenna didn't know if it was because of the pregnancy or Darrin.

In an effort to save Angie as many steps as possible, Jenna hurried toward her and hugged her. "You should be at home," Jenna chastised her.

Angie grunted, rolled her eyes toward the ceiling. "Are you kidding? I've been chained to my bed for four weeks so that I could attend. I couldn't miss your show."

"I'm glad I rank so high on your list." Jenna curtsied. "But for me, would you mind sitting down? If necessary, the museum has a wheelchair."

"Don't you dare bring that thing! I'm just pregnant with twins. I'm not some old woman."

Jenna laughed. "OK, but please sit down. You're making me nervous."

Darrin stared at Jenna, but said nothing. If it had been Ansel with Angie, he would have made sure she was sitting down. Darrin just stood there like a moron, not doing anything. Men!

Chapter 30

"All right, Jenna," Angie conceded. "You need to go wow those people. I'll be right here rooting for you."

After an hour of talking, shaking hands, and discussing her work ethic, Jenna was parched. She walked to the bar, wondering what had happened to Dawn and Chad, when she noticed them mingling with the guests.

She ordered a glass of mineral water, and hurried to her friends. She hugged Dawn, who looked radiant in a white silk pantsuit. Chad was dressed in a traditional black tux. They both hugged Jenna.

"Girl, this is wonderful. I told you this was your time. Everything else pales in comparison. The picture of Dez is excellent. Absolutely perfect. I wish my picture was hanging on the wall," Dawn said.

Chad turned to his wife, then looked at Jenna. "Jenna, I want to be present at my child's birth. But I can't do that if Dawn's picture comes out of hiding because I would definitely be in jail."

Jenna knew he was joking. Only partly, though. Chad had a serious jealous streak when it came to his wife. "Don't worry. That picture won't see the light of day on my watch."

"Thank you." Chad put his arm around Dawn's waist and pulled her back into the throng of people.

Jenna finally found herself alone. She quietly left and headed for the restroom. She just wanted a few quiet minutes, then she'd go back and face more people. Just as she pulled the door open, she heard a familiar voice.

"Hello."

She froze. Too afraid to turn around, she merely said, "Hello." Would he have the nerve to show up this late?

"The pictures look great. I knew you were going to ace this. Congratulations, baby."

That small term of endearment made her turn and face him. "Baby? Shouldn't you be at Katonya's bedside?"

Zyrien winced. "Can we talk?"

"We're talking now. Did you see your family? How's Katonya doing? I heard she's going to be off for at least six weeks," Jenna chattered needlessly. She just wanted him to leave.

"I came to see you." He walked closer to her. "I'm sorry, Jenna. I was wrong for not telling you about Katonya and her claims. I just thought I could handle it on my own."

Jenna wanted to believe him. "Zyrien, I understand things happen. Condoms break. I get it. But to demand she get an abortion is too much. You told her to kill your baby. I thought you were a stronger man than that."

"It wasn't my baby," he said in a small voice.

Jenna opened the door. "I'm not going to ruin the one night I've been looking forward to most of my adult life with this nonsense. You have so little regard for me that you would show up at my opening with a bunch of mess. You know how much this means to me and yet you show up trying to ruin my moment. I'm not listening to anything you have to say tonight. Maybe another time, when I'm more in the mood." She walked inside the ladies' room.

* * *

Zyrien stared at the bathroom door. He had only one option. He had to go after her, but Ansel's voice stopped him. Or rather the tone in Ansel's voice stopped him.

"I'd let her alone, Zyrien. This is her night and you should let her have it. You hurt her bad and Jenna doesn't take hurt well."

He liked Jenna's brother and knew Ansel was just looking out for him, but sometimes a man needed to be humiliated. And this was where Zyrien was in his life. "I appreciate it, Ansel, but Jenna won't even hear the truth, she won't talk to me."

"Give her a few days, Zyrien. She's more disappointed than anything else. Why would you tell someone to kill a life?"

Zyrien felt his shoulders sag with the task of trying to make everyone understand. "Ansel, I didn't. Yeah, I went to the hospital with her because she begged me to. The actual culprit in this has been transferred to another office. I would never ask anyone to do anything like that. You should know me better than that and I take my responsibilities seriously."

"I should, but right now the cards are stacked against you. Why don't you take the time to decide if Jenna is really what you want or is it the challenge of an older woman?"

Zyrien knew he wanted more from Jenna. He wanted her in his life forever, but he couldn't tell her that until she actually talked to him. "You're right, Ansel. Tonight is not the night for it. I'll back off for now, but tell her this is not over."

Ansel shook his head. "Good luck. 'Cause you're definitely going to need it."

"Tell me something I don't know," Zyrien said as he walked away to rejoin his family.

His mother met him as he entered the main gallery. "Well, did you talk to Jenna?"

"Yeah, but she wasn't buying what I was trying to sell. And Ansel reminded me how important this night was to her and that I shouldn't try to force the issue now. So I'll wait for the right time and try to explain."

His mother didn't look like she was buying it, either. "Zyrien, you've always been the one in the family who could solve all our problems and guide us in the right direction. That was my fault. I placed too much responsibility on you at such a young age. You let that girl almost ruin your life because you didn't think you had anyone to tell your troubles to." She wiped her eyes. "It's my fault that you lost the woman you loved."

He hugged his mother. "Mom, it's not your fault. It was something I thought I could handle on my own and I failed. I was wrong and I hurt my family and my woman."

"Baby, I just know you guys will get over this."

Zyrien hoped so with all his heart.

A few hours later, Jenna walked through the museum making sure she hadn't forgotten anything. It had been a grueling day, but was worth every moment of smiling, schmoozing, and discussing her art with the guests that evening. She'd accomplished her goal. She was in a museum and had an order for several paintings for another museum. It felt good when a plan came together.

She rode home in silence, wondering about Zyrien. He'd made sure to stay out of her way during the rest of the night and she was very thankful for that. The last thing she needed was to lose her temper in front of all those people.

Zyrien was waiting for her when she arrived home.

He was leaning against the car, still dressed in the suit he had on earlier. Jenna parked next to him and sighed. *Might as well get this over with,* she thought, and got out of the car.

"I was beginning to think you weren't coming home," he said, closing her door. "Ansel got here an hour ago."

Jenna was tired and wanted to go to sleep. "What do you want? I'm tired and want to go to bed."

"I know you are, Jenna. I am too. But before I go, I want

you to know the truth. Then if you don't want to see me again, I'll deal with it."

She knew he wasn't going to leave, so she invited him inside. "If you could expedite this, I'd be ever so grateful," she said in her most sarcastic tone.

"Sure, baby." He led her to the couch and took a seat.

"My name is Jenna. Not baby."

"Oh, it's like that?" Zyrien asked, defeated. "OK, I asked for a chance and I guess this is it. So I'm going to tell you the entire story and you can check with Katonya, the hospital, and your former boss."

Jenna nodded.

Zyrien relaxed a little and started his story. "Well, I guess I should start from the beginning. Yes, I did date Katonya for about two months; we broke up a few weeks before you started working here. Well, last month she told me that she was pregnant and it was mine. She also said she was past the point of an abortion. I told her that I knew it wasn't my baby because I used protection every time we had sex and that's all it was, Jenna."

"What did she do?"

"Well, I told her that when the baby was born I wanted to do a DNA test. If it turned out I was the father I would have assumed responsibility. But I also knew that she had started seeing someone else who worked at Duncaster. That's why I broke it off. I don't share. You know that."

Jenna didn't say anything.

"Well, about a week ago, she threatened to go to my bosses and tell them that I was seeing you. I told her to go ahead and I was going to mention she was seeing Kyle. She denied seeing him, but she also didn't tell Mr. Duncaster. Last week when she got sick, she asked me to go with her because she was scared. That's when she confessed that it was Kyle Storm's baby and he didn't want it."

"So why did she tell you that?" Jenna could see where things had gone horribly wrong.

"Because she knew I'd marry her or at least take care of the baby."

Jenna let the sentence soak through her brain. "How was she going to explain a biracial baby as yours?"

"I don't think she'd figured her plan out that far," Zyrien said. "I guess she'd figured I'd get scared when she threatened to go to my boss. But they did find out about her and Kyle and he has been transferred to the Minnesota office and demoted to assistant accounts manager."

Jenna thought of all the run-ins she'd had with Katonya and Kyle over the course of just a few months. It was because of Zyrien and had nothing to do with her.

"Jenna, I'm sorry for not coming clean about my situation, but I'm used to being the go-to guy. I'm not supposed to have this kind of drama in my life."

Jenna laughed at how silly they both were. Her for thinking Zyrien would forego his responsibility and him for thinking he wasn't human.

"Jenna, I love you. I will do anything you want to get back in your good graces." Zyrien reached for her hand and kissed it. "I promise to be more forthcoming with anything that's going on in my life from now on. Nothing will ever come between us again, if you just give me one more chance."

"What do I get for giving you this one more chance? This has been about you not wanting to share your world with me. How do I know when something else happens again you won't close up again? I'm not trying to take over your life, Zyrien. I can't afford to be blindsided like that again, especially with my career taking off now."

"You get all of me. Today and every day. With all this craziness that's been going on this last week, I have realized one thing."

"What's that?"

"I don't want to lose the one woman I truly love for being stupid." He reached inside his jacket pocket and produced a box. "Do you forgive me for being so stupid?" He kissed her gently on the cheek.

"Do you trust me?" Jenna countered. "I mean not just enough to sleep with, but do you really trust me?"

"Yes," he answered without hesitation. "I trust you so much I got you this." He gave her the box.

Jenna's heart thudded loudly against her chest. Was he actually proposing? She opened the box and laughed. It was a ring all right, but it was a key ring with three keys on it. "What is this?"

He kissed her on the mouth. "You asked me how much I trust you. I trust you enough to give you access to my house, and my car."

Jenna knew her heart was melting and fast. He loved and trusted her. He gave her keys to his house. She wiped away happy tears. "Thank you, Zyrien." She kissed him hard and long with the pent-up frustration of a week of misunderstandings and doubts now taken away.

He chuckled against her lips. "I have another surprise for you."

"Zyrien that's not necessary. I told you gifts aren't needed. I forgive you. I'm just happy you weren't the dog I thought you were."

But he wasn't through with her yet. "You have to close your eyes this time."

Jenna complied and felt him touching her hand gently. What was he going to do with her hand? He slipped something heavy and cold on her finger. "OK, you can open them."

She opened her eyes and gasped. "Zyrien, are you sure?"

"That I want to marry you? Hell, yeah, I'm sure. Will you?"

"Will I what?"

"Jenna, please don't joke. This is way too important to me.

Will you marry me and make me the happiest man in the world?"

"Why don't you marry me and make me the happiest woman in the universe?"

Zyrien shook his head. "I can definitely do that." Zyrien pulled her into his arms and kissed her. "I can definitely do that."

Epilogue

A year later

Zyrien leaned back in his office chair, relishing a few quiet moments after his meeting. Finally, everything was in place. The new employees were acclimated to the new software and the government was happy, which meant his bosses were happy.

He was enjoying his new status as a junior partner in the firm. He was also enjoying his new marital status and looking forward to impending fatherhood. Jenna filled a gap he hadn't known was there. The only bad spot was that Angie divorced Darrin right after the twins were born. But at least his sister was happy now, especially since she was dating her divorce attorney, who adored her children.

"How long are you going to sit there with that silly look on your face?" Brenna asked.

He sat up instantly. "Sorry, just happy."

She smiled at her boss. "That's called being in love. By the way, Jenna is on line one. Isn't her first sonogram today?"

"Yes, this afternoon." He glanced at his watch. "It's early. Oh no, something's wrong." He snatched the phone to his ear. "Baby, what is it?"

His assistant shook her head and left the room. Jenna's laughter through the phone soothed his ruffled nerves.

"There's nothing wrong, honey," she cooed. "I was calling because your mom wants to come to the sonogram."

Zyrien took a deep breath. "Jenna, I don't know. We already have Dawn and Ansel coming. The room isn't that big." Zyrien knew he was just being selfish, but he wanted Jenna's first sonogram to be a private affair.

Nine months into their marriage, Jenna found out she was pregnant. She'd given him the greatest gift possible.

"Zyrien, it will be fine. I'll make it worth your while," she said in a voice dripping with innuendo.

"And how do you plan on doing that, being that you're twelve weeks pregnant?" He was smiling into the phone like an idiot. Luckily, Brenna wasn't there to witness it.

"You'll have to see, won't you?" She ended the call.

Zyrien replaced the phone and rose from his chair. "Might as well go home and get that surprise now." He picked up his briefcase and headed home.

As he parked in the garage, Zyrien shook his head. He was actually living in the arts district of Dallas. Before they married, Jenna put up a good fight about keeping her house and he did the same with his. So they compromised Jenna-style. They bought a bigger monochromatic house in the artsy section.

His mother's Suburban was parked out front of their house. He entered the house and called out his wife's name.

"We're in the studio," his mother answered. "Come see my picture."

He took a deep breath and walked to the front of the house. Jenna's studio was what most would consider the den, but much larger. Jenna wouldn't let him look at his mother's portrait while she was working on it, which suited him just fine. He had no desire to see his mother in the buff.

"I'm coming," he said and walked to the studio. "Hey, babe. I decided to come home early." He walked to where Jenna sat in front of the easel and kissed her on the lips. "Shouldn't you be resting? I thought we agreed to you taking morning naps."

"It's a sonogram, Zyrien. Not a physical. You can be such an old man, sometimes." Jenna caressed his face.

He laughed nervously. She was right about that. "I just don't want anything to happen to you. You know the doc said you needed to take it easy and no paint fumes."

"She meant like painting a room. That's your department. You're the designer for the baby's room."

He nodded and glanced at the portrait on the easel. It was his mother. She was dressed in a black peignoir, looking like a very classy and beautiful woman sprawled out on a couch. "Mom, this is beautiful. Jenna, this is great." He kissed his wife again. "I can't thank you enough. Mom looks like a queen."

Jenna wiped the tears from his eyes. "Actually, it was Mom's idea."

Zyrien walked to his mother and gave her a kiss on the cheek. "You are one special lady, Bella Taylor."

Bella hugged her son. "You're pretty special yourself, Zyrien. Or how else could you have attracted this miracle worker?

"What?" Husband and wife asked at the same time.

Bella sighed. "She brought excitement into your life and she got you to fall in love. That, my son, took a miracle."

Zyrien thought about his mother's words and looked down at his wedding band. He was never without it, much like his love for his wife. "When you're right, Mom, you're right."